ZAX

Richard M Clements

Richard M Clements

Published by
Chipmunkapublishing
PO Box 6872
Brentwood
Essex CM13 1ZT
United Kingdom

http://www.chipmunkapublishing.com

Edited by Mary Dow

ZAXXON

Also by Richard M Clements
and available from Chipmunka:

"Defender: Adventures In Schizophrenia"

Richard M Clements

ABOUT THE AUTHOR

Richard M Clements was born at Colchester Garrison Hospital in 1969. He overcame Dyslexia as a child thanks to the avant-garde Head Master of Felstead Junior School. After five years at Langley Park School in Norfolk he dropped out of 'A' Level studies aged seventeen to work on a building site.

Richard's first published work is his memoir entitled: *"Defender: Adventures in Schizophrenia"*, the story of a latent illness catalysed by his experimentation with LSD in 1989. He developed a love of creative writing over the next decade while trying a number of careers around the country.

'Zaxxon' is his debut occult thriller. Richard enjoys cinema, café culture, and sunny weather. He is currently working on his third book. Richard lives in Essex.

Richard M Clements

ZAXXON

ACKNOWLEDGMENTS

I would like to thank Dennis and Tonia of the Colchester Mind Advocacy Service for finding a publisher for *"Defender"* and for their unflinching excitement in its promotion. Thanks to all at the *Chipmunka Publishing* for their work. It is a brilliant idea that has given many people many opportunities. Gratitude must go to the staff in my sheltered accommodation for their support - for letting me stay so damn long - and for feeding my fish on the rare chances I get to go on holiday! Blessings (and a few apologies) must also go to my parents for their unceasing enthusiasm for all my writing. The war between us ended long ago and you never gave up on me. Thanks goes to all the mates I have made here in Colchester: Andrew, Paula, Terry 'D', Stuart, Nick, LEAP, Roger, Aron, Dizzy, 'G', Sam, Paul Bonus, Lee Stearn, Katherine and Carlito (and all the others at the Boudica Rio Samba drum batteria) and in particular to Leigh Smith. He is a gentleman who knows more about computers than I will ever, and without whose help much of what has happened would never have transpired. It just goes to show you can't have too many good friends!

Richard x

Richard M Clements

ZAXXON

CHAPTER – 1

"Sol.stice"

Rupert had never been caught before. The fear was like a swallowed tooth, a taste of blood. He had experienced a few close shaves, everyone did, but this time he hadn't been sufficiently vigilant to avoid a harbinger of the school rules. Someone had seen him cross a public path into one that was quite private, and Out Of Bounds. The June sunlight seemed clouded to him, and to him only: a bright chilled emergency that seemed to spread through every nerve ending in his stooped body. The noise came again, closer this time. Leafy branches somewhere over to his right twitched with a noise like rats scuttling across crusty newspaper.

In his adrenaline befuddled mind he was already running in the opposite direction, had already dropped the cigarette butt under his regulation black shoes and crushed it into the nicotine flavour spit that speckled the mud inside the bike shed, but in reality he was rooted to the spot. Not knowing how many were closing in on him, his right hand rose to his lips. To alleviate the fear he took another quick puff like a murderer absentmindedly scratching his head with a bloody dagger. A twig crackled. It was a subversive sound. He needed to hide behind a squeeze of toothpaste. He needed to go back about five minutes to when he had left the cafeteria after lunch, at twenty past one, to do anything other than come to this dismal shed for an illegal pleasure, but it was too late. He could hear the panting of his stalker.

His biology tutor, whose skin was as tight and only slightly greyer than his suit, swept around the side of the corrugated iron wall like a phantom. Rupert's heart leapt against his ribs and his acne flushed like a rash. Mr Marshall was as tall and thin and as forbidding as a cane, and he had a reputation for swinging one, but the price for being caught smoking was in many ways worse than that brief pain in the arse. The rapid breathing that Rupert had heard was his own. The teacher pronounced his surname like an insult, a stupid name identical to that new brand of cheap yoghurt.

"Empty out your pockets *Thornberry*," demanded Marshall. "I want to see all of it. Now! All your filthy works."
The moist stink of Rupert's crime and the butts of others was a smell soaked into the mud like embarrassment.

"Yes sir!" said Rupert, reaching into his loose trousers.

"Do you know what some people call 'works'?"

"No sir!" He pulled out some coins, a magnifying glass, and a tube of Colgate. But he knew that there was no point messing this teacher about. So he took a deep breath and also revealed a half empty packet of red Marlboro, a blue Clipper lighter, and some green acorns wrapped in a tissue. He couldn't recall why he had collected the acorns. He sneezed.

"Heroine users. Addiction, young man! That's what I'm talking about. Do you remember what I said about the habit of smoking to the 4th Form last year?"

"Yes sir, you said… I don't remember…"

"I said *two per day* probably doesn't make any difference to the lungs, but the habit can grow. And *I know* who smokes more than ten a day in this place." Marshall took the lighter and the Marlboro out of the boy's hands. "And you had better believe it!" He licked his lips.

Rupert was starting to relax now, to accept it was over, that he had been caught.
"It's the GCSE's sir… it's my last one today and exams make me nervous," he said.

"Your health is equally important to your betters, Thornberry. Biology – understand?"

"I do sir: I've got a touch of the Flu."

"All the more reason not to smoke. Report to your Housemaster at five o'clock for gating." He placed the Colgate tube back into Rupert's hand. "Now go and brush your teeth. Don't be late for Games."

*   *   *

ZAXXON

Rupert Reporting he thought, and walked down the concrete flags between the rhododendron bushes that joined the wide gravel path. The path led from the changing rooms, past the huge imposing Edwardian edifice at the front of the school, to the classroom blocks. Just before his sweaty shoes crunched on the gravel he heard a similar sound from behind him, from the scene of his crime, the unmistakable noise of a Clipper being lit. He smelt a wisp of smoke but felt too tired to be angry. His dreams had been upsetting him.

He started counting his coins, his mind already working on from whom he could purchase a few cigarettes. He had started the habit to be 'one of the lads' about two years ago but he had only been legally allowed to buy them for the last three months. He had turned sixteen, cursed with the greasy skin, the stinking feet and the berserk hormones, which come with the age - but his life was as mysterious as ever. His memory was as hazy as his motivations. Sixteen had brought with it no answers.

He wanted to lie on his bed, if only for an hour. His steps bisected the gravel path. He walked past the warm dead smell of the wheelie bins arranged in the sun at the back of the kitchens, and headed for a door leading into a corridor made of wire reinforced transparent plates. It surrounded the changing and locker rooms on the exposed sides of the red brick wall like a glass snake skin. He walked in the other direction. Infiltrated the annex adjacent to the main hall and then stood still to take stock. It smelt of old books and varnish. There weren't any people about so he slipped up the stairs and crossed the landing, hearing no noises from any of the 6th Form study bedrooms. It was against the rules to be in a dormitory between the hours of nine thirty am and half past four in the afternoon but Rupert didn't care. He was in the worst kind of trouble already.

He sat on the edge of his bed and unwrapped the incomprehensible pouch of acorns. He took off his thick glasses and examined the nuts closely, his woefully short focal length allowing a macro perspective. There were twenty of them. Like the date, he thought: June 20th. They were all green and hard. Rupert yawned and took a bite of one. His mouth flooded with bitter juices and he gagged and spat on the floorboards. That obviously wasn't why he had collected them; they weren't for eating. He sucked some toothpaste out of the end of the tube and sneezed.

The school doctor had offered him sleeping pills if he needed them because of his vile dreams. The pills had a weird name. Something like 'Zimmer frame', and the Matrons kept them for him in a bottle in the Surgery. Since he had exaggerated the symptoms of his cold he had also got himself put Off Games and this meant he had a couple of hours to brush up for his last exam. He was due to take paper two of the French G.C.S.E this afternoon but his memory was so terrible studying it probably wouldn't make the slightest bit of difference. He lay down and his head sank into the softness of his feather pillow. A cool breeze through the open window ruffled his black greasy hair, bringing with it the distant sounds of tennis and cricket. He yawned again and laced his hands guilelessly across his chest. He was going to sleep. He hoped that he wouldn't dream of his estranged parents, nor that other dream. That the light of day behind his eyelids would keep the old woman at bay, the witch that called herself Lilly, who raped him in his sleep.

It had begun seven weeks ago and he had tried to write some of it down but his notes were a scribbled mess of phonetic Dyslexia and over-pressed biro. Back at the beginning of term there had been only hazy images, like out of focus photographs. The nights of the week passed by and the scenes gained resolution as though rising through shallow water. It was like the transmission had been growing, somehow, then rippled into three dimensions and took on substance like a *fourth* dimension. Rupert could be taken sexually in his sleep, and a part of him could be taken to other places in his sleep where it would happen. He wanted to hate it.

ZAXXON

In that reality he sensed the old woman's strength. Lilly had bones like Titanium rivets yet he could feel her gentleness working on him, her soft hands, her hot mouth. Her paper-soft skin left behind a smell on his own like bird's nests and bruised grapes and he would awaken sweating, unable to recall much detail. Only essences: exotic words; a kiss; leaves. And that geriatric smell lingered in his nostrils for a while as he dried up his secret shame.

Except for one older friend, a sensitive 6th Former named Julian Rant, he had decided not to tell his colleagues about this. He could imagine their taunts. Kids could be cruel sometimes, Rupert knew that. 'Dirt-berry' and 'cheesecake', the common insults, might become 'Ghost-fucker' or 'Dream-wanker'. Most of the time he couldn't control his body odour either. He was harassed for being unable to accept that he was dirty. He didn't actually like water and he often felt too exhausted to shower before breakfast. His feet were a mess of fungal infection and smelly skin with a sweaty appearance like a wrinkly pink frog, and he hid his shoes under the blanket at the foot of his bed to muffle the smell. He hated the feel of starched cotton and wore his shirts for as long as the collar wasn't dirty enough to be seen like a black firework in daylight.

He did not dream of Lilly that afternoon but he woke up crying anyway, about having been sent to boarding school at the tender age of nine, too young, and about a lack of memories of his mum. He hadn't seen her since last Christmas when the atmosphere at his Dad's had been as cold as the turkey. He'd had only three photos of her but they were gone now. One day he'd been sitting alone in his dormitory looking at them and because his collar was so dirty that maniac of a House Captain, Tom Hudson, had tried the rip the shirt off his back. Rupert had called him "a son of a bitch" and Hudson had said: "let's see how you like *your* stupid life without *your* stupid bitch!" And ripped up the precious pictures.

Rupert could recall so little of the days before she had walked out. He wept. She had left him and his dad in a barrage of slurred insults and wobbled out of the front door like a thousand valiums being washed away in a flood of vodka. He pulled a pair of Y Fronts from out of his bedside locker, wiped away his tears and blew his nose in them. It was a noise that seemed very loud in the silence. He dropped the pants, his panic rising. He could no longer hear the smack of leather against willow, nor the shouts and thumps of the games of tennis... because there were no Games being played outside. They were all in exams! He had somehow slept through *both bells* and according to his Casio he was twelve minutes late for his own exam, his last test, the French paper!

Rupert swung into action feeling like the iron in his blood was being pulled out of the top of his head with a giant magnet. He re-knitted his tie, re-knitted it again, and then scrabbled about for his old pencil case. The adrenaline was making him feel as though he was breathing with lungs that were outside of his body and trying to take on enough substance to open the door and escape without the rest of him. For a few seconds he couldn't find his shoes then he saw the twin bulges under his blanket. For a disjointed moment he misinterpreted them as a pair of woman's breasts although he had never actually seen any in his life outside of a magazine. He bolted onto the landing. Inside the dormitory the sun shone on the dubious posters, the seven beds covered with the identical red counter-panes, and the identical bedside lockers. The door snapped closed, quietly.

He tore down the back stairs, his steps like beating drum sticks wrapped in cloth, and hit the vinyl floor and ran right, around the foot of the banisters into the main hall. "Je suis, tu es, ills son, vous et," he thought madly, his steps echoing on the parquet floor. He pushed open the heavy front door like he was a horse in a steeplechase and ran along the side of the East Wing; passing the windows of tuck box alley and the library block in a blur of ochre and grey granite. "Amo, amas, amat, amamus, amartis..." he thought, his shoes making a satisfactory crunching noise on the gravel, then: "No, dammit, that's *Latin!*"

He forced himself to adhere to another rule: to walk past the Head Master's house. It was a small modern building with much glass and a balcony from which to view the cricket. Within a few breaths he was running again, until he passed under the great Chestnut trees that led onto the concrete paths between the classroom blocks. He fancied people were taking a moment from their writings to stare: eyes watching, inwardly laughing. His acne felt like it was on fire. Strands of greasy hair were plastered over his forehead with sweat. He approached the double doors to the theatre, which had been commandeered again as the 5th Form hall because of its huge space, and a sign tacked on the glass bore the wounding legends: "SILENCE – EXAMS IN PROGRESS!"

The teacher overseeing the event was at a table on the front of the stage. He had a giant clock on his desk facing the boys that Rupert could read from where he was standing, the minute hand swooping toward the half hour like a knife. Rupert met the teacher's frozen eyes through the window and froze himself. It was Marshall. Without any idea how to undo the giant metaphorical lock that had closed these doors since he had become twenty minutes late, Rupert felt he couldn't knock. So he waved his old pencil case weakly in Marshall's direction. The teacher shook his head and made a decisive 'shooing gesture' to go away with flicks of his hand. It was over. He walked back very slowly, thinking about killing someone - himself.

*   *   *

At five o'clock Rupert walked into the main hall to receive his four weeks 'gating'. It was as though the floor was a tight rope that he could fall off at any time, fall a long way into a warm chasm. He knocked on the Staff Room door and waited. He felt a fear like he had felt when he had been caught in the first place. The door opened. Someone looked at him; then it was closed. Momentarily it opened again and there stood an icon for some and a dread for many, his ageing House Master, Mr Copeland. The stocky man was blocking the Staff Room doorway as though hiding secrets. His grey hair was combed into the shape of a 1940's Royal Air Force flying cap, his face red and wrinkled, and his moustache was tinted from pipe smoking. Many believed Copeland had always wanted to be Head Master but he had never made it, and now he was nearing retirement age; yet he still had eyes like a hunting leopard and was snaring Rupert's own with their full force.

"Here for castigation on time, I see, Thornberry," said Copeland. "I'll say good to that but to nothing else. You've been caught smoking red handed, haven't you? Again?"

"Yes Sir."

"You were bound to eventually, Thornberry, you cheeky pup. It was on the cards. Like the cards I seized from you last year when you were caught gambling."

"Yes, sir."

"And those filthy magazines!"

Rupert looked over Copeland's head. "I'm sorry sir!"

"That is a small word that doesn't mean very much. You are gated. You will wear full uniform in the evenings, *clean uniform*, and you are barred from leaving the school grounds at all times. At the weekends you will report to the Duty Master on the hour, every hour."

"For how long, sir?"

"The rest of term."

"But that's five weeks, not four!"

"If you violate any of these conditions I will recommend that you be expelled. Now go and shower. I can smell you from here."

Rupert took his shower and found three cigarettes in his changing room locker, hidden in his running spikes: an antidote for the pain. He couldn't remember having put them there but his frontal cerebral hemisphere felt warm and his mouth and lips and cheeks were stretched in a strange way. He realised he was smiling! Probably the first time he had smiled for a month. After towelling himself dry he put his dirty clothes back on. He intended to get as far away from the school's main building as possible before he lit up. He walked around the side of the Games Barn, along the tennis courts at the rear of the school, passed the large pond by the cedar tree with its round stone border and its unknown depths; headed for the trees, glancing into water that looked brackish yet inviting as he walked by. Over his shoulder he saw the main building had been swallowed up in the trees, losing him to the deep woods. Rupert was going to his Thinking Place where he was going to solve the last problem of his miserable life.

It's a lovely evening for such grim business, he thought, *like walking under water.* The sun was piercing the leafy canopy and dappled the ground with shards of light. It was almost an honour to walk over this rich soil, through these bright green textures. The forest floor was like an endless coral reef in crystal water that ebbed to and fro, fresh as a cool breeze, gentle as a lover's whisper. Rupert took his secret path. His destination was hundreds of paces away from the Scout Area, the school chapel, and the cadet's little assault course. In those places the earth was worn without much vegetation under foot and a sense of tiredness about the trees. *'But not here'*, Rupert thought, as he pushed through the bushes and between scaly trunks into his glade. This was his Thinking Place, a circle of grass with a tree stump to sit on near the centre hemmed in on all sides by the overhanging boughs of healthy trees.

Rupert sat on the stump and took out his magnifying glass to light a cigarette using the glass as a makeshift laser. He had seen this done on a TV show when he had been younger, and happier. The days when his parents had been together, when he hadn't known the weight of the world that bore down upon his rounded shoulders now. He took a deep pull of the cigarette, his body quickly suffused with the elixir of nicotine. The exams were supposed to have been opportunities to open a better future, chances to make qualifications, to choose 'A' Levels that might have led to a university place. But unless he thought about it really hard he couldn't even remember what subjects he had taken. He had an overall essence of the breadth of his failures but the details were just pieces of paper, dim, and fluttering with desperation. The final decision to make was here, in this place, how to end it all: rope, wrist, or roof.

Then came the noise of breaking branches from the same direction he had taken himself. He had been hearing similar sounds for at least a minute but he'd been too deep in thought to register it. Someone was beating down stinging nettles with a stick, twigs snapping underfoot, blundering along Rupert's own secret path. Whoever it was obviously didn't care if anyone heard the noise. Rupert looked at his cigarette with a rueful sense of disappointed amusement. He was caught again - for the second time in one day - but what difference did that matter to someone who was going to commit suicide? The intruder popped into the glade like a bubble of wax rising to the top of a lava lamp. It was a 6th Form prefect, a figure of authority yet Rupert's good friend. Julian Rant walked up to the tree stump.

"What are you doing here?" Rant asked.
"I'm thinking about death."
"How did the French paper go?"
"I was late and the sheriff wouldn't let me take it."
"Marshall *didn't let you in?* You should complain!"
Rupert looked at him. "How did you find me?"
"I saw you out of my window, and came round the back." Rant sat cross-legged on the lush grass. "You could make a formal written complaint to Oxbridge, you know that?"
"It isn't worth bothering with. Even if they let me sit the thing again I'd still make a total cock up of it."
"That's the only definition of the expression 'cock up' I don't like."
Rupert was surprised to find that he was chuckling at this. "It gets worse."
"Yeah, you got gated for smoking, I know. That's why I followed you. I figured you might need a shoulder to cry on."

ZAXXON

"Actually I've been crying a lot recently Julian. I'm low on my new mother's to do list. My old mum, she's sober these days but it's like she's embarrassed about what happened and she's re-married an idiot. I'm still with my dad but he's in 'corporate entertainment' now, whatever the hell that means, flitting all around the world shagging a girl in every city. He sends me a tenner every couple of weeks and seems to think that makes everything alright but he's left me here in this opulent hypocritical shit dump excuse for a school!"

"You're babbling," said Rant.

"I've got a load of younger step-brothers and sisters from my old mum's new husband that I've never even met before and I can't remember their names: I can't remember anything!" He leaned forward. "I remember their surname though, oh yes. Why can't I have a cool name like that? I used to like the name Thornberry but then *Thornberry Dairy Products* came out with a load of yoghurt – and not milk yoghurt either but that stuff with friendly bacteria in it. How can bacteria be friendly? And the cheesecakes; and milk shakes and trifles and low fat... what's that crap called? yeah – 'fromage frais', yeah, I hate my name!"

"Calm down, Rue."

"Rupert's a stupid name too. I want to die!" Rupert stubbed his cigarette on the side of the tree stump then dropped it on the grass and pushed it into the soil with a finger.

"Things will get better."

"Even if they do I won't remember. You know when we talked the other night, when you said that the human mind has a way of blanking out the bad stuff?"

"A defence mechanism. Yeah."

"Well, I don't remember anything *good* either. I'm gonna kick the bucket, I swear it."

"Rupert, show some back-bone!"

"Suicide for me, yes, but not for the reasons you might think."

"I feel it's my responsibility to cheer you up. Can I change the subject, Rue?"

"Okay."

He thought about the subject for a moment, then said: "Do you think you'll be in this place forever?"

"Don't talk to me about forever. I might learn what forever really means, and soon - even though I've never had a girlfriend. Never even been kissed! Except by Lilly."

"She isn't real."

"She seems pretty bloody real to me! I used to think that she was like a grandmother with the sex drive of an eighteen year-old."

"But, *you* yourself are young."

"And that witch isn't, if you don't look at her right. What's it like to have a girlfriend?"

"How should I know? I'm gay, remember?"

"She ties me up sometimes... 'I'm coming! I'm coming!' She says."

Rant reddened. He seemed to pause to think; then said: "This dream. It might mean too many years have gone by to reconcile your relationship with your real mother."

"You saying I want to screw my mother?"

"No, God forbid! When your real mum is the age of your dream demon she won't act anything like that. No, what I'm saying is that you want to be your dad, and go back into the past to sort it out, make things right before your mum is too old."

"But there are a few points you don't know, what I call the Main Points. Lilly's actions are very real; *more* than like in a dream, and progressive," Rupert explained. "My sleeping tablets "will always equal sleep", that's what the Doc told me. He also said that I wouldn't dream so much, that they would cause "black sleep", but two nights ago I took some and had a vision. She teleported a part of me, my astral body if you like, into a room full of red drapes and mirrors. And I can remember exactly what she said, the Main Points. Why do I remember?"

"Even a broken clock tells the correct time twice per day."

"Eh?"

"It's something I read. Did you know that Picasso painted a picture with three clocks in it melted everywhere like fried egg whites? He called it "The Persistence of Memory.""

ZAXXON

"You're kidding!"

"No, it's true... so, what did she say?"

"She said: "I'm coming, I'm coming Rupert *soon, for us* to merge in the night when part of you will die and part of me will be born," she said that, and then she said: "After three hundred years our lips will conjure it and I will never be old and ugly again: we will both be beautiful to behold forever.""

"Interesting."

"Isn't it? What is really fascinating, though, is that when I caught sight of her in a mirror out of the corner of my eye I saw she had changed. She had become a little over my age, sexy and slim and feminine. She had streaks of silver hair, but not like grey, like a newly polished silver cigarette box that seems to glow. I saw her true essence in that reflection and she is beautiful."

"So now you've got two things that you didn't have before," said Rant, with a smile.

"What?"

"A dream-girl *and* a reason to live." His stomach rumbled. The time on his watch obviously surprised him. "I think we'll have to run for it if we want to eat."

"It can't be dinnertime already. Look at the angle of the sun."

"It's the longest day of the year tomorrow, Rue, the Summer Solstice." Rant stood up and stretched like a long bow. "You going to run with me?"

"No, I've already done enough of that today. And I don't feel like eating either. I'll stay here."

Rupert lit a cigarette with his magnifying glass thinking about the sun, and the Solstice. But in his mind it was a black festival, the shortest night. He let his friend go without telling him that he himself was going to get a classmate to steal something for him: the key to the Surgery and the four digit PIN number for the security keypad on the medication cabinet. Because if Rupert saw Lilly in all her loveliness again - tonight - and she accepted him, he was going to die to be with her. He would sacrifice his daydreams for his nightdreams and do it tomorrow using a massive over-dose of sleeping pills.

His mind drifted in and out of the past like a blind person surfing the web with their Braile keyboard at arm's length. Sometimes he didn't think at all and did not realise it. The noise snapped him out of such a fugue, like a scream in a church. He stood, a snarl of pain and pleasure a few hundred feet away echoing into the silence, and he realised that there was something more wrong than the sudden fear the sound provoked. There were no birds singing and it was getting cold. He started breathing faster and his fingertips were pressed into his palms. His bladder felt full and he lowered his head as though he had the eyes of soldier peering into hostile jungle. He needed to return to the main building. Wanted to get back amongst people that were cruel but at least predictable. The forest he knew had gone, become a fear of horror. He started walking.

The growling noise happened again, moaning with desires Rupert could only guess at. It was a noise terrifying and yet lonely, a hollowness that needed to be satiated with more than sex, perhaps with another of itself. Rupert continued walking and trod in the mess before he saw it. The ground beside an ancient oak tree was covered in stinking green stuff that had been shed from a hole in its trunk. The roots of the tree were a confusion of bark that was gnarled and dark and dripping. It was on his shoes. The hole in the massive girth of the tree's trunk gaped, and was scored with downward claw marks and dripped slime as though some kind of monster had been born here, had torn its way out of the side of the tree. Rupert could sense a presence. He looked around but didn't see anything else unusual. Whatever travesty of nature had taken place here it was clearly over but that didn't stop him from starting to run. On a tree branch thirty feet above the ground a new-born demon watched him go and rubbed its groin on the wood.

*　　　　　　*　　　　　　*

Russell Chase, the "Man Who Could Get Things," was Rupert's age and they slept in the same dormitory, yet

ZAXXON

Chase had a blonde #2 head shave that was like the opposite to Rupert's black spikes, and Chase was also taller. He looked down at Rupert's ruffled jacket and grimy collar and dirty shoes. Then he noticed Rupert's newly washed hair. "Hell, Thornberry, you've had a shower and you still smell terrible! Is your cheesecake passed its sell-by date?!"

"I suppose so."

Rupert stepped agitatedly from foot to foot, loosening tiny bits of green crust from his shoes onto the wooden floor of the landing. "I need you to get something for me."

"Sorry, it's Light's Out in three or four minutes. We'll talk tomorrow."

"Ten pounds," said Rupert. "Cash." He sneezed.

The taller boy became brusque. "Chase by name Chase by nature: what can I get for you?"

"I want the key to the surgery and the PIN number to the medicine cabinet."

"What *the fuck* do you want that for?"

"I need them, please, Jack –"

"Stow that!" Chase poked Rupert in the chest with a finger in step with each of the syllables of: "Don't. Call. Me. After. A. Dog."

"I'm sorry, I'm really sorry, Russell. But I need them."

"Why?"

"Personal reasons." He coughed.

"The only personal thing you need is a clean uniform. Tell me the reasons." Chase's expression suddenly dawned with understanding. "Drugs, right? I don't deal drugs Thornberry, you know that!"

"I'll give you fifteen."

"No way."

"Twenty!" Rupert's hands grabbed the neck of the other boy's England football shirt. Chase looked surprised because he, himself, was strong. No one ever got into a fight with him. "I need sleeping pills," blurted Rupert: "Twenty quid, OK? – Cash, tomorrow!"

"Get off!" exclaimed Chase.

He took Rupert's wrists and tried to prise them away from the collar of his expensive shirt. "You smelly drug user addict, get off!" Rupert shook his arms and the taller boy's head wobbled backwards and forwards, then Chase snapped his forehead forward a fourth time into Rupert's in a head-butt. BANG! Rupert's vision was swimming with white stars. With the strength of his anger against life Rupert shoved the taller boy against the wall. Chase tried to get him into a head-lock but they both lost balance and fell sprawling.

"What *the bloody hell* is going on here?" shouted authority.

It was their House Captain, 'The Hammer' Hudson, standing over them with his arms crossed. The fighters let go of each other. Rupert rebalanced his thick glasses onto his nose and blinked about myopically. The fight had attracted an audience. To Rupert they looked like ghosts rowing a phantom long ship in a rough sea. Hudson adored Mr Copeland and was known to be the old man's lap-dog; a prefect feared yet often considered dull-witted. 'Hammer' was a nick-name he had developed for himself. Hudson had been known to be a brute.

He turned to their spectators and said: "Alright lads, back in your dorms. I know you like to watch a good scrap but there's nothing more to be seen here. Off you go."

The crowd dispersed; wandering back into their rooms stealing whispers and glances. Hudson leaned over the two dazed boys, took a long look at them, then pulled Rupert up by the scruff of his jacket back onto his feet. "You are late for Light's Out, Cheesecake, and as usual you smell awful." Russell Chase climbed unsteadily to his feet, also. He opened his mouth to begin an explanation but Hudson interrupted him: "On your way now, Jack. I can see that this was obviously not your fault." Chase backed away. "Oh, and by the way," said Hudson, "that century you scored on the field today was the batting of a master." Chase paused inconspicuously in the shadows, watching, silent and quickly forgotten. Hudson looked Rupert up and down, particularly down, and wrinkled his nose.

"How did your shoes get like that? Have you been stepping in and out of goose shit?"

Rupert avoided Hudson's eyes, focusing anyplace else. Floorboards. Light fittings. Doors. The small pieces of paper on the huge landing notice-board. "Guano," said Rupert, because he couldn't muster a way to answer Hudson's question.

"What did you call me?"

"I didn't... I mean, guano means bird-crap... it's like the goose, you -"

"I don't care about the goose! How could school uniform get so mashed with muck?" It was one of Hudson's favourite phrases. "What's the matter, cheesecake, forgotten what amnesia means?"

Rupert looked at him. "That's not fair."

"Try this on for size: report to my study at half past six tomorrow morning in running kit."

"I'm sick of this place!" Rupert cried, "I just want to go to bed, I'm not well!"

"Don't raise your voice to me, cheeky pup!"

"What, you're like Mr Copeland's bosom buddy now, or something, that you have to use his expressions?"

Hudson pistol-whipped Rupert in the face with the back of his hand. The pain was a sudden surprise to Rupert but the attack itself was, to anyone watching, perhaps predictable. The younger boy felt an agony that cancelled his anger as his glasses spun off and broke against the wall. Hudson raised his hand a second time when a young man intervened.

"Hudson, stop this!" shouted Julian Rant. "That's enough!"

The senior prefect raised his hand further still, until his elbow was level with his shoulders.

"Step away from the boy, Hudson!" Rant said.

Hudson dropped his hand and stood blinking at Rupert as though he didn't know where he was. Rant stepped up and squeezed Hudson's forearm to capture his attention.

"Take deep breaths, now... OK, good?"
Hudson shook himself. "Yeah...yeah, I'm OK." He looked at Rupert, who was hesitantly exploring his face for injuries. "Get back in your dormitory, Thornberry. And remember: six thirty tomorrow in running kit."
"I'll do their Light's Out for them," said Rant, "A S A P."

Hudson thanked him. Rupert walked into his dormitory doorway nursing his broken glasses. They were retro 'Harry Palmer' type plastic glasses and one of the arms had snapped off. The shapes of Rant assisting Hudson towards the back stairs became increasingly hazy, and he heard Rant saying, gently: "Come on Hud, I'll make you a nice mocha."

A few minutes later Rant put a fresh scented bundle at the foot of Rupert's bed. It was a complete change of school uniform. "You've only got the one jacket, Rue," he whispered, "so wash it before your first report to Marshall tomorrow. And clean your shoes." Rant waited for him to wrap sticky tape around the hinge of his glasses and then switched the lights off. The boys discussed their G. C. S. E.s and cricketing achievements, and talked about what they would get drunk on first when the long holidays began. In the dark there was some talk of Hudson and Rupert. It seemed to him that his colleagues thought his actions out on the landing had been crazy as opposed to brave. The talk petered out like a glider being released to fly noiselessly into the night. *Well, at least I won't have any bruises in my sleep*, he thought. Then, suddenly, Chase's voice whispered: "You've got some pluck, Thornberry. Fifteen pounds. I'll have it by morning."

*   *   *

ZAXXON

Rupert dreamt of waiting for a train in the London Underground, but there were no trains. He was alone and felt hungry enough to eat two rare 'T' bone steaks. He realised he could see without his glasses. He had pure 20/20 vision but that didn't prevent him getting lost whilst looking for a chocolate vending machine. The tunnels were all illuminated in deep red light, and the stations had trees growing either side of the track. None of them were on any map. The branches that stretched around the domed roof of these stations looked as though saplings had been planted and some mad engineer had anticipated their growth and built the ceiling around them. He could smell grilling meat on the warm air wafting downstairs, a fast food smell from above that made him salivate. The problem was the escalator: when he was half way up, alone with its electrical rumbling droning motors, he disappeared: had a flash of running into the night holding the hand of a beautiful woman, and then re-appeared at the bottom. He tried it twice and on his third attempt he noticed he was holding a feather in his free hand during the transition.

On the eighth attempt he actually managed to tear the feather out of that subliminal moment. Once again standing at the bottom of the stairs, he found he now had a quill pen in his left hand with 'BIC' written on it and wet ink on its tip. Food appeared on the escalator moving in the opposite direction. There were takeaway boxes of it coming down, which disappeared when they brushed the bottom step. He picked one up and opened it. A joy! Inside was a delicious steaming cheeseburger in a toasted sesame seed bun with relish and lettuce and tomato. But when he closed his lips around it, it disappeared. His stomach growled with anger at this deceit. Wondering what to do with the quill he suddenly had an idea. He snatched up another burger box and wrote "FOOD PLEASE!" on it and placed it on the steps going upwards. About a minute later he saw the box coming back down the other way and grabbed it excitedly. It rattled.

Inside were about twenty acorns. He paused to recall the bitterness he had spat on the dormitory floor earlier that day, but whatever dream-weaver was controlling this fantasy had chosen these as food. He put one into his mouth, and crunched it. Unlike the sap of a freshly pruned daffodil, it actually had a taste that was wonderful; and, somehow, also *emotive*. The flavours of hot roasted chestnuts and dark chocolate, and revenge. He dropped the empty box and burped. Still hungry, after he poked the quill feather (end down and nib upwards) in his top pocket, he wondered whether there were any more acorns to be had and walked through two tunnels.

It was comparatively quiet in the next station. It had a smell like a beach under a holiday sun; perfume and sunscreen and sweat, yet paradoxically cool. It was the smell of the trees. They towered above his head like wax-work representations; the work of an artisan mimicking nature's beautiful and unfolding chaos. He stepped carefully amongst the tree roots foraging for acorns. A lot of the lower limbs were burrowed, impossibly, into the concrete. He heard a scuttling sound and straightened up. He listened... and there it was again, the scratching of animal claws. He figured they belonged to a tunnel rat - a very big rat coming up behind him – and, like a man who doesn't wish to face a threat, fear turned his feet slowly.

Rupert's eyes met the sight of a scrawny little dog skipping along towards him. It was white with black and tan patches, its tail wagging with a happy determination. It was a Jack Russell that looked like its food had been unfairly taken away in much the same way as Rupert's burgers. It sat on its haunches directly in front of him and dropped a key out of its mouth onto the floor. It made a tinkling noise when it hit the stone flagging, a shiny door key that made a sound that was definitive and exciting, like a gold coin dropped on a mirror. Honing Rupert's sense of disorientation the Jack Russell said: *"You've got some pluck, Thornberry,"* and then it jumped off the edge of the platform and ran off along the track.

ZAXXON

The key had a number '18' engraved on it. Rupert put it in his trouser pocket and took a hike along the tracks himself. The tunnels were larger than you might rightly have expected if you were looking out at them from a train, seeing the blackness and the reflections of people inside the carriage in the windows. All the tunnels were lit in this anxious red light, apparently without the use of electric bulbs. The deep red glow suffused the tubes and made Rupert feel as though he was walking along the arteries of a beating heart. His shoes echoed his steps, and he didn't know how far he had walked. In the fourth or fifth new station he noticed something that jogged his own heart, both emotionally and physically. Almost walking passed it on the track he saw a poster on the wall of a beautiful woman over the lip of the platform. He mounted it, breathlessly. The woman had a face that was slim and lovely, the image pasted up between the trunks of two wrinkled trees.

It was a shot from the waste upwards of Lilly, the young bodied Lilly. She had long black and silver hair, and teeth like hooked incisors. They poked out slightly from between her full lips and looked as though they had been extended for a fantasy film; or had been filed down by a dentist, or that they were a physical fact and somehow part of a nastier reality. Her breasts were full and her nipples were visible beneath the silky dress. He loved the evidence. He walked up to the portrait and the closer he came to her image the more his own crotch seemed to glow. Initially he felt embarrassment about this, which was ridiculous since he hadn't seen another living thing in this underworld except for a small talking dog: he was alone. Thinking of the dog reminded him of the door key in his trouser pocket. He took it out and found the source of the glow, glittering now with white purple light. Rupert held it aloft: Key #18, blazing with ultra violet light that shone upon the image of Lilly. It revealed a secret Yin Ylang configuration, missing the 'S' shaped balancer, drawn on her upper lip, and words hidden across her ample chest, in italic letters, saying: *BURY THE KEY IF YOU WANT TO LIVE.* Beneath that, in smaller letters, was written: *Our lips will conjure it: inscribe the symbol.*

He understood this instinctively as though he had a different mind in this place. As if he knew well the mind of his beautiful lady, but he did not know her. Rupert had only an inkling of Lilly's secret self and he was trying to bury that in the deepest parts of his mind, because being with her may have a price, a cost to his eternal soul that he didn't want to dwell upon. He took up the quill and noticed again the letters BIC written along the side of the feather. He traced the whole shape the Yin Ylang, paying particular attention to the reflective dividing curve, then he dropped the quill and blew on the inscription. The ink soaked into the paper, and he leaned forward and kissed the likeness of her sensuous lips. The whole of that reality wobbled like a rock thrown into a lake.

A subdued electric whining noise began from down the track. An approaching train was pushing warm air before it out of the tunnel into his face. The noise got louder and the ground shook. Then the image of Lilly fell away, the picture falling in flakes onto the floor. He watched the appearance of the bones underneath, the bones of a beast's skull, and then that crumbled also into a pile of silver shavings that blew away as the train rumbled into the station. The picture was gone... and in its place was a green door with letters reading: FIRE EXIT. He looked back at the train, rubbing the key in his left hand without thinking. The doors were opening and clearly there was no one on board. He looked back at the door and saw a key-hole in it about the size of key#18. Suddenly a woman's voice spoke from a tannoy up in the branches:

"To leave the school grounds, please bury the key, or use the nearest exit."

Rupert thought about it, and he knew that he didn't have much time to decide. The words on the disintegrated picture of Lilly had said to 'bury' the key, and a train was clearly another source of exit, but how could you bury something in the floor of a train? Time was almost up. As the announcer said: "Mind the Gap," he noticed again the key-hole in the door. He rubbed his nose. Logic dictated that he was *far less likely* to get up to the surface on a train than through an exit, and then the carriage doors slid closed. The train moved off, its motors whining as it accelerated into the tunnel and disappeared round the bend.

Rupert stood for a while, tapping the key on the door. The sound was paradoxically a blend of excitement and boredom, and it echoed to and fro in the empty station. *"What the hell,"* he thought, *"It's all just a dream anyway."* He pushed key #18 into the keyhole and found it was a perfect match. The worst that could happen was waking up with acne puss on his pillow. The door unlocked with a subtle a click, and he opened it. He opened it wider. Through the doorway he saw the rear of the school at night. The cusp moon was bathing the gardens in blue and casting all else into black shadows. Judging by the position of the pond, and the tennis courts, and the angle of the gravel path below where everybody lined up for roll call after breakfast every morning, Rupert realised that he was looking from the third floor out of the leftmost window of his own dormitory. A cool breeze blew into his face and he swayed with sudden vertigo because there was no glass to prevent him falling sixty or seventy feet.

You're awake my little thorn, said Lilly, telepathically. *I'm down by the pond, see now?*

Her mind speech had an accent he had never heard before, a strong youthful voice with a haunting brogue like that of the Irish. He peered deep into the dark panorama and saw her. Indeed she was there, it was true: a slim person in some kind of flowing garment standing by the pond about four hundred feet away. "I see you!"
Come to me now if you want to love me, said Lilly.
  "I've been waiting to dream of you."
Who said you have to be asleep?

"I want to be with you forever," said Rupert, "I'll die to do it!"

Then gain nothing, she whispered into his head. *Come to me next time…*

Suddenly his mouth was filling with pills. The coating wore off quickly to introduce a taste of foul chemicals. They were clogging his tongue and went spasming down into his stomach. More tablets spilled from his lips and got stuck in the back of his throat. They sprinkled the ground, spit soaked clods of white sleeping tablets, and he felt increasingly faint. Sick like on a taste of bleach. Rupert swayed then fell through the doorway and dropped. The wind whistled past his face but instead of being smashed into shattered bits of oblivion on the gravel path below he landed on something soft.

He no longer felt sick but he couldn't see anything, and he couldn't stretch his toes or his arms. Cramped in a tight place, after pressing his fingertips into the satin cloth above his head he realised he was in a coffin and started to panic in earnest. What day was this? Had he taken the over-dose already? Actually done it, *for real?* He kicked and punched and shouted for help. None came. Then his screams were drowned by a gushing noise from outside, from all around. He started to get warm and smelt smoke. It began to fill his nostrils. Quickly he was getting really hot, coughing, and dripping sweat as the box was cremated. This was the FIRE EXIT.

*   *   *

Rupert sat up in bed in a tangle of bedclothes, breathing hard, and fighting with his duvet. He thought he might have screamed. With a hand clamped over his mouth he listened to the others. The room was silent but for sleeping breath. The 'beep' of his digital watch announcing midnight seemed comparatively loud. They were all asleep and Rupert slowly lowered his hand. He had got through the nightmare without waking anyone! However much he needed one he wanted to save his last cigarette for after breakfast. He also wanted to have dream sex with Lilly but he didn't think he would get to sleep for a long time.

You're awake my little thorn, said Lilly, telepathically. *I'm down by the pond, see now?*

Rupert's body petrified with shock. His skin prickled with anxiety; was the nightmare not yet over?

His laboured breathing went unnoticed and his mouth felt dry and crusty. He couldn't move for the Déjà Vu, frozen in a reality crisis about whether or not he was awake.

Except for the kind of dreaming all react to everyday, you are not asleep. Look out at me.

He slapped himself, trying to do it quietly; then bit his hand. He drew blood and the pain verified he was awake. He sensed her amusement in his mind. Was she laughing about the taste of his blood? Was she a monster, or a messiah? He put his mended glasses on his face and looked around at what was normal: here, this dormitory, wrapped in humid tranquillity, his friend's beds indistinct. But perhaps he was about to cross some kind of border to be with Lilly? Did he really want that? Absolutely, yes!

Rupert took several deep breaths then climbed out of bed. He tip-toed over to the left hand window, crossing the room as though it was mined, and opened the musty curtains. He smiled wistfully at the daunting panorama of the night. The cusp moon was low on the horizon, casting long shadows through the gardens and forest as he had seen in his sleep already. When his eyes were drawn to the pond, he gaped: for standing near it by the trunk of the great cedar was a woman; pale and slim, who appeared to be wearing a flowing dress. It was Lilly. Her appearance was identical to the 'reality' of his bizarre dream-life, but here she was waiting for him to hold her and kiss her in the real world!

"I see you!" he hissed.
Come to me now if you want to love me.

He crept back to his bed, picked up the bundle of fresh clothes and emptied them joyfully onto his duvet. He dressed. With a dirty jacket and rank shoes, and only that token of Celotape to hold his glasses together, Rupert slipped quietly out of the dormitory. His watch read 00:04 on the night of June 21st.

Midnight to midnight, thought Lilly. *Two nights together and then the rest of time.*

He crossed the landing then walked stealthily down the back stairs. He moved through the hall into corridors that smelt of the vinyl flooring. It was a maze here, with essences of boot polish and useless advice, and all lit by dull orange night-lighting. The colour had an aura of excitement and cast strange shadows, the bulbs positioned in places no one would rightly expect. Rupert covered the ground floor like an escaping convict. He listened at doors. He kept his steps quiet... and he was sly, always cautious being 'pinched' would not hinder his new destiny. All the while he was attempting not to whisper: "She's real, she's real, she's real!" over and over, and aloud, so as to understand the evidence of his own eyes, that Lilly was flesh and blood.

Flesh and blood, she thought into his head, amused. *Life... oh, and what a taste for it!*

He sensed a darkness in her but her laughter was a gentle tinkling noise that made him smile. He passed the cafeteria doorway and then furtively entered the extension of the main building, through a swing door into the glass corridors that skirted the changing rooms. The secrets of the night lay beyond. His dirty shoes squeaked on the tiles as he walked up to the final door. With hands trembling, and a sheen of sweat threatening to snap the tape on his glasses, he pushed through the last doorway out into the night. Along the concrete path beside of the Games Barn he went, the sound of his steps vanishing when he stepped onto the grass. His breath was coarsening with rising excitement. The breeze was whispering in the trees. He walked towards the pond along the tall netting that marked the boundary of the nearest tennis court, his senses heightened with adrenaline. Which was perhaps why he smelt the woman before he saw her: an edgy, animal-like musk sweetening the night wind blowing towards him.

Hello, my little thorn, she thought, happily. Then she made a kind of *"sssssss"* sound in his head, but not a snake's hiss, more like the word 'sex', yet unfinished and lingering.

The pond water had an odour he picked up also. A spunky smell, like the answer to the first, strange enough to frighten him, but over-all things were looking good. His erection suggested that none of this was his imagination and nor, for the first time, were the events that were to follow. He walked faster and then saw her; beautiful, *real.* She had a strong back, and silver-streaked hair cascading over her shoulders that seemed to glow in the moonlight. He closed the distance between them but when he was about ten feet away his eyes slid out of focus. He had out-guessed this already and took off his glasses, slipped them into his top pocket. Now he saw her, and with clarity unlike anything he had ever seen before.

Her eyes glittered like emeralds. She wore nothing under her diaphanous robe; it was a delicate weave as transparent as spider web. Her breasts were rounded and proud, moving gently with her breathing, and her calves were long and firm. He drank in her curves. She wore a belt around her waist made of what appeared to be a woven vine. He reached out nervously and actually touched it!

"Did you make that?" he asked, his mouth going dry.
"Yes, does it please you?"
"It's very pretty... like you."
"Thank you," she seemed gratified. "I made it just now!"

"Yours is the same voice I've heard in my dreams. Are you Lilly?"

"Lillith."

"My name's Rupert." Oh, how he hated that name!

"I know about you," she said, "- *all* about you." He was a little disappointed, but not surprised. It was logical considering the recent history of his sleep. "And I can promise you, now, that no 'friendly bacteria' have ever passed my lips!" She chuckled musically. "Nor *fromage frais,* nor any other artificially influenced milk produce!*"*

It was funny, but he sensed that darkness in her again. He wanted to dive in and swim in it forever. She took his hands in hers and his skin prickled. Not with sensual frisson, but with an electric shock. He saw glints of blue light sparkling around his knuckles and fingers: the ache of the bite to his hand evaporated and the teeth marks disappeared!

"You have many enemies," she continued. "Hate them. By this time on the morrow you may be invincible. I know also that you are not happy with your body, but remember the depth of beauty. To me flesh is putty." (The alternative to the word 'putty' he gleaned telepathically from her mind was something like 'food', but he didn't care. An amazing transformation was happening). "Let me show you!"

Lillith's hands gripped his with firm reassurance. Electricity with a taste like peaches surged through his body once again. He couldn't pull away. It sparkled up his arms and neck and into his face as Lillith closed her eyes. His mottled acne dwindled into skin as smooth and as pale as hers. His hair became weightless and soft, as clean as if it had been washed with moonlight, and he laughed with amazement. "Lower your eyelids, also," she instructed. He did.

His spine straightened with a delicious crackle of his vertebra. His bones braced up like steel bars. Sinews thickened and fat became tempered muscle. His brain fumbled.

ZAXXON

"Trust Lillith," she said. "It's real. Open your eyes now."

She withdrew her hands and he sensed in her a powerful pride. Rupert found himself over three inches taller than he had been, and with a startling new perspective: he was looking down at her! He was conscious that his clothes were small. His body was buzzing, ready for anything like a gigantic battery at full charge. He felt he could crunch a snooker ball into dust with one hand.

"Satisfied?" she asked.

"Yes," he whispered... then dried up. The crotch of trousers was standing up like a tennis racket!

"No, you aren't, go and disrobe. Our needs are... mutual." She looked down at the evidence of her sway then giggled and ran off.

"Hey, where are you going?" he cried, then engaged the new machine of his fitness with a fierce smile and gave chase.

She ran into the forest and looked like a ghost weaving between the trees. The vicinity was as black as pitch because clouds were covering the moon but his night vision pierced this obscurity. He found he had eyes like that of a predatory animal and pursued her at a fast yet leisurely pace with an uncanny almost complete silence. This was instinctive. He was enjoying himself: a hunter for sport, for sex. He heard her laughter up ahead and chased her through the Scout Area realising they had run almost in a complete circle. Then somewhere between the pond and the rear of the Head Master's house she suddenly dropped into the ground: and disappeared!

He was relieved when he understood that she had jumped into the sunken garden. Slowing to a walk, and ready to run again if she bounded up the other side, the hunter crept curiously along the top of the bank. The clouds uncovered the moon, casting bright blue light onto Lillith, who was lying by the steps at the far end of the tract of grass, smiling at him with her head propped up coyly on one arm. He went down the bank in a controlled stumble, straightened up on the lower ground, and then walked towards her. His blood stream shuddered when he saw that she was naked. She had fashioned a bed out of her robe on a patch of soft old leaves and he was overcome with pre-nuptial timidity. The sexual predator became Cheesecake Thornberry again, with the same athletic physique but timorous rather than ravenous. Lillith started squirming erotically on their bed, fingering herself: sensuous, snakelike. His erection returned speechlessly. He watched her caress herself, then lick her fingers. She said:

"Divest your attire, and have sex with me, hmmm?" It was a juicy question as delirious as her movements.
"What are you?" he asked. He had to know.
"Lillith," she replied.
"No - *what* - are you?"
"I'll tell you after I've opened myself to you... pleasure me... bury your thorn in me!"

At this his hesitation dissolved. He tore away his clothing in an over-powering seizure of lust and leapt on the woman, kissing and licking and scratching. She egged him on as he took her, encouraging his ravishment with arcane language and warm spittle as he drilled into her, abandoning his whole self inside her heat. All Rupert's repression burned in this conjugal fire. He re-mounted her, again, and often, with a passion that had always been within him. She was the catalyst, so he thought. She had chosen well.

He was blissfully ignorant of the virtually impossible number of orgasms they made for each other that night. A few hours before dawn he was peaceful, and went to sleep in a comfortable euphoria and a great quantity of last autumn's gossamer thin, fragrant, leaves. At daybreak the woman dressed and vanished to a destination as mysterious as the evaporating mist.

Rupert no longer had to die to be with Lillith. He could *live* to be with her, and thus he had a *reason to live* at last; truly, as

Rant had said. He was fulfilled, but he would be lucky if he would remember her answer to the query that really bothered him: about *what* she was. Not only because of his amnesia, but because she had told him as he fell asleep. She had altered herself into another of her semblances and scored a message for him deep into the stone steps with a fingernail. Then she had leant over him and answered his question, spoken the word in a dozen languages. She had said it as if she enjoyed wrapping her forked tongue around its dark intonations. She told him to call her '*Succubus*' and then she had crawled away like nothing on Earth.

CHAPTER TWO

"Water.shed"

Tony Newman was walking to meet a lovely girl that he hadn't seen for three months. He ambled along apparently aimlessly through the Broadmead shopping precinct, deep in thought. He had left Sussex on the train journey to Bristol two days ago. Stepping onto that platform at Temple Meads station he had felt like a soldier about to join the front line of a battle, such a contrast to when he had initially arrived in the city last autumn. He had been eighteen, then: an art student wanting to learn and make friends and find his vocation, but in spite of his optimism he had started mixing with the 'wrong people' and had eventually been expelled from the college. That had been three months and ten days ago. He had returned to the bosom of the family in disgrace, did jobs with no prospects and gained no respect from his parents for his promising art. So he went back to the city, returned to face the challenges of creating self-esteem - and would begin this very afternoon by dropping an envelope of seventeen photographs of his finest work at Gillows Gallery Of Contemporary Art. He was also going to see Samantha.

Along with his luggage and the one-way ticket he had travelled upon, he also carried the perception of a man unemployed to these, almost familiar, surroundings. En route to the flat he shared with Demitrius Kiriacou he had looked out of the taxi-cab window. He saw a dreaded exposure, the barely concealed chaos and uncertainty of the streets. He had heaved his bags up the stairs hoping that the rest of his property remained in his room. It was there, still: his easel and canvases, his hog's hairs and his Windsor and Newton. The bed was musty and soft; on the wall was a poster of the latest super-model. The room was a mess of stolen tyres and alloy wheels and car parts but it still retained a feeling of anticipation, like waiting for the launch of a huge but harmless rocket. Demitrius, his mentor, had welcomed him back with coffee and advice. That had been two days ago.

ZAXXON

To Tony, Bristol was like a huge soft poisonous plum. His C.V. was riddled with a pox of redundancy and defective qualifications, and the umbrella of college could no longer protect him from the randomness of life. He felt this most particularly when on foot. It caused a mild paranoia in him that he felt marked him like a layer of sweat. On his way to meet Sam he didn't want to think about the possibility of her rejection. That although he had told her several times on the phone in the last three months to move on, to find someone else, he now sincerely wished that she hadn't. Her last text message had been dubious: *do not B 2 late it's not 2 late. I have a surprise 4 U.* He groped the pocket of his black Levis for cigarettes but left them there. He hardly smoked at all anyway. He could make a packet last for a fortnight.

His mind shifted from alleviating his nerves to the imagined kisses of victory: that their lips were together, now, the urgency of her tongue and the warm red wine taste of her mouth. She had been his anchor during the suicidal boredom before he was kicked out of college. Unable to see a future for their relationship was why he had told her they might not have the chance to be together again; the reason he had uprooted that anchor, not knowing if he was ever going to return to the city beyond collecting his things. Now he was back from Sussex, and dared to wonder if Sam would be there for him. Slim, red-headed, her hazel eyes gleaming with mischief; yet needing him, he hoped, needing him to complete her like an unfinished canvas waiting for the definition of his brush.

He wandered through the multitude of Saturday shoppers on his way to where they were to meet, at The Watershed arts centre, at two pm. He watched the people surreptitiously through his mirror sunglasses, people with families and mortgages and jobs; people that walked through the hot June sunshine with purpose. At least this afternoon he was to share a smoke and a glass of chilled beer with a lovely girl. Whatever the outcome, today he had set out with a fine purpose of his own.

*   *   *

Just over a mile to the west Sam Lingard thought she might be running late. She took her hand off the steering wheel long enough to glance at her slim gold plated watch, and rolled her honey coloured eyes. Tony never had any money so she wanted to withdraw some of her own, over the counter as quickly as possible, but she had a typically student relationship with her bank. She would have to use her 'secret account' because her cash-point card had been confiscated and her credit card was maxed out. She also needed petrol, although she absolutely hated the smell of it. She had passed her driving test only recently, but she drove her dilapidated Beetle like an expert; nay, like a wild woman. It had been a gift from an old boyfriend; had vexed her father when it had been parked on the verge outside the house for so long. Finally it had been moved, sent for its M.O.T, and Sam thought the patch of yellow grass it left behind was the most interesting feature of the street, still did.

She needed to park as soon as she could and honked her horn at a bus driver who was hesitating at an intersection. She passed it in third gear, her long hair streaming out behind her in the draft through the open window. She had dyed it to look like Tony's: that was her surprise! The digital sign in the N.C.P on Nelson Street indicated that the car-park had fifty five spaces available. Whoever had designed this facility couldn't have imagined the sheer weight of traffic that floods into the centre of Bristol nowadays. Trying to find those last spaces was like looking for fleas on an elephant.

The ageing attendant raised a bushy eyebrow at the pretty blonde girl driving the old Volkswagon, as it passed by his booth and puttered up the entry ramp. It was at least twenty years old, bumped and scratched with patches of rust. He sat back, reminiscing. He could remember a time when there had been dozens of those shiny little Kraut cars using his place, but no longer. These days he could hardly keep up with the vandalism and he'd been raided three times since last Spring. What was the world coming to? He reached under his desk and patted his 24" machete affectionately. This was a very good question.

Sam lived with her father, who was a district councillor specialising in tourism. They shared a big house on Cherry Garden Hill. Her mother had passed away of a ruinous illness two years ago, and her two older sisters had both left long before that. They had families of their own now. It was a lot of space for just the pair of them yet the place felt paradoxically claustrophobic to Sam because her father was ever present, and over-protective. She was his last remaining company in the house. She liked driving her old Beetle, not because it had been a present from an old flame but because it was a symbol of independence. Her eighteenth birthday had been celebrated six months ago but her father never had, and still didn't, been able to accept her coming of age. He still enforced strict rules. She lived in hope that one day, maybe, he would learn compromise.

They still argued, fiercely. Shortly after Tony had left Bristol her father had severed her allowance, completely. Means testing indicated that she couldn't even get a basic grant because he earned too much, so she started working evenings, served tables in a local restaurant and this funded her 'secret account'. It wasn't much of a job but the added financial independence turned the loss into a victory. Since employment she hadn't had to fight quite so hard for her freedoms. She wanted to slip into college life like a pair of tights, buy the occasional glass of red wine if she wanted one, legally, and to make love; yes, that too. Her experience with boys was limited because of her father's prejudiced screening processes, but she had had sex on one occasion. She had lost her virginity in a fit of alcoholic rebellion at a party the Christmas before last. She had made a night of it, and then dumped the guy the following morning in a parallel fit of regret.

She had expected him to go on his way, having had his fun, but the geek had followed her around for ages professing undying love. That had been startling. Sam pitied him because of her own guilt, but a few months later she didn't want to be reminded of it anymore, didn't want to feel any of it - so she decided to get brutal. Just before the holidays began she told all his friends about his deluded notes, his stalking, and his embarrassing generosity. He had never returned to college and Sam never found out what had befallen him. It was a more drastic result than intended.

Even without his hovering pressure she found herself drawn into further guilt. *She* was the one that had been drunk at that party, after-all, and yet she hadn't thought she was 'that kind of girl'. Her father had taught her it was the *men* who behaved like that, which was an educational irony. She hadn't had sex or gotten drunk since but the resolve never fully settled her mind because drunkenness doesn't exactly create vices but bring those hidden to the fore. Still, she had convinced her father about the basic biological benefits of a little alcohol. He allowed her, and more important *she* allowed *herself*, the odd glass of red wine if it was distinctive, not too many units. The rich smoothness and sour fruitiness of good wine was a favourite taste upon her tongue. With the car parked Sam started walking to the bank as quickly as her heels would allow.

*   *   *

Half a mile to the north-east Tony walked into the welcoming shade of the Watershed's veranda and dropped off his packet of photographs at Gillow's art gallery. He then picked up some pamphlets from a rack and took them to an empty side table. The furniture was situated across the walkway by a railing over-looking the river. A cool breeze was blowing up from the water and the ducks that bobbed up and down there seemed to be asleep. He looked at his watch: it was five minutes to two. Tony took a chair and opened a pamphlet. Ripples on the water sent sun sparkles over where he sat, flickering like a magic mirror, or a cool drink. He started reading an example of the marketing of Sam's dad. Tony had been stigmatised by him in the past, usually at a distance, but the man was evidently good at his job: he had boosted tourism in Bristol almost single-handedly. August was in the distance and July had yet to begin, yet the city was already making big money.

According to gossip gleaned from Sam, the campaign's success had been catalysed by the heat-wave and had caused few surprises. Record takings were forecast but it may have provoked a few headaches in the more astute of the councillors. Tourism had been just a reliable crutch, in the past, and now it was the city's only growth industry. Nobody complained about it but then nobody knew whether or not it was really a good thing. Sam's dad, an insider who had lived in the city all his life, and his marketing team, had put in nine months work into the pamphlets, flyers and posters. Albeit, Tony thought as he read, a little unscrupulously: yes, the place is 'steeped in history', but it was only 'beautiful' if you saw it from the angles of the photos in the guide. "Your personal safety is solely dependant on never straying from the routes recommended in this glossy brochure," was something they could not have written. Could they?

It was a matter of crime.

The Cypriot with whom Tony shared his living space made pizzas as a façade for felony, and claimed whatever government D.W.P handouts he could get. This was a crime in itself; Demitrius Kiriacou knew the benefits system back to front. 'Demi' as he preferred to be called (maybe after 'demi-god' Tony had quipped, but only to himself) had befriended Tony in a pool hall on the Gloucester Road. They had talked a lot and played dance music on the juke to accompany their games. The man was twenty one and looked like a gipsy: 5'3" with long black curly hair, a thin moustache, and a powerful physique. His stare was as dark and as blank as a shark's, like there was a super-computer operating behind his eyes.

Demitrius was boss of a three man crew, a car thief and renowned get-away driver. He was an enigma and it was a notion that may have been reciprocal. They were utterly different. Although Tony always enjoyed his stories, he had never gone out with them himself. They stole as many car stereos and good vehicle parts as they could carry off. Tony had always been aroused by danger, ideally on the screen: Third Person risks; violence from a distance. Demi and himself went dancing together and talked about girls and drank beer. In mid November Tony moved into his flat. 'Kiriacou' was the only name on the tenancy agreement and he sub-let Tony's room to him cheaply, and unofficially. Moving into such close proximity to this alternative life-style was, unarguably, a reason that Tony had been expelled from college.

An old man arrived from nowhere and wiped the table. Tony looked at his watch again. "Is she worth waiting for sonny?" croaked the pensioner.

"Yes, I think so," Tony replied. It was a quarter past two.

"Women are all mad," said the old man. "You only have to look in their hand-bags to know that!"

"Do you think you could fetch me a couple of drinks? I don't want to abandon my table."

"What, you think I'm a French maid?"

Tony smiled. He was relieved to have his mind taken away from brooding thoughts. "If you were, and forty years younger, I'd get three drinks."

"I wish I was!" the old man laughed, a growling coughing noise. "What do you fancy?"

"I'd like a pint of your strongest lager, and a glass of your best House red."

"Coming right up, young man."

By the time Tony paid for the drinks he had only a few pound coins left in his wallet. He looked at his watch again. It was twenty past two. His mobile phone had a flat battery and he didn't want to dwell on the implications of this disorganisation. He didn't want to think about anything. He held his glass up to the light, as he always did, to ensure its quality, then took a draught of the cold beer. The sun made him sneeze. He picked up a Save-The-Whale pamphlet from his collection.

*   *   *

Fifty meters to the southwest Sam was walking scared, and running late, towards the Watershed. The Saturday queue at the bank had been longer than a factory production line and she didn't know if Tony was still waiting. Sam ached for him with the same yearning she experienced on the phone after they hung up. Tony's mobile was unobtainable today, of all days! She paused to check herself in a shop window: the reflection of her left side, then her right side with a hand on her flat stomach, and then straight on. She looked good. She was wearing her favourite blue summer dress. It was cut up at the knee, open at the neck, and flattered her figure very nicely, but she would still have the dress tomorrow - and she might not have Tony.

Sam had found him attractive from the very beginning. She had observed him strolling around the college with his lazy gait: the close blonde hair, his smile, and his beautiful blue eyes that looked anywhere else when their gaze met. During the 'fresher's week' dance in mid September she had watched Tony's lager fuelled antics with chuckles and a secret smile. Three weeks later she was wondering if he was gay, or whether or not there was something wrong with her she didn't know about, because he had made no move to break the ice. It had surprised her yet in some deep part of herself Sam just knew he found her attractive. Her returning looks across the cafeteria had not been unresponsive, yet he remained stoical. So, to break through this, Sam understood that at the right moment she would have to make the first move herself.

In the Student Union bar on the evening of November 2nd she anonymously bought him a pint of lager. She bound over a friend of his to strict silence then waited behind him sipping at a glass of rather poor Bulgarian sauvignon. She watched Tony's friend give him the drink and saw him lift the pint to the light, as he always did - as she had seen him do, covertly, dozens of times - to check its quality. Then she leaned closer to his ear. She had guessed how to press his buttons:

"Don't you think that the colour of my eyes is very much like that Carlsberg Export?"

He looked round and recognized her. His skin went pale and he gulped three huge mouthfuls of beer. Looking closely into his eyes Samantha felt as though she was falling into an ocean. "Yes," he said, "yes… it does."

She flicked her long red hair from one side of her face and popped her eye-lids at him to ensure his full attention, both unconsciously. "I'm Sam Lingard. And I think I like you."

"I like you too."

"Well, thank god for that!"

"How d'you know what kind of lager this is?"

"I cheated."

"How?"

"I bought it for you!"

And that's how they met. They were kissing before Last Orders, but had never ever, since nor then, made love. Her slim watch was now showing twenty-four minutes past the hour. Sam crossed the road to the edge of the canal and approached their rendezvous, sliding her hand along the railing as she walked, feeling anxiety rising in her chest with every step. The Watershed had been designed for students and young executives and it was her favourite meeting place. Even from a distance the building had the essence of a crystal castle. It incorporated an art-house cinema, a restaurant, two bars, several expensive gift shops, and an art gallery.

She could see people walking too and fro under the veranda, and paused to take a small bottle of perfume out of her cloth shoulder bag. She gave her neck a little spray. She put it back and walked onto the promenade, into the cool blissful shade of the sloping roof. She saw Tony immediately, seated alone at a table by the canal. He looked... older. She felt electrified from toe to top and laughed into a cupped hand because it looked like he was feeding bits of torn paper to the ducks! The moment alleviated her nerves. She walked up to the table and stood before him, inadvertently holding up the sides of her dress a little, feeling like a Faberge egg after an auction, just about to be picked up delicately in the fingertips of its adoring new owner.

*   *   *

"Ducks can't eat paper!" she blurted out.

Tony looked up and felt a shock that was all consuming. Seeing her cheeky face, and her becoming summery dress; seeing the way the thin shoulder strap of her bag pressed along the side of a firm breast, flooded his nervous system with joyful terror. His relief was powerful like his heart had been arrested and re-started - with Sam's own hands applying the defibrillator guns! And on her face was an expression that mirrored his own. She sat opposite him, and he noticed her pink tongue flick across her lips; and then, again. Seeing that her new blonde hair was the same colour as his own was a revelation. Its length and softness, the way it glittered in the sun ripples reflected off the water, he understood that she was his, and "I am yours," he said, and leaned toward her. Gradually their lips drew together across the table with the inevitability of gravity. Each inhaled the other's sweetly remembered scent and they kissed with the fervour of re-united lovers. The passion was a surprise to the both of them. Their mouths parted sensually. Tony took a couple of swigs of his pint.

"I'm sorry, Sam, but your drink's been in the sun," he said.
Sam examined the colour of her wine by swilling it around the rim of the glass. "Don't be silly," she replied. "Red wine is supposed to be served warm." She put her perky nose over

the liquid and inhaled the fruity musk of it, then took a mouthful... she smiled at him: "Beaujolais - not bad!"

"I've just delivered seventeen photographs of my best paintings to Gillows," he said.

"That's brilliant," said Sam. "I can't stop smiling!"

"Why did you dye your hair?"

She thought about it, then said: "It's the 'new me', the me that wants to be with you. And so that everyone can see we're together. Is it okay to say that?"

"Definitely!"

"Do you like my hair like this?"

"Definitely!"

She preened. "I don't think I've felt this happy since I passed my driving test!"

"I wouldn't know about that." But he thought that it must be amazing to have such freedom. "You'll have to give me a few lessons sometime."

"You're already living with a bloke who knows more about driving than either of us will ever know. That Greek guy, Emetrius, I don't like him, Tony, I really don't."

"He's Cypriot. And his name is actually Demitrius. How can you judge him so fast when you've only met him once?"

She took a long sip of her wine, then said: "You know people go around saying 'I don't judge anyone, I'm not a judgemental person' but it's rubbish. Everyone does, instantly, when they first meet, because if they don't they might get hurt. It's a mechanism. And he scared me, Tony, he made me feel like I was see-through, and I didn't deserve it."

"I'm sorry... but Demitrius is going to help me now that I'm back."

"It was Demitrius that got you chucked out of college in the first place!"

"I came back for you."

"That's lovely -"

"- and for me, and my parents, also. I've come back to prove myself."

"That's silly."

"I have to do it."

"Why?"

50

"Because all my life my parents have been helping me, too much. Because I've never done anything that they ever admitted is good. I felt like an angel, when I was a child, but that was not because they made me feel like one. They actually put a stop to it. I've never finished anything, except paintings, but they say the odds that I can make a career in Art is well nigh impossible. And they won't back me up now because I've blown the latest chance of a qualification high enough to make a difference." He took a crumpled cigarette pack from his pocket and lit one. "I'm cut off, Sam." He exhaled. "I need to create a little self-respect. Try to make my way without the help of anyone - except Demitrius."

"Oh, so now he's an art expert!"

"I think in his way he likes my paintings too, or at least respects me for it. Demi is my mentor. I feel almost honoured to be his acquaintance."

"That's crap and rubbish! You like danger. He's just another streetwise speed-freak that thinks he's God's gift to women!" She didn't know that for certain but she remembered the lethal charm he exuded all too clearly. "So, where do I fit in? What about my help?"

"Demitrius is my guide in a shitty world."

"The world is *not* shitty! *His world is shitty*!" A droplet fell down her cheek.

"Oh, Sam, that's because you're not seeing it from my side: you're still living at home."

"You think that isn't right?" she exclaimed. "You think a teenager's parents aren't supposed to help their children? To protect them, pay for things, make rules. Isn't that normal?"

"What's 'normal'?"

"Normal is what everyone else says it is!" She took a tissue out of her bag.

"At this moment my life sure as hell isn't normal; I'm all alone out here, I know."

"For God's sake, Tony, you're not alone anymore," she cried, tearfully. "Not now that I'm falling in love with you, you fool!"

"Hey! Hey! Stop crying!"

She shook her head. "You know every time you phoned and told me to go and find someone else, do you know what that felt like? It just made me need you all the more!" She sniffled. Tony jumped around the table, took the tissue out of her fingers and started rubbing it gently around her big hazel eyes like he was cleaning fine porcelain. "It made me want you so *desperately*... damn you," she pushed him away with one elbow, "you said you weren't coming back!"

"Well, I am back."

She recovered her tissue and quietened. Suddenly she looked grim. "It's not that simple, Tony, mark my words." She blew her nose and then told him to sit back where he had been.

Tony returned, feeling apprehensive. He took a deep pull on his cigarette. "What is it?"

"I can't deal with the rest of the damage, of the possibility that you could be hospitalised, or arrested, or go to prison." She leaned forward: "So if I *ever* find out that you've gone out stealing with that man, or his two stupid friends, I'll leave you Tony. We'll split."

He drained his pint. "I will not go," he said... then he asked her if she wouldn't mind buying him another beer.

She laughed hard, with relief. "Alright, big boy, I will, but you'll have to kiss me for it!" Tony gave her a series of kisses, pressing their lips together in delicious little pecks, then Sam picked up her shoulder bag and crossed the terrace. Tony stubbed out his cigarette and sat alone, emotional; full of terror and happiness. She came back and placed a pint in front of him. He lifted it to the light.

"What do I look like through that glass?" Sam asked.

"All bulbous and yellow," said Tony. "Same as always!"

"Cruel man."

Tony looked at her glass. "What have you got there, orange juice?"

"Yeah, and proud of it! This old guy at the bar asked me if I might have an Ormolu Bracket-clock in my handbag..." They paused thoughtfully to sip their drinks.

"So, how are things going with your dad?" asked Tony.

"Improved since you left."

ZAXXON

"You mean he hasn't had a reason to slate me since I've been away?"

"I told him you were back, and he just looked like a balloon deflating. But he still enforces dozens of rules, some really petty. I got a job on the quay, and I've got the car, and I don't let him fix dinners for the both of us by himself all the time, and still all these bloody rules! But the final battle is worth it, when he accepts me as a woman, truly, he may let me spend the night with you." She smiled at his blushing. "All night: just the two of us."

"Oh, y-yes," he stammered. "That w-would be good... I suppose."

"Are you still a virgin?"

"No. Yes. It's kind of embarrassing."

"That's a shame!" she lied happily, and rubbed her hands together. "Tell Aunty Sam all about it!"

He took a deep breath. "Before you and I got together, Demitrius and I talked a lot of 'man's man' stuff. I couldn't believe how many women he claimed to have had but I've found out since that it was true. When he asked me how many I'd had, I replied 'about seven' but I lied. Even given half the chance I couldn't find anyone who wanted me as much as I wanted them. *He knew I'd lied* and one afternoon in the middle of college this note arrived on my desk." He sipped some lager.

"What did it say?"

"It said: '*Three girls will be coming round to the flat tonight. Nine pm. Jo, Sue, Karen. Entertain them until I get off work at mid-night then fun times - Demi.*' I recall mixed feelings about it. Fear, mostly."

"Why not excitement?"

"Because I had to keep these three girls amused, alone - for three hours - with my lack of experience, knowing that we were going to have an orgy. I was desperate for Demi to get back but dreading it at the same time."

"What happened?"

"We drank white wine. Demitrius put some R&B on the stereo and spread out some duvets on the... y'know, on the floor... then we all got down to it. The five of us." She stroked his hand. "You see although I put it in... I couldn't finish. It was really bad... I was disillusioned. It was just a sweaty disappointment."

"It won't be like that with us, Tony. With us it'll be great. We'll be in a real bed with soft music and dimmed lights and lot's of soft stuff, y'know?"

He eyes misted over. "Yeah, that'd be nice."

She watched him lick his lips and she flushed unexpectedly. Imagining the grind of their bodies she squirmed pleasantly, watching the sky over his shoulder. "Look at that sky, Tony!"

He looked round. Sinister clouds were gathering on the horizon, vast banks of cumulonimbus with dark, swollen undersides. "It's going to rain," he stated.

"Yes, you can almost taste it." She shivered. "It's weird how things have a habit of going wrong just when they seem to be going right, don't you think Tony?" Thunder rumbled. "Tony? Don't you think?" She waited a long time for him to reply.

Eventually, he said: "It's the Summer Solstice today," and the storm began.

*   *   *

Long ago the Montpelier district of Bristol had been a haven for the gentry of the city. In the sixties the developers had given up and the builders had moved on, taking their Rotoring pens and lunchboxes with them. Montpelier began to resemble its neighbouring area, St. Pauls, the most crime-ridden district in the Southwest of England. The flat was on the third floor of a crumbling tenement called Launch Terrace, and the door had been assaulted while Tony had been in Sussex. Heaving his luggage onto the top landing he had found a gaping hole in the wood. He learned later that three weeks ago Demitrius's party had disturbed the tenants below and a large man had come upstairs. The sound of his knocking had been overwhelmed by club anthems so he had armed himself with a masonry hammer and proceeded to break into the flat. With splinters clinging to the sweat on his huge biceps, he had told them all to shut up, and they did so, out of respect. The next afternoon Demi had gone downstairs and threatened to kill him with a pool cue if he didn't pay up for the damage. He did so, out of respect, and the following night Demi had used the cash to stage another party!

Demitrius's love of the combustion engine had begun the moment he had arrived on British soil, age thirteen. As the youngest of six he had been patronised for life and had never had any influence over anything. It was the power of cars and the number of them roaring around London that were his first impressions of the other streets with which he was destined to become so familiar. The control of the power over the weight of metal. He befriended lads that taught him to drive in ways no legal driver would ever need to know. As the hot sweet scented dust of Cypress faded from his mind, he was overcome with an exciting new smell: petrol, and the amazing vehicles that burned it. By the age of sixteen he had spent several nights in police cells, crashed two family cars and dented his parent's own precious Mercedes SLK three times. He had nothing on the cards except reform school. So, he had hooked up with a couple of soft drug dealers who were on the run, and they fled to Bristol in a recreational vehicle. They lived in it near the Avon Gorge for the summer months and used to wash in the river.

Their education in survival had led to a place in underground society, where the Cypriot found a niche for his intelligence and driving skills in crime. Being addicted to adrenaline and the wealth it spawned this was where he belonged. He displayed no guilt. He had his own flat by the time he was nineteen and entertained a great number of women. In spite of being short he was prepared to thump anyone that bothered him, so no one ever did, thus he never needed to. He couldn't remember the last time anyone had thumped him back and was starting to believe no one ever had. By the age of twenty-one he had the flat in Montpelier, a crew of expert thieves, contacts, respect, and a reputation for being a fine driver. Yet he was dissatisfied.

Sex and money didn't generate the excitement it had. Tony brought with him a new facet into Demitrius's life, clay to be manipulated into the shape of a man that Tony was never supposed to have become. Once he had moved into Launch Terrace, and been booted out of college, Demitrius began to teach Tony the survival techniques of the 'real world'. It was a far cry from the upper-middle class background within which Tony had been brought up. He had scorned that, and wanted a different kind of further education. The Cypriot was providing it. In public Demitrius fenced off questions and insults about Tony's background with agreements and insults all his own, but he liked the arrangement. Tony's terror was a good basis for a master / apprentice relationship. Now Demitrius's sadistic hand was becoming tempered with paternal feelings towards him - in both their thoughts, but never discussed.

Demitrius had an impulsive nature that was most reflected through non-sequiturs in conversation, as if his brain was working faster than his mouth. He had no long-term future plans and a past of discarded chunks of memory like set-pieces arranged on a shelf. In Tony's opinion his benefactor was dangerous because he cared little about anything and armoured this by living the few values he did have to the brink of obstinacy. When coupled with charm and the implied capacity for indiscriminate violence you have a highly beneficial friend, or a formidable enemy. Tony could have packed up and left the flat, of course, but what he had to learn from this weird friendship kept him there.

*   *   *

"Is that you Tony?" Demitrius yelled from the cramped bathroom. His melange of accents, the Greek inflection and the south-western brogue, was charismatic.

"Yeah, it's me," said Tony. Then he shouted: "You're not washing your hair *again*, are you?"

The blustered sentence that followed somehow involved his having swum in the sea off Western-super-Mare. Tony began the laborious task of tidying his room and decided that swimming in the pea soup that masqueraded as water off Western-super-Mare was a good enough reason for *anybody* to need to wash their hair! When the incessant whining of the Cypriot's hair dryer had stopped, time seemed to pass quickly while he tackled the mess; clothes by the window, stolen articles to one side, art articles to the other. The sun was setting when Tony wandered into Demi's bedroom, which doubled as a lounge. The Cypriot slept on a sofa bed, part of a grey three-piece suite. Sophisticated posters of fast women and sexy sports cars added vitality to the atmosphere. The Technics stack stereo in the corner was silent; Demitrius was talking on the phone.

"Yeah, I know, rained like a bastard for hours... five so far, yeah? Including the Pioneers and we're game on for the rest later... I've already told you, the Blaupuncts are knackered - that's why I need you to fix 'em, Jason... Tonight – yeah, of course tonight, and bring your brother Patrick with you... I don't care! This is a two hundred pound deal so you're going to have to chill the same as the rest of us... sweet. Your tools are here: come around in... I can't believe it, it's half past nine! Better come around now. Chow man." He hung up and looked at the dreamy expression in Tony's eyes. "Well, how did it go?"

"Fantastic," Tony replied. "I'm going out with her later."

"I'm talking about the DSS you idiot!"

"Oh, yeah, that went well too... but I still can't work out why I can't claim Housing Benefit."

"Because if they knew that *you* were paying *me* I'd get less Income Support money, understand?"

"Okay. Look at how tidy this place is! I thought you usually got women to clean it up for you."

"Don't pull my pecker."

"I'm just saying!"

"Okay. So how do *you know* I didn't?"

"Because I can't smell any perfume and you're wearing your Slush Puppy tee shirt so you're dressed for business."

"True. That's good observation, Tony. I didn't exactly clean it up anyway, I just chucked my rubbish into your room."

"I saw." The younger man sensed trouble. His mentor was hiding something, tugging his earing, tapping his index finger to his lips. Tony found himself wanting to placate the Cypriot for something that hadn't even been revealed yet. "Would you like coffee?"

"Yes. Did you drop those photos off at Gillows?"

Tony wandered into the kitchenette and filled the kettle. "Yeah. Let's let them steam over them for a while."

"Who's this fly bitch you were saying about?"

Tony leant against the fridge and ran a hand through his hair. "Her name's Sam. She's lovely. You met her once, before Christmas."

"The red-head, I remember. She looked like a bomb."

"Don't you mean a 'bomb-shell'?"

"No, a bomb – she looked like she wanted to throw me out of a window. She liked me about as much as a traffic cop!"

Tony handed him his Playboy mug. "I've given her this phone number, if that's okay."

"I don't care who calls but if I catch you ringing out on the sly you won't forget it." He sipped his drink. "Have you checked her yet? Have you put the cigar in the waffle toaster?"

"No, I've never seen her... y'know, like that... but she could be staying over tonight."

"Yeah?"

"She said she had to clear it with her old man but if she wasn't here by ten thirty she wouldn't be coming at all."

The response was unemotional. "That's cool, because she can't come round tonight anyway. Jason's fixing the duff stereos so we need a third man on the job. You."

Tony was crestfallen: he had sensed this coming. "You never take me!"

"Well, this is the time for you to prove your worth then isn't it?"

ZAXXON

How could Tony talk of love to a man that had the sensitivity of a house brick? "I can't do it, Demi."

"The hell you 'can't do it'," Demitrius continued, "we're not twocking cars and you won't have to pop any windows. We just need a lookout."

"I'm scared of being caught."

"Bullshit! Don't lie to me Tony. Don't even try. You won't be able to."

"I promised Sam that..."

"Don't mix women with business."

"I've never had a problem with that, it's just Jason and Patrick think I'm soft so I haven't been out on business with you before, and I've never had a girlfriend here to mix it *with*. We love each other, and -"

"- Love? Is that all this is about? Love! You've never had sex with her and now you want to get a taste of it using the excuse of virgins and assholes!" He impersonated a girl: "I won't give you my body until I love you." He returned to speaking normally. "Sex creates love, Tony, amplifies it: *it's the other way around!*" A press on the front door button downstairs made a buzzing noise in the hallway. "Look, are you coming out with us tonight, or what?"

"Shall I answer the door?"

"No!" bellowed the Cypriot, seething with sudden anger: "Answer me!"

Like a wet dog shaking itself, the younger man shivered. "Okay, I'll do it, I'll go."

"Wonderful. Great." Demitrius pushed his face into Tony's, who saw sparks of lunacy in his eyes, and, with a frightening placidity, he said: "I don't know what the fuck's up with you."

The bell buzzed again.

"I'd better get the door," mumbled Tony. He was in a cold sweat.

"Do it."

The stairwell had a worn crusty carpet that smelt like a condemned warehouse, dusty dry rot playing host to the occasional insectile house guest. He switched on the ceiling lights as he went down and found his breathing easing in the absence of darkness. He couldn't remember if Demi's attack had been warranted. Trying to understand him was like being a ship's captain trying to navigate a mine-field without sonar. Last January, when Tony had finally been ready to show Demi his paintings and pastel drawings, the man had changed. No one had ever asked his opinion of art before and he liked it. After that he developed an interest in the occult and the super-natural, when Tony sensed that he was dissatisfied with his life-style. Most importantly, he didn't think anyone else noticed. Having thrice the common sense didn't necessarily make Demi the better man because he was a destroyer whereas Tony, however muddled, was a creator. It seemed Launch Terrace sustained a balanced pair of tenants on its top floor.

Tony opened the front door and the two Dreyer brothers pushed past him into the hallway. The elder brother Patrick was a fine driver and dressed like a country bumpkin, massive but humble. Tony was the same age yet slightly shorter than Jason, the younger, and each had no bones about which was the most practical. Tony's commitment to art was the equal of Jason's to electronics but what negated their worst insults was a grudging respect for the other's vocation in life. Demitrius enjoyed studying Tony's side in this jousting but ensured their petty arguing didn't escalate. If it wasn't just a matter of harmless cynicism it may have got in the way of business. Both brothers' hair was grimy and usually their clothes seemed to have been trampled on by the same horse, but tonight Jason had revamped their wardrobe with a black leather trench coat belted at the waist.

"Nice coat," said Tony. "How much was it?"

Jason replied he'd stolen it, as if the question had been thoughtless. "Why, do you want one?"

"No thanks, it wouldn't suit a real man."

"I could get you a dozen if you want," continued Jason obliviously.

"Great! We could all wear them at an identity parade and look like identical idiots!"

"You could paint on them."

ZAXXON

Tony thought about it for a moment, then said: "Each a grand master!"

Patrick chuckled at this. He advised Jason to 'leave it out' and then they walked into the flat. Subdued garage music was playing from the stereo. Demitrius had closed the blinds; he had changed into navy blue combat trousers and a black sweat-shirt. "Come in lads. Tony – coffee."

Tony walked into the tiny kitchen and set up the kettle. He shuddered. This time his cold sweat wasn't directly due to provoking the wrath of Demitrius, it was because of his own weakness in not being able to save himself from coercion into crime. He hadn't stood up to it, and it would happen again, but this time the cost was steep in his opinion of himself - even if Sam was never to find out. He was going to break the promise he had made to his loved one only this afternoon at the risk of all he cared about.

*   *   *

Jason Dreyer withdrew the last of the screws from the back of the Blaupunct. He placed it with the others laid out on a hand scribbled quadrant map to remember where they had been located. He unclasped the rear cover, re-poised the lamp, and then leant further forward over the glass-topped coffee table with a hand roll-up of marijuana hanging slackly between his lips. He squinted into its lifeless innards. The land-line telephone rang.

"Bollocks," he muttered, dislodging ash into the gaping stereo. Instead of blowing the machine clean he turned it upside down so he could take a long puff of the aromatic smoke. The phone continued ringing. To Jason it sounded like a sheep that had been breathing nitrous oxide. He was stoned and smiled as ash rained to the tabletop - followed by a switch, some circuit boards, and a spring.

"Bloody hell!" he shouted, leaping off the couch.

The movement knocked the lamp to the floor. He put it back on the table and then balanced his joint on the edge of a sticky upside down coffee mug. He crossed to the windowsill and picked up the receiver.

"Yeah," he growled breathlessly. "Who is it?"

"Is that Tony and Demitrius's flat?" It was a girl. She sounded classy.

"Yeah, it is."

"Is Tony there? I was supposed to –"

"No, sorry, he's out, Demitrius too. I already asked once, who is this?"

"I'm Samantha."

"Never 'eard of you."

"I'm Tony's girlfriend."

"Then I guess it's safe to say they're out on business."

"What kind of... 'business'?"

"How long have you known Tony?"

"Just tell me what kind!"

"How long?"

"Over five months!"

"Then you should know y' silly slag!"

"What... they've gone out... stealing?"

"Give the girl a magic mushroom!"

"Tony wouldn't do that."

"Oh, you reckon? You think I'd lie about it?"

"Alright then, tell Tony what this sounds like. Tell him *exactly* what this sounds like."

She hung up.

CHAPTER THREE

"U.x.bridge"

Rupert was sleeping, back amongst the red tunnels and tree abundant stations of the bizarre underground. The FIRE EXIT to him, last night, was now like an exhibit in the wet ashes of a burnt museum. A spent firework scorched and blackened with no function other than to warn him that his choices mattered in this place. Then he heard the chilling sound for the third time: the footsteps of something terrible walking towards him along the blood lit tunnel, an augury of doom. The hair on the back of his neck prickled and wherever his sleeping body was laying it filled with adrenaline as his dream-heart beat faster. The warm air that blew gently to and fro around the strangely scented trees carried with it the sound of its inhuman relentlessness, the walking of a monster with each step having the essence of slicing guillotines.

Wishing he had a weapon, a gun particularly, Rupert walked up to the edge of the platform. He looked down at the track as though he was about to run away from a man-eating lion by diving into a river of piranhas, experiencing the basest fight or flight instinct. He struggled to temper it with logic because there was nowhere to run. The forthcoming creature would never stop until it had bitten his head off and in this version of the London Tube the escalators didn't work and the tunnels could go on forever. The steel rail carrying the electricity to power the trains looked shiny and dangerous, like a pearl handled pistol with a chrome finish.

The paradoxically gentle steps of what was stalking him did nothing to ease his fear of it. He felt the doom of being a victim about to die at the climax of a hunt. He needed to hide. It would appear at any time so Rupert crouched back against the wall behind two trees. His right hand absently stroked a root that felt comfortable: it had a smooth nugget under his index filter that felt like a trigger. Unable to tell the creature for the trees Rupert didn't see the thing when it emerged from the tunnel. But at the sound of it mounting the platform he suddenly inhaled something, smelt the musky scent of a woman he recognised. A giddy feeling of relief swept through his whole body. He sneezed. Someone walked up to where he was hiding and peered around the tree trunk at him. It was Lillith.

"What are you doing here?" he asked her, amazed.
"I'm in your dream," she said. "I'm testing you."
"How did I do?"
"Nothing inspiring, little thorn, but you survived."

He coughed. Lillith was wearing what looked like a pair of black Levi 501s, a black sweatshirt with *Dolci & Cabana* written across it, and pointy boots. She reached down and took his hand. As usual her small frame belied her strength as she pulled him onto his feet with remarkable dexterity.

"Where did you get those clothes?"
"After sucking the experience out of a woman in the village I conjured them from nothing. But I like modern garments. In this reality one's imagination can become solid when you have learnt the way. The natural state for one such as myself, in a hell, is to be naked."

Rupert felt himself erecting. "What's my next performance then?" he asked, smiling lewdly. He licked his lips and pressed himself against her. Lillith pulled away.

"You have to kill someone Rupert. To get a special book that we have to return to the Nefarious Library." From the small of her back she drew a shiny automatic pistol out of her jeans. "Take this sword, such as you wanted three times. Your desire for it shone like thunder flashes in a tinder box." Rupert hesitated. "Take the sword, Rupert."

He took it and found it was surprisingly heavy. The gun was a Walther CP88. It fitted snugly into his hand and was loaded without a doubt. He stared down the sights. He felt its deadly potential and pulled the slide to cock it as he had seen done in a thousand movies.

He held it to his face. "This is outrageous!"

Lillith jumped lithely off the platform like a cat. "Come with me," she commanded, "come into the tube."

Rupert dropped gracelessly down to the rail beside his loved one. He followed her, traversing the gun before him, left to right, right to left. The glow of the tunnel was crimson and had an emotive essence like a vein itself fearing the surgeon's first cut.

"Why was I so scared of you earlier?"

"Because I was projecting my carnivorous enmity toward you. Testing you, the predator in me sharpening my teeth on the distance between us."

He coughed. "Well, it worked… you know if I could crap myself of terror in a dream I probably would have done!"

"You can."

Unexpectedly, ahead of him, he saw a shape, a ripple in the air walking towards him. He blinked and gaped. The shape was transparent, man shaped, and he aimed his weapon with his index finger closing around the trigger.

"Don't shoot it!" hissed Lillith.

Rupert moved out of its path. It was a melancholy thing and it passed him by without incident.

"What was it?" he asked her.

"A Searcher."

"What is this place?"

"It's Hell 47. A place haunted by lost souls."

Their steps echoed loudly back and forth.

"But I'm not a ghost."

"You're here because you are under test conditions. Twice, only. As a living sleeper you will not return here again after tonight. The Searchers come to walk, and to consider problems of memory. When they think the right things a train arrives to carry them to the next level."

"Amazing!" He sneezed.

The ambient light was changing colour from red to a greyish blue as they emerged from the tunnel.

"Here we are," said Lillith, "- an Uxbridge."
Rupert climbed up slowly and awkwardly. Lillith flexed her knees then leapt onto the platform and landed on her feet like a gymnast in one fluid movement.

"Prepare yourself," she said. She was leading him towards a door in the wall. "Prepare to become a Zaxxon demon!" The door was red. It had FIRE EXIT written on it.
"No, no, I'm not going through one of those again!"
"It's a cusper."
"What's in there?"
Her voice was becoming a bass booming noise. "Use the sword on it. Now!"
"I can't!"
"Now is your fork. Open it - and open fire if you wish!"

Shuddering, he took a deep breath and tapped the barrel of the Walther on the door.
A familiar voice spoke beyond it, Copeland's voice. "That had better be you, Thornberry, that had just better be you."

Rupert grimaced, raised the gun as the door was opened. The old man stood in the staff room doorway. He was hugging a large black book to his chest, a book that looked very old, and in his right hand was a bamboo switch. "You know what's going to happen to you now, don't you, cheeky pup? I'm going to cane you!"
Rupert applied pressure to the trigger. He was squinting along the sight, tearfully. "I'm no killer!" he exclaimed. Copeland flicked the stick around the gun barrel into Rupert's jaw-line. It stung his face with a bright and sudden pain.
"If you blatt him, it's for us both!" said Lillith.
"It's not supposed to matter, it's a dream!"
"Not quite."
"What do you mean?"

ZAXXON

"Your physical body has a cold, yet you cough and sneeze here. Deeds done here have an echo in the real world, and back. You can slay him *from this side*, give or take a few hours."

Copeland whipped his bamboo stick across Rupert's cheek-bone. It hurt like a burn. "Stop it you old fool!"

The old man raised the stick again and Rupert lowered the muzzle of his weapon. He fired it four times, with his eyes shut, into Copeland's chest. It kicked hard in the palm of his hand with bright flashes of orange light behind his eyelids. There were huge discharges of noise. He peered through the dispersing smoke and he saw the old man's body lying motionless on the staff room's green Axminster. Three bullets had struck the wrinkled jacket of the old book, shiny clods of lead stopped by it as though it was made of Kevlar. The fourth bullet had gone through Copeland's left eyebrow and killed him instantly.

"Platch!" said Lillith, "you did it!" Her voice was normal again, musical. "You have crossed into a place from which there is no return, your Uxbridge. How do you feel?"

"Sick... steady... I don't know. I feel powerful."

"You may feel that power for many centuries. Fetch me the grimoire."

"The book?"

"Yes."

He noticed the gun had disappeared. He picked up the book and the three distorted lumps of lead fell off the cover and dropped noiselessly onto the carpet. They disappeared also.

"What is this thing?"

"It is the *Necronomicon*, a book that we have to find in the real world and return to *him*." He handed it to her and she walked with it through the doorway. "Our chances of succeeding are much more likely to come to pass since your action at cusp."

"Where are you going?"

"I'm returning the dream ghost of the grimoire to an adjacent level." Her shape became indistinct. "An Uxbridge like this is purely functional," she said, and her voice strained as she threw the book through the window with no noise of breaking glass. "It has a limited surface area and exists only as long as the portal." She emerged beside him and cocked her head to one side, listening. The surface of the FIRE DOOR folded up bizarrely like origami and disappeared. "Ah, do you hear that Thorn? It's on time!"

Rupert heard the sound of an approaching train blowing a warm wind into his face. He sneezed. It emerged from the tunnel like a gigantic horse and slowed down, squealing and growling, to a halt. The doors opened with a noise like loud roller blinds, and Lillith took his hand. She led him on board and they sat next to each other. The doors closed and they kissed. The train moved off.

Rupert drew back his lips. "Usually, I can't recall my dreams in my waking hours, and when I'm asleep I can't remember my waking hours. Even someone without amnesia would get in a muddle!"

"You must try to. Do you remember the key, the acorns, and the quill from the last time you were here?"

"Yes, clearly. Key number eighteen has to be buried, the acorns are for you, and I have to draw a curve on my lip with the quill and meet the circle on yours in a kiss. Something like that. But how will I remember in the morning?"

"I have taken precautions. We will be together again, tonight, shortly before the second midnight of the Solstice, when all dreams stop."

They kissed again. The train rumbled and wobbled occasionally from side to side. He pushed his hand up beneath the hem of her sweatshirt to her breasts. She moaned.

"Do you remember last night?" she asked.

"You were there, weren't you?" he said. "On the leaves! We made love on the leaves!"

ZAXXON

"Many times."

The carriage was brightening, filling with a peculiar light. He reached down between her legs and started to pop undone the buttons at the crutch of her jeans.

She opened her thighs. "Kiss me my love," she demanded breathlessly.
He did. Yet the luminescence was brightening, becoming a glare as white as daylight, and her voice was disappearing.
"What are you?" he asked her. "What is the price?"
"Kiss me, my darling... kiss me..." she said.
Again he asked: *"What is the price?"* but then he didn't care anymore.

It was as though she was drifting away, as the train's angle of travel started to tilt upwards, running impossibly up towards the surface. He felt as though he was shrinking, and leaving that place, falling into her wet mouth.

"Take me," she muttered, "...take me!"
Rupert twitched, for a split second. Then awoke.

       *   *   *

In the brightness of daylight Rupert Thornberry opened his lids and squinted into the hot June sun, shining directly into his eyes. He sat upright with a crackling of leaves. He was in the sunken garden, for some reason; and he found he was naked. He sneezed and coughed, which bit into his lungs as if his cold had evolved into influenza; he had a sore throat and a slight temperature. His vision was a haze and his defensive instinct demanded that he be able to see. He could hear a droning voice at the rear of the school and clear vision was mandatory. He needed his glasses. On the embankment was a thing like a black island in a green sea, and he guessed that it could only be his jacket. It was, and he retrieved his glasses from the top pocket. The sticky tape holding the broken arm together was intact and he recalled that Hudson had broken them last night, hitting him.

He collected up the rest of his uniform and sat upright crossed-legged on the leaves with the clothes in his lap. He coughed. The monotonous voice at the back of the main building continued. It was Hudson's voice and Rupert's watch read 9:04 am on a Saturday morning. The repetition was a list of names being read out, which meant he had missed roll-call, so he crept up the slope like an infantry soldier to reconnoitre. It was obvious there was no way he could infiltrate the line of boys without being 'pinched' and he would be reported missing within minutes. He was gated, but his uniform was a mess. And he had missed the six thirty report in running kit to Hudson's study. It was a catalogue of disasters. He slid back down the slope.

He took deep breaths to melt the ice in his blood and surprised himself with a huge yawn. He felt tired as if he hadn't physically benefited from his sleep, and confused about his sore penis. All his muscles ached, but then the evidence of his flesh prompted the sex of the previous night to break through his amnesia. Lillith: her firm breasts, her long dark hair with its silver streaks, the heat of her. His own chest and neck, emblazoned with love-bites and scratches, as his memory served him well with images of their coitus. Yet questions arose, also:

"What are you?"
"Lillith," she replied.
"No – what – are you?"
"I'll tell you after I've opened myself to you… pleasure me… bury your thorn in me!"

Shortly after that he had lost his virginity in a spectacular fashion. But she had never replied. Another unanswered question echoed from some other place: *"What is the price?"* Again, she had given no reply that he could remember. Lillith was an enigma who existed out of all probability. She had materialised from his dreams and vanished without leaving a mobile phone number or a forwarding address. She was not human - of this, at least, he was certain, and yet he loved her. The column of boys trooped off, to practise singing for chapel the next day. After that they would enjoy free time. He put his clothes on. The black material soaked up the sun like a pelt of fur and he lost his balance pulling on his trousers. He fell back into the leaves and yawned again. He relaxed into the detritus like it was a feather bed. He buttoned his trousers and closed his eyes. He fell asleep.

Ssssonthesstepssssssoonthestepssssssooooonnnnttthheessstt eeppss!!! hissed quiet female voices.

Rupert opened his eyes. The sun was nearer its zenith. He wasn't sure whether it was the telepathy sighing in his brain or thirst that woke him up. Maybe it was sunburn. His lips felt sore and his acne was enflamed in the heat. He shuffled through the leaves in a panic to find his glasses, then realised they were balanced on top of his head. It was 11:15 am. He stood up and swooned for a moment with a jumble of confused images; neither memory nor imagination. A montage of rhetorical questions and questionless answers. His cold was worse. A sore throat and a headache had conspired with his cough. He acutely needed medicine, but if he fetched it from the school Matrons he would find himself standing on the Head Master's front porch waiting to be expelled.

He needed his own key, to the Surgery... and then remembered that the key was almost his already, from Russell, for fifteen pounds... and then he remembered Lillith, and key#18 and the acorns and the quill! *Onthessteps* the voices had hissed. There were six stone steps that led out of the sunken garden, and there were words engraved on them in Roman style script. A stone mason would have taken at least sixty minutes to engrave so deep into this hot granite. Lillith had cut it with her fingernail with casual flicks of her hand in under twenty seconds.

THORN - MEET ME, SAME PLACE
BRING THE OFFERINGS – 12 AM

DRESS TO TRAVEL
- SUCCUBUS -

A fierce joy filled his heart, and drove the aches and pains out of his body like being plugged into mains electricity. He bounded up the steps, sloughing off his school blazer and taking in a breath to shout. Up to the cedar tree he ran, swinging the jacket around and round above his head, and he yelled some words which were almost too gleeful to be human, like the roar of a Neanderthal child. He threw the jacket into the pond. He watched while it sank gradually into the water and stood there doubled over, with his hands on his knees, laughing till tears came to his eyes. Someone came panting up behind him; it was Rant, staring breathlessly into the pond.

"Rupert, what the hell have you done?"
"My hat off to you, Sir Julian," said Rupert, "for noticing the crime of yonder varlet!"
"It cost someone over a hundred pounds."
"May I be the first man to congratulate myself on this direct action against the establishment?" said Rupert, chuckling even harder.
Rant pulled the hem of his tee shirt out of his jeans and wiped his face with it like a mechanic. Rupert noticed he was wearing tan trousers.
"Are they leather?"
"Yeah, my most flattering and attractive civilian cloth," Rant said proudly.
"Does the material breathe in this heat?"
"No, of course it doesn't breathe. It's a dead animal skin."

Rupert bellowed laughter, his hands on his knees.

"Stop laughing, OK, Rue? We've serious things to discuss, and sooner rather than never."
"OK, OK." Rupert clutched one side of his ribs. "Oh, thank God for that, I didn't think I'd ever stop." He sat down with his back to the tree. He took some deep breaths.
"They've been waiting for you to make an appearance."

"Who's looking?"

"A few prefects that report to Marshall. He goes off duty after lunch –"

"- and then Copeland takes over."

"That's right. How did you remember that?"

"It figures. And no police. The school would look incompetent."

"Russell told me earlier that he saw you leave the dormitory at about midnight. He said that you never came back. Have you been out here all night?"

"Yes."

"Doing what? For goodness sake, tell me what were you doing!"

"I was having sex. Repeatedly. And I fell in love." Rupert enjoyed the way that expression felt on his tongue; meaningful words, precisely articulated.

"Sounds to me like you should be locked up."

Rupert jumped to his feet. "I didn't expect that kind of crap from you Rant!" He started to unbutton his shirt. "I thought you were a friend!" He revealed his sweating torso, dropped the shirt to the grass. His chest and neck were blemished with bites and scratches, unmistakable evidence of sex.

Julian gawped. "Oh, my God!" he whispered.

Rupert sat back down against the tree. "She's lovely, you know? Long silky hair spun with silver... so beautiful... I can't stop thinking about her."

"God!" said Julian, again.

"Do you want to know what happened?"

"Yes! Tell me now!"

Rupert told him. "So then," he finished, "somehow, this Tube train started moving *upwards,* which was when I woke up in the leaves. That was just after nine this morning. Physically speaking I'm back to my normal self, but I missed roll-call. And Lillith was gone."

"That's a very interesting word, *succubus*, and it's lighting up neon signs between my ears," said Julian. "Where did you first hear the word?"

"She left it in a message. It's what she *is*, engraved on the steps that lead in and out of the sunken garden. Take a look for yourself, if you want."

Rant came back half a minute later. "It's totally weird," he said, "but that doesn't make it any the less real."

"Undeniably real."

"No, you have to understand, Rupert, it's totally fucking bizarre!"

"I know! Brilliant isn't it?!"

"It couldn't have happened to a better man!"

They beamed at each other like a couple of kids at a party.

"I guess school stuff is irrelevant now."

"That's part of it for me, Julian. Without Lillith I had no future, and with her I've got a chance for something that... isn't *normal*. For a destiny-line that is far beyond what anyone could imagine. And God help anybody that tries to stop me."

Julian grimaced at this last, then asked how he may help.

"I need to talk to Russell."

"He went down to the pub, as far as I know, about half an hour ago."

"Then the pub is where I'm going. The thought of a cool pint of lager with lime is driving me mad."

"You're the least crazy mad person I've ever met," said Julian.

"Don't make me laugh again." Rupert stood up. He put his shirt on with the collar open, then put his tie in his pocket and rolled up his sleeves. "I'm going on a short cut through the woods beside the top cricket pitch. That way I'll walk on the main road as little as possible."

"I'm going down to the library," said his friend, already walking away.

"Why?"

"- To look up 'succubus' in an encyclopedia!"

*   *   *

ZAXXON

Going Out Of Bounds reinforced the annexe to that which Rupert had committed himself to in regards to the school. Putting one foot in front of the other turned the theory of it into a reality far scarier than he had imagined. Leaving the grounds was like destroying a familiar picture; like a landscape painted on glass bought in the days when its beauty still mattered, and smashing it. Now the empty wall begged for a new picture as a reference to the now, a portrait of Lillith; a romance, or perhaps a horror. The pub frequented by 5th Formers was the last of three, at the far end of the village. Walking along the dried mud of the hedgerow, which led almost directly to the beer garden behind it, Rupert counted twenty-five pounds in his wallet and was well pleased. He mounted the fence.

It was cool and dim in there, busy with the noise of continuous yet somnolent conversations. Several of his acquaintances were seated at a round table by the window drinking beer. He slurped down a pint of tap water with ice then bought a pack of cigarettes and pushed between the customers to where Russell Chase was playing the gambling machine in the corner. The man looked stressed.

Rupert said 'hello'. Russell tore his gaze away from the bars and sevens long enough to say: "This bitch is taking me for a ride to a bottomless pit! Do you have my money?"
"Yes fifteen, as agreed. Have you got the key?"
"Yeah, come over here," he said. They stood together under a still life of a basket of dead grouse between two horse brasses. "Where the hell have you been?"
"I woke up at eleven and then came down here for a couple of beers."
"That's a fantastic attitude, Thornberry, but you're in so much shit you'll probably be expelled."
"I don't care about that anymore."
"Really?"
"Really." He sneezed and then coughed.
"Wow, Cheesecake goes Section Eight as well as AWOL!"

"Don't call me that, Russell, OK?" He opened his wallet and took out fifteen pounds. "The key?"

Russell unwrapped a handkerchief and took out the key and placed it into Rupert's hand. Although Rupert wasn't surprised that it was identical to the one in his dream, shiny, with the number eighteen engraved on it, its existence in this reality nevertheless stole his breath.

"Russell, could you get me a large Scotch?"
"Yeah, if you give me the money."
"How else?"

The whisky burned down his throat and set off a bomb in the pit of his stomach that took the edge off the world. He put his empty glass down beside a beer mat that said 'Teachers' and then gave Russell some more money for a pint of lager and lime. After he had won his war against the fruit machine, with a jackpot repeated, Russell outlined the secret workings of the school Surgery.

"When they find out the key is missing they're going to change the PIN number on the medication cabinet, but they always write down the new number in the surgery Communications Book. And I know where it's kept! Chase by name, chase by nature! You just tell me when you're going in and I'll get the new PIN for you. It's that simple."
"It's OK, Jack. I don't need it anymore."
"Well, thank Christ for that, but only my friends can call me after a dog!"

Last night this key had originally been intended to thieve sleeping tablets, to engineer his own suicide. It had represented death, then, but it seemed to Rupert as though a lifetime had passed by since.

"All I need it for now is to self-medicate a bit of flu mixture."

ZAXXON

"I can't say I'm not relieved," said Russell. "Fifteen pounds for your own flu mixture, fuck me! Let me get you another drink to celebrate."

It was typical of Russell to buy just a small glass of lager, a half pint, but Rupert felt fine and he didn't need more alcohol. He sat with the others by the window. Sneezing, half drunk, his anxiety was loosened so much that he found himself wanting to tell them everything. But silent alarms were warning him not to jeopardise Lillith's love, not to disparage the superstition that could become fact after darkness fell this very night. So he left the pub. He walked up the field without fear. He had already taken enough Dutch courage to face Copeland, and he was actually whistling when he crossed the cricket pitch onto the road that led down to the main building. But before he could accept whatever the old bastard dished out he had to visit the surgery.

His foul smelling shoes crunched on the gravel as he walked up to the portico, passed Copeland's BMW. Many more executive cars could be seen parked there during the week. He knotted his tie in his reflection in the front door. He pushed through it and then walked onto the cool parquet floor of the front hall. Acting as calm as he could, he walked passed the notice boards, passed the tuck shop, and up the back stairs beside the kitchens. There he would find, at the far end of a corridor of 6th Form study bedrooms, the back door to the Surgery.

Rupert fished out Key #18. He listened at the door. He could hear nothing from inside then suddenly sneezed loudly! He froze like a rabbit trapped in truck headlights, and in that brief eternity he considered aborting his attempt at self-medicating to return to the Surgery later, on an official basis. But he had his own key - and with it he wielded a sense of power that he knew would help him deal with Copeland. So he stood there, hunched over by the door to ride it out, trying to breathe as quietly as possible. No one came. He scratched his acne and pushed the key into the lock. He turned it anti-clockwise and the door opened on greased hinges.

Inside was a large square room that looked different to him, at this moment, because he had never seen it before without the overhead fluorescent lights on. The white paintwork seemed to glow in the ambient afternoon sunlight shining through a small window. The room smelt of iodine and disinfectant. It was the scent of bandages, a smell that he was too young to realise was horrible.

There was a couch, some sterilised dishes, and tidy cupboards. And then he saw some large bottles on the main counter that was parallel with the windowsill, including the only brand of cough mixture he had ever known in school: the classique flu remedy *Squill Linctus*. It was ideal.

Mentally preparing himself for its vile taste, he tiptoed into the room and reached out to grasp the bottle. Then stopped his hand. There was a pen lying on the counter, a black Biro with no cap - and its nib was pointing at the name label of the syrup - indicating, in fact, a word within a word: *QUILL*. For the second time that day Rupert was amazed by the way his dreams bled into the real world. He picked up the pen and knew it was manufactured by BIC even before he read the name along the side of the barrel. He put it into a pocket in his loose trousers then unscrewed the cap of the cough mixture bottle and took a gigantic swig from the neck. Its taste seemed to spread from his offended tongue into the bones of his skull like a rotten toffee apple. He put the cap back on the bottle and locked the room behind him. It was time to see Copeland.

He found himself dragging his feet down to the front hall as though his steps were more reluctant than his mind. There were no certainties. He knew that as he walked up to the staff room door and knocked on it, knew that it could go either way, from awkward to awful. Copeland's commanding voice came through the door sounding like a wrecking ball wrapped in a silk suit.

ZAXXON

"That had better be you, Thornberry, that had just better be you!"

Rupert frowned with déjà vu. Then the door opened and there was Copeland, the haft of a pipe in his mouth, staring levelly at him with an expression of pompous confidence in his own power.

Rupert felt a twinge of anxiety without focus, like tossing and turning in bed being unable to sleep, like it wasn't his own body standing in the doorway. Copeland ordered him inside, but before the door closed Rupert looked over his shoulder and saw Hudson standing behind a small number of morbid juniors who were gathering like vultures near the tall windows, watching and whispering. He stuck his tongue out, and needed to override the resulting sense of his own silliness. Then the dead bolt clicked into place and sealed him in the staff room alone with the old man.

"You have no jacket," Copeland began. "And why do your shoes smell so terrible?"

"I stepped in cow manure, sir."

"There are no heifers on school grounds. Tell me where you've been all this time – now!"
Copeland considered Rupert's explanation whilst puffing his foul smelling tobacco, his red face wrinkled with scepticism.

"Do you really expect me to believe that you wandered down to the woods at midnight, last night, because you felt ill, and you didn't wake up until *five minutes ago*?"

"That's correct, sir," said Rupert.

"But it's half past three in the afternoon, boy!"
The young man chuckled inside. A single thought of kissing Lillith and his fear was evolving into alcohol borne humour. He looked at his watch and said, with an exaggerated deference: "Half past three in the afternoon – so it is – sad!"

"I'll give you something 'sad' boy!"

"But one wonders: what *actual day*, is it, today?"

Copeland took him by the lapels of his shirt and shook him. "You'd best keep your sarcasm to yourself, you cheeky pup! You stink of alcohol. What do you take me for? A lemon?"

Rupert grimaced at the old man's rancid breath. He pulled out of Copeland's grasp. "A lemon? Yes, I think I agree, definitely a lemon!"

Copeland demanded: "Shut up!" as loudly as he could, which sounded like a rusty hinge. Then he declared, with his full power: "The Head Master has reached a decision. Rupert Thornberry, you are officially expelled from this school and must leave the premises within one week. The reason he asked me to tell you is because he doesn't like wasting his breath on cheeky young pups! What do you say to that?"

Rupert thought about the key, the quill, and the acorns. "I say you suck the Head Master's tit behind the bike sheds, and that you always have!"

"*What?!* My God, boy," Copeland exploded, his forehead sheathed in moisture. "You know what's coming to you now? Eh? Come here laddie!"

Rupert leant nonchalantly against the staff room door. "You can't intimidate me you old fart."

"Intimidate you be damned!" screeched the old man, virtually drooling. He slammed his pipe on the table. "I'll tell you what I'm going to do to you." He paused, breathlessly, to shuffle over to the massive prize cabinet against the wall. "I'm going to" – he started coughing.

"What are you going to do old fatty?" Rupert chuckled, amused by his own frivolity. "There's nothing you can do, you can hardly even walk, coffin-dodger!"

The teacher's bronchial fit had not subsided by the time he opened the cabinet. "I'm going to give you a painful lesson, cheeky p-p-pup," he wheezed, took a bamboo stick out of the cabinet and closed it. "I'm going to c-cane you!"

"Yeah?" Rupert was laughing and bent over: "Kiss my arse!"

"I'll whip the hide off you," Copeland blustered, his face now an alarming sweaty purple. He wobbled across the room weakling brandishing his stick and knocked his pipe off the table.

ZAXXON

"Pig's giblets!" cried Rupert. "Old pork scratchings! Big fat, fucking, fatty, fat - fats!"

"You've gone insane," whispered the teacher, dropping to his knees. His eyes bulging alarmingly from the hunted look on his face.

"Let me help," said the young man, jovially, and walked over to where Copeland knelt swaying beside the table.

"Teach that pup," the old man kept muttering, when his lungs presented the opportunity, else he just clutched his chest and coughed and dribbled.

Rupert took away the cane. He snapped it in half. Copeland stared balefully at Rupert then fell forward flat on his face and lay as still as the cooling pipe beside him.

A voice from another place and another time, said: *platch!*

A cool breeze was stirring the smell through the room. Rupert stared down at the body and stumbled backwards and swore. His left hand wandered into his mouth. Copeland's face was a waxy grey and his lips were blue. "Heart attack!" Rupert exclaimed through a mouthful of fingers. Steeling himself, he wiped his hand on his trousers then fumbled passed two seats to kneel beside the body. With a dry mouth, he checked for a pulse at the old man's wrist like he'd seen done on TV, and felt nothing. The arm flopped back onto the carpet with a cold thump. Copeland was dead.

This was the first corpse he had ever seen, and there was no point wishing that he hadn't killed the man. Whether he had been drinking or not, he had murdered Copeland with words, yet he had to accept that there was no room for remorse. It wasn't difficult. He had crossed a metaphorical line (and perhaps also a *metaphysical* line) and he already had one foot in another world. Copeland's fate was now nothing more than a factor in the running. He was committed to his Succubus. There was nothing without her.

While Rupert imitated a discussion for appearances sake between himself and the dead teacher, he was developing two escape plans. No one could have witnessed the crime from the tennis courts because no one was playing. Rupert's breathing sounded loud to his own ears and according to his watch he had been in the staff room for almost twenty minutes. The length of his imitated conversation could have become over-extended, and that might become troublesome because of the eavesdroppers outside. There were several young sadists in the front hall, including Hudson, who were waiting to hear a whacking. So Rupert decided to make some noise. He selected the longest half of the broken cane and looked around for something to hit. On the table was a large book called "Monsters In Art" by Mr J.R. Copeland M.A. Rupert didn't know that pig's giblets had written a book, and for that reason it was the perfect whipping post. He brought his vocal performance to a peak, levelled the book up with the edge of the table, and whacked it with the cane. He groaned... then hit it again... and so on.

Originally 'Plan A' had seemed workable: to prop up the old man's body in front of staff room television and escape through one of the back windows, then to hide in the woods until he met the Succubus at eleven forty five pm. The problems were myriad. The front door was the only way in and out of the room so what would the audience outside do if Rupert never re-appeared? Sure, he could have locked the door shut - from the inside - before he took off, but they would have broken it down eventually. And Hudson was out there with them, who loved Copeland. According to school mythology Hudson was psychopathic. The younger man didn't know whether there was any truth to this, or not, but Hudson was a muscular son of a bitch and there was certainly no reasoning with the man when he was pissed off.

However similar, 'Plan B' was the better alternative. If he *dealt himself* the cane and walked out clutching his arse, Hudson and the others might leave him alone. Rupert also wanted the chance to say goodbye to Julian before he left and he didn't want to touch the body. Copeland was the only master on duty between Saturday and Sunday lunchtimes and the Head Master never came up to the main building. These procedures existed because there weren't many boarders in school at weekends so the Governors could save money by letting the prefects run the whole show. All Rupert needed now was some way to ensure that the staff room remain undisturbed for the night and he thought he had that one sussed out as well! His mind dwelt on wisps of images; of fire exits, and underground trains.

As his mind drifted through what little of his dreams he could remember, he stopped hearing his own hit count. When his concentration returned he noticed a number coming out of his mouth. He had actually whipped Copeland's book twenty eight times! Torn between worrying and chuckling laughter he gave the old man's *magnum opus* another two hard thwacks while begging himself to stop, then put the stick on the table beside a box of matches. He used the matches to light a cigarette and then looked around for anything else that might prove useful later. Although he was running away, the extravagant silverware in the prize cabinet was not a temptation. The glittering display only served to remind him of his lady's hair.

A blue glow in the corner captured his attention and he went to investigate. He found a computer running a state of the art 'Windows' operating system. There was a compact disc half in and half out of the 'A' drive slot, with *PERSONAL RECORDS* written on it, and Rupert's breath caught in his throat. The information on this disc was legendary. He couldn't resist accessing it, so he decided to bring up Hudson's file. Date of birth, quality of eyesight, latest information on his height and weight; none of it was revelatory. And then he saw Hudson's I.Q, which was 85, and beside it was the word IMPAIRED. Rupert did not have any time to waste, but he had to know why - for what could amount to his own safety.

Subject: Hudson .T. Diagnosed V.23'H409 deficent. Psychiatric evaluation indicates a quadrilateral disorder moderated via narco-reality therapy (Carbomazapine, Lithium). Symptoms inc. bi-polar manic depression, nocturnal epilepsy, neurasthenia, and latent schizophrenia. Therapy course outlined in Med Disc B. Reacts well to responsibility. Encourage paternal role-model within school framework. Withdrawal from medication or trauma may result in fits of extreme violence.

"Oh shit!" whispered Rupert. He ran his hands down his face, still staring at the screen.

Hudson's role-model was almost certainly Copeland. And Copeland was dead. As if to rid himself of the bloody fantasies featuring what Hudson could be capable of when he found out, Rupert ejected the disc and cracked it in half, then dropped the twisted plastic into the bin beside the desk. It felt a little like spitting in a policeman's face but he wanted to hurt the school, wanted to put it back by at least the number of years that he had suffered there as a pupil.

His hatred of the place rose to the surface yet brought with it other emotions that were not so welcome. Like doubt and fear and guilt... but nothing specific to hold on to because his memories of her were already growing dull, and being replaced. They were being blended with inferior imagination that was papering over the cracks of his amnesia, finite yet unmeasurable. He opened the desk drawers and destroyed every disc he could find. While he was ramming a screwdriver in and out of the computer's smoking disc port, he discovered he was crying. At least he wouldn't have to fake it.

*   *   *

Julian Rant had not gone directly down to the library after seeing off his friend. The impact and importance of Rupert's revelations, however supernatural, seemed to fade; perhaps because such things aren't supposed to walk abroad on a summer's day. Julian went swimming and watched TV and slept in the sun. Finally he went to the library that evening at about half past seven. If he had discovered the full meaning of the word *'succubus'* and its implications to his friend, sooner, maybe events would have taken a different path. Fate was with neither of them, and up to its usual inscrutable tricks with space and synchronicity. Julian sat at a table between the shelves. He had no access to the Inter-net and opened The Collins Dictionary. It seemed to be the obvious and logical place to begin. He idly flicked through to the letter 'S', hoping that if there was a reference - at all - it may fire up his curiosity. It did far more than that.

STILT – STIMULOUS - STINK
He turned over another two pages.
SUCCEED – SUCCINCT – SUCC'OUR
Then he found it:
SUCC'UBUS   n. *female demon fabled to have sexual intercourse with sleeping men.* [pl. – BI]

In spite of the facts of Rupert's story, Julian wondered what this nonsense was doing in a modern dictionary. It was exactly this question that prompted him into digging further. He commandeered a pencil and a few sheets of paper from a librarian's drawer then moved into the occult section, where bunkum like this was commonplace, but which was beginning to make sense. He had intended to be half an hour investigating Rupert's woman, but he ended up spending over three hours - before he sought out his friend to stop him leaving because of grave knowledge. She wasn't a woman at all. Even after the first hour Julian was convinced that Rupert was in real jeopardy. But not of his life - of his soul.

CHAPTER – 4

"Be.quest"

In her shop there were glass cabinets on three sides. They contained a plethora of delightful silver jewellery presented on velvet, as in the window display. The shop floor was lit by purple and ultra violet spotlights. The wall hangings were dark with Diamonte stones arranged into star constellations like looking into space. Quiet music was always enhanced by the burning of incense and the moon globe hanging from the ceiling cast an eerie light over the hand-made pieces. The shop was in Covent Garden, and it was called The Silver Tortoise. Owned by investors that were close friends of her family and run by one Stephanie Ashcroft, it had been open for just a year and yet it was trading at the pace of its rivals already. The woman had attracted a few celebrity clients, and some media attention herself, but owning and managing a jewellery shop in this part of London was more tiring than prestigious. It seemed that by mid-afternoon everyday she just wanted to go home and rest.

She had chuckled with her staff, Marcel and Caroline, when they suggested that she put up a camp bed in her office, but the joke was wearing thin. In school she had suffered ME, what the press had then dubbed 'yuppie flu', and it had hit her hard. She was an only child and had spent most of her time in bed, her hands shuddering when drinking tea from fine china, and creeping aimlessly around her parent's house like the ghost of an old woman. It had taken her eight months to recover, using Bach flower remedies, and she suppressed the occasional thought that it could recur. Even now, fifteen years down the line at the age of thirty-two, Stephanie always took her herbal teas from pottery because she couldn't hold fine china without her hands shaking.

Stephanie had had to drop out of her 'A' Levels. Not going to university had seemed like a disaster but it had not held her back. It emerged that she had a good head for business and elegant hands for the paper-work; a thumb and forefinger of her right hand that one ex-boyfriend had poetically compared, when she was counting money, to being like the sensitive tongue of a cat lapping milk. She was tall and had long dark hair. She liked to wear hippy style dresses in pastel colours and carried her things about in a hand woven shoulder sack that Celtic shamans call a 'crane bag'.

She bustled about her office, at the rear, with that 'Saturday feeling'. It was early today to be putting cash and cheques into the deep rectangular mouth of her wall safe. Doing so made her feel as though the time was later o'clock than it actually was. She spun the dial to lock it, and swung the mirror to cover it. Usually this was the last job before going home, hence her choice of concealing the safe behind a mirror so she could check herself before walking onto the street. She examined her face now, with a sense of alarm tempered by fighting spirit. She looked pale, washed out, and she felt it. She took a cover-up stick out of her bag and blended some under her eyes.

The holiday in Cornwall tomorrow was what she needed. Her father was driving them down in his classic MG. It would be just the two of them, for two weeks. They were going to stay in the same cottage that Stephanie and her parents had enjoyed visiting since she had been little. Inevitably it would remind her of her mother, who had passed away just a year ago of a tumour, but she wanted to pull herself together. The last year had been very hard. They would visit galleries and National Trust attractions, she would draw pencil sketches, and they would see by how much the Eden Project had grown since last they saw it. It would be a fun escape from London, and a relaxation self-therapy worth its weight in wrought silver!

She sat on the leather seat, on her side of the desk. The view through the small window beside the NO SMOKING sign was dismal. Claustrophobic red brick, dead grass and smelly dustbins. The tourists on the other side of the wall who drank coffee and bustled around the markets looking for a bargain could never have imagined mess like it could be so close! She leaned forward over the desk with her head in her hands thinking of Rhoda's clotted cream. The intercom crackled. Caroline's voice, with her slight East London accent and tone revealing always that she felt there was a chance of a pay-rise, said: "Miss Ashcroft, there is a nice gentleman here to see you!"

Stephanie smiled tiredly at the girl's enthusiasm. None of them would be getting a pay-rise for a long time yet, not even a mediocre bonus, and that included herself.

"Who is it?"
"It's Mister Hawthorne."

Stephanie briefly raised an eyebrow. Nigel was an old friend of the family who had personally invested money in the shop. He was most likely here about her dad because, like him, Hawthorne was also a professor in the British Museum. Sometimes he used Stephanie to manipulate her father in personal matters that decorum dictated should be kept within the family. In other words Hawthorne needed her because he was pernickety and her dad was a stubborn old goat.

She pressed the intercom. "A pot of mint tea for two, please, Caroline. And send him in."

Hawthorne entered the office. He was smiling, under his huge moustache, and she came around to peck him on both cheeks. He was short and stocky yet had an imposing bearing. They sat either side of the desk and studied each other. He favoured Tweed suits, and bow ties from a massive collection. His Queen's English and gruff politeness was an endearing anachronism, and the mints he had been chewing for so long had become a part of his personality. There was an icy scent to his crunching the XXX extra strong variety. The paper rolls were always in his breast pocket, had been ever since he had given up cigar smoking fifteen years ago! Stephanie pushed her chair out a little. She crossed her legs.

ZAXXON

"Its nice to see you," she said. "You're looking good."

"And you, Stephanie, are not. In fact you look like you could fall unconscious at any moment," growled Hawthorne, popping a mint into his mouth. "Are you sleeping alright?"

"Yes, fine."

"So what's the trouble?"

"It's no reflection on you, Nigel, I'm sorry."

"Friends never apologise to one another unless it's an emergency. And never for hard work, if that's what it is."

"I suppose so. I've been under the weather lately but it's nothing a summer holiday won't cure. We're bringing in new stock every week and selling more than ever, but somehow it feels difficult to keep it together. Like I've been trying to push large pieces of jewellery through a very small hole and winding up unable to do anything new because my hands are full."

"Pure poetry," he boomed. "You should have been a writer!"

Her face clouded with an ancient regret. There was a knock on the door and Caroline was told to come in, and put the tray on the desk. Stephanie poured the tea as she sidled courteously out of the room. She passed one to her visitor. "Mint tea," she said. She smiled and Hawthorne laughed.

Absently swirling the tea around her earthenware mug, Stephanie said: "Since you're obviously not here to buy the finest jewellery in town, you must be here about my father."

"That's very astute, my dear. And quite correct."

"Tell all!"

"Last Tuesday at work Stephen and I were downstairs and he came up to me, looking dishevelled, and questioned my trust. After I had assured him that whatever it was would remain just between the two of us, he took me aside and starting babbling. He said he was close to unearthing a great revelation about an ancestor of your family, Angus somebody-or-rather. That kind of thing. I really kick myself for not recollecting the name but I don't think I ever heard it before, which perhaps is also strange. Stephen said the ancestor disappeared about 160 years ago and that he was close to uncovering the truth of his fate." Hawthorne put a mint into his mouth and crunched it. "Did you hear the way I said 'ancestor'? That's how he pronounced it at the time - like there was no other word as important in the whole English language!"

"Nigel, I know about this OK? Dad's been researching Angus McLoughlan Ashcroft on and off for three decades. And imitating the way he says one of his favourite words isn't going to do anyone any favours. What are you trying to say?"

"That he's back to the genealogy. That he's as committed to it as to any other of the pet obsessions he goes through so often. But this time the compulsion is geared purely to his own ends."

"So? So what? You know he does this sometimes!"

"In this example Stephen's doing it on the Museum's payroll, and during the Museum's time. He's missed three seminars this week."

"Oh, I see... that is worrying."

"I'm afraid there's more. I don't wish to be melodramatic but he talked about devil worship, and mercenaries... or maybe it was buccaneers? Anyway, he said to me that this secret could prove the existence of magic. I suppose I've broken my word telling you all this, but his mental state seems flaky and you are the only person he'll listen to. While on holiday you must try, at least try, to talk him out of it. Or his position as Head Keeper of the Adriatic Department could be jeopardised."

She stood up suddenly, and anxiously brushed her hands down the waistline of her dress. "You mean he might get fired?"

"The Curator has turned a blind eye - until now."

She sat down again. "OK, OK, I'll go there this afternoon. But I want to relax first. I have to!"

"Try a mint."

"No thanks, Nigel, that just wouldn't do it for me." She opened the bottom drawer in her desk and rifled about in it with her hand. "That tea is lousy!" She took out a Mars bar and declared: "I need *chocolate!*"

Hawthorne chuckled. "Most great people do."

*   *   *

ZAXXON

His research was complete. Stephen Ashcroft, who was sitting at his usual table in the basement archive of the British Museum, had waited for this day. He put the cap onto his pen and dabbed his receding grey hair-line with a handkerchief, experiencing rapturous achievement. That feeling of realisation, like the last block of his own skyscraper had just been cemented into place. His head still swam with manorial rolls, war office and criminal records, censuses and electoral registers, but the paper-trail was over. He wondered for how long his quest had been going on. In terms of time, the comparison of thirty months continuously to thirty years on and off, seemed accurate. The last books and manuscripts on the subject, which he never need open again, were piled around him on the table like a fortress.

Tracing his ancestor had been a reverie of excavation. Angus McLoughlan Ashcroft's nickname had been 'Black Fist', and his turbulent career as mercenary and Satanist in the early nineteenth century had demanded a labour of love. The Professor remembered most of it now as having been like a huge jigsaw of names and places and times. And after so much sweat, after the moments of frustration and stoppage, and the frenzied blur of discovery, he had the name of it at last. The name of a remote fishing village on the north-western coast of Scotland. A tiny place with no notable history that should have withered away or fallen into the sea long ago, called *Ravencliff*. Angus had visited it 165 years ago and had never left alive. And it was even older than that. Somehow it had existed for six centuries and exists still, allocated the smallest spot in the biggest atlases, and apparently with only five phone numbers in the entire location that were all unlisted. On the best authorities the Professor had concluded that this was where Angus had died, during his last and most diabolic experiment. And he had left his body and the experiment behind.

A polite voice from behind him: "Professor? Will you be needing anything else?"

The old man took a sharp inhalation of breath, his trail of thoughts shattered as though splashed with a pint of cold water. It actually felt good. He swung his chair round and recognized the young bespectacled man at his back, the Junior Archivist.

"Thank you, Edmond, but no. I'm finished here now. Hopefully I'm done with this horrible dusty place for the foreseeable future!"

"I wish I could say the same thing, sir. I'm stuck here all the time."

The Professor put an Ordinance Survey of Scotland into his brief case, took his jacket off the back of his chair, straightened his tie, and tried to smooth down his unkempt mop of grey hair.

The archivist stared at him curiously, and asked: "Professor, are you... feeling alright?"

"I'm better than 'alright' son. When you get promoted to a position that involves research you may understand how I'm feeling."

"Oh, I see." Edmond didn't, but it was getting late enough already. "It's ten to six and I have to lock up. Your daughter's waiting for you in the lobby again."

"Then what are we waiting for?"

Edmond didn't know that, either. He locked the doors of his department and followed the Professor upstairs. Stephie's eyes met her father's the moment he walked into the entrance hall. In comparison to the basement, the foyer had a high ceiling and was full of air and light. Her hair looked different, a bundle of curls, and she was standing tall and graceful by the doors in an autumnal floral print dress. She smiled at him infectiously. It touched the few dimples around her generous mouth and lit up her whole face like the sun glinting off the still waters of a Scottish loch. A mechanical voice from the Tannoy echoed around the exhibits: "All visitors, please make your way towards the exits at the front of the building. The museum will be closing in five minutes."

ZAXXON

"Look at you, Stephie!" He said, and gave her a bear hug. "You're beautiful and you're hair's gone all curly!"

She seemed proud of herself. "I've just had a perm. You like?"

"Love it!"

"I thought I'd have it done for the holiday."

"Let's get out of here."

"Where are we going?"

The Professor paused. *Ravencliff*, he mused. A forbidding name, dark and smooth to the tongue yet with a bitterness that fades pleasantly. Like a pint of Guinness. "The pub," he exclaimed. "Let's go to the pub, immediately!"

Her car was parked in a cramped side road adjoining Museum Street. On their way to the Curator's Arms she needed to have a quick look at it, just to make sure the Audi was alright. Satisfied no one had interfered with it they sauntered through the evening sunlight that lanced between the buildings like transparent gold. Walked with the languid pace of tourists killing time, disturbed the occasional pigeon and discussed Nigel Hawthorne's visit to the shop. Her father called Hawthorne "a back-stabbing walrus-faced tit with all the brains of a mint!" And the word 'tit' was the closest he ever came to swearing. Stephanie had thought it was really funny and he was gruff with her but in face of such a victorious achievement, this day, his anger was brief. She tried to make him understand that it had not been fair on his students to miss three seminars this week, and he was typically cagey about the extent of the obsession that had driven him to this, but he revealed nothing new - except that he had never been happier. She had no wish to taint that.

They approached the door to the pub in an amiable silence. Stephanie could accept, at least, that his research into Angus 'Black Fist' McLoughlan was over, finally, and that it was a great day for him. He seemed embarrassed that he couldn't stop grinning. Once inside they walked up to the bar with different thirsts. He seemed to radiate his happiness like good music through quality speakers and when their drinks arrived it was like turning up the volume. She had a glass of vodka and orange juice; he, a pint of Guinness Extra Cold. And once they were seated Stephanie felt, just then, for the first time, the proximity and reality of their holiday... but they didn't stay even long enough to empty their glasses because the plan changed.

"Last time you got drunk there you fell off the stern of that fishing boat," she said chirpily. "Christ that was funny! The captain hauled you out and you threw up all over him! I *love* Cornwall!"

"We're not going to Cornwall anymore," her dad said.

"We aren't?"

"No. Have you packed your bags yet?"

"Yes. But where are we going?"

"Don't be defensive!"

"Where are we going?"

"Northwestern Scotland."

"If you think I'm following you all the way up there to hunt for an old skeleton on a bloody museum trip, you're very much mistaken!"

"It's beautiful, Stephie. You've never been there. It's a beautiful place." He leaned forward. "There are glens of heather that wave silently beneath the sun; grass carpeting huge valleys of granite cut by glaciers. The lochs have water like liquid lead under the clouds, and the bleak grey rocks of the Highlands are inhabited by wild animals with long hair whipped by the wind."

"I'm moved."

"It was the best holiday with my parents I ever had." He beamed.

She was starting to smile back, she couldn't help it. "We'll need our hiking boots."

"I know that... and I say we go tonight!" he exclaimed.

"I can't believe I'm agreeing to this, but... if we *do* go I'd like to stay in a nice hotel, a really good one with satellite TV, and room service. And a little fridge of drinks."

He grinned. "Breakfast in bed every morning! What do you say?"

"You actually want to leave *tonight*?"

"Yes! Shall we do it!?"

ZAXXON

"Just go?"
"Yes. Now. And leave our beverages."
"OK! We'll do it!"

*   *   *

Inevitably, the plan changed again. To break the journey they booked a room in the Lake District and finally left London at half past eight PM. They listened to the radio and didn't talk much. When Radio Four switched to the BBC World Service, the newscaster's voice flowed over Stephanie's head and blended with the droning engine and the rumble of the tyres on the road. She drifted in and out of sleep, and awoke at oddly disconnected times to look around myopically before going back to sleep. That's how it seemed, to her. From the passenger seat in the darkness one motorway looked pretty much the same as any other, but, by two AM in the morning, they were safely tucked up in their motel room beds.

On Sunday, after an early room service breakfast, they tugged on their walking boots and hiked into beautiful weather over rough hills and around serene lakes, and Stephanie began to sense a change in herself. Down in some claustrophobic part of her the shackles of her London life were being gradually dismantled, and her continuous worry about her shop was relaxing into fragments. They found water-smoothed wood to use as walking sticks. Sometimes she meditated about the strip of silver in a bank note, and if Marcel the Frenchman could cope with managing the shop for two weeks without her. Hand crafted silver was coveted. Unlike the animal it was named after, The Silver Tortoise moved quickly, but she didn't want to think about work. Yes, Marcel would be fine. They walked back to the motel and after a bar meal continued their journey.

Sometimes Stephanie nodded off to sleep and dreamt of flying. She awoke to an increasingly barren landscape. Their arrival time was supposed to be just shy of nine pm. At half passed eight the grey skies faded as darkness fell. They seemed to be no closer. Her dad was tense with concentration, and was increasingly becoming as cold and as harsh as the weather. They drove ever northwards and it started raining. With no further traffic they seemed to be in the middle of nowhere. By the time the Ordinance Survey map had gained a more vital importance, the MG had consumed almost two tanks of lead replacement petrol. Her dad had chewed two packets of gum and drank an entire one-litre Thermos of coffee! The car was Stephen Ashcroft's pride and joy, a classic 1974 two seater MG BGT, with a leather top, spoked wheels, and radial tyres. The engine was a 2.5 litre V.8 capable of 220 BHP. He loved it.

Drawing closer to what she assumed was their destination, the winding excuse for a 'road' narrowed into a pot holed stumbling mire. It was little better than the rock-strewn marsh it was supposed to negotiate. Her dad desperately wanted to get back onto some excuse for a main road but the map was becoming increasingly vague about the whole area. Hunched over the steering wheel, as he drove, the mud splattered MG slid clumsily on into the wet darkness. The rain soaked leather top was dripping into the interior. She switched off the radio to aid her father's concentration and at nine thirty he stopped the car and gave the engine a well-deserved rest. To Stephanie the silence was like an anxiety made more oppressive by the rain gusting against the chassis. The map crackled.

"If you had installed a Sat Nav this wouldn't have happened," she pointed out. "Do you have any idea, at all, about where we are?"

He re-started the engine and slid the gear stick into first. "Of course."

"Well? Where?"

"Still about fifty miles away I'm afraid."

"Yes? Fifty miles away from *where*?"

"From the focus of dark magic, where all the cross-references of my research meet."

Simultaneously worried for him and angry at him, these words verified what Nigel Hawthorne had told her on Friday afternoon. "And I thought we were here to give Angus a proper burial."

"That was collateral damage. It's what killed him I want."

"What are you talking about?"

"I'm talking about stunning the whole scientific community, about undermining the laws of physics with metaphysics, with the proof that magic exists!"

"How do you intend to?"

"Just you wait."

Stephanie didn't want to 'just wait', or feel fear for him. Anger was easier. "It's gibberish!"

At this the Professor changed into third gear, over-revving angrily. "Don't be so prejudiced young lady." The car snaked about slightly in the mud.

"I'm the most open minded person you know."

"Then believe me."

"I'm stuck with it, dad, OK? What are you really here for?"

"To find a book with amazing power that Angus found in 1829. *The Necronomicon*, written hundreds of years ago. It can awaken the dead and raise demons and open doors into other realities. I wouldn't expect you to understand."

"How *dare you* say that?! You won't find any magic book, not anywhere in the real world, because there's no such thing. Typical!"

The old man pursed his lips and changed down a gear grimly. The headlights illuminated a right hand bend and he swung the car into it. The vehicle broadslid towards the verge, spraying up gallons of mud from its rear tyres, and he rode out the skid. The windscreen wipers revealed a hill. He put his foot down and hurtled up it into the heavy rain.

"For heaven's sake," Stephanie panicked, "could you slow down?!"

"I thought you liked a fast pace like London."

"That's ridiculous!!"

He changed up a gear, and relaxed the accelerator. The MG slowed down but it was still too fast and Stephanie felt no better. They tore up to the apex of the hill.

"I'm going to wipe the smiles off their smug faces," he muttered quietly.

"Are you talking to me?"

He had no time to say no. At the top of the hill, the tyres bit into unexpected black-top and flung them across a road parallel to huge cliffs. The Professor had time, just, to gather that it had not been on the map. He slammed on the brakes but the inevitable skid catapulted them straight over it. They felt, more than saw, a fragmented panorama of yawning cliffs on either side - and up ahead nothing. Stephanie cried out, shielding her eyes, as the car leapt out of control up the grass embankment. Then they both screamed. Those horrendous seconds, as their innards rose in a fall they might never forget, assuming they survived, had seemed like an eternity. Their deaths had been certain but with a sudden bone-jarring crunch the doomed car landed earlier than expected, and on solid ground.

*　　　　　　　*　　　　　　　*

Stephanie heard a mingling of sound that pulsed rhythmically back and forth through her brain. Her own laboured breathing, steam hissing from the bonnet of the car, the ticking of metal cooling. She was shuddering with shock. Her whole body seemed to be aching, particularly her neck. Exploring the injury she found a whip-lash burn over her right collarbone and under her chin. Stephen Ashcroft groaned. In the absence of the SRS air-bags that she had wanted him to fit, any way possible – which he hadn't - she felt it was lucky that she hadn't broken her neck. The remains of old fruit and chocolate wrappers and empty drink cartons had spilled from the glove compartment. One headlight had survived. Coughing, she blinked disbelievingly outside.

ZAXXON

"Can't be," burbled her father. "Can't be Ravencliff... still forty miles away..."

She ignored him. They were on an expanse of wet Tarmac enclosed on three sides by grassy earth. Thirty yards away to the left were two buildings, small and white, which were no bigger than sheds yet perhaps solid enough to have been built of brick. Windowless buildings with small signs written on each composed of words that were too far away to read. She looked down at the ground. The whole area was segmented by white lines.

"I don't believe it!" she exclaimed.

They had landed in a car park! Stephanie wearily disengaged the seat-belt and her dad cranked his door open and stumbled out into the drizzle.

"Where are we?" he asked. "This is a car-park!" After a pause he added: "Oh no, look at my car!"

She got out and slammed the door. And kicked it. "Never mind this, you almost killed us!" She kicked it again, her eyes blazing.

He was pacing around the MG, clutching his beard. She followed him around it wanting to rant at him but saw the damage. The radiator was ruptured, the bumper was mangled, the left front wing crumpled - and that was just the visible havoc. Stephanie knew he had nurtured the car for many years, and it was in ruin. Her anger subsided into compassion, and then he did a funny Laurel and Hardy thing. He picked half the number plate out of a puddle and started making small mewling noises! She walked up to him, and hugged him. He dropped the twisted piece of metal and clutched her back hard.

"I'm sorry, I'm so sorry," he gasped.

Gently, into his ear, she said: "Don't worry dad. It's insured and if it doesn't start we'll find an engineer, somewhere, I'm sure we will. What's important is that we are alive."

"Of course, that's right!" he said, and pulled away from her with a gradual sensitivity. "I suppose we had better make a move. This *is not* Ravencliff. According to the map I don't see how it could possibly be, and I admit we're lost, but at least it's stopped raining."

She could no longer see any of the parking spaces. Mist had crept up and shrouded the place. In the bright cylinder of light from the remaining headlamp, it looked like they were floating, as if they *had* died but hadn't realised it yet, and she swore softly. Her imagination was being overactive and grim. Stephen Ashcroft rooted about in the trunk of his car and walked over to his daughter carrying their luggage: two large suit-cases, her shoulder sack, and he extracted a torch from a gym bag of archaeological equipment. "Take this," he said, and gave it to her. He ducked into the cabin of the MG, switched off the headlight, and then locked the doors.

"Who's going to steal that?" asked Stephanie. "It's shutting the stable door after the horse has bolted, if you'll forgive the cliché!"

"I'm so hungry if a horse bolted to me, I would eat it."

"Well, you can't eat mine!"

This was an old joke and they both laughed. She slung the crane bag over her uninjured shoulder. Her dad picked up their suit-cases and his gym bag. They started hiking. She shone the torch too and fro like a searchlight, and asked him how he knew, for sure, that there was a village down there.

"Where there's a car-park there are cars, and –"

"- where there are cars there are people," she finished.

"That's it."

"But what if there really *is* nothing there? What if those two sheds are loos and this car-park is just for tourists to look at the view?"

"Put your bags down, just for a moment." He put down his own. "Now stand facing the sea, and switch off your torch." She did. "Now - look at the sky."

"I can't see a thing!"

"Wait for your eyes to adjust…"

She was momentarily baffled by the blackness. And then she discerned an undulating gulf of clouds receding out to sea. A storm like a mountain range was moving inland, by slow degrees, and the base of the cloudbank seemed to be glowing underneath like a bangle in candlelight. A reflection emanating from beyond the car park, from the lights of a village somewhere below.

"Yes, I can see it now," she said, with pure relief. "You're a clever man."

"And you are a clever woman. You get it all from me!"

She started walking directly along her sight line, towards the sea.

"Where are you going, Stephie?"

"I want to see the town properly! I have to see it!"

"Be careful then."

She walked to the edge of the car park and up the grassy bank. She was stopped at a flimsy railing and held onto it. Looking down into the bay laid out below her it seemed to be at least two hundred feet down, she thought, probably more. The houses had been constructed between two headlands. Spurs of granite crags silhouetted against the volatile sky, with the continuous rumbling of waves crashing in the distance. The houses had lights sprinkled through the fog, little yellow lights like fire-flies, or fairies. She sensed her father standing beside her.

"A drop of hundred and fifty feet, I would hazard," he said. "It's amazing, but hell its cold!"

"We need to find an inn or a hotel or something." She shivered. "What's the time?"

"About half past ten. If we're fast enough getting down there it won't matter."

"Then let's move."

They squelched down the embankment and she switched her torch back on. The light was as welcoming as watching TV in her favourite armchair with a blizzard outside the window. She illuminated the two buildings and beyond them they saw the exit from the car park, a wide track of rough stony ground winding down into the bay. She scampered towards the sheds and left her father behind with the heavier luggage. She was much fitter than he was but in their family the large bags were always the man's responsibility.

"I bloody well hope these are toilets. It smells like they must be." She walked round them, and there was a pause. Then she said, with a noticeable lack of enthusiasm: "Dad, I think you're going to want to see this…"

He walked up to the nearest shed and read the sign by the light of Stephanie's torch. Written in dark blue capital letters was an expression that made fact out of impossibility, two words that spelt: R A V E N C L I F F   F I S H E R I E S.

*   *   *

The track that led down into the village was like a meandering river and fifteen minutes later the compacted dirt gave way to cobblestones. Their footsteps echoed back and forth through the fog and they passed the first of the houses in the main street. They could smell peat burning from chimneys and found the buildings were all white washed and built long ago. Constructed of the rock of the cliffs, the houses were small and located closely together as if to protect them from the terrible storms that raked the coast in winter. Closed net curtains divulged no secrets, and there was no one else in the street to direct them to somewhere they could eat and sleep.

The Professor lagged behind his daughter, often, because his muscles ached. The combined weight of their luggage and his archaeology kit was almost too much for a man of his age to bear for such a distance. He was breathing heavily and if not for the torchlight dancing ahead he would have regularly lost sight of Stephanie, but every so often she stopped to allow him to catch up. He was sweating, even in the moist coldness of the fog, yet also excited to actually be there. Amazed to be in the reality of Ravencliff, a place annexed by geography that had risen from the whispers of words in books. It was an insignificant village yet it concealed a history of devilry and was apparently protected by maps that lied.

When his daughter waited for him again, he said: "Stephie, I don't think I can carry all these bags anymore."

"I didn't realise." She walked to him.

"I'm just an old professor." He put her suitcase down. "Take this heavy one, which is yours. I'm tired and hungry and I can't work out whether I'm hot or cold."

"Have you got a fever?"

"No, no, nothing like that. It's this place. I'm frustrated and happy and nervous all through. But mostly I'm just exhausted."

"I'm very sorry dad." She picked up her case. "I feel young when I'm with you, like I'm always sixteen and you're always thirty two. I never think of you as being old."

"I try to avoid thinking about it myself."

Then they heard footsteps approaching them, a fit of diseased coughing blurted with a grotesque suddenness out of the fog. A hunched figure passed them like a balloon drifting along the edge of the street. It stopped and seemed to look at them, then it burped and shambled away up the hill.

"Stay back," whispered the Professor. "He's drunk!"

Ashcroft begged his pardon; this was greeted with no reaction. Walking briskly he followed the old drunkard, who had an irritating pace for one so frail and bedraggled. The hunchback stopped when the Professor overtook him. He had white hair, a red face, and had a surprisingly determined expression on his wrinkled features that somehow didn't fit the aroma of strong malt.

"We want to find an inn," Ashcroft clarified. "A bed for the night. Some food. Won't you help?"

The man looked blearily at him seemingly for the first time. Then he said something gutturally in the common local tongue.

"What's that language?" asked Stephanie.
"Gaelic."
"What did he say?"
"You don't want to know." The Professor was grinning. After a pause for thought on sentence construction, he countered the man in his own language.
The hunchback looked surprised, and respectful. He smiled toothlessly and said: "For a man of my age, sir, that would be a wee bit difficult!"

The Professor held out his right hand. The hunchback's eyes glittered when he held out his own because at some point in the past it had been severed just above the wrist. He raised his eyebrows in a mocking challenge. Ashcroft grasped it after a brief hesitation. His eyes never left the madness in the eyes of the other and the tissue covering the bony stump felt dry and papery, but soft as silk. His own skin crawled but he squeezed the limb until the hunchback pulled it back to himself with an expression of admiration. He cleared his throat.

"Name's Duggon," he said. "John Duggon."
"Stephen Ashcroft. And this is my daughter Stephanie."
"Hello, Mr Duggon."
"Just Duggon." He turned away. "A fine looking lassie, she is too," he muttered to himself hoarsely. "Fine, she is!" He was dribbling a little. His tongue slid in and out over his lips like a slug randomising bites out of a lettuce. She reddened under his gaze. He shook himself and looked back

at the other man. "What are ye doing here, if I may be so bold?"

"We're on holiday," said the Professor. His daughter looked at him reproachfully. "We left London on Friday night and stayed last night in the Lake District."

"Aye, London. I thought as much, there's nay room here for the likes of *tourists*," he spat. The statement was unexpectedly venomous.

"It's a working holiday," said Ashcroft, dryly. "Could you direct us to the inn?"

"What kind of work?"

Stephanie uttered: "I don't see that it's any of your business! Just direct us to the nearest inn!"

"Och, keep your hair on, lassie, it's just doon the road for gawd's sake!" Duggon pointed to a side street. "It's doon there." The Ashcrofts picked up their luggage. "D'you fancy buying us a wee drop o' Glen Morangie?"

They didn't answer. It had been a very long day, and the welcome of an inn was within their reach.

"Ashcroft," yelled Duggon, "I want to ask ye somethin' else!"

"What is it now?"

"Are ye, by any road, related to Angus 'Black Fist' McLoughlan?"

The Professor dropped their luggage and he took a deep breath, staring down at the cobblestones. This was impossible. He turned. "I am his ancestor. Why do you ask?"

"Yea, you," said Duggon, turning on his heel to dodder back up the road. "Y'think I'm only a crippled drunkard, Ashcroft? I know things!"

"Dad, let him go."

"I can't let him get away," exclaimed her father.

Both of them went up the street after Duggon, but he was already being swallowed up by the fog. They had time for one last glimpse of him before he disappeared, and they gawped at the sight because the hunchback had actually started running.

"Unbelievable," whispered Stephanie. She walked back. The Professor stayed on the corner of the street gazing into the mist as if for answers. "The *bastards!*" she shouted suddenly. He was at her side in an instant, and her sentiments echoed his own exactly. Except for the crane bag over her shoulder, their luggage had disappeared. Stephanie offered up an unexpected perspective: "At least they didn't get the chocolate."

"Give me some of it!" demanded her father. He liked it as much as she did. She gave him a Toblerone and he ripped the wrapper off it and chewed off several chunks. "Alright, alright..." He was thinking hard, and speaking with his mouth full. "There are few secrets in a village this small. We'll start asking questions in the morning and since I still have my wallet we could loosen their tongues with sterling. I'll bet someone will know where our bags are. The immediate problem," he said, looking at his watch, "is that it's ten passed eleven, so we need to get to the inn. Now!"

He started walking down the side street and his daughter followed. They stopped at the front door of a public house called the Raven's Nest. The door was made of oak reinforced with old shiny bolts. And it was locked. The Ashcrofts made their pitch to be allowed to enter.

"No," said the Land Lord, from inside.
"Be serious!" cried the Professor.
"It's a quarter passed eleven. I can't let you in. I'm sorry."
.   It was starting to rain again. "We've been on the road for two days," yelled Stephanie, tearfully, "we don't have anywhere to go!"
Silence.
"Our car is smashed up -"
"- and our luggage has been stolen!"
Continued silence.
"She needs the loo!"
"Sleep in your car," suggested the publican, when the net curtain in the window beside door twitched fractionally to one side. The kind face of a middle-aged woman peered at them, frowned, then ducked back behind the curtain.

ZAXXON

"William McTavish!" said the woman, clearly. "That wee lassie out there is starving and you want to leave them both out in the *Harr* to freeze to death!"

"They'll be alright my bonnie strawberry."

"Utter nonsence!" cried the woman.

Stephanie giggled.

"I didn't think you would want to cook again. Let's go to bed, my sweet posy."

"Hogwash!"

The Professor whispered: "Custer's last stand!" into his daughter's ear.

"Bed? Think? You should be so lucky!" Then she said, quieter: "If you think you're goin't'ave your way with me later, you'd better be bringing them in." The door opened.

At that same moment the hunchback was in the village church on the far side of the bay. He was facing the true power of Ravencliff, a priest named Raul Caine. It was a quiet community that hadn't seen a crime, except for the priest's own (of which no one but Duggon would ever be aware of) for over twenty years. He controlled the Post Office, the telephone system, the fisheries department and he had a hand in all imports and exports to and from Ravencliff. He was law, jury and judge. He ruled with words of iron from the pulpit and an antique knife to keep the village as far away from the social infections of the rest of the world as possible.

Caine's right hand was currently in the pocket of his black robes, running his fingertips back and forth over the smooth haft of the knife. It had belonged to the priest's great, great, grandfather. It was seven inches long, razor sharp, and Duggon knew it intimately. He was fearful of losing his other hand to it now! The priest spoke Gaelic gutturally and his face was sallow. He asked the hunchback, for the second time, if he had been drinking that night. Duggon looked around at the cold unforgiving rock of the vestry. He hoped that telling the story of meeting the Ashcrofts might keep Caine's knife in his pocket.

"If I was drunk I wouldn't be in this place," said Duggon.

"Bold," said Caine, "but I do smell it upon you, alcohol fiend."

"I beg you to hear me out before you make this judgement!"

"Alright. You may speak."

"The son of the Black Fist is with us." The hunchback watched the other man recoil at the possibility. "He is here."

"You're certain?"

"Och, he admitted it so! He has been travelling with his daughter from London."

"His name is Ashcroft?"

"Aye, I spoke to them not ten minutes ago. They are staying at the pub."

"Then it seems my blade will be wetted this night. Is he here to plunder McLoughlan's tomb?"

"I don't think he even knows about it. Will you let him have the legacy?"

"No. It was not written for the eyes of a mortal man. *And the sins of the father's shall be visited on the sons, and in turn upon the sons of their sons.* Vengeance for God, vengeance for the community, and vengeance for my ancestors - who were bound over to keep McLoughlan's secret down all the generations. The only thing he'll get from me is death; both of them. You have done well, John. Stand up now."

Duggon was surprised to be kneeling. He hadn't realised that at some point he had dropped to his knees and he hadn't felt so desperate for a drink since last Sunday when he had left church.

*   *   *

In the outlying villages of the Scottish highlands and along the rugged coastline, the takings of competing pubs can be affected by the hugeness and efficiency of their 'inglenook' fireplaces. These could be cold parts of the world, even in late June. The inside of the Raven's Nest was confined, yet cosy – small, in every way, except in the size of its fireplace.

ZAXXON

The bar had a single counter, a low ceiling of exposed beams, and bare floorboards. The room was warm and had a pleasing aroma of peat smoke and liquor. Outside in the road, through the leaded diamond pane windows, lay darkness and cold driving rain. The Ashcrofts were relieved to be indoors. To have a drink, with the prospect of hot food and a soft bed; it was hospitality that several times seemed would be denied them. The simple oak and pine furniture was comfortable and worn smooth over the years. They leaned over the bar reviewing the small menus.

"I'll have the Cullen Skink to start, and then... the venison. Will this be too much trouble? I mean, isn't it late to be cooking?"

"Don't worry, sweety," said the buxom landlady. "I have one of those new microwave ovens."

"What are you having Stephie?"

"I haven't a clue what most of these words mean!"

"D'you like fish?" Stephanie said she did. "Then you just trust Nanny McTavish. I'll set your table with the fish specialities of the house. Your broths will be ready for you very shortly." She bustled out of the room.

"Come and sit by the fire with me, Stephanie," said her father. "I have a tale to tell you."

Stephanie sat beside him. "Tell me all of it," she said.

He placed his pint on the low table in front of them, closing his eyes. "Angus McLoughlan Ashcroft," he murmured: "The 'Black Fist'."

"Yes!"

"Born to a poor family in Glasgow; 1794. It was an interesting year... Napoleon's wife is arrested. Robespierre and his followers are executed. The French begin their offensive against the Spanish with the crossing of the Tech. Angus's family were simple folk; crofters mostly. They moved to Ireland when he was eleven, to escape involvement in the never ending Napoleonic wars, but found themselves starving. He was over five feet tall when he was thirteen, and educated himself with stolen books. To keep the family alive during the famine he thieved life-stock, and was caught twice. A few years later found himself in the worst kind of trouble, mortal trouble. At the age of seventeen he was gaoled for stealing a pig and, as a repeated offender, he faced the gallows."

Mrs McTavish came over and put their cutlery on the table. Then she proudly placed earthenware bowls of chowder in front of Stephanie, and a steaming broth of Cullen Skink in front of her father. They tried a spoonful each; then another. They smiled.

"Kind of makes you realise how lucky we are to live in this part of the world."

"What? Here in Scotland?"

Stephanie chuckled. "So how did Angus escape?"

"Some say he died. Others say that he made a pact with Satan. But I think this is when his reputation was forged, when he earned the name 'Black Fist'. Young Angus was six and a half feet tall at the age of seventeen and I think he punched his way out of gaol with his bare hands." He ate some soup. "The story picks up in England two years later, after he crossed the water to join the British Army to fight the French in the Peninsula Wars. Since he didn't have enough money to set out as an officer he took the King's shilling and joined the ranks in the Royal Artillery. He fought the French under Lord Wellington, in Spain and Portugal, as a gunner." He ate some more soup. "In 1813 there was a fierce fight on the French border, called the Battle Of Vitoria, full of blood and gun smoke. The huge number of cannon positioned on Arinez Hill won the battle for the British, but in spite of his part Angus found himself behind bars again."

Stephanie pushed her empty bowl away, looking content. "What did he do?"

"After the battle his regiment overran a French baggage train on the road to Pamplona. It was stuffed with loot: pearls, jewellery, art, silver, gems, and millions upon millions of gold coins. The undisciplined mass of gunners took everything they could carry. Allegedly they used paintings by Grand Masters as umbrellas! More treasure than even the King would ever have seen, and Angus wanted his share.

Unfortunately, as he whipped his loaded horse into the sunset he was intercepted by mounted Huzzars, and got in a row with one of them. He killed an officer who was trying to take his treasure and faced a Court Martial. But, once again, he got out."

"How did he do it this time?"

"Apparently he smuggled some choice gems into the prison using a part of his body where the sun doesn't shine, if you follow me."

"Yuck!"

"Anyway, he could not return to England. After the Battle of Waterloo he married a French girl and they took to mercenary life in North Africa."

"What, his wife fought beside him?" She seemed entranced by the idea.

"Yes. Fought and died, when the power of the sword deserted him. Angus became disillusioned and turned instead to the Black Arts, a very different power altogether. Over the next five years he searched for the necromantic rites necessary to raise his wife from the dead."

Mrs McTavish replaced their empty bowls with steaming platters of food. Lobster served in a half shell with melted cheese and breaded herring for Stephanie, and venison in mushroom and red wine sauce for her father. He ladled potatoes onto his plate.

"After her death, the Black Fist would take no woman. He travelled the world, alone, his quest fraught with disappointments. The books and manuscripts he uncovered were all false prophets. Then he got lucky, or very unlucky, depending on how you look at it." He cut into his succulent meat.

"Stop stalling will you!" demanded Stephanie.

"Give me a break, I'm trying to eat!"

They ate for a couple of minutes.

"Alright," continued the Professor. "What the Black Fist was looking for he finally found much closer to home than he could ever have guessed. Settling in Paris, not far from the cemetery where his wife was buried, he joined a group of Devil worshippers. These cults were growing in popularity in the 19th century. He learnt the basics of alchemy from the relative of a famous spiritualist named Alistair Crowley. Then discovered his magi was using an ancient book called the *Necronomicon.* It is the unholy grail of the Black Arts, which could conjure demons and raise the dead. It could open dimensional windows into other realities and also held within in it the secrets of the very fabric of time and space. McLoughlan killed him for it, and stole it. The book was bound in human skin and had been created in the 11th century by a French monk possessed by Satan. But Angus murdered his guru before he learned that the book was written in a coded language that no one else had been able to understand for a thousand years. The magi took the key to decipher it to his grave. And once again Angus was on the run."

Mrs McTavish came over to collect their plates. "Did you like your suppers?" They agreed that they had. "Would you like anything else?"

"Coffee," said the Professor, "- with a shot of whisky in it, please."

She looked at Stephanie.

"Do you have Camomile tea?"

"No, I'm sorry."

"Have you got honey?"

"Yes."

"Then normal tea with honey. Thank you!"

The landlady took away their plates.

"Angus fled to England. In London he found a man who could de-code the grimoire who, by an amazing co-incidence, was a master of languages at the British Museum."

"Always assuming you believe in co-incidences."

"Quite so! Anyway, the text was composed out of an encrypted form of cuneiform, the first known form of writing, which I have studied extensively. Angus took the work back to Paris with him and visited the cemetery where his wife was buried. He dug up her coffin, in the middle of the night.

Standing at her graveside, he re-animated her into an accursed semblance of life. By the light of his lantern she came forth as a mindless zombie and he had to use his shovel to put her back to her rest. The sight may have driven him insane."

"No wonder it was written in the 'Dark Ages'." She thought about it. "I'm glad I've already eaten!"

"He captained a ship, after that, and sailed around the world for a number of years at the whim of his appetites. He had one bastard son, my ancestor, but accounts of his exploits become garbled from this point. As a pirate he committed atrocities that history has elected to forget. It is obvious to me now that the more of the Necronomicon he translated, the more twisted he became - until he reached the climax of the book and took to the road one last time. He travelled to a small village on the western coast of Scotland, called Ravencliff - this place - and it was here, in this village, that the Black Fist constructed a chamber to protect the outside world from the most dire and terrible conjuration of them all."

"What conjuration?"

"I don't know."

"What happened?"

"Nothing. As far as I know he never emerged."

"Here are your hot drinks," said Mrs McTavish.

"Bless you!" said the Professor.

"- Very much!" echoed his daughter. "Well, that's about all the intrigue I can take for one evening. It's a quarter to midnight," she added. But the night was only just beginning.

*　　　　*　　　　*

"Permit me to introduce myself," said the tall man as pleasantly as possible. He propped up his umbrella beside the fire place. The woman was eyeing him with what looked like instinctive suspicion. "I am Raul Caine, minister to this community." She looked pale, discomforted. Maybe he should have worn the Arran sweater and water-proofs stowed in his bag, instead of his black cassock, but he was not a part-time priest. All his waking hours he wore the uniform. Her father stood up to take his hand; and the priest was impressed. The man's palm was dry, his shake vigorous and firm.

"I'm Professor Stephen Ashcroft. And this is my dau -"
"It is your name that I wish to discuss with you."
"Ah. I see."
"I doubt it."
The Professor sat down again. "You want me to prove I am the true descendent of the man that long ago they called 'Black Fist'?"

The priest squatted expressionlessly on his haunches before the hearth, and pursed his lips. He threw a block of dried peat onto the fire, and warmed his hands to the flickering flames. It was a consolation to be dealing with a man of wisdom. "It's a windy night for such business," said Caine. "And cold. I hate the cold."
"Thus fitting. Wouldn't you agree?"
"Aye, I would at that."

Unlike the dumb happy-go-lucky fortune hunters that had preceded him, which Caine had buried alive with his own hands, this Ashcroft was no fool. To kill him, to kill them both, was the ultimate challenge. It would alleviate the weight that his family had carried for so many generations and lift the essence of responsibility that Caine had hated and personally carried all his life. He inclined his head towards the daughter. She looked away. Throwing her dead body into the bay would demand absolute clarity of mind. Caine thanked God that he had steeled himself against the temptations of the flesh.

"I have my passport," said Ashcroft: "It would be of use."
"In this the proof of your ancestry must be unequivocal."
"But our bags were stolen," said Stephanie.
"That's true. All my documents were in one of those cases."
"Not to mention my clothes."
"Don't fret. I had your baggage transferred to my rectory."

ZAXXON

Both started complaining vehemently.

"Return them, forthwith!"

"We want them back!"

"You can't sleep here anyway," Caine said. "The Raven's Arms is a public house, not an hotel. Didn't they tell you?"

"They said nothing of the kind! And if you wanted to wander off with our luggage you should have sought our permission first, you really should. It's tantamount to theft!"

"I did both of you a favour, young lady. It is no short haul to my house, particularly on such a night. I offer you safe beds and you just spout anger. I say now, you can take it or leave it!"

"We'll take it," said the Professor.

"The hell we will!"

They started gesticulating like stranded seals. Caine returned his attention to the fire. He had assumed that this Ashcroft was the genuine descendant. He had killed enough charlatans to wonder if this was so, but it was too late. He had already thrown their bags off the wall of the harbour. The priest felt for his blade. This was going to be a long night.

Turning his gaze back to the Ashcrofts, he realised that they had stopped arguing and were watching him silently. "Well?"

"I think you will find my passport sufficient evidence. It quotes my full name."

Caine took the slim red booklet from the proffered hand and examined it closely. It was genuine. He opened it and his eyes scanned the holder's name with unbridled curiosity. It read: STEPHEN McLOUGHHLAN ASHCROFT. He closed the booklet. Suddenly it seemed to be very hot in this place. He took a shuddering breath and returned the passport to him who was the True Son of the Fist.

"That is satisfactory. Will you accept the hospitality of my rectory?"

"I'm afraid my daughter wants to leave tonight."

"- If we can't sleep here, that is, or in a B&B."

You'll sleep with the fish, the priest thought. Loudly, he shouted: "McTavish!"

The landlord emerged from the rooms behind the bar looking as white as a bleached sheep. He stood behind his counter, terrified, with a plate in one hand and a dishcloth in the other. "Yes?"

"McTavish. Prepare your spare room for these two tonight. The Professor and I will be returning in about forty-five minutes."

"You're going out?" Stephanie asked. She looked flabbergasted.

He removed his robes and put the thick woollen sweater over his shirt. "We leave for the 'crypt on the spit' immediately." The priest then pulled on an oil-skin jacket, and covertly transferred the knife from his robes to his trouser pocket. Did she see?

"For God's sake *why*?"

"It's alright," said her father. "I expected something like this."

"It's the middle of the night."

"I have to."

"But it's dark and you don't have the slightest idea what's out there. Aren't you tired?"

"No."

"I won't allow it!"

"I'm sorry but I have to go..."

"Can't it wait 'til morning?"

"I won't get a wink of sleep tonight if I don't. I've been waiting for this all my life. Allow me."

"Ok. Go. But don't trust him."

"You're rudeness has been noted," said Caine.

"Chin up, girl. You're only allowed to travel once you've passed customs! Anyway, look out there now – it's stopped raining." He zipped up his coat and picked up the torch from under the table. He started walking with Caine towards the door. "Will we be needing tools?"

"I have all that we need." Caine lit an oil lamp and lowered the glass cover. "Just this lantern."

ZAXXON

Stephanie followed them to the doorway. "Dad?" The priest looked at him carefully. He looked at Stephanie carefully. *"Be careful,"* she said, *"OK?"* The Professor nodded.

The unlikely pair left the pub. They walked between the sleeping houses on a cobbled road to the far side of the village. To the Professor the cold dampness seemed as though it could be pulled apart like the paper wrapping around an expensive fish. Caine asked if he had a vehicle, and it seemed to be important to him. The Professor explained what had happened to the MG.

"Where is it now?"

"What's left of it is up there in the car-park. Why? Do we need it?"

"No. I was wondering whether my services were in order. I'm the only mechanic around here."

They continued walking along a sea wall until there were no houses left, and then walked down a ramp onto the beach. The tide was out and Caine explained that the fastest way to the crypt was vertically up the cliff face on an old path. He said he was familiar with it. The Professor traversed his torch across the rock and fancied that he could see their route: a disintegrating trail of worn steps going up two hundred feet and finally disappearing in the midnight sky. They mounted the path.

The Professor was pleased the northerly wind couldn't touch them in the shadow on this side of the headland, and happy for the priest to be leading the way. He couldn't have navigated it alone and needed to go tonight because he wanted the *Necronomicon* so desperately that he couldn't have waited for daylight, as he had said to Stephanie, so upwards he climbed, torn between euphoria and mounting terror. The dancing light seemed to accelerate nature's process. Rocks moved in the shadows, fissures became gaping maws, and cracks laughed at him. He could feel his own mortality when compared to these awesome surroundings, magnified by the ocean's hypnotic rumble and the fragments of rock kicked spinning into the abyss.

At the top he waited for Caine to haul himself over the final ledge and dimly registered a stone embedded in the man's boot. The priest stood above him, holding the lamp aloft. Ashcroft gritted his teeth. He expected perhaps a foot pushed into his chest to send him screaming back down to the beach, or a kick in the face, or the lamp smashed over his head, all with the same result. He could die. He scrambled to safety, his hands aching, but no attack came. He rested on his back breathing hard and stared up at the volatile sky. He had never felt more alive. "Come along," said Caine. "This is no time to be lying about."

The Professor got to his feet. Even with the battery-powered torch it was impossible to determine the length or breadth of the headland, but he guessed it was thin. He could hear the waves crashing below on both sides now. He followed the priest over course grasses and heather, through the ruins of an arch and over the crumbled remains of low walls. The place must have been a church. They walked on among ancient gravestones. There were a few wind-whipped trees that didn't seem to know what season it was, until Caine stopped. He waited no more than nine metres away from the very tip of the edge of the cliff, and lowered his lantern. Ashcroft caught up with him. At their feet was a one metre square slab of stone, what the priest had called 'the crypt on the spit'. Immediately in front of the last monument was a Celtic cross of worn granite.

"This is the place?"
"Yes," said Caine. "In a few years the chamber and all these ruins will fall into the sea. The Black Fist took the oath of my ancestor to keep it a secret, in the event of the failure of his magics, to protect the world outside from calamity - and this village, from the world outside - until his true descendant came to finish what was begun. Now my waiting is over, as is your's."
"It leads underground?"

ZAXXON

"Of course. It was constructed in 1837."

There was no name or epitaph upon it. Only lichen and moss covered the stone.

"How can there be a grave so close to the entrance?"

"There is no grave just there. My Great Grandfather moved the cross to hold the weight of the block upright."

"It has been opened?"

"Many times. Can you imagine whole lifetimes of maddening curiosity? But you worry needlessly Professor. Nothing has ever been removed from below this stone."

Stephen Ashcroft hadn't felt so thrilled since hauling up armfuls of Aztec artefacts in South America with Nigel Hawthorne twenty years ago. It had been the basis of the Ashcroft family fortune, all but spent. The house, a share in Stephanie's shop, and the MG BGT were all that remained of that money, but the treasure he sought now was worth infinitely more than gold.

"It looks heavy. How do we open it?"

The priest reached behind the old cross: "With this," he said. He picked up a three feet long crow bar and placed his lantern to one side. He hunkered down in front of the stone. "Now, you get your hands into the crease, as I lift it..." He wiggled the tip of the bar into the gap. "Take the strain!" he advised, and levered the slab upwards a few inches.

Ashcroft was kneeling beside him, and pushed his hands palms upwards into the opening. He tried to lift it the rest of the way alone, but couldn't. Using the traditional measure it must have weighed over sixteen stone. When the priest withdrew the bar, he was worried that his fingers might be crushed but the other man was at his side in an instant, pushing his own hands into the gap. Heaving and grunting, the two men lifted the great stone together until it was standing on one end. Then they pushed it a little further over the vertical until it leant against the cross. A terrible smell vented from the hole. Dismissing all thoughts of Caine's threatening quality, Ashcroft picked up his torch and shone it, with his hands shaking, down into the crypt. There seemed to be a huddled figure lying at the bottom of a set of steps. But he couldn't see the chamber beyond.

"There's a body down there."

"Of course," Caine retorted, peering down himself, "probably more than one. Angus took a few of his acolytes with him. When his experiment failed they didn't emerge either."

"So, you're not coming down now?"

"No. This is your affair."

With no need for further discussion, the professor walked down into a claustrophobic darkness that smelt of old vegetables. Waving his torch around he counted seventeen steps. His excitement was almost indescribable; possibly alike the strings of a harp vibrating beneath the fingertips of an impresario playing exquisite music. He shone his torch over the body at the foot of the stairs and found yet another corpse sprawled on the chamber floor beside a huge altar of stone. And then he realised that he had made a terrible mistake. Both had obviously died of hunger and thirst, their bodies thin as sticks and their dried features stretched into permanent leers, but that was not the problem. The problem was that they hadn't worn track-suits and Reebok trainers in the 19th century!

Ashcroft immediately pivoted on his feet and ran back up the steps - but too late. The huge slab was already crashing down. He ducked under it at the last possible moment and narrowly avoided a fractured skull. He was sealed up in a rain of mould dust, and soil, and in its final resting position the underside of the stone was actually touching his hair. "Caine! Caine!" he cried, with his heart hammering under his ribs. He tried to push the slab upwards with his shoulders and arms, using added strength born of his love for Stephanie, but it was too heavy. "In God's name, Caine!" There was no answer. He was buried alive.

Caine chucked his crow bar over the cliff and jumped up and down on the stone like a kid that has won a gold fish at a country fair. The responsibility of the secret was undone. He felt the weight of years lift from his shoulders and he laughed into the storm. There was just one final deed to perform here, before he dealt with the car and Ashcroft's daughter, the creation of a legitimate tomb. He reached behind the Celtic cross and took out a mallet and some chisels that had waited for a long time for his hands to carve Ashcroft's name. The priest had enjoyed fashioning gravestones for a decade and deployed that skill now to find fulfilment; to honour the ghosts that had been released from old promises this night. He knelt on the cover stone by his lamp. After warming his hands on it, because he hated being cold, he started chipping a letter 'A' into the rock.

It was obvious to Stephen Ashcroft that the priest would murder Stephanie also. The Professor wept. He hoped that his daughter's demise was quicker than his own was evidently to be. Sitting on the steps, considering how to commit suicide, he raised his head and bellowed: "Damn you forever, Caine!" and suddenly felt the temperature drop. He noticed static in the air and realised that his torch was now not the only source of light in this room. There was a blue glow emanating from the other side of the altar, accompanied by a subtle vibrating noise like a muffled engine.

He stood, with his joints crackling, and walked around the side of the giant stone. There was a third corpse sitting against the wall. A dusty skeleton with large bones dressed in scraps of crusty leather, the mortal remains of the 'Black Fist'. Clasped in its bony fingers was the grimoire that his descendant had sought for so long, the infamous *Necronomicon.* The other victims, with whose doom he would share, had left it alone. Perhaps they had put it back, or felt it irrelevant compared with escape. He reached for it. The blue light was illuminating a seam in the pages like a fluorescent bookmark and it was the first example of true magic the Professor had ever seen. It flared, as cold and as bright as a laser, when he grasped the book and slowly pulled it to himself, tearing it away from cobwebs, with pieces of bone dropping to the floor. He squinted into the brightness. His breath misted in the frigid air. The human skin that covered the book bulged with patterns of skulls and gargoyle faces in relief. The latent power of it thrummed in his hands.

He let the book fall open and found the source of the luminescence spilling out of the centre of an exposed page of pliant vellum, and above it he saw the wedges and slashes of a column of Cuneiform writing. This was the first known form of writing and it looked like Sumarian. But when the professor tried to read it from right to left, the only way, it made no sense. Perhaps it was a dialect he hadn't seen before... or maybe it was the encryption that had purportedly baffled his ancestor. He was pleased to see that an old scholar had notated the sentences and the word pronunciations at the base of the page - in raw Latin! The Professor read:

Damn your enemy for all time, trigger the spherical lightning of Canderra to seek and condemn, burn him, and break him on rock and stone, forever, by speaking the conjuration: I never need strike twice.

"I never need strike twice," said the Professor. And nothing happened. Then he smiled and re-phrased the imperative as though he was speaking to the book itself: "*YOU* never need strike twice!" And everything wobbled as a ball of blue fire rose buzzing and crackling out of the page with a noise like thunder ripping through a dark sky. It flashed through the room and up the steps, with a scent of ozone, leaving trails of light on the backs of Ashcroft's retinas. It hit the cover stone and exploded like a bomb smashing the slab into a hundred pieces.

Caine died instantly in a flash of blue incandescence and granite shrapnel. His body was thrown twenty feet up in the air and fell back shattered and bleeding, on the grass not five feet from the exposed crypt. But Canderra was not done with him. The ball of lightning pressed to the dead priest's pineal eye, sucked out his soul, and carried him screaming silently into the multi-dimensional fabric of the book itself. To the prison from where it took its power, a blue hell that was always cold.

The dust settled.

The Professor walked up the steps. He took deep breaths of the fresh air then started walking back, the long way, towards the car park. He hiked inland, with the torch held out in front of him and the *Necronomicon* tucked under one arm like a schoolboy going to an evening detention. And considering the cataclysmic nature of the book he carried, a child was essentially *all* that he was.

CHAPTER – 5

"Trans.figure"

By killing his House Master and destroying the school's precious discs Rupert had taken another irrevocable step beyond commonly accepted reality. He stood in the Staff Room loosing himself in regret, with no apologies or second chances. He was swaying in a blackness soaked with tears that led to another world. No one could be blamed for his amnesia yet was not the school partly responsible for the rest of it? Hadn't the bullies and the stupid rules driven him to the divine madness of loving a woman that existed out of all probability? That was point: he was in love with her and he had a date tonight. He would have to be prepared to fight, or even kill again, if necessary, to keep it.

Rupert found the TV remote and filled the room with noise. With eyes wet, looking as sullen as he could possibly manage, he backed out into the front hall clutching his rear. For the assembled eavesdroppers he had given himself thirty lashes. Most of that original leering crowd had doubtless become terrified by their own morbid curiosity and departed. They wouldn't be sleeping well tonight. For the rest of them, including Russell Chase but mainly for Hudson's benefit, Rupert briefly turned back to the doorway and mumbled: "Yes, sir, yes. I'll tell him." And then the door swung shut like the final curtain on a theatre of blood.

He hobbled into the Hall. Those standing against the radiator beneath the portraits of long dead teachers seemed almost embarrassed by their own sympathy. Pale with shock, they were picking their teeth and shuffling their shoes; trying to look anywhere except at Rupert.

"Got the whacking you deserved, eh?" blurted out Hudson. "Thornberry, I'm talking to you!" Rupert ignored him. "Answer me this, Cheesecake, do you need a fire-extinguisher for your arse?"

"Oh, for heaven's sake give it a rest," muttered Russell, sickened.

"What the hell's up with you?"

"The man's just taken one hell of a beating and I think it would be fair of us to cut him some slack."

Hudson found Rupert by the back stairs reading the notice of his own expulsion on the Head Master's board. It was dated June 21st, another nail in the coffin of a dead reality. The rest of the world thought he was going home in a few days, but in fact he would never see his parents again. He choked back further tears. Damn it, but he needed to be stronger than this.

"A sight for sore eyes indeed," said Hudson. Next, in the drawl of an old sea-dog: "An' I ain't lookin' forward to the journey 'ome neithorr!" He cackled at himself.

Rupert was despondent: "Hudson, you're mentally ill." And, of course, according to his medical records, this was a fact.

"Yeah, but thirty smackers, eh? That's some sort of record!"

"Mr Copeland has instructions, for you."

Hudson drew his hand over his nose and then down his mouth. He raised his eyebrows. "Yes? What is it?"

"He says no one is to disturb the Staff Room tonight and that he wants you to do Lights Out and Lock Up."

"Why?"

Rupert started walking away. "Because he's watching television."

"Oh." Hudson loosed a sickly smile. "What's he watching?"

Rupert stood at the bottom of the stairs. "A film called 'IF'" he replied, and then walked up and crossed the landing. It was nearly half past nine. The time surprised him and when he knocked on Rant's door there was no answer.

*   *   *

"And it came to pass, when men began to multiply on the face of the Earth and daughters were born unto them, that the Sons of God saw of the daughters of men that they were fair: They took of them all which they chose."

GENESIS CHAPTER SIX, VERSES 1 – 4.

Julian Rant yawned. He leaned over the table and wrote with the commandeered pencil on lined spiral bound notepaper: *CONSENTUALLY OR BY FORCE?* Then he added: *WHO ARE THE* SONS OF GOD? He returned to the shelves. The investigation was leading him through many branches of the school's huge library, a macabre excursion into legend and superstition, and although much of what he uncovered was clearly nonsense, some of it wasn't. He took some books to his table and realised that the genuine answers were often obvious, more particularly since he had witnessed at first hand the evidence of sex with the Succubus on his friend's skin.

REFERING GENESIS 6 - QUOTED BY POPE BENEDICT 14TH.
"This passage has reference to creatures known as incubi and succubi."

Rant flicked through to the index, then forward to another chapter.

TAKEN FROM BOOK OF CHURCH DOCTRINE [HELD BETWEEN 1100 AND 1700]
"The Succubi are evil angels… a hierarchically organised army in the service of Satan working for the perdition of the faithful. Satan and his hosts also tempt human beings into service, and these human beings become the visible agents of diabolic power."

Some of these references displayed an insight that warmed him, to a cold idea, that much of the superstition of yesterday had become the science of today. He didn't know whether or not this was cause for fear. He opened another book.

'STUDIES IN DEMONOLOGY' – (PAGE 96)
"It has been estimated that during the witch-hunt centuries almost 200,000 people were burnt at the stake , 97% of these being women. There is rare documented evidence to suggest that a small number of female demons, known to theologians as 'Succubi' may have been implicated and unwittingly tried alongside the innocents. It seems that repeated attempts to execute them all failed. They escaped..."

Rant returned to the shelves. The occult section was nearly exhausted, and time was flying by. His research had uncovered some tracts that were actually quite funny, like the story of French witch-hunter Pierre de Lancre. The cusp moon was already shining from high through the library window.

One day, in 1550, Pierre de Lancre decided he needed a holiday so he took a few days off to visit the neighbouring Labourd District. For reasons that are obscure, but reputedly sexual, de Lancre became convinced that all 30,000 inhabitants - including priests – were witches, and subsequently 1000's fled their domiciles. This caused a breach of trade between the two districts sufficiently disastrous for De Lancre to be executed the instant he returned home!

If someone had told Rant, just yesterday, that his best friend was going to fall deeply in love during the following night he would not have believed it. If someone else had suggested, a week ago, that he was going to spend most of Saturday night in the library investigating the demon that his best friend had fallen in love, with, he would not have believed that either. He opened his last book at half past eleven pm and what he read there was the last of all he needed to know.

"Throughout history there have been poems and stories written about them, but where is the divide between fact and fiction? Take the strigae *of the Latin writers: the* lamias *whose lust for love was immortalised by the poet John Keats; the* Valkyrie, *who could change at will as they flew their wild rides; but before all of them the archetypal* Lillith, *whose loveliness and silver hair was more than human, but whose true nature was revealed by a single flaw – her feet were great, sharp claws!"*

This was enough. Rant fled.

*   *   *

Rupert's fantasies before he met Lillith had not been entirely sexual. Since the end of puberty he had looked forward to the give and take of material gifts in a relationship, to the exchange of romantic cards and presents like a learner driver desperate to carry passengers. He had often dwelt upon this, the fulfilment of giving carefully chosen presents to a lover. So, shortly before Light's Out, he sneaked down to the drying room to assemble just such a package for Lillith. He sat in the heat of that confined space, in the clean smell of freshly washed clothes, and used scissors and sticky tape to wrap the pen, the key, and the acorns in brown paper. Afterwards he looked down at the parcel for a moment, then drew vampire bats and little flowers on it with a ball-point pen.

Before he went back upstairs he needed clothes for his getaway. Rifling among the rails, dropping pegs to the cement floor, he stole a pair of jeans, a blue athletics shirt, and a black Navy cadet's jumper. They were all selected for their dark hues to blend into shadows. Also, they were all slightly too big for him, to accommodate the metamorphosis that his body had undergone yesterday night when he had first met Lillith. Too amazing to forget? He folded everything and bundled it into a dustbin liner with a pair of size nine Army boots, and went up to the dormitory. He wanted the bag close to him from now on because her present was in it. He slid it under his bed with five minutes to spare. With no more than a perfunctory: "Keep the noise down cheeky pups," Hudson switched the lights out. It was ten o'clock.

He wanted to stay awake but he was feeling hung-over and it had been an afternoon of extreme stress. He put his pyjamas on without thinking. He set an alarm for twenty-five minutes to twelve and put the watch on his bed-side locker close to his ear. The bag under his bed felt like an egg that he needed to keep warm, like he was a nesting hen. With these motherly sensibilities he drifted off to sleep. Of course, he dreamt of Lillith, saw a montage of vague images washing over him like the sea up a beach; sex, violence. And in the sea water, always, he saw the eyes of the dragon.

The images sharpened... and here she was standing before a wall of mirrors wrought of pure silver, resplendent in a million glittering reflections, and pulled the pin out of a hand grenade. She placed the heavy lump in his hand, and the safety clasp popped off and spun into the darkness. "Wake up!" was written on it tiny white letters. And suddenly - as it always did when the dormitory door was flung open hard – the grenade exploded as the door smacked into the side of Rupert's bed with an ear-splitting BANG, and someone blundered into the room, breathing hard. *Jesus, it's Hudson!* he thought, feverishly.

A hissed word; quiet but full of urgency: "Rupert!"

It was Rant's voice and Rupert felt his whole body relax with relief, but there was a new imperative. He had missed his alarm, and according to his watch it was a quarter to midnight.

"What the bloody hell is all this noise?!"
"Come on, Rue!"
"Woz wrong?" burbled Russell, waking up. "That you Rant?"

"Yes, it's me. Now, all of you, go back to sleep."

"What's the matter?" Rupert whispered.

"I have urgent news and you have to come with me now. We can't stay here."

"Well, I know that."

"Come to my study."

"I'm not dressed!"

Another voice: "For God's sake shut up, we're trying to get some kip in here, alright?"

Rupert pulled his bag out from under the bed. "I have clothes in this."

"Bring it." Rant grabbed his hand and yanked him out of the room in his pyjamas.

They crept quietly through the musty darkness and tip-toed past Hudson's study. They needn't have worried, then, because he wasn't in there. He was walking down to the staff room to get the keys for Lock Up from Mr Copeland. Once in his study Rant put his ear to the door and closed it slowly. The wholesome sound of the latch as it clicked into place had a satisfying essence of safety.

"This had better be important," whined the younger man, tipping the contents of his black bag onto the laminate floor. "I'm supposed to be meeting her in ten minutes!"

"That's what I have to discuss with you. I'd like to say that it's lucky I woke you up, but it isn't at all. Now you have to listen to me, carefully."

But Rant suddenly looked unsure. If he could have paced up and down his study he would have done, but the room was too small; just a single bed, a sink, some basic furniture and a work desk by the window that apparently doubled as a kitchen counter. Rupert began to get dressed as Rant leant back against his Queen poster and frowned. He clasped his hands to his mouth. Eventually he began:

"Things happened to you last night that you obviously feel were wonderful, yet maybe far from the truth. I want you to think about them."

"What's to think about? Wonderful things shouldn't be questioned."

"I've been to the library, Rue, and I found out in there that 'Succubus' isn't her name, it's the monster that she is."

"What is she?"

"Some kind of... demon." He looked vague. "Of an ancient race, and with terrible power."

Rupert spoke without hesitation. "Even if you are right I'm willing to risk losing myself in her. It doesn't matter to me what she is. I have to go."

"No, Rupert, you don't, because if half of what I've read about this thing is true we have to call the police, or a priest, or something."

"You're missing the point, Julian. I've fallen in love with her." He lifted the black cadet's jumper over his head.

"Then, you may be in love with your own doom."

"I understand that. That's clever, Julian, but do you remember what it's like to be in love? Do you remember Michael?"

"That's below the belt Rupert. You know bloody well I do, but Michael wasn't a monster - he was a man, a human being!"

"I never troubled myself with the belief that the Succubus was human, rather that she isn't!" He pulled on an Army boot and started to lace it. "Lillith is supernatural, like her energy, like the whole of her. I need this undiluted purity because of the boy I have been, and I'll take the consequences."

"Yeah, well, it might cost you more than your life."

"Like I said, I'll risk that." He laced up the other boot. "I need to get out of this school!"

Rant chuckled in spite of his disquiet. "So what's new about that?"

"I er..." Rupert sniffed. "I killed Copeland, earlier."

Julian stared at him. "You did *what?*"

"Well... I didn't really."

"What do you mean you 'didn't really'?"

"He must have had a weak heart. I was just –"

Suddenly someone knocked on the door, three times. The young men gawped at each other in shock. Three louder knocks followed.

"Christ," Rupert whispered, staring wildly around the room.

"Open up, I know Cheesecake's in there, Rant!" It was Hudson.

"Oh man," hissed Rupert, scared badly. "Where can I hide?"

His friend answered through the sudden fusillade of Hudson's hammering fists:

"---- in the ----- obe!" Julian's face had gone white.

"What?" Rupert stood in the middle of the room, turning round and round on the spot, spilling tears of mortal terror.

"Rant, I'll give you five seconds before I smash your door into firewood."

"Hide in the wardrobe!"

"Five, four, three –"

Rupert slapped himself in the face. "Brilliant!" he said bravely, and jerked the wardrobe door open. An avalanche of cricket equipment fell out like ghosts jumping out of a coffin.

Rant pushed his suits along to the far end of the rail and then they both started moving the gloves and pads to the back. Rupert climbed in. A sudden deafening thump on the front door made the entire room tremble. Rant couldn't close the wardrobe and remembering hiding Michael in that exact same piece of furniture before the guy had been expelled was inevitable. A second thunderous attack followed. Plaster dust rained from the ceiling and the wood of the front door audibly splintered.

Rant pushed and prodded at Rupert until he was inside it, hidden for what it was worth, as the third onslaught opened a split down the middle of the door big enough to post a shoe. The fourth knocked the Yale lock out of its chamber and after the fifth blow the corner of a large metal object was withdrawn from a gaping hole. One of Hudson's eyes replaced it. And, yes, he was insane.

"Hi, Julian," Hudson said conversationally, "Cheesecake's killed my house-master. Hand him over now or I'll kill you as well."

Rant took a shuddering breath, then said: "Hey, I'm your mate Tom. I'm pleased you want to... to do that."

The eye opened wider. It sparkled with madness. "Yeah?"

"Really, I'm right up for that. Come in and have a mocha."

"Alright."

The front door opened with a slight squeal almost as easily as a feather blown across a tiled floor, and the maniac stood in the warped doorway flushed and sweating after the exertion of breaking in. He was grinning with uncertainty and dangling from his left hand was the biggest sledgehammer Julian had ever seen. Hudson hefted the tool proudly:

"Look at this! It's got a sixteen pound head of pure steel block. Wicked, isn't it?"

Its handle was three feet long and its business end was the size of a small loaf of bread. Julian realised that he was staring at it. "Yeah, it's wicked... that's for sure. Where did you get it?"

"Don't tell anyone," Hudson confided, drooling, "but I nicked it from the tool shed!" He cackled.

"Goodness me." Rant filled his kettle and plugged it in. "Two sugars?"

The maniac frowned. "Eh?"

"- For your mocha." Rant tapped the kettle's power button. It was a Haden that his mum had given him last Christmas. "I was asking because you look like you need more choc and sugar today." The kettle was the plastic kind with a transparent window so you can tell how full it is. Rant sat at the desk and idly glanced at it. The scale was showing two and a half pints and the appliance was rumbling already. It could boil that much water within two minutes. He nibbled his index fingernail.

"Don't pansy about Rant, I don't like it."

"I was just asking. You look like you need a little less coffee in your mix right now."

"You don't know where he is then?"

"Who?"

"Cheesecake." His eyes glittered.

"No idea... what's he done this time?"

"He killed my house-master."

Rant watched a tear form in Hudson's eye that was a more disturbing sight than the sledgehammer. The maniac seemed embarrassed to be seen upset. He closed the front door of the study, as well as was possible, and added: "He was your house-master too."

"Damn that Cheesecake. He'll disappear for that later, I'm sure."

"Can I sit?"

"Go ahead."

Hudson yawned. He sat on the bed and perched the huge hammer across his lap. Rant looked away from the makeshift weapon and glanced at the floor. Initially his brain didn't recognize what he was looking at, a brown paper bag speckled with skeletal doodles, and then he understood that it was Rupert's. It was just a few inches away from the maniac's left foot. The kettle was beginning to rumble more intensely but Rant wanted to fake a confidant ruse to retrieve the package. The maniac and the younger man stood up simultaneously and spoke at the same time.

"Oh, there's that pressie for my mother –"

"I'm far too knackered for this bastard –" Hudson dropped the hammer to the floor with a resounding thump. "Can I borrow your base-ball bat?" He was turning towards the wardrobe.

Rant forgot all about Rupert's parcel. "No, hey, no!"

"I'll play careful games with it, I swear."

"It's in my changing room locker, downstairs, I'm sorry man!"

"That's okay, I'll borrow a cricket bat instead."

ZAXXON

Hudson opened the wardrobe door and his jaw dropped open. Rant picked up the bubbling Harden by the handle and jerked it out of its plug socket. It was heavy with boiling water. The maniac turned his frighteningly blank visage to Rant, who heaved the contents of the kettle at his head. The lid disappeared. Two and a half pints of burning liquid hit Hudson full in the face and cascaded steaming over his shoulders and down his back. He collapsed screaming on the floor and kicked about like a speared fish, his face red and wrinkling already.

Rant shouted: "Rupert, we're leaving!" and the younger man didn't need to be told twice.

He fell out of the wardrobe in a second eruption of cricket equipment, and to escape the room he actually walked over Hudson's writhing body in his army boots. Out on the landing dozens of scared looking boys were standing about in pyjamas and dressing gowns. There were no living masters awake on the whole campus. Rupert looked at his watch. The time was ten past twelve. He was about to follow Rant downstairs when he stopped and pulled himself up. Something was wrong.

"Julian, wait."
"Come on!"
"I've forgotten something important."
"What is it?"
"That's the just point, I don't remember!"
Rant walked up some steps. "Is it a brown paper parcel?"
"Yes! Yes! That's it!"
"It's near my bed, but forget it. You can't go back in there."
"I don't have a choice."

Rant clutched his head with anxiety and the audience of worried boys stepped back as Rupert walked up and listened at the door. He could hear a noise like someone bashing a coconut, and he peered through a splintered hole.

Hudson was kneeling in front of Julian's gaping fridge smacking a tray of ice cubes on the floor, muttering to himself. His blistered face had long shadows drawn down it under the ceiling lamp and appeared demonic by the fridge's interior fluorescent light. The younger man could see his package beside Julian's bed, and when Hudson placed ice cubes onto his eyes with murmurs of relief, Rupert wondered if this was the time to go in. But he hesitated. Hudson dropped the ice cubes and pulled a bag of vegetables out of the top compartment of Julian's appliance, and ripped it open with his teeth. He started rubbing handfuls of frozen peas on his face.

Rupert went in suddenly. He crashed through the door reaching for his parcel and plucked it off the laminate floor. He thought he was out of reach but it was a small space. As he turned to leave the maniac lunged at him across half the room and brought him crashing down in a rugby tackle by one foot. In spite of his adrenaline enhanced reactions Rupert still managed to retain, in one hand, his precious parcel and he kicked out hard and backwards with his free foot. The heel of his boot connected with Hudson's nose with essences of punching a tomato, of smashing a light bulb with a mallet. Groaning, Hudson rolled onto his back exploring the injury with blood pouring through his fingers, and Rupert scrambled outside onto the landing. He found himself surrounded again by dozens of boys with pale, terrified, faces.

"I'm to be expelled soon," he exclaimed, "as most of you already know. But in fact I am leaving tonight, to be with my girlfriend. We are very much in love and you will never see me again. I will never return to this place." He raised his voice: "But Hudson is in that room, and he has lost his mind, and I need some of you brave lads to delay him." No one answered. There were noises of movement and groaning sounds from Rant's study. "As you can see, by what he has done, Hudson has gone insane, yet if enough of you join against him he can be stopped."

"Come on!" yelled Rant, from half way down the steps, "it's a quarter past twelve!"

"Answer me!" Rupert was desperate. "Isn't there anyone here who's man enough to help us?"

"I will, I'll try," said Russell Chase, from the back of the crowd. "But I can't promise anything."

Rupert started downstairs. "Thanks a lot Jack."

"Hey, my friends can call me after a dog anytime. Give a kiss her for me! I always hated that Hudson anyway. He's an overgrown outspoken bullying twat! So, who's with me?!"

Rupert never heard the rest of Russell's dialogue because he was already sprinting towards the kitchens through the orange night lighting. Although his life may have depended upon an immediate escape, he wanted to spend his last few moments with Julian. He found the older man sitting on the bench in the glass-covered corridor that ran along the sides of the changing rooms. It was dark and lonely, and cold, but for the half moon shining down through the ceiling.

"I tried to get the others to delay Hudson," said Rupert.

"God, I hope they do," said Julian.

"Did you see his face? You messed him up pretty bad."

He walked over to the light switch and flooded the passageway with three yellow tungsten lamps spread high up along the wall. After the sudden thrashing of a fire door in the distance, there was a strangled wail of pain. Rupert sat on the bench, and turned to his friend, feeling compassionate and apologetic.

"You can't come with me, Julian, you know that?"

"I know, but it's okay... is she there? Is she waiting for you?"

Rupert closed his eyes, and his hands tensed on his knees. "Yes, I can sense her... I feel her!" He made subconscious kissing noises. "So sexy!" He grinned. "She wants to know if I've got the parcel." He opened his eyes and looked at his friend, eyebrows raised.

"That's amazing." Julian said, and smiled woefully.

"Shit! Where's the parcel?"

"Don't worry, it's under the bench. You put it there when you switched the lights on."

Rupert picked it up and held it in his hands. It crackled as he squeezed it. Noises of violence arose again, closer this time. A scream and another fire door being whacked about echoed along to them like a paper with bad news printed on it blown into their hands. Hudson was coming. They stood.

"Are you certain she's a monster?"

"Yes. Make any difference?"

"No."

"What about you?"

"I'm staying. I've got this –" Rant picked up a cricket bat from the bench. "- as insurance." It was an expensive Grey Nicols bat with a single red scoop down the middle. "I found it before you caught up with me." Thirty feet away in the adjacent corridor there was a scream cut off by thumping sounds. Then dragging footsteps.

Rupert was horrified. "Surely you don't intend to fight him?"

"I will, he'll catch up with you if I don't."

"You can't!"

"Hey, what makes you assume I can't win? If I knock him out maybe I can call the police later. It would buy you some time."

"But he's probably hurt a lot of people very badly to get to us!"

"That's why, partly. And also because of you." He looked at Rupert with a complicated expression, a passionate coalescence of sadness, fear and love. "I wish I could have danced with you, Rue. Just once..." Rupert felt the need to kiss him, briefly, on his lips. He did. They hugged. "Now go," cried Julian, pushing him away. "Go! Go to her, and be happy forever!"

Rupert backed outside into the darkness and saw Julian turn away and raise his bat. In the same moment the door at the other end moaned open and Hudson limped into the corridor. He was badly burned and brandishing a broken snooker cue, covered in blood from head to foot with a Swiss Army knife sticking out of his left thigh. Rupert offered up a silent prayer to whatever new Pagan gods ruled his destiny in these times, and stole a moment to watch the combat through the distorted glass. Wood clapped on wood as the fighters lunged and parried with a force that made Rupert's own hands ache sympathetically. Then without warning one of their armaments struck the frosted pane before him.

Rupert ducked instinctively as the window exploded with a loud and revitalizing crash. He was showered with glass. If not for his spectacles it was likely he would have got shards of it in his eyes. One of them cut him just above the cheekbone and he felt it bleed a little. He also felt the telepathy of his succubus as an almost physical manifestation: her tongue licking the blood from his face, her lips kissing his with unbridled passion. He stepped back from the jagged hole in the glass and watched Hudson chanting: "thirty lashes for cheesecake, thirty lashes for cheesecake," again and again, swinging his snooker cue with more ferocity than his enemy could counter, attacking Julian with the greater strength of madness. His friend was going to lose.

*Come to me now, above this brave disaster…*whispered Lillith into Rupert's head. *You have kissed him, now kiss me.*

He unconsciously turned away from the fighters and looked towards the future. His eyes sought the pond under the great cedar tree but from where he stood he could not see either. Yet he felt her presence as a cuddly warm tugging at the middle of his chest.

Bring me your precious parcel, she thought, *for which you are to be lifted above all such mortal endings.*

His shadow, cast by the lights of the glass corridor, lengthened and faded as he crossed the gravel path and walked along the tennis court. He felt as though he was becoming a part of the night, like the moist darkness after a bedside lamp is switched off before nervous lovemaking. Yet in his need for Lillith he thought of the opposite, of light. Seeing her he became as excited as a child playing in the summer sun, his love bubbling up with volcanic passion. His eyesight changed focal length and he threw his glasses away forever.

Her smooth face and silver-streaked hair were emphasised by the moon rippling on the water, and he looked upon her as if she were a statue in alabaster, as though the sculptor had perfectly captured the component parts of her beauty. The woman, the knowledge, the monster, and the magic. She was wearing a black dress, belted at the waist, and she welcomed him into her arms. In her embrace he felt like a soft puppy going to sleep in a basket; and time, just briefly, seemed to stop. She spoke of it, aloud:

"No, Rupert, time does not stop. And we do not have much of it."
"Then you had better open this, my gift," he said.

The brown paper crackled as she tore it open. She poured out the collection of nineteen acorns into her right hand and led him away from the pond. She returned the package to him, and, as they walked towards the skirt of the deep woods, Lillith started scattering the hard green nuts to and fro. She was muttering something like: *"Latent seeds be food to make a tree beyond me,"* and it was spooky, a mantra she repeated as the acorns were distributed across the mossy earth, disappearing in the night. Soon there were none left, and they stopped by a tree. Rupert judged that it was old, by the wrinkly bark and the girth of its trunk, but he didn't recognize the variety because he couldn't see the leaves.

"It is an oak," said Lillith, "inevitably. Perhaps the oldest in the forest. Three hundred years since it was a nut, when I was last here in the Material Plane, and was burnt for a witch."

ZAXXON

"This is a new millennium," said Rupert. "That can't happen again, my sweet."

"Usually we made ourselves cold, and tore free."

"These days all the witch hunters are psychiatrists!"

"The mob scattered before us like wheat before the scythe, but I had lost my lover to the rope. I had no will. My spirit was locked into a tree like this ever since. Take out Key#18."

He reached into the paper bag, and experienced a mild electric shock as his fingers closed over the metal. The key felt important and unnaturally heavy. He passed it to her feeling excitement.

"Now dig a little hole between the bole of those roots. Just there."

He hunkered down onto his knees and dug into the soft soil with his fingers. When it was done she placed the key into it, and he noticed it radiated a blue luminescence. Lillith picked up a twig and drew an upside down pentagram and a cartouche of strange symbols around the hole, and then she spoke reverently:

"We are burying this key instead of the poisoned body of Rupert Thornberry, and we cover it with earth for him to transcend the shackles of mortality. The boy inside him will meet his spirit's ending in the imminent conjuration, to become his Yang to my Ying. In this new age we will be the Zaxxon. Never the prey. In return we will deliver the *Necronomicon* to the Dark Lord." The key flashed, once, like lightning. "We are blessed. Bury it," she said.

He did so, patted down the soil with his hand like a child finishing a sand castle. "Bring out the quill," she asked him. He crumpled up the empty paper bag and dropped it. "Use it to draw a circle on my lower lip," she said, and he marked her full lips with the Biro, wanting to kiss her, by the light of the stars. In turn she took the pen and drew a 'S' of the same width on his own lip. "The Eternity Circle will meet The Propeller in fusion. It is ready."

They observed each other, then, for some long moment. She looked into his eyes with a stare of such intensity that he felt transparent. She nodded.

"You are aware of my enmity," Lillith stated.
"I am."
"The Thornberry was an accident."
"My parents always thought so!"
"We will complete the conjuration forthwith."
"Will it hurt?"
"Give up entirely in the exchange of the kiss without fear."
"But I am – very fearful!"
Lillith took his hands and she squeezed them gently. "You will know no doubt, nor fear, nor pain. You will overcome all these with magics of your own." She leaned forward and licked the scabby blood from the cut above his cheekbone. She swallowed it with a little gulp. "I will make you an incubus and you will live forever. Laugh in the face of death."
This was what he wanted. "I love you," he whispered.
"You can love me for a million years."
Shockingly, the voice of Hudson rang out from the direction of the main building. "Hey Cheesecake! I'm coming for you! I'm gonna deodorise your stink once and for all!"
"Ignore it. He's meat," she said, and leant forward to lick the last dribble of dry blood from the cut on his face. "Ready?"
"I want to see you first. The Succubus, the true Lillith."
She stared into him. "Your mind is a confusion of hatred."
"What do you mean?"
"I mean you are perfect." She closed her eyes and her voice was distorting noticeably to bass. "We will enjoy each other's heat, long passed the next Ice Age, after half of the world is frozen. Know me now, Rupert," she growled gutturally, "for I was born again to hate this world!"

ZAXXON

She looked at him and his stomach flipped with happiness and terror. Her pupils were vertical black slits in hazardous pools of yellow, the eyes of a lizard beast; beautiful, terrible. Here was the real Lillith, not some façade of fragile humanity, which lasts but for a millisecond when compared to the universe, but eternal eyes. She emanated a latent power like a bomb that was his, to have and to hold, which could kill everyone and everything, except himself. And in spite of distended fingernails that were decorated with strange markings, like 'scrimshaw' ivory knives, she was still beautiful to him.

The demon spoke: deep, gutturally: "Do you still *want* me?"

"I do. But will I..." He looked away for a moment. "Will I *remember* things?"

"Yes," it rumbled confidently. "Everything."

"Cheesecake!" yelled Hudson. Rupert looked over his shoulder. Somehow the maniac had found them. "I'm gonna kill you *and* your little friend, you damn pervy!"

Rupert turned back decisively: "Take me!"

"Then you will become my reflection. Now kiss," she growled.

"I'm ready..."

She threw back her head and howled in triumph, like a wolf, a chilling caterwaul that echoed between the trees. He looked down into her mouth and noticed for the first time how her teeth had evolved. They looked sharper, shrunken. A succulent mouth to kiss, a fact, yet fitted out now with hooked spikes ready for tearing and chewing. And when he recalled her enjoyment of his own blood he understood, then, and was horrified. These teeth were for eating human flesh.

"It is part of the pact," she snarled. "Now kiss me!"

That aspect of Rupert Thornberry, which was about to die, was exactly the part that was indecisive. Yet barely for a second.

"Your batty boy Rant died like a stuck pig," shouted Hudson.

I want him dead first, he thought, *and I want him myself.* He took her in his arms and their lips drew close.
He's yours, my Thorn, she thought, *and we'll share the meat together.*

With the sound of sirens wailing in the distance, their tongues intertwined. She ground herself against him while Rupert shuddered as his body morphed into something that was akin to a warrior athlete. The energy of the succubus flooded his mouth and passed along his blood stream like a virus that had the taste of honey. Crackling sparkles of electricity jumped around his skin as his old self poured down the inside of him like melting wax. His musculature braced up like car suspension springs, his bones like steel bars; the very essence of his brain was evolving into a new and higher state. They kissed as the dying Rupert melted. Slid down and disappeared like there was a drain between his boots, but Hudson died a lot slower because when the lovers finally parted they were hungry.

A short time after Thorn had enjoyed his vengeance, their first kill together, blue lights were flashing along the edge of the Head Master's house. Torch beams were flickering and dancing towards them. Thorn dropped a torn chunk of Hudson to the ground.

We must leave, now, Lillith thought.
They turned away from the bones.
What is the Necronomicon? wondered her other half.
Ah! Your mind is as sharp as your teeth, my Thorn! It is a book that our Master lost two centuries ago, which has been uncovered and may be rekindled. We must return it to Him within sixteen days. Torchlight picked them out like two skittles on an unlit bowling alley. *What price eternal life?* She started pulling him toward the deep woods.
Then we will do it, he thought.

ZAXXON

"You two! Stop!" shouted a police officer.

The pair started to run. They felt like predatory birds; free as Golden Eagles to fly this way or that, yet with keener eyes and sharper claws.

"Halt where you are!"

But they did not stop. And like most things that are not supposed to exist, they disappeared. The policemen heard them giggling like young lovers as the forest took them, and then the oddly appropriate sound of that gradually disappeared also. Rupert was dead, and the demons quest had begun. They merged with the night, satiated, and hand in hand.

CHAPTER – 6

"In.timid.ate"

Samantha was dreaming. *They left the lights on after leaving the fair*, she thought. She walked among the flashing of thousands of bulbs, alone. It was like an empty cinema: the screen, loud with punctilious excitement, yet without an audience it seemed listless and disconnected from life. The place had rides and sideshows from every amusement park she had ever visited; the huge futuristic globe of the 'Space Ship Earth' in Epcot Centre, Florida, to the tiny ghost train in Blackpool. Yet there was no music. No one else was here. She could smell sweet foods, and wanted to eat a toffee apple or a stick of candy-floss, but there were no people to cook it. The rides groaned and rumbled automatically like broken promises. Then new actors came onto the scene. She sensed them, and suddenly felt fearful and exposed. She had to move quickly.

Samantha climbed over the side of a booth offering goldfish for skilful dart throwing, and the prizes were swimming about in bags of water hanging from the ceiling. More life than Samantha had seen so far, in this lifeless place. She peered over the counter to watch the board-walk and within moments the unmistakable figure of Demitrius came into view and stopped near to where she hid. He was wearing a red FCUK shirt with big baggy denim shorts, and was carrying what looked like a huge bar of chocolate close to his chest, but she felt its energy. It was a powerful book. He stood still, sniffed the air, and Sam wanted to have a shower because he was sniffing her personal scent. "I take everything I want," said the car thief. "And I'm going to take you - before Tony does." Then the man tilted his head. He heard danger that Sam could not detect with her own ears but which she felt poignantly as a gazelle being stalked by a lion. Something terrible was coming.

Demitrius walked faster, and vanished into an alley beside what looked like the roller coaster from Great Yarmouth.

Sam looked to her left, her skin prickling with a cold that was indistinguishable from terror. She saw two pairs of yellow eyes. They were glowing, and belonged to a couple of young people walking into view that weren't human. A tall teenager with perfect skin and a woman with streaks of silver in her hair. Both were following Demitrius, and both radiated a shadow that leached colour from the surrounding lights. When they passed her hiding place Samantha felt her blood thicken like she was going to faint, and every prize goldfish floated dead to the top of every hanging bag. They followed the car thief into the alley, and the shadow moved with them. She could breathe again.

After waiting to be out of danger for less than a minute she heard her boyfriend shouting her name like a bucket of cold water given to someone dying of thirst. She looked to the far right and saw him standing by the façade of what appeared to be the Maze Of Mirrors experience from Clacton Pier, looking pale and worried. He was turning on the spot, grabbing his head anxiously, and Samantha winced when he cried her name again, too loudly to be safe. She climbed over the counter and ran to him. They fell into each other's arms murmuring their love and smiling and kissing.

"So loud you might as well have called for me, instead," said Demitrius.

The shocked lovers saw the car thief standing beside them. Sam noticed he was no longer carrying his book. Demitrius unconsciously licked dribble from his lips, and his eyes were emotionless except for burning sexual desire. Sam clutched Tony hard.

"Let's do the wild thang," cried the older man, "let's get it on, woa!!"

He lunged forward. Tony's only attack was aimed at his lower chest, but his swinging hand smacked into something that felt as hard as a block of wood. He retreated, clutching his bruised fist. Demitrius lifted the hem of his shirt to reveal his book, the shape of it having been concealed by the red material. "Seems the pen is as mighty as body armour!" Demitrius exclaimed, and laughed humourlessly. He started unbuckling his belt.

"Let's go," said Tony. He pulled his girlfriend sideways towards the Maze of Mirrors. "I'd like to see him find us in this place."

Samantha had had the same thought combined with a suspicion of this attraction, but that was diminished by her dread of the car thief. "We must stick together," she said, "it's absolutely crucial!"

They pushed through the doorway and entered a world of confusion.

They turned left, and looked around them at dozens of reflections. Walked on, and saw themselves sideways. Turned right and saw their own backs, then moved on and saw millions of themselves going on forever. Turned right again, and bumped into the same corner they had just walked around.

It was a maddening conspiracy of mirrors. One-way, normal, double sided, and plain sheets of glass as well. Demitrius entered the maze himself and then it was terrifying. One moment he was walking away from them, or passing by them in the wrong direction, and then he was directly in front of them and attacking, with no way of knowing where he really was. Although his assaults always ended with a bumping noise from somewhere unexpected, and a growl of anger, how long would it take before he actually had them in his grasp?

Samantha held tightly onto Tony's arm, trying to recall a lost memory from her school days. Greek myth, learnt long ago, and now floating about just out of reach like a leaf on the wind. *We need a ball of string,* she thought, and the hand that held on to Tony's arm disappeared. It reappeared at her side. She gaped into Tony's hands, because he was unravelling a ball of white twine!

"Where did you get that?"
"It's alright, I've got plenty of it."
"How long have you had it?"
"I've been threading it out since we walked in."
"No, you haven't. That's impossible."
"- It's so we can find our way back."
"Obviously, Tony, but that string wasn't here a minute ago. It appeared just when I thought of it."
"We have to kill the monster," said Tony, and abruptly Samantha remembered the whole thing.

In the story, Minos, the king of Crete, had a labyrinth built to contain a monster that was half man and half bull, named the Minotaur. In vengeance for the death of his son in an old war, every nine years seven young people were sacrificed to this creature, until a hero called Theseus arrived. He had a magic sword and the daughter of the king gave him a ball of thread to lead him out of the maze. He slew the monster and emerged victorious.

"I don't have a weapon," Tony muttered, then said: "There it is - duck!"

They crouched down and Samantha watched the huge creature pass by. It was Demitrius yet changed, taller and stronger, and his head had become that of a bull. The thing reeked of sexual potency, stripped to the waist and slick with sweat. The denim shorts were tight now and just roomy enough to keep the weird book tucked up at the small of its back.

It stamped about with its wet nostrils flaring as it spluttered and snorted. Its horns were long, and sharp, and Samantha also wished for a weapon because she realised again that it didn't want to kill them, it wanted to rape her. The thought trampled through what little was left of her composure... yet a jewel encrusted scabbard appeared in the belt at her boyfriend's waist. Tony gasped with relief at the serendipity of it. He took hold of the hilt and withdrew a short sword of shining steel. It had *Vorpal Blade* engraved on it

"It must be Theseus's sword. It's beautiful," she said, sincerely.

"Fantastic," he agreed.

They moved on. Tony unravelled the string with one hand whilst waving the sword back and forth ahead of them with the other, the hands of an artist. They ducked and dived, continuing to avoid the monster. This went on for several minutes until the status quo changed when Samantha noticed a disastrous problem reflected in a small detail. The creature wasn't as stupid as it was strong. It had intersected the back trail of Tony's twine and picked it up in its mouth. It was sucking it up like spaghetti and coming up fast.

"Pull it back!" she hissed.

"What?"

"The string, pull it to you, quickly, quickly!"

Tony did. He put down the *Vorpal Blade*, wrapped the twine along the whole length of his crooked forearm, and reeled it in, reeled it in, reeled it in - and pulled it right out of the Minotaur's mouth! It bellowed with anger. The monster had thought it was on top of them. It found it was just another illusion, and it was furious. The scared couple watched it from one side as it drew back its fists and punched through the glass. The image was shattered into a thousand pieces and vanished. The creature's reflection popped up instantaneously beside the original mirror, but facing the other direction. It saw them also, out of the corner of its eye, swung both of its fists at the second mirror and smashed that also with a loud noise. Tony dropped the redundant twine and picked up the sword.

"It's cheating," he said. "How many years bad luck is that?"

"Fourteen."

ZAXXON

"How are we going to return without the string?"

"The same way as the monster. We'll smash our way out!"

Samantha could see that Tony's bravado was failing him. He looked terrified, the tip of his sword pointing at the floor. The Minotaur rubbed its bloody hands together, before punching through a third mirror. Glass crashed audibly over the floorboards nearby, and Tony and Samantha could now hear heavy breathing from the other side of the last thin wall. It was right beside them.

"Don't let it get me!"

The monster crashed through that partition as well and almost fell into their laps. Sparkling fragments of broken mirror were thrown everywhere like diamonds and blades. Sam stumbled backwards, and Tony lost grip on the sword. It slid away, out of reach and forgotten, and the Minotaur lifted Tony bodily off the tiles and then crashed him through the wall into the adjacent corridor where he lay unconscious. To Samantha it was already over.

The Minotaur overpowered her with its size and weight. It pushed her to the floor and dribbled saliva with a noxious musk. It pressed down on her but suddenly howled with an inhuman amplification, and over the creature's shoulder she could see the sword - stuck, stabbed into the middle of its back - and Tony standing over the creature with its book in his hands and an expression of total astonishment. It bled on her dress and bellowed its pain with breath like a warm and foul wind blowing into Samantha's face. It shuddered, spasmed, and it reached back for the sword but it could not grasp it. Gradually the fury of its body weakened and Sam looked into the bull's eyes and saw the life go out of it. It sank heavily on top of her, in death, and she pushed the stinking thing off her, onto its side.

She sat up and studied the thing altering back into the old Demitrius, with a sense of amazed revulsion. Its body hair receded into the Cypriot's natural olive skin. The horns slipped back into his head and lush hair sprouted outwards with a fall of black curls. Its bovine snout sank into his face, and its supernatural musculature deflated to Demitrius's original size; then, lastly, his moustache appeared. It was uncanny. She looked up at Tony and he made a hand gesture towards her as if to say: *"I don't know what's going on, but let's not question it."* He still held the book.

"What are you doing with that?" Samantha asked.
"I wasn't going to let him have body armour a second time, so I pulled it out of the waist band of his shorts - before I shoved my sword into the same place!"
"Brave."
"Thank you!"

Tony tucked the book under one arm and reached for the hilt of the sword. It wavered like hot air in a desert mirage; wobbled, and disappeared.

"Damn it!"

Then he saw something new to terrify him, in the corridor behind her, and his face went white. She looked over her left shoulder and suddenly felt like she was lying cold and naked in a dank basement. The woman with streaks of silver in her hair and the athletic young man were watching them, the couple that may not even be human, that had killed all the fish when they had passed her hiding place at the booth. The woman raised her hand.

"That book does not belong to you," she said.

Samantha looked back at Tony, and nodded at him, once, and briefly popped her eyelids open. It was a silent instruction. He understood this and walked past his girlfriend to the one laying claim to the book, his shoes crunching on broken glass. He hesitated.

"What is this thing?"

ZAXXON

"Power through knowledge," replied the woman. "Addiction through evolution. Destiny through structure. And death."

"It's not ours either," said her companion, "but we will return it to Him that it belongs to."

Samantha guessed that Tony's skin was prickling with a cold fear as he handed it over. He stepped back quickly.

"Good," said the woman, running her fingertips over its wrinkled cover. "You have been asleep young Samantha. You are dreaming."

"I thought as much!"

"And you have done well. Understand *this test has been an allegory of your best possible future.*"

"Remember," said the young man.

Tony disappeared and the floor opened up beneath her. Sam fell into own her body and awoke.

*   *   *

Tony was unable to sleep in his own nightmare. He was using his leather jacket as a pillow in a cell that was fifteen by fifteen feet square. The bunk he was lying on was actually a bench, upholstered in gouged red vinyl. It had been adorned with the eternal graffiti of attention seekers. Scribbles of love and hate and sexual frustration that he had quickly become bored of reading. At five o'clock in the morning he couldn't tell whether it was getting light outside, or not, because the halogen ceiling lamp had been burning shadows into the grout between the wall tiles all night. They were chipped and stained, like antique crockery. The toilet was a sorry affair in an alcove, and the windows were composed of what he supposed were archetypal squares of thick opaque glass. Terror and regret awoke him quickly from brief moments of sleep to the crushing reality of his situation.

His future lay in his art. In college Tony had been top of his class for half the term, until the skid that had led him to being thrown off the course. Now painting was his vocation, his only source of self-esteem, and he knew he was good at it. Demitrius thought so also and although the Cypriot was no aesthete, his praise counted for a lot. Tony tossed and turned in his cell. His portfolio was at a sufficiently high standard to have submitted photographs to a gallery, and he surprised himself often with this thought. Yet he hadn't applied any new gouache to his latest work for a week, and kidded himself it was because he had just come back from his parents' house. If only he could stick at it, instead of running around the Avon countryside in the night like an overgrown child. Of course it was fine to chastise himself now, since being locked up in Princess Street police station, but last night he hadn't felt like a child at all, far from it. He had felt the same adrenaline buzz as the other two.

Patrick and Tony had left the city at half past midnight, driven by Demitrius in the direction of a used car lot on route to Western-super-Mare. They had travelled in the Cypriot's souped-up and lowered black Honda Civic, nick-named the 'Vampire', with a list of pre-ordered stereo systems. Demi had previously arranged for a 'mole' in the garage to leave them the key to the back door of the office, the number to disengage the inside alarm, and the padlock key to the box containing the removable facias of the sound systems; and all awaited them around the back of the garage in a pink watering can lying beside a pile of old tyres.

They had 'gone equipped' last night. Gloves, old keys, bin liners, torches, flat head screwdrivers, pen knives, scissor jacks and a pair of heavy pruning secateurs. During the journey the secrets of the night's crime were revealed to Tony. The powerful clippers could kill three birds with one stone: be used to cut a hole in the fence on one side of the garage; snip the wiring to the CCTV cameras, and then cut the power to the forecourt floodlights. While Patrick reconnoitred mid 90's saloons (and tried to open a few by 'jiggling' old Ford and Vauxhall keys) Demitrius would raid the watering can and enter the site office. He had explained that with more men it would have been common to drive off all the best cars straight away, but not then. Last night they had a list of twelve specific stereos to supply and only three men on the job, and one of those was a rank amateur.

It was surprising how apparently easy it was to open a car without setting off the alarm. When getting into the older BMW '3' Series, Mk 5 Ford Escorts, older Vauxhall Astras and VWs, you just slide a screwdriver into the rubber window seal, lever open the side of a door, and lift the latch. Neither a wire cut, nor glass broken. The alarm is disengaged and all the doors open simultaneously - because of the wonders of central locking!

But maybe Tony didn't want to know all this. He was there because he hated confrontations and had been coerced by the Cypriot's indomitable pressure. He was horrified about breaking his promise to Samantha yet he may have felt slightly better knowing he wasn't a career criminal, and that he never would be. He was truly an amateur. He was only to be a lookout. Demi, himself, had said both! The older man had sensed his fear and said that being terrified of the police was a good thing because it made for a better watchdog. So Tony took up his position on the pavement, waiting for the night to end, and for dawn to see him tucked up safely in bed. That didn't happen.

They departed the crime scene at 3 am. There were twelve stereos systems in the back of the Honda locked in an aluminium case. As a kind of parting gesture they had also raised a model similar to the Vampire, on jacks, and had stolen four low-profile alloy wheels. Two had been stored in the boot, and two wedged behind the front seats. Tony had begun to relax when they were on their way back to the flat, like being driven out of a storm in a Lifeboat. The operation ran as smoothly as a newly greased axle, but in the eleventh hour Demitrius made a glaring misjudgement. He could suss C.I.D officers in unmarked cars from a hundred yards, so the Cypriot had claimed often, even at night, but he failed to do so on this occasion.

To change the stolen wheels that very minute because of a lack of privacy at Launch Terrace, he pulled over into a closed petrol station - with another vehicle coming down the hill in the distance. He passed the shop, passed the inanimate pumps, and drove around the back to stop the car against the wall in an area reserved for an air-pressure hose and a jet-wash. Demitrius switched off the headlamps. Tony would recall, later, that Demitrius seemed to know they were caught prior to it actually happening. He swore softly before the unmarked police car even left the road. Its headlights became visible, brighter as it swung around the side of the shop, and then stopped opposite them with its lamps casting a glare beneath which there was no escape.

Demitrius assimilated the situation and went to greet the approaching policemen but he was stumped by their first question: *"What are you doing here?"* It was almost a quarter to four in the morning. For the life of him, Demitrius could not think of an answer. The four stolen wheels and the stereo systems had been quickly discovered. More officers arrived on the scene; they milled about like aliens wearing yellow fluorescent jackets that flickered in the strobe lights. Patrick and Tony had been asked for identification, but Tony had none. He gave a false name and address of a boy he had never got along with at college. The three were arrested on suspicion of theft and driven in separate cars to the station. That absence of collusion had been bad for Tony. If the Cypriot was telling a tall story he wouldn't know a thing about it. It was embarrassing to name himself and after being searched for sharp objects he told them he had lied about his address because he had been scared. The desk sergeant said he looked like an amateur as well. Tony was locked up.

The stark reality of being in custody wasn't the cause of his insomnia. His fear was about Samantha, always. He hadn't set eyes on her cheeky face for eleven weeks before yesterday and he had broken his promise to her within a few hours. Of course, she did not have to know of this night's work. She need never learn of his treachery, but how else would he alleviate the weight he carried around in his chest if he didn't tell? He wanted to hold her, to kiss her wet lips, and cuddle her under a soft duvet, but at some very deep level he felt dirty inside. A thing like paranoia, a creeping guilt that he did not want to recognise, which meant the naïve happiness of their love could become tainted. Become, at the very worst, a living lie, if he did not confess.

Tony did not have his mobile phone with him. Its batteries were flat, wherever it was, but he was allowed one phone call in the morning, in a few hours. He would call Sam and lay it all down, and he started to chill-out at the decision. His eyelids began to close. He would place his desperate heart in her hands and accept her ruling. He fell asleep.

*   *   *

Later, a policeman brought him a breakfast of beans and a greasy egg on a paper plate, and a cup of tea. It was eight o'clock in the morning, on Princess Street, and daylight found Tony with the new worry of being charged, and re-terrified of losing his beloved Samantha. Soon he would be interviewed by officers of the C.I.D. His short sleep had been a great escape and numbed his mind as well as his body, but waking up had promptly returned him to the reality of his cell and much apprehension had flushed through his clenched flesh like a virus. Believing he might reduce this anxiety with breakfast, he ate his ration. The officer who had delivered the food returned for the left-overs the instant he was finished, like a psychic. The cigarette he gave Tony was the finest he had smoked for an age. Tony asked for his phone call. The constable replied that it wasn't up to him, but that he would pass the request up the ranks, and then Tony remembered something that relaxed him. It was June 22nd – a Sunday. Samantha wouldn't even be awake yet!

He wanted the Cypriot to help save their relationship. To tell Sam that he had forced Tony into the crime. If Demitrius would agree to this or not he didn't know, but it was the truth and the plan made Tony feel optimistic. He felt good when he reminded himself that by tomorrow the gallery would have seen digital stills of his best pictures and he felt happiness about finishing his latest painting. He could probably take it from moist to completion in under two hours! With so little colour left to apply he wanted Sam to come up and watch this accomplishment. It was one of his finest, a portrait of Samantha herself from a photograph in varying shades of blue / green gouache, and oils. His love was there in its essences, lived with his fingertips in the raw paint.

This unexpected optimism countered his fear of interrogation, as the cell door was opened with a cat-like squeal of metal hinges. He was led to an interview room of white washed brick with a battered table and two chairs. Tony sat on one of the chairs and felt like he was sitting on the wrong end of shooting range with a target glued to his chest. The two C.I.D. officers introduced themselves. The younger was named Detective Sergeant Johnson, who had a kind face and a blonde crew cut like Tony's; and the elder man was tall and thin, Detective Inspector Higgins, a serious policeman with an aquiline nose and a receding hairline near baldness.

"You got yourself into a mess last night, didn't you?" Higgins asked, with a Scottish accent.
"Definitely."
"Did you sleep alright?" asked Johnson.
"A little."
"Eat some breakfast?"
"Yes."
"Would you like to have a solicitor present?"
"No. Thank you," Tony replied. He didn't want to complicate things.

Uncomfortable under their intense appraisal, Tony found that he couldn't meet their eyes. He stared instead at the corner of the room; at the table top; and then at Higgins's nose, which seemed to have been broken and reset badly at least twice. Tony started daydreaming about how this had happened. The Inspector's index finger came unexpectedly into view as he rubbed it along the side of his nose. It jolted Tony awake. He didn't know if the Inspector had done it unconsciously or on purpose, so it had different meanings, yet they were quickly extraneous, because the old man said:

"That's good. You don't need a brief, and I don't need to record this interview."

Tony grasped the implications of this, slowly. He couldn't believe his ears. "You mean you're letting me go?"

"Bull's eye," said the Inspector. "We're satisfied that you and Patrick Dreyer were picked up by Mr Kiriacou, in his car, after the fact, so you had nothing to do with it. Mr Kiriacou has accepted full responsibility for the damage and the stolen radios and wheels. It's easier for us, since we save time and it's easier for him, since he can have it taken into consideration when his case is heard next month. So you are free to go. No criminal record, Mr Newman."

Tony hadn't known that the Cypriot was due in court. "Brilliant!" he exclaimed, getting up from his seat.

The Inspector extended the open palm of his right hand to impede him. "Whether it's brilliant or not is irrelevant," he said. "We've had young Patrick in here many times as you probably know, and Mr Kiriacou more, but you don't look like a criminal. I take it that this is the first time you've been in custody?"

"Yes."

"- And the last, I hope?"

Tony nodded.

"That's good!" said DS Johnson.

"Yet you share a flat with Kiriacou?" asked Higgins.

"Yeah, but my girlfriend, Sam, she wants me to move out soon. I'm hoping to start an art studio."

"A sensible girl," said Johnson. "And you do that, because –" The older man interceded: "– because repeat offenders like Kiriacou and the Dreyer brothers reckon they are so very 'street' but they're just yobs. They are fools and won't get anywhere in life, probably won't ever lead 'normal lives' and when I say 'normal' I mean that by which society dictates it is, by the way everyone else behaves." Tony could recall Sam saying the same thing. "Like you, Mr Newman. Normal." Higgins took a deep breath and shuddered.

"If you really are an artist, you've got a chance for a good life," said the younger detective.

"- For a well-spent life," said the old Scotsman. "You can go, now, Mr Newman. DS Johnson will show you to the front desk where you can collect your belongings."

Tony got up and followed him into the corridor.

"It's refreshing to talk to someone in here who isn't a no-hoper," said Johnson.

Tony had been harbouring a small, unimportant, suspicion. He looked back, briefly, at the old detective slumped in his seat. It was true. Higgins hadn't lived a normal life either.

*   *   *

Samantha awoke at eleven o'clock with the last tendrils of the nightmare clinging to her consciousness like the ivy climbing the wall outside her bedroom window. She thought that the long tee shirt she wore as a nightdress was still soaked in the Minotaur's blood; that the stink of it was still in her nostrils. The smell lingered with her long into the shower, a hot smell like drying animal skins, and she scrubbed herself hard as though the nightmare had physically dirtied her body. Emerging refreshed she towelled herself dry and sat at her dressing-table blow-drying her hair, wondering what part of her psyche had prompted the dream.

The potency of the beast, and the abhorrent intimacy of its rape attempt, might denote that Demitrius was the epitome of a fear she had of sex. The monster's assault on Tony, when he had thrown him through a sheet of glass, meant that she was afraid the Cypriot was taking Tony away from her. When she had discovered his betrayal on the phone last night, that seemed to have happened already. Her first impulse after slamming the receiver down on that foul-mouthed boy had been to break-up with him.

ZAXXON

This morning she did not want to. It wouldn't solve anything. They would both just be confused and heart-broken, but she needed to know why he had done it. Maybe if he got arrested it would teach him a lesson. She wasn't tender in life: the blood of the Minotaur had made her tender, but that was just a dream. When she finally spoke to Tony she was going to be hard.

Samantha tied her hair into a pony tail and selected a yellow cotton frock. It was a warm day outside and she was considering taking her spaniel, Winston, for a walk, but she decided to give the house a clean instead. Her father was away at a conference in Birmingham and she wanted to ask Tony around tonight. Her dad wouldn't be back 'til Monday. Whilst dusting, her thoughts drifted to when she had so nearly invited Tony to stay yesterday. The invitation had died on her lips. It had seemed forward. They had seen each other only once in the last two months, but she wanted to make love to him tonight, beat her fear of the act and go on all night - if that's what it took to break Demitrius's hold over him – and, of course, Sam expected to enjoy it. The telephone rang at eleven thirty. She switched off the vacuum cleaner and walked to where the phone was perched on a small occasional table in the hall. In her ear there was the clunking noise of a coin being pushed into a slot. She inquired:

"Hello?"
"Sam, it's me."
"I thought it was you, Tony. Don't bother trying to conceal what you did last night, I already know."
"How?"
"A disgusting boy told me when I rang your flat. He insulted me."
"That was Jason."
"Why do you hang out with these lunatics?"
"I can't afford to live anywhere else."
"I'm not asking *why* you live there, I'm asking why you *associate with them*."

"I don't know. Part and parcel I suppose. I'm sorry."

"You betrayed me."

"I didn't want to go, I didn't!"

"How long did your promise last? A few hours!"

"He forced me."

"If Demitrius forced you to tell me to sod off and leave you, would you do it?"

"I don't know... No."

"But can't you see it's the same thing?"

"I was in a difficult position."

Another coin was pushed into the slot.

"You mean he would have beaten you up if you hadn't agreed?"

"I think so."

Samantha leaned forward, frowned, and pinched the bridge of her nose. "I figured as much. Anything else I should know about?"

"Yes. I got arrested. I was released about ten minutes ago, without charge, and rang you straight away. Please don't dump me, Sam! I was in a cell almost all night worrying about you dumping me. This will never happen again," Tony expressed. "I'm very, very sorry." And he sounded as though he meant it.

"It's OK, Tony, we'll talk about it tonight. I'm not going to leave you."

"Bless you, I love you!"

Her heart skipped a beat. "Take the bus from outside Debenhams at half past seven. You'll get to Cherry Garden Hill by eight and my house is at the top of the hill, number ninety-two. Buy yourself a one-way ticket and bring your wash kit." Her heart was thumping hard, her cheeks flushed, and her hands were shaking. "I want you to stay the night with me, Tony."

"That's lovely."

"Dim lights and soft music and lots of soft stuff, remember?"

"I do, but I'm nervous."

"Trust me. Everything will be fine. Say the same to me!"

"Everything will be fine. And I think it might be... see you later, then?"

ZAXXON

"Yeah. Bye, bye." Tony replaced his receiver. Samantha put down her own. She was smiling.

The coins fell noisily into the belly of the payphone. Tony fingered the change compartment unconsciously and emerged penniless. He didn't even have the bus fare back to the flat but he had already adapted to the prospect of walking there. Everything would be fine - Sam had said so! Arriving at the flat he made lunch; dumped hot ravioli on toast. It was how he prepared most of his meals and he ate it sitting cross-legged on the floor in front of his easel. He was winding himself up into the mind-set to finish this painting whether or not Sam watched him do it.

He stared intently at the whole picture at once, the wider vision of an artist. He used his 'whole eye' rather than the small focal point of most everyone else. Blues and greens could be thought of as cold colours yet Sam's pretty expression was full of warmth. In a way it was better for the work that she didn't watch him. He did not want to interact with two loved ones at once, and he did love this painting. The portrait was accurate to the last hair... and then it went beyond that original digital image to the essences of fine art, a place where nothing is finished yet is full of the almost indefinable passion of love expressed in the paint. He washed his plate and cutlery before he began.

For the first time he could remember his room was clear of stolen goods. The wheels, tyres, stereos, bicycles, tools, and dirty motorbike parts that had littered the carpet were gone and he wondered whether the police had confiscated it all this morning. If they had they would never let Demitrius out! Tony began blending paint on his palette into colours that could be argued had never existed before, nor would again. He mixed it delicately with the tip of a '000' sable brush when Demi himself came into the flat and walked into Tony's room.

"Nice to see you working again," he said.
"Demi, what happened to all the stuff that was in here?"

"The tooth fairy took it."

Tony stepped back from his easel as though he hadn't heard the typically caustic reply. "What do you think of this?"

The Cypriot walked up and leaned closer to the painting. His eyes, usually blank and unemotional, showed a fierce interest. "Who's the babe in blue?"

"Samantha," Tony replied proudly. "My girlfriend!"

"It's safe. The sea-green colours make her look like a mermaid. I like it a lot. You're not going to be Mister Popular when she finds out you got banged up last night are you?"

"Do you care?" Tony asked suddenly.

Demitrius paused, putting the knuckle of his right index finger against his lips. Eventually he said: "Yeah, I think I do. You did a good job last night. Getting nicked was just bad luck. Shit happens."

"It needn't have. What really happened in here?"

"I used my call to tell Jason to stash the gear in his van, and drive it as far away from here as possible. It looks like he did a good job of it, too, but the bill never searched the place anyway."

"That's good." Tony turned back to his painting, holding his wet brush horizontally at the level of the middle of the canvas. "I wouldn't have liked a bunch of strangers messing about with my art."

"Oh, aren't we full of ourselves today?" Demitrius smirked. "You're lucky Jason Dreyer didn't carry off your art as well."

"That's a very bad joke."

"If it's so important to you, you should work on it everyday instead of messing around trying to find a job you're never going to enjoy. You're good at it, you should make it pay. Why not call Gillows about those snaps first thing Monday morning?"

Inside that gallery many careers had flopped or taken off. It was the gold medal for an aspiring painter, a place of white washed walls and air conditioning and high quality exhibits. If this new portrait was not fine enough for them then nothing would be. Tony believed that, but he was young, he had decades of potential still to explore. It was not true. What he believed was a driving realism at the heart of his personality was in fact a pessimism born of disappointment and bad choices of which he was ignorant. He had had to break through that to even submit photos!

"I'm not sure. A lot of them may not be good enough," he said, needing Demi to deny that, to encourage him, but the man was dismissive.

"Maybe they aren't then." That was the end of what the Cypriot had to say on the subject. "What did you mean when I said 'shit happens' about being arrested, and you said 'it needn't have'?"

Tony froze. He had hoped Demitrius wouldn't pick it up. The man was sharp. Tony fumbled for phraseology: "It seems to me, and I'm inexperienced in these matters, but it seems to me maybe you shouldn't have pulled into that garage, that you should have realised it was a police car coming down the hill."

"How the hell am I supposed to suss every car on the road?"

The young artist was sliding, out of control, into a red and black place at the hands of the Cypriot's violent temper. It was a call to action, time for the other's rage to be placated with soft words. "I know you were tired last night, and that it was difficult to do it at night, but with all that stuff in the car you should have been, maybe, more vigilant."

Demitrius's right arm slipped around Tony's neck, suddenly, and clamped him from behind in a head-lock. Tony started gasping for air and dropped his palette, wet-side down, on the carpet. Demitrius pulled the younger man's ear close to his mouth: "Don't you ever criticise my style again, you don't know enough about it. I got you and Patrick off the hook this morning, have you forgotten that already? You ungrateful shit!"

"I never should have gone in the first place," Tony wheezed.

"There you go again, criticising my judgement!"

"I'm not cut out for it. Everybody says so, including you. I don't want to end up in prison."

"And I will, is that it?"

165

"It's an occupational hazard."

Demitrius relaxed his arm. "It is… and I probably will." Demitrius released him.

Tony stumbled forwards wondering for how long he would have to take this abuse. He rubbed his bruised neck, breathing raggedly. The thought of actually hitting the Cypriot never occurred to him, because the man was a psychopath who reigned Montpelier with the myth of picking up anything at hand for a weapon. It didn't even matter if this was false. The last thing Tony wanted to risk was being on the receiving end of a blunt instrument. When his breath was back under control, he asked:

"You 'probably will' what?"

"I'll probably go to prison."

"Does this have anything to do with that court appointment you've got coming up?"

"How do you know about it?"

"That Scottish policeman told me."

"Yeah, well, he shouldn't have done. But he was right."

"What happened?"

"I took three bikes last Christmas, took one off this geezer at knife-point. They were all ringered and re-VIN numbered so sweetly I got blasé about wearing gloves and one morning this nosy copper found them, calls in the forensics, and there I was - back in Princess Street - again. I've been told it's likely I'll go down but I've been inside before. It's no big deal."

Losing freedom meant more to Demitrius than he was making out, but Tony was not about to contest the issue.

"It won't do my rep any good," the older man continued, "but obviously I'll have to cancel the deal for the stereos." He yawned, and started walking towards the door. "I need some sleep."

"So do I," said Tony. "But I have to get the bus from Debenhams at half past seven. I mustn't miss it because the busses are dodgy on Sundays. D'you think you could wake me up?"

"I will. But clean up that paint you spilled. If I see one drop on the carpet, when I get up, I'll smash that painting over your head."

"Alright, there's no need for threats."

"There usually is with you." Demitrius smiled coldly. "You twat!" He left the room.

Recently Tony had overheard Jason and Patrick discussing an example of the Cypriot's violence. About three weeks ago he had been riding a yellow Saracen bicycle from his snooker club to the flat, when a middle-aged man in a Ford Focus had 'cut him up' at an intersection. The man, who was maybe a minor executive, had caused Demitrius to take a nasty tumble and had compounded his error by leaning out of his electric window and shouting: "Get out of the road, sonny!"

So Demitrius had taken out the heavy end of his two piece pool-cue from its velvet lined box and had hit the Ford's windscreen with it until it was a smashed mess. The executive opened his door, probably in two minds, Jason had supposed - between dealing with this mad boy or staying in the vehicle and locking it - but he had had the chance to do neither. Demitrius had pulled him the rest of the way out onto the road and whacked him in the teeth with the stick. Once, but caused terrible damage, then he had calmly ridden off into the traffic. Apparently no one witnessed the assault. What scared Tony the most was not that the story was true, but that it was not even embellished.

All the more reason to clean the paint spill, he thought.

Tony assembled a pan of water, a nail brush, and a half empty bottle of white spirit. He hunkered down on the carpet and scrubbed at the spillage, grudgingly. It wasn't his fault he had dropped the palette in the first place. What really annoyed him was the fact that the carpet was covered in mud and oil stains already, because of Demitrius and his two friends, and he wondered what difference a small splat of paint could make in all that mess. He cleaned it up anyway.

He spent twenty minutes, doing it on his knees, and afterwards he stood up slowly with his joints popping, and remembered Demitrius's threat to his picture. It was enough for Tony to come to a decision. He would call Gillows tomorrow and learn if his ambitions were realistic. It was a powerful urge, however worrying the risk to his ego, but if they were exhibited and sold... well, that would be one of the Cypriot's suggestions that Tony would be happy to have acted on! Could something so amazing take place so soon after something so terrible? Maybe. He would complete the painting and let the warm air from the open window dry it while he snoozed until he went for the bus to see his girlfriend. Tony had a long hot shower and got into bed. He stared at the finished portrait across the room until his eyes slowly closed and the perfection of it followed him into sleep.

"Hey! Tony!" Somebody was shaking him. "You slob!"

Tony's eyelids opened a fraction. He woke up quickly when he saw Demitrius looking down at him with that typically bland expression. "I cleaned up the paint, I swear it!"

"I know that you wing-nut. It's five past seven. This is the alarm service with a punch, so get up or I will."

"Will what?"

"Punch you."

"OK. I'm there." Tony swung out of bed and looked at his watch. "Bloody hell! I'm supposed to be catching the bus in twenty minutes and I don't even have the fare!" He went to the wardrobe and took out his best suit. "Could you lend me a quid?"

"I never lend money to friends, only to enemies at extortionate interest rates."

"Oh come on, I'm going to have sex tonight!" He sprayed deodorant liberally under his arms, and pulled on a chequered shirt from a hangar.

"That's a convincing argument," Demitrius said. "And it's about time, too." He fished a coin out of his jeans.

"Thank you," said the younger man.

"But I want you to help me TWOC a car next week."

"You can't ask me to do that, Demi!" He belted his trousers as though constricting the flow of icy fear in his blood. 'TWOC' meant Taken Without Owner's Consent.

"You must do. It's a classic MG in a dodgy location and Patrick and Jason are in London. You're all the help I've got."

"I'm not cut out for it. Remember?"

"Don't fuck me about again. What if you could take whatever you want from inside the car?"

"We only got arrested last night!"

"What if I promised to get you off the hook if we got caught again?"

"OK, OK." Tony adjusted his tie. "I'll do it. But only if you swear you'll never ask me to go out with you again. This is the last time, Demi, right?"

"I agree."

"That's great." Tony tied up the shoe-laces of his Hush Puppies. "It's a big day for me tomorrow. I'm going to phone Gillows."

"Well in that case I do swear it – see, I didn't before. Now you go and catch your bus."

"See you later."

"No, Tony, say: 'laters'."

"Laters," said Tony. He left the flat, and went down the stairs feeling a fear that was indistinguishable from excitement.

*   *   *

"Good gracious," Sam exclaimed, "but Tony, you're wearing a suit!" It was a charcoal grey pinstripe and she realised she had never seen him looking so smart before. It was a dated design, but could nevertheless make a good impression at a gallery interview.

"And that's a lovely dress, Sam. It's so... *red.*"

It was figure hugging and cut half way up her thigh, which she called her 'sexy dress'. Obviously her Dad didn't approve of it, but he wasn't here. It was their time. Winston the spaniel was locked up in the laundry room with a huge bowl of dog biscuits, and she had lit candles in the dining room and upstairs in the guest bedroom, her sister's old room, selected because it had a double bed. They were going to do a lot of other things tonight that her father wouldn't approve of!

"Give me a hug," said Sam.

He took her into his arms but their kissing shamed such platonic invitations. They ground themselves together; touching, tasting. They parted reluctantly. "That's a really lovely perfume you're wearing," Tony commented. It smelt like trees, like a forest after rain. "What is it called?"

"Ralph Polo Sport."

"What's so funny?"

"You gave it to me yourself last Christmas!"

Tony appeared embarrassed but not for the reason Sam was thinking, about his lapse of memory over the fragrance. Nor was it because of the exertion of walking from the bus stop. It was because he felt intimidated, had done since first laying eyes on her tonight looking so scarlet and curvy. He chastised himself for this unfairness and tried to quash the idea that her carefully prepared dinner was just a formality before sex. He guessed that her own version of the thought was much deeper in her mind than his. While they ate their appetizers of prawn salad, Tony made himself stare at her unfettered cleavage through the candle flames, and to enjoy sexy thoughts. Then they had steak. What really mattered was that he was lucky to be seeing her at all after breaking his promise, and now he knew that, more than anything else, he wanted to be her lover.

He complimented her cooking and she smiled with an infectious cheek. Sometimes her face seemed to glow like a wistful child's. Her choice of sweet was a chilled pudding wine with portions of Tiramasu. They ate it slowly.

ZAXXON

"We should do this again with your Dad here," Tony said.

"It wouldn't be so fun."

"How else will he meet me?"

"When it comes to boyfriends his standards are very fussy. He's due back at ten o'clock in the morning and you'll have to be out of the house by then because if he finds you here he'll blow up and demolish half of Bristol!"

"You mean I'm an unemployed criminal."

"Being arrested once doesn't make you a criminal, Tony."

"But he wants you to go out with a solicitor or an accountant or a doctor, or something?"

"Yes… or perhaps an exhibited artist."

This made Tony feel good. "Actually, I've got a batch of pictures ready for Gillows the moment they accept me. I guess I'm in with a chance. I'll get Demi to help transport them in his Honda, and sooner rather than later. He'll be banned soon."

"Good thing. Make the roads safer."

"I've actually got some information about him and me. Do you want the good news or the bad?"

"Neither."

"Sam, I 'm working hard, now," he said, leaning forward. "You are my muse, my inspiration. Part the guide of my moral senses. It's as important for you to *know* that I'm trying to create some kind of future for myself as it is for *me to do it*. And this is the thing: if I help Demitrius steal a car with him next week he'll no longer be a threat."

"You're not going to, right?" She pushed her empty bowl away from her.

"I've already agreed to, because he's promised that, if I do, it will be the last time. The last job. He'll never ask me to go again."

"How can you trust that man? He's got the ethics of an alley cat!"

"I know him very well, better than you. He does have some ethics. He's given me his word and I believe him."

She sat swirling the sugary white wine around the rim of her glass, then she exclaimed: "Do it!"

"That's what I was thinking," said Tony. "What I'd hoped you would say."

Sam stood up and walked to his side. "If we wash the dinner things now, Dad won't see them in the morning."

It didn't take long. When Tony had dried his hands, they felt soft, and warm, and sensitive.

"Let's make love," Sam said. She led him up the cream carpeted staircase.

"I was hoping you'd say that, too."

They undressed, shedding their anxiety like their clothes, with a gradually increasing joy. Jasmine incense swirled around their meeting bed and mingled each with the scent of the other. They watched every breath and euphoric expression in the candle glow, lost themselves up to the peak of it, and arrived together. Then they started falling asleep, sharing a bottle of red wine, contented under the soft duvet in the flickering light. Neither heard the empty bottle fall off the bed as they slept. And that night, in each other's arms, there were no bad dreams.

CHAPTER – 7

"Per.severance"

The demons shared a motel room on the outskirts of Norwich, registered under the name of Mr and Mrs Frost. It was just after midnight in the infant hours of Monday morning. They were lying in each other's arms but did not sleep in the normal sense. They drifted through oblivion without altogether losing touch with their surroundings, like a pair of super-computers linked at some deep level that never completely log off. If they didn't deploy their psychic arsenal they could go on for several days without sleep, but they could almost completely shut down their bodily systems, at will. It was a pleasing escapism. When they did they never reached REM. The Succubus lay with her eyes turned inward, accessing her 'memory cards' of this morning's newspaper.

What she hadn't read was represented as blank patches in the columns. The remainder of what she had read was as clear to her now as it had been to anyone, when it had rolled off the presses. The front page described murders, most of which were attributable to them, although the assailants were unknown at the time of printing. The banner headline exclaimed: "CANNIBALISM AT LOCAL SCHOOL!" A finger-tip search, in the woods, for sixteen year-old Rupert Thornberry, was not expected to find him alive. The Succubus knew that they had to get out of Norfolk by dawn. She was just assessing her extra-sensory digital clock, which read 00:32 hours, when she suddenly felt a shock that made her hair stand on end. Even in her half-sleep, she saw a blue flash of light behind her eyes originating from somewhere in the northwest. It was part of a huger power, and she quickly grasped the meaning of it.

Thorn abruptly sat bolt upright in their bed. "What!? *What was that?*"
"You felt it also?"

"Like an axe falling." He looked around the room and then pointed into one corner. "From that direction. But far away."

"I know."

"What was it?"

"We just experienced a power flux from the *Necronomicon* on the western coast of Scotland!"

"Could we have sex?"

"A pox upon your todd-end! The book has captured a soul and that's where we must head: Scotland! We have a destination. That is good, isn't it young Thorn?"

"I suppose so... could we have sex now?"

"OK."

*   *   *

The Professor took the long route back to the pub because he could not navigate the cliff by himself. He had been walking for about half an hour with mixed feelings of worry and elation. The problems with the car, worry about Stephanie, fear of the police, but it was all cancelled by the elation of having survived an attempt on his life using magic - the magic of what maybe the most powerful book ever written - and it was in his possession!

He had retreated from the site of the priest's death with the grimoire tucked under his arm; where, for some reason, it felt the most comfortable. The restless fingers of his left hand fondled the dry wrinkles and ridges of its ancient cover. Soon he was on the road back to the village, his other hand traversing his torch back and forth in the darkness. The metal 'blakeys' on the heels of his hiking boots echoed eerily on the tarmac. Sometimes he shone his light behind him to allay the fear of being followed. He berated himself. In reality he had problems that were more pressing and in many ways worse than a silly paranoia that Caine's crippled body was shambling after him.

Stephanie wanted to leave Ravencliff, tomorrow, he guessed. If the car proved too damaged to drive that would prove impossible. He would have to get an AA engineer to come out especially and, if that failed, they could be in even worse trouble. The MG was a classic car and most of its parts were rare and expensive. If it needed to be towed away to a specialist they could be stuck in this dismal place for several days, and they would have to face the police. The Professor had already decided to call them himself. At some point investigators would turn up under their own steam anyway – and, since foul play was involved, it would most probably be a crime not to report it.

Three bodies were lying in the bottom of that mouldering crypt, and two of them were obvious victims of murder. The Professor had almost suffered the same fate, himself, but had been saved by the magical explosion that had killed his antagonist. But how could he explain it? He couldn't bring up the preposterous truth even to his own daughter. He did not want to mention the *Necronomicon* so how could he convincingly explain what had he been doing at the scene of these crimes? What had brought them to Ravencliff in the first place? What connected him to the other victims?

Stephanie was worried sick for her father's life. She had been sitting in the Raven's Arms pub on a worn oak chair in front of the hearth for over an hour and a half. As her gaze moved fitfully from the burning peat logs to her watch, again, her head swam with the legends that her father had told her during their dinner. Her imagination was over-wrought with pirates and strange books and devil worshippers, but they were just stories. Although these visions could not harm anyone, they coalesced with something very much worse that could. Had the priest transferred a knife from his robe to his trouser pocket just before they left? She hadn't been certain but with even the suspicion of it she should have tried harder to prevent her father from going. Try was all she could have done. Nothing short of a heart attack would have stopped him.

With his passport close to his chest, as if he had expected Caine's inquisition, her father had proved he was the genuine descendant of Angus the 'Black Fist' McLoughlan.

Then they had both left the cosy warmth of the pub into a cold night. They hadn't returned, for an hour and a half. Her father had told her what he was after, but it was on the fuzzy edge of Stephanie's memory. He hadn't dragged her across the country for a holiday, or to see the bones of an ancient relative, or for treasure of a financial nature. Her father was not driven by money, it was something else. In this example he was driven by... the occult? And then Stephanie remembered. Angus's legend, his zombie wife rising from the dead, and she shivered and hugged herself. Her father wanted the *Necronomicon*, the Black Arts. That was his legacy and Stephanie felt despair. As time crept by like a gravestone eroding too gradually to measure, it seemed less and less likely that he would come back. No one knew they were here. And if Caine murdered her father he was going to come after her.

She took one of the last cuttings of peat from the wicker basket beside the hearth, and tossed it into the fire. It burnt with an enchanting smell that reminded her of garden bonfires when she had been little. The fire crackled noisily but the sound of footsteps squeaking and groaning down the creaky back stairs was louder. Stephanie looked behind her, at the bar, and saw Mrs McTavish appear behind the counter in her dressing gown.

"Goodness me!" exclaimed the landlady. "Have they not come back?"
"No. I've been waiting for them for an hour and a half."
"D' you fancy a drink?"
"Yes, please. Whisky."
"Poor lassie." She took two tumblers and measured generous quotas of the best from an optic, then opened the flap in the bar and carried the glasses over to the fireplace. "It's Laphroaig, my favourite. A very special malt from the Islay distilleries." She pulled up a chair.

Stephanie took a small sip and found it had a smoky taste like the peat logs. She had been feeling warm on the outside and cold on the inside, for ages, the wrong way round to be comfortable. A large mouthful re-dressed the balance, warmed her in places the fire had been unable to.

"Thank you, very much," she said.

"That's alright, sweety," said the landlady. "I often have a drink in the middle of the night for my arthritis. My copper bracelet doesn't seem to work anymore, just turns my skin green. I really should get some pain pills but I never seem to get around to it. It's always so busy around here!"

Stephanie laughed.

"What's so funny?"

"I live in London."

"Horrible stinky place," said Mrs McTavish. "What do you do there?"

"Have you ever been to Covent Garden?"

"Once, long ago. Big crowds don't agree with me."

"I own a shop there that sells hand-made silver jewellery, in a wonderful position opposite a famous café called the Rock Garden."

"It's not famous to me," exclaimed Mrs McTavish. "D'you run it yourself?"

"I have two permanent staff. I've called it 'The Silver Tortoise' because it's a quirky name that sticks in the mind, in a tradition of London jewellers like 'The Great Frog' in Carnaby Street."

"Must have cost ye a wee mountain o' pound notes!"

"I inherited most of the investment capital from my mother when she passed on. I hardly needed to borrow a single penny from a bank. The other share-holders are all friends of the family and they seem well satisfied with the progress." Stephanie leaned forward, earnestly. "I just wanted you to know, Mrs McTavish, that I really appreciate you giving up your time to talk to me, to take my mind off things."

"Call me Ellen."

"I will. You know? - I'm feeling much better!"

"I thought you were. And I was just thinking that your father is absolutely fine too."

"Really?"

"Aye. And that's not just the Laphroiag talking."

Stephanie discovered she shared the older woman's optimism, which meant that the priest had not been so fortunate. "Ellen, do you and your husband own this pub?"

"Aye, it's been passed down the generations like most things in Ravencliff. Especially the boats."

"Do any good car mechanics drink in here?"

"The best man in the village for that is Reverend Caine, he's brilliant with engines."

Stephanie sighed inwardly because her instinct told her they were going to have to get the car mended somewhere else. Reverend Caine was not going to come back this night; not ever.

The Professor walked up to his MG in the cold drizzle and fished out his keys. If it was drivable he and Stephanie would somehow get their luggage out of Caine's rectory, wherever that was located, and get the hell out of Ravencliff tomorrow at the crack of sparrows. He slipped his key into the ignition but felt it would be prudent to look around the car before he started it. He left the keys dangling and switched on the headlamp. The remaining bulb filled the misty car park with a bright cone of light. The other was smashed.

The front left wing was crumpled but salvageable. The rear number plate was lying several feet away in an adjacent parking space. The bumper was broken on one side; hanging down and touching the tarmac impudently like a broken arm in a photograph. The Professor well remembered the hissing sound of the ruptured radiator immediately after the accident, but at first glance the rest of the damage seemed relatively cosmetic. Although every panel appeared to have a least one dent, he was beginning to hope they could drive it away tomorrow with a minimum of sweat. He shone his torch under the car, and the news from this angle was bad. His sump had broken open like an old fruit and a huge pool of engine oil had collected under the car. If he had started the engine it would have seized up within moments.

ZAXXON

He straightened up with a sigh. The car was not drivable. They were stuck here for a while and Stephanie would have to make the best of it. In the bright light of day she would find Ravencliff as pretty and singular as most small villages in the West Country. Even without her sketch pad and pencils she would accept any break from the noise and fumes of London as a holiday.

So that was fine.

After wrestling with a brief (and unexpected) reluctance to let the book out of his sight, he opened the MG and locked the *Necronomicon* in its boot. It was out of harm's way in that black pocket. He turned up the collar of his coat against the drizzle and started to walk along the rough steep path that led down to the village. He had concocted a story to explain Caine's death so plausible that even forensic analysis might back it up! Thinking about this now gave the Professor a renewed enthusiasm for the walk. He lengthened his stride and soon his iron-clad boots were clatting along the cobbled street between the squat sleeping houses. Feeling excitement, a bone-tired relief, and an urge for chocolate, he banged on the door of the pub at half past two AM.

Stephanie jumped out of her chair as if the noise were gunshots. She almost dropped her whisky tumbler to the floor, a latent destruction like the threat of flooding from a passing cloud heavy with rain. She fumbled with the glass then placed it on the table. Now she would know the truth. Was it her Dad in the street, or the deranged priest waiting with 'bad news' and thoughts of murder, bloody apologies, sham sympathy? Stephanie had been waiting for either of them to return for over two hours. Ellen McTavish padded over to the door in her old slippers and dressing gown and unbolted it top and bottom. It swung open, inwards.

He walked in - and Stephanie's pent up breath was released with a 'whoosh' of relief. It was her Dad! His long torch hung down from his hand like a rolled up newspaper, and his smile was kind of sad, but wide and warm. He looked as tired and as wet and as cuddly as a bedraggled puppy! She ran a few steps into his arms, almost tearful with happiness, and they hugged as though they hadn't seen each other for years. Ellen McTavish waited for them politely, for a little while, then asked:

"Where is Reverend Caine?"

The professor let go of his daughter, and turned to the landlady. Grimly, he said: "I'm afraid there's been an accident. Reverend Caine is dead."

"How?" she exclaimed.

"What happened to you out there?" asked Stephanie.

"First thing's first," said the Professor, shrugging out of his wet coat and sitting by the fire. "I need chocolate, and a drink. Something strong." He warmed his hands to the flickering flames of the last burning peat log.

"I'll fetch you a Mars Bar, and whisky," said Mrs McTavish.

"You're in the right place for that," said Stephanie. "The Laphroiag is delicious."

"I'm in the right place for more reasons than that."

"So? Tell us!"

"You Stephie, for one..." He accepted the proffered tumbler and took a large swig of the liquid. He squinted happily and said: "Phew, great stuff!" He ripped open the Nestle wrapper and bit off a large mouthful of the Mars Bar: "Mmm!" Beyond matters of her temporary spiritual protection he had never lied to his daughter. When they were back in London he might tell her the truth about the book, but for now he felt ready to test pilot his story. He would reveal, right now, how close they had come to being killed at the priest's hands, and see if the rest of it would fly.

"We walked through the village passed the quay-side to the beach. Then Reverend Caine led me up the cliff face of the far right hand spur. It was a very difficult path. At the top we found the ruins of an old church with graves that are falling into the sea."

"Excellent!" exclaimed Stephanie.

He chewed some more chocolate. "When he and I reached the cover stone of Angus's tomb, Reverend Caine used a crow-bar and slipped into the gap between the slab and the border. But he never raised it more than a couple of inches. I was in fact standing several feet away when he started heaving it up because he didn't need my torch light. And then - boom!"

"What happened?" Stephanie asked.

"A spark from his tire iron ignited the gas inside the chamber. There was an explosion. Hot chips of rock went everywhere, and a foul smelling fire. I was lucky to be unharmed but the priest was killed instantly." He gave a considerably brief description of the body. "So, there I was, standing around looking into the chamber for a while, needing more and more to investigate what was down there in spite of what had taken place. I could actually see the steps! It was like I was an iron bolt being drawn toward a giant magnate."

"You did investigate it?" Mrs McTavish wondered.

"Yes. And this is where my story becomes revelatory macabre. I found three bodies down there. One was old and skeletal, clearly my ancestor – Angus 'Black Fist' McLoughlan, but the other two had died within the passed two years. They were fresher looking, wearing modern clothes and foot wear, and must have died of starvation because their limbs looked as thin as sticks."

Ellen McTavish gasped and spoke. "I remember a young man came in here about nine months ago asking about this place you've been telling us about. I remember him because I didn't know what 'archaeologist' meant and I had to ask my husband. Reverend Caine took him away and we never saw him again. He never came back but I didn't think anything of it because the Reverend told us the man had made a mistake coming here and had driven away."

"Big mistake, coming here," said Stephanie dryly.

"Think hard Mrs McTavish: did you see an older man come into the pub about a year before that, maybe telling people that his name was Ashcroft, like mine?"

The landlady screwed up her rosy-cheeked face with concentration... then opened her eyes. "No," she said, "I'm sorry. I just can't remember. Maybe my husband saw him. I can't remember, Professor."

"It's alright," he replied.

"No, it's not!" cried Stephanie. "You're trying to say that a priest locked up these poor souls in a hole in the ground and left them to die!"

"Yes," said her father.

"That he would have done the same to you, then killed me?"

"Most likely."

"Over a stupid *book*?"

"Reverend Caine was driven by other forces."

"This is terrible!" cried Ellen McTavish. "We'll have to call the police."

"Tomorrow. First thing."

"Deary me! Nothing like this has ever happened in Ravencliff before."

"Oh, I think stranger things have happened here," said the Professor. "It has a long history."

The irony of this did not escape Stephanie. "Well, I hope the damn thing was worth risking our lives for."

"Maybe."

He was being deliberately evasive, and knew it was not the answer she wanted, but for now he was satisfied with his invention. It had held up like a precise history discovered in an un-raided tomb; and the more complex version that he had concocted for the police did not mention the *Necronomicon*, but they may yet find it a palatable investigation. Like a larger burial place full of golden artefacts eclipsing the due process of documentation. Yet he didn't know the science of their procedures, he couldn't forecast their reactions. It was difficult to be realistic and easy to be over-confident if you had just cheated death - and were sitting in front of a warm fire with half a bar of chocolate and a glass of Scotch. He watched his daughter yawn. She watched him do the same; each smiled. They had been on the road for several hours before their hair-raising arrival and it was after three o'clock in the morning.

"I need sleep," he said. "It's way passed my bed-time, and probably passed Stephanie's as well."

"That's agreed," she said. "Ellen, do you have beds for us tonight?"

"Aye, we've got a nice guest room. Follow me."

The Professor finished his chocolate as the landlady led them through the bar counter, into a hallway then past a sitting room. The private features of the inn were small and full of old timber. The Professor felt as though he and his daughter had been miniaturised and were exploring an antique doll's house. Mrs McTavish led them up a rickety set of stairs and showed them the bathroom. Their bedroom was a simple affair at the end of the corridor. It had a tiny window and thick walls, and two beds with starched sheets.

Initially Stephanie didn't like the feel of the bed linen. She switched off the light, got into bed, and told her father it was like trying to sleep in a paper envelope. She closed her eyes and listened to the night outside. The wind blew in intermittent gusts, and the rain smattered on the window. Soon she felt comfortable and safe; sealed up like a changeling butterfly in a cocoon. She asked her Dad, in a tired voice: "Is it a magic book?"

"Yes," he replied.

"Is it cursed?"

"No."

"Well that's alright then," Stephanie decided. She fell asleep.

*   *   *

The Professor rose early the following morning, Monday 23rd June, and the weather was fine. Ravencliff was basking under the rising sun in an azure sky. He had chosen to phone the AA *before* the police but first he would eat whatever kind of breakfast he could get. He had showered by half passed seven and dressed in the same slightly moist trousers, shirt, and sweater he had worn last night. He would ask for access to Caine's rectory so they could recover their suitcases. They both needed fresh clothes, and Stephanie particularly wanted her sketch-pad and her pencils.

Over kippers and eggs, and mugs of strong coffee, the Professor told his daughter that the car was too damaged to drive. She looked out at the street, at the brightness through the window, and actually smiled. She resigned herself to a few more days without rancour. Stephen Ashcroft argued a price with Mr McTavish for a further three days room-and-board, and then got on his mobile cell phone to the nearest AA office, which was in Ullapool. He was surprised to have a signal. Half an hour later they phoned back:

"I'm afraid you were right, Professor, your car will have to be towed," said a polite young Scotsman. "The nearest garage that can repair the damage you've described is called 'McEnzie MG Classics', in Glasgow. I suggest you claim the value of the bill with your insurance company."

"How soon can you get a truck here?"

"We can have a tow-truck with you by early this afternoon, at about two. Our driver will give you the number of McEnzie's before he takes it."

"How much?"

"Nothing for the tow. According to my computer here you have full coverage. In the matter of repair costs, you must deal with them yourself, separately... they could be steep."

"Fine. The car is stranded in a car park at the top of the cliff. I'll be waiting in the public house in the village down at the bottom of a steep hill on the left. Get your driver to call this number when he arrives." He quoted his mobile number.

"Aye, got it. And if you can't get to Glasgow when it's mended, we can deliver it back to you."

"That's a terrific service."

"I hope you have better luck when you're next behind the wheel."

Slick young lad, thought the Professor.

He switched off the receiver then dialled Directory Inquiries. He was put through to the digital switch-board of Glasgow police   station.

"North West Highland's Police, how may I assist you?"

"Yes..." He took a deep breath. "I need to speak to a detective."

"What is it regarding?"

"I have to report an unmarked grave, an accidental death, and two murders."

"Could you give me your name and location then a number so we can contact you?" He did. "Thank you, please wait..."

He waited for thirty seconds then heard a confident and unexpectedly Welsh voice. "I'm Inspector Alquin Wilkey."

"I'm pleased to be talking to you."

"That's Alc-win –wil-key, understand? I won't be interviewing you in person but I will be selecting the investigating team. If, indeed, there is anything to invest-I-gate. OK?"

"Yes, Inspector."

"Where were these bodies found?" He answered.

"Did you see these deaths personally?" He described Raul Caine.

"Did he try to hurt you first?"

Stephen Ashcroft steeled himself grimly. The questioning had already begun.

A few minutes later the policeman called back: "DCI Greenwood has been assigned to the case. A full team has been dispatched and will be with you in under two hours."

"That's excellent."

"In the meantime don't leave Ravencliff."

"I won't."

CHAPTER – 8

"Re.inforce.ment"

"Sunset," said Thorn. He was looking out of the caravan window. "At last!"

"We can't leave, yet," said Lillith. "Only when the hour is late, and full of blackness."

The abandoned trailer smelt like a wet cardboard box although the sun was warm. The light was bathing their torn seats and the old folding table with bright hues of orange and red. "It looks like blood. I'm so hungry!"

"We will harvest later. Be patient and let time stretch along with you for a little longer."

"I'm so bored."

"How can you be apathetic after what I've showed you?"

"Because I can't do any of it!"

"I'll perform them again. Close the light."

He stretched through the tiny swirling dust particles and shut the curtains, lithely, his arm musculature like the armour plate of a self-propelled gun.

"We have five abilities, and our eyes change colour when each are used. Red, blue, green, yellow, and purple."

"Tell me again, why do they glow?"

"Because our optic nerves are connected to the neural nets of our 'conjuration drive' with filaments that glow when the eyes transmit an attack or defensive action. We have an allocated brain that is far along the time-lines of common evolution. The first are faculties of sight, visual abilities called 'ultra sight' and 'infra ranging'." Her eyes turned inward. Her expression drifted, became lost.

"How do they work? Go on!"

"Even with no moon we can interpret shapes around us in shades of black and white because some objects absorb different amounts of ultra violet and some reflect it." Her eyes opened and had the appearance a rich purple pigment painted over light bulbs. "This is 'ultra sight'. Do you see?"

"Yes - and I want to do it too."

"So now you try."

Thorn's eyelids creased together with concentration, but a moment later he said: "I can't do it. It's hopeless!"

"Attempting to change how your eyes perceive the world won't work. They are just projectors. Try to feel the optic fibre going back into your head, like loading a cannon. Roll an invented ball backwards until it rests against the black powder of your conjuration drive, against the source. Can you feel the dangling bits?"

"Sort of…yes!"

"These are neural pathways connecting your conjuration drive together. They are also triggers fired by extrasensory guesses called 'Reaching'."

"My eyes feel odd."

"Platch! Look around you now, Thorn, but just peep; it's very bright."

"Black and white," he exclaimed, his eyes widening with shock. "No, white and white. White and white sun-glasses! Help me!"

"Calm down, Thorn, 'Reach' to undo it…"

"Oh it's gone. That was really cool."

"Maybe we ought to wait before we do the others."

"No way, do them now!"

"So be it. At the other end of our visual spectrum is an extension called 'infra ranging'. With this we interpret objects according to the amount of heat they radiate. Our eyes see the scene, infrared is detected through our 'imagination drive', where you visualise pictures, decoded in the conjuration drive and sent back to the imager with the distance to the target broadcast by your Reacher Core. Your eyes will exhibit a red incandescence - but you need not try it now. You just select the trigger on the opposite side. It's a throwback. In the long past we were demon soldiers of the Zaxxon."

"What happened?"

"In an Age when the church was strong, we were the Succubus and the Incubus. We moved in pairs like a witch and a familiar except that our familiars were each other. We were covert revolutionaries, assassins, until the Lower Planes realised that the church was doing more damage quite by itself then we ever could, even as an army. So they cancelled our re-incarnation tickets."

"Until now."

"Yes. For returning the *Necronomicon*."

"I see…let's continue. What about attack and defence?"

"Which?"

"You decide."

"These two take a lot of physical and cerebral energy, the 'air spike' and 're-collection'. We can kill with a thought and we can strip a man of his entire memory, but even after meat and sleep we can only do either once every twenty two to twenty four hours."

"And here's me thinking you are invincible!"

"By the time I've finished explaining our capabilities you may think so again."

"Just don't try them on me, OK?"

She sensed his worry over memory. "You need not worry about that anymore. It's the old Rupert that couldn't remember, the rest of you is infallible and photographic."

"Go on…"

"The triggers are located on opposite ends of your conjuration drive, also, second to the left and second to the right. When 're-collecting' you hypnotize your crop at close range and picture yourself reaching into his fore brain. Your eyes will glow bright green as you extract his experiences in what is known as a block of 'memory-cards' and merge them with your own brain, which has six hundred times the capacity of a mortal."

"What about the killing thought?"

"The 'air-spike' is when you lock your vision with the meat and draw strength from your whole body, like drawing back a bow string, from your toe tips to the top of your head, while your eyes shine blue. Suck from your every limb and muscle until you have a needle of bright cold fire in your conjuration drive, and then stick it into his head. It is invisible; imagination made solid. Your hand won't even move but the energy will dissipate in his brain like compressed air and cause a fatal embolism."

"Cool!"

"...Merely fragments of extra brain tissue."

"What about X-ray vision? Like seeing through walls and clothes?"

"Don't be silly, Thorn, that's impossible. There is one altered state that combines both defence and attack. The trigger is in the centre of your conjuration drive and it is called a 'bestial deflector body', or just a 'feeder'. We change into the beasts we were below. Feel like you've done it before..."

He looked at the fiction Lillith was broadcasting into his imagination drive. Pictures of running through a forest after a woman on a horse, chasing her low to the ground, her white dress fluttering and so very clean, faster and faster with twigs, branches, whipping his face painlessly, and then the last leap, teeth first.

"Like becoming a were-wolf?"

"More. I've known a few were-wolves in my time. Their hearing is keen and their eyes are sharp, but we are much stronger and more in control than they are. Our eyes shine yellow like sulphur with claws like knives and teeth like a shark's that can taste blood in the water ten miles distant. We can multi-task infra and ultra-sight simultaneously and become ravenous for killing with the strength of twenty men. We can lope on all fours like a leopard and our metabolism is so fast it can heal even the mortal wound of a sword within a moment, and without a scar, as though it had never been. We are terrible. Wonderful."

"Both."

"That's true. Now, wake-up!"

"What?" He opened his eyes groggily.

"Didn't you know you were sleeping?"

"No." He saw it was twenty passed nine on his watch. "What happened to the time?"

"I tweaked your perception of it because you were bored. Are you ready to harvest?"

"Let's do it!" He stood up feeling strong and unclasped his watch and slipped it into a pocket.

"Engage telepathy inter-lace!"

Inter-lace linked, Thorn thought excitedly.

Change to feeder body.

He pulled off his army books and stepped out of the trailer experiencing the mutual ecstasy of their metamorphosis. They made incomprehensible empathic noises of pleasure and dropped onto the wet grass. Their sinews stretched and their jawbones jutted out, dislocated, with huge teeth, and re-formed. The night was filled with the grey shapes of other caravans looming around them like pale monoliths. There was only a sliver of moon. Some windows were ablaze with small light bulbs and others were unlit except for the heat of bodies cocooned in them within illusions of safety. The demons' muscles thickened and their bones braced up with a sound like twigs crackling underfoot. They moved off.

On the outside of the field they found a caravan coloured with the rolling clashing heat of two men having sex. The demons swiftly closed their distance to the target and broke into it quietly, and so quickly that the men had no time to scream. They were dead before they could even begin to understand what manner of creature was killing them. The demons fed, then rutted amongst the soaked, coppery smelling sheets. Their bodies were physically normal when they dried off after showering, and then they searched the caravan for cash and clothing. They found £90 and different sizes of similar clothes that fitted them both: khaki combat trousers, sweatshirts and leather jackets.

They also found an AA Road Atlas of Great Britain.

Lillith liked to think of it as an Omen, an 'indicator'. That the map had been placed there in a destiny-line engineered by the Lower Planes. She flipped through the book recalling a dream she had experienced three times. She had seen a granite cliff featuring two white lobster claws painted on the face of it like a map in itself. Huge outlines, composed of the guano of ravens nesting amongst outcroppings and crevasses, black feathers ruffled by chill digging winds. She scrutinised the survey of a northern section of Scotland in the atlas. West of a town called Ullapool was an unnamed bay made of two headlands that jutted out into the sea like lobster claws. She recognised them immediately. Her Reacher verified it like the muzzle flash of match-lock musket. The name of it appeared in her mind like it was engraved on the edge of a sword.

"Look here, Thorn, this is it!" Lillith passed him the atlas. "Ravencliff!"

On indicating the place with a fingertip, he stared hard at where she was pointing. There was no name. It looked like any other random chunk of rocks on that coastline.

"It's unnamed," he said. "There's almost no chance at all that a place would be unidentified in this map." He considered the state of her sanity, briefly, and then completely rejected the question.

Thank you for your faith, dear Thorn. She took back the atlas. "We are going to move north as rapidly as possible."

"Neither of us can drive."

"I can 're-collect' a lifetime's driving experience." She opened up the map on the grid square of central Norfolk. She looked at it until it was recorded, for about three seconds. "Platch! We want the East Deerham road. Take that satchel and empty it. Put a couple of kitchen knives in it."

"What for? My finger-nails are twice as sharp and ten times stronger."

"- Only in your bestial state. Put them in."

Thorn rifled the kitchen cupboards and found two bread knives. He dropped them into the bag with his eyes picking through the rest of the detritus in the drawers. "Hey, Lillith. I've found a tiny little compass!"

"We don't need a compass, tiny or huge. I've got one already." She tapped her forehead with a fingertip, and smiled and chuckled. "Put the map in the bag as well; I'll learn the rest later. It's nearly eleven pm so let's go or we'll be too late to catch a mount."

They made off for the edge of the campsite, walking passed the caravan containing the still warm remnants of their feeding. The Succubus thought that she recognised some of the constellations glittering above from a previous life. The stars seemed to have moved; she didn't know the science of it. They climbed over a gate and progressed breathing easily across a field of plump dry wheat. The tall stalks brushed their legs like whispers in closed a museum.

If we leave tracks they'll know where we went.
Don't fear the law, Thorn. They have less than nothing.

When the police examined the wounds on the two dead men they would assume that the murder weapons were handfuls of knives, but would not find even a fragment of metal. The test results of blood samples taken at the scene would show DNA traces of a bat, a dog, and 25% of it totally unknown. Forensic dentists measuring the bite radius and teeth shape from castes of the wounds would conclude that they were looking for two strong people, probably both men, and both with hideous facial deformities. They did have less than nothing: confusion. Even after making the connection between the cannibalism at the school and the murders at the campsite, they still had no chance of understanding what had really happened.

"Lie down here, Thorn. In the road. Act dead."
"Where are we?"
"Half a kilometre from the slip road onto the A47. This lane is north."
"I dunno which way is north, but everybody drives on the left."
"Fine. Put yourself there, divergent with the way."
He lay down on the asphalt feeling like a fresh fish on ice at a supermarket counter. "What if I get run over?"
"You won't. We need one driver, only; you stop his mount and I'll re-collect him."

"You're sure this will work?"

"I will protect you with my Reacher Core. Get you out of the path of unsuitable vehicles. Or at least I'll try to."

"Try to?!"

"It's not an exact discipline. Put your feet across the centre line... splay out. That's it! Now I will hide in this hedgerow." She crossed the road and found a ditch. She jumped down into it.

Employ verbal silence.

Five minutes passed. Like they were standing still on an ice rink in flat shoes. The Incubus was getting grit in his hair and the Succubus was getting her clothes caught on spikes of hawthorn.

Something's coming.

Thorn couldn't see or hear anything coming, but he sensed her muster power like the rising outburst of an express train as it growled out of a station. He raised his head and saw two headlights swinging down to the flat of the road from low on the horizon. His vulnerability rose with the engine noise. A car was coming over the brow of a hill not fifty yards from his position and he was blinded by bright lights. He felt like a target, hadn't felt so hunted since before Lillith in some bleached memory of cigarettes and spit.

? ? ? ?
Get out of the road Thorn, it's a family of children!

He scrambled to his feet without looking at the oncoming car - as if at any second it might knock him down. He leapt towards the hedgerow and unexpectedly fell into a ditch with Lillith in a tangle of limbs. It was an executive car. It drew level with their hiding place and slowed down to a crawl to allow the passengers a look for the bizarre person who had been running about in the road. There was a menacing pause, then the car moved on and Thorn felt like laughing.

He leaned over the edge of the ditch on his elbows and watched the brake-lights disappear.

I want to buy you some flowers, Lillith, he thought.
What flowers?
I dunno… red roses, maybe.
Just get out of this trench and back on the road, you dunderhead, you nincompoop!
OK, relax! He lay in the pose he had been arranged in before. *Look, I love you Lillith, and if you don't want a little romance from me maybe I should let the next car run over me for real.*
Fine, I apologise, she thought. *Stay down.*
Something else is coming.

He had more warning. The engine noise was louder, and the vehicle was casting more intense light above the road. It came grumbling over the brow of the hill and it was gigantic. It was so wide it took up both lanes of traffic. His slitted his eyelids against the blinding glare of three large round headlamps: *This thing's got three lights! What is it?*
I don't know, Thorn. Just get out of the way!

He stood up, frozen in the middle of the road like a mesmerised rabbit about to be shot. The single light bearing down on him from his left side was travelling faster now, breaking away from the other two. The Succubus scrambled out of the ditch and ran at Thorn and knocked him off his feet onto the other side of the road. A motorcycle drove passed them, orange lights flashing to indicate the rider's return to the left hand lane, and that was followed by a large white van. Both thundered passed and left a gush of exhaust fumes that quickly faded.

That was close, Thorn thought. *You saved me!* He was trembling; in shock.
Please see it as a romantic gesture. Now let's get back to the plan.
I don't know if I'm up for it anymore.
You want me to do it? Be brave, my Incubus!

ZAXXON

He took some deep breaths. And then he thought: *it's a test isn't it?*
Yes. Of gallantry in the Material Plane.
Alright. I'll do it.
Third time lucky, eh? She crossed over the road to re-conceal herself in the ditch.
He stretched out extravagantly back on the asphalt. *You told me there was no such thing as luck.*
I'm trying to make you feel your strength. You can't forget who you are, but you need to try to understand <u>what</u> you are. After that you will fear nothing. Can you hear it?
What? He heard the sound of a small engine in the distance, quiet on the night wind. *I hear it!*
Tell me your Reach of it? The car was getting louder.
What d' you mean reach? He lifted his head and saw the dark sky over the top of the hill was becoming grey on paler grey.
What do you guess - Reach - about the car?

Brightening beams of lamplight were moving relentlessly down to the road surface. He made an extrasensory guess and felt movement in a strip of his brain around, and above, the nape of his neck.

One middle-aged driver, he thought quickly. He felt the back of his brain twitch again: *alone, a reformed alcoholic but sober behind the wheel. No immediate family.*
Excellent, Lillith thought. *Estimation of accuracy 85%. What is the colour of the car?*
The headlights swung over the hill and suddenly blazed into his eyes. He lowered his head. *Dark green,* he thought, visually dazzled.
Good. Stay down.

The car was rolling towards him at speed. He assessed he wouldn't have to play dead anymore, soon he would actually <u>be</u> dead, because it seemed unstoppable, approaching where he lay with the implacability of a falling meteorite. He had to battle the urge to jump out of its path, stared up at the sky, and gritted his teeth. The car finally pulled up with the subdued chattering noise of anti-lock brakes. His heart was pounding as though it had swelled to the size of his entire ribcage. It stopped under one metre from Thorn's head. He sat up feeling exhilarated with adrenaline.

The car was the latest Peugeot, a small yet powerful diesel hatch-back. Thorn's last Reach had been correct: it was British Racing Green. The door opened and an old man staggered out into the road wearing a natty tweed suit. He had a crown of grey hair around his liver-spotted bald patch, and he was alone - Thorn had been right about that too. The old man had the red face of a drinker, where the Incubus's extra-sensory performance collapsed, because the old man was quite drunk. Many times over the legal limit. Lillith crossed the road swiftly and silently like her shoes weren't even touching the ground. The old man swayed and burped.

This guy's wasted! thought Thorn. *You said my guesses were excellent!*
I said they were 15% inaccurate, she replied.
So you let this old bastard drive up to me, in a two tonne vehicle in the middle of the night, and you knew he was drunk?
That was my Reach. That he was drunk was half of it: the other half was that he definitely would not have hit you.
Oh. So I wasn't in any danger?
None. Now clip the inter-lace. I am re-collecting him.

The Succubus seized the drunkard by the lapels of his jacket. His terrified expression was lit by the green shining power in her eyes.

"What's this happening?" he asked Thorn, desperately, "this is impossible!"
"Look," insisted Lillith, "look at me!" She pulled his face closer.

Her eyelids opened wide to capture his full attention. He shuddered and went limp in her arms as she raped his mind. His pupils dilated as if to the size of archery targets. The old sop moaned, and dribbled. His memory-cards started to come up like transparent postage stamps being sucked up by a vacuum cleaner, and were sorted and logged by the Succubus almost in real-time. She looked amused. Blood ran from his ears before she let him go and he stumbled backwards against the bonnet of the Peugeot making mindless baby noises. The green light in her eyes faded.

Re-tying the inter-lace.
Is that it? asked Thorn.
Yes. Throw him in the ditch.
What's so funny?
Old Arthur, well, he was a very naughty boy. When he wasn't drinking cheap vodka he was giving his little todd-end a bit of a tickle with a porno disc collection the size of a hot air balloon; pun intended. Actually, he's given me some choice sexy ideas…
Really? Let's do them now! In the ditch: "Right now!!"
Keep your verbals down, Thorn. We're running out of time. She picked up Arthur by his legs and started to pull him towards the ditch. *Give me a hand with this.*

Thorn took him by his left elbow, and together they dragged the body across the Tarmac and flopped him unceremoniously into the hawthorn. The demons climbed into the car, and Thorn hid the satchel of knives under his seat.

What will become of him? he wondered.
I suppose they'll put him into an old people's home. He had a wife once you know.

Infantile gurgles were being uttered from the hidden tangled bottom of the ditch.

Did he? It seems he fell a long way.
He was an international rally driver, until he had an accident. He came off the track after a drink and ploughed into a group of spectators.

The engine caught immediately when the Succubus twisted the key in the ignition. She put the Peugeot into first gear and moved off at low revs as if she had been driving for thirty years. She picked up speed and made for the motorway.

They lived in Scotland, the Succubus thought.
Who?
His wife's family. The day he asked for her father's blessing, to marry her, he drove all the way there at over one hundred miles per hour.

"Then let's drive all the way there at a hundred and ten!" cried Thorn.

"Platch!" exclaimed Lillith.

She manoeuvred their car onto the motorway, then into the fast lane, and accelerated.

CHAPTER – 9

"Invest-I-gate"

Chief Inspector Giles Greenwood brought with him a coroner's van and three car-load's of men. There was a photographer, crime scene investigators, a mobile forensics team, a few uniformed officers, and an enthusiastic young DC named Garrick who followed Greenwood around with the devotion of a blood-hound puppy and recorded everything anyone said in a spiral bound notebook.

The only house in the village with enough space to set up an HQ was the rectory of the dead priest; a cold sterile place marred with a bachelor's sour smell, on the far side of the village. Once Greenwood's entourage and equipment were installed on the ground floor, the hole in the ground was cordoned off to protect it from nosy villagers. The two detectives spent some time at the site, then they went for a pub lunch.

Mr McTavish was impressed by both men. Greenwood was about forty-five, and tall, with large hands and an intense gaze. His smooth baritone accent was as confident as his air of authority, intrinsic and unaffected, built over many years in the Force. His assistant, DC Garrick, was at least ten years younger and thinner and better dressed. He wore a three-piece suit the high quality of which the landlord hadn't seen for many years, except on television. An expensive ball-point pen hovered over a note book in his right hand. His boss held an old walnut pipe and puffed on it contentedly. Pleasant smelling smoke drifted across the table.

   "What can you tell us about the hole in the ground on the edge of the cliff, Mr McTavish?"
Garrick licked the tip of his pen and started writing.
   "Nay much. Some locals hereabouts call it the 'crypt on the spit'. There is a professor staying here at the moment, with his daughter, and they seem to know more about it than anyone else in the village and they don't even live here."

"What are their names?"
"Professor Stephen Ashcroft, and Stephanie Ashcroft."

The senior detective raised an eyebrow at his assistant, who quickly flipped back through his notes and came across the relevant entry. He nodded. Greenwood turned his gaze back to the landlord.

"Look, am I in trouble or something?" asked McTavish.
"Why? What have you done now?"
Garrick chuckled. The landlord looked distressed.
"It's alright, Mr McTavish. I'm just having a joke."
"Well, it's nay funny."
"Can you tell us where the two Ashcrofts came from; and when they arrived?"
McTavish leaned forward, and peered at him. "You'll have to speak up!"
"Where did the Ashcrofts come from? And what time did they arrive?"
"They came in last night from London." Garrick licked the tip of his ballpoint and continued writing. "They arrived late, at about five past eleven. The Professor spoke to Reverend Caine in the bar and they left for the crypt at about ten to midnight. The Professor took maybe two and a half hours to come back and my wife stayed up especially to keep his daughter company, till past three o'clock in the morning!"
"And the Reverend never came back?" Greenwood sucked on his pipe stem until the bowl was burning evenly. The tobacco had a nice grandfatherly smell like furniture polish and rosehips.
"That's correct."
"Do you know *when* this underground room was constructed; and its purpose?"
"Pardon?"
Greenwood repeated his questions louder.
"Ah! According to legend the crypt was built near two hundred years ago by a man that wanted to conduct some kind of dangerous experiment. It's poppycock. He asked to be sealed up in fear of releasing 'demons' into the world, or some such nonsense."

"So the nature of the experiment was, what? ...occult?"

The landlord said: "Aye."

"Occult," muttered Garrick. "Good!" He jotted it down and smiled around the table. The Chief Inspector shot him a withering glance and his grin disappeared like a soft toy falling down a well.

"Do you happen to know the name of the man that arranged the experiment?"

"Aye. My wife overheard them talking. His name was Angus McLoughlan Ashcroft, the Professor's ancestor."

"Thank you, very much! Do you know where the professor is?"

"His daughter's gone out to draw a picture. He went out to see her, just before you arrived."

"Would you like to be present while we talk to your wife?"

The landlord stood. "For certain."

"Could you fetch her?"

"Aye." He set off to the counter.

"And bring us a couple of massive drams of whiskey!" cried the DC.

"How about *Three Bells*?"

His boss glowered at his subordinate. "He was just having a joke, Mr McTavish."

"Pardon?"

"- MAKE THAT TWO TONIC WATERS!"

"There's nay need to shout, Chief Inspector. I'm not deaf, I was just having a joke."

*   *   *

It was a beautiful day. Stephanie was sitting on a rock on a footpath that was covered with coarse grasses. The path meandered up the left hand spur on a much more gradual slope than the cliffs on the opposite side. Curlews and black-headed gulls and terns squawked and glided in wide circles in the hazy blue sky. An on-shore breeze tousled Stephanie's curly hair as she paused to admire her drawing.

Ever since childhood she had occasionally enjoyed sketching. Age eight, whilst spending a couple of weeks in

Cornwall, her mother had given her a pad of 30gm cartridge paper and a set of Rowney pencils. She liked to draw the places they visited every summer, and always packed similar tools in her luggage. It had become a traditional part of a holiday and it wouldn't be the same if she didn't. She had collected all the pictures (she kept ten pads of them in her wardrobe!) and they were a visual record of her improving skill over the years that were so much nicer than photographs or commercial post cards. She was a stickler for detail; a style reflected in her choice of jewellery, both personal and that which she sold in her shop.

She lifted the pad, compared it to the vista of the village below. It was a beautiful day and a stunning view for a drawing. There was the quay - at least two hundred feet away - with all its colourful miniature aspects, an organised chaos of tiny coils of rope and baskets and palettes of shiny fish. Stick-men were preparing boats for sea that looked like bathtub toys. The harbour walls curved in a decisive little hug. The white-washed houses looked as tiny as a child's building blocks but they had an essence of strength, a determination to keep their occupants safe. They had survived floods and storms and lightning for many hundreds of years passed, and would still to come.

The drawing had so far taken her an hour. Equipped with only Ellen McTavish's 2B and HB pencils Stephanie began to sketch the shadows around the houses. She was really enjoying herself and would have liked to share it with someone. Lost in the softer pencil she was surprised when her father shouted her name, and pleased to see him coming up the path with an old book tucked under his arm, which could be only *that* book, the *Necronomicon*. Although her Dad was a stubborn and cuddly bear of man, whom she loved very much, she believed he had been hare-brained in the book's acquisition, and that he may soon not be as reliable as he used to be because of it. He placed it on the grass and sat beside her. She didn't want to bring up the subject of the *Necronomicon* so she asked him if he had chocolate, her mouth salivating.

"No, I'm sorry, I'm out," he said. "And the inn's dry as well. I was hoping that you had some!"

"None. Maybe there's a grocers. I could eat a whole *Diarybox* in two minutes!"

"Been there, done that."

She handed him the sketch. "What do you make of this?" The wind was getting stronger. Out to sea the waves were flecked with white caps. It caught the pages of Ellen's McTavish's drawing pad and threatened to send it fluttering out of his grasp. "Be careful Dad!"

"There's great feeling in it," he declared. "But this perspective here, of the houses nearest the harbour, it's out of joint." She watched him indicate this with his finger.

"They are a bit askew," she admitted, "but if you weren't actually sitting here looking at it you wouldn't notice."

"True. It's a grand effort."

"You've brought that book with you, haven't you, the one from the tomb?"

"Do you want to look at it?"

"I suppose so. Yes."

He handed it to her and she rested it on her lap and found it was as heavy as it appeared to be. She touched the crusty human leather. Ran her fingertips over its Braille of skulls and demon heads and gargoyles, and grimaced at its dusty black-board texture.

"It's horrible!" she exclaimed. She opened it and noticed in herself an unintentional and surprising flick of her tongue over her lips. The parchment inside was softer and more pliant than she had expected. Every gilt edged page was covered in writing the like of which she had never before seen, a strange array of wedges and slashes. "How old is it?"

"Eleven hundred years."

"What is this writing?"

"It's called cuneiform, read from right to left, the first known form of writing. Sumerian cuneiform is well over three thousand years older than the book itself, and it's supposed to be my speciality. Unfortunately it's been encrypted with some kind of code and I can't crack it."

She handed it back to him. "Are you going to give it to the Museum?"

"No. I think I'll keep it for a while. At least until I've translated it. I need to know: would you keep it a secret with me?"

"From the police?"

"Yes. They may take it. It would be obvious the other two men who made that place into a grave had also been after it, which would draw attention to it. They have their own museums here, you know. The book is *mine,* yet the research that proves my rightful claim to it via inheritance was so painstaking and took so very long, I don't think I could ever get it together in one document."

"Is it valuable?"

"I don't think an average antiquarian book dealer would offer more than a hundred quid for it without authentication. Carbon Dating, that's easy, but a note of providence... well that would take a long time as well, and
beggar belief."

"What's the top end?"

"To someone that 'knows' it's worth an awful lot of money. Millions. But that doesn't interest me, and it wouldn't interest anyone with enough money to buy it, *if they knew* what it is."

"Dad, I think you should sell it, because it's useless. It can't raise the dead. I don't believe it was wrote by a monk possessed by Beelzebub, or that it has supernatural powers. Of course it hasn't. It's just an old book full of nonsense."

"I can't sell it."

"Well don't go get all obsessive about it, OK?"

"Alright. Will you keep the secret?"

"From the police? What would I need to say?"

"If they don't ask you about it directly, you won't be lying. Just say you accompanied me here for a holiday and to see where our ancestor is buried."

"I'll follow that," she decided.

"Bless you, daughter!"

Stephanie observed her father deflating. He expressed his relief with a hearty kiss on her cheek. As far as she was concerned it was a minor deceit to give him much needed peace of mind.

She opened her sketch-pad. "Let's just sit here quietly for a while. OK?"

He agreed. He tucked the grimoire under his arm. It was bulky, and felt safe there in its usual place, as reassuring in its potency as a powerful battery. He looked across at Stephanie's drawing and wondered about his own horizon, his own future. How many people had died because of the *Necronomicon*? Even without a working translation he had already had his life saved by its magics.

He had witnessed it kill and he wanted to immerse himself in that reality, perhaps with a reckless lack of fear for his own safety. He wanted to harness its power, and couldn't conceive it may kill him also. Coercing his daughter into lying to the police was an act he never could have foreseen, even last week, but maybe the book was altering him. It was his property, all his, the *Necronomicon*, the most important recovery in the history of the occult.

*   *   *

"I saw the younger man," said Mrs McTavish, "but it was ages ago. He told me he was an archaeologist interested in the ruins of the old church. He called himself Doctor Ashcroft."
    "How old was he?"
    "About thirty."
    "What happened?"

She watched DC Garrick lick the ball-point of his pen.

"Well, this local man named John Duggon, he overheard us talking and brought Reverend Caine back to the inn. They left together at sunset and the doctor didn't come back."

"Were you not suspicious?"

"Reverend Caine told me he had made a mistake and left."

"I was, a wee bit suspicious," said her husband. "An older man in his late forties came in to the pub about seven months before the archaeologist and he said his name was Ashcroft aswell. The priest took him away and he didn't return either."

"So this professor also claims to be an Ashcroft?"

"He's the only the true Ashcroft of all of them," exclaimed the landlady eagerly. "I know that because I saw him show Reverend Caine his passport before they left together, at about midnight."

"And this time it was the priest that didn't come back?"

"Aye."

Garrick lowered his notebook and voiced a mutual question. "So, what were they all after?"

"I think his daughter Stephanie doesn't know either," said Ellen McTavish, "but she wants to."

A short round man entered the bar, wearing a dark brown suit. He pushed through the smoke like an air ship thrusting through light clouds. The smoking ban had not reached this place. He came up to Greenwood's side of the table and leaned into his ear. Ellen McTavish had never heard anything overly loud in her life and she had sharp ears for her age. She overheard their brief and whispered conversation. In spite of the noise of the socialising locals she learned that an empty jam jar containing severed fingers had been found in Caine's rectory and she felt she should speak of it.

"Thank you, Cobb," said DCI Greenwood. "Now go and push those lab boys a wee bit harder."

Mrs McTavish watched the rounded Cobb with her eyes until he was out of the room, then said: "Excuse me, Inspector, but I overheard what that man said to you about the fingers, and I think I can shed some light on it."

"Please do," invited the policeman.

He nodded to Garrick, who turned over a page of his notebook, and suddenly the landlady didn't want to talk about it anymore. She was still terrified of the priest. Garrick licked the tip of his pen again and she wondered whether or not the habit was leaving ink smudges on his tongue.

"Why don't you use a tape recorder instead of that pen?" she asked him, distractedly.

"Cassettes can be doctored, Mrs McTavish. This kind of statement is always taken on paper."

"Please continue what you were saying," asked Greenwood, "about the fingers?" He studied her face perceptively, and then nodded. "I can assure you, he is quite dead."

"Well, alright then...there have been these rumours going around that Reverend Caine was being horrible to drunks. Some say he cut fingers off at least three of these poor souls, and now I know it is a dreadful fact. John Duggon, the man I was telling you about, has got only the little finger and index finger remaining on his left hand and he hasn't got a right hand at all. He can hardly hold a glass!"

"How did he explain it?"

"Fishing accidents," said her husband.

"Duggon will **be** coming in here earlier tonight," she explained. "The other men who were victimised have left the village since, and who can blame them?"

"No one," the Inspector intoned heavily. "It seems our Right Reverend Caine was a psychopath."

Nothing new but a collection of oriental knives was found during a second search of Caine's rectory. The Ashcroft's luggage remained missing and they were informed of this. Duggon re-iterated most of what the Inspector already knew about the crypt. It had been built to exacting specifications one hundred and sixty seven years ago and guarding it had been the Caine family's responsibility for many ancestors. It seemed the last of their line had a personal vendetta against anyone bearing the 'Ashcroft' name.

As a man of the cloth Raul Caine might have detested that his secret had links to the Black Arts, a rotten apple that fell so far from his tree; or vengeance for having no son of his own, or it was because of the inconvenience caused to his family down the generations. For whatever reasons: motives to kill. The Ashcrofts staying in Ravencliff now were lucky to be alive. He would interview them tomorrow. Duggon needed a dram of whisky before Greenwood could wheedle out more of the story.

"We were all terrified of Caine, ye know," Duggon began. "He cut two fingers and a thumb from this hand," he raised his glass, "and cut off my whole right hand."

"We know. We found the remains in a glass jar in Caine's bathroom."

"He also took bits off other men that drank a wee bit too much, spitting Bible quotes while he went about it."

"Why not call the police?"

"Because the man had... *presence*. I'm just a simple fisherman, he was educated. There was nay law in this village but him, and all feared him. It was a mass terror, stronger than curiosity."

"Stronger than the curiosity to discover what was hidden in the underground chamber?"

"Aye."

The books and other occult paraphernalia of the 'Black Fist's' experiment should still have been somewhere in the tomb when Greenwood's men had arrived at the scene, yet they had found nothing. Presumably this stuff was worth quite a lot of money. It was concluded that Caine didn't take it. Maybe the Professor got his hands on it, but most likely the tomb had been pillaged decades ago. For one certainty, at least, the two men now lying on a mortuary slab in Glasgow had been treasure hunters. Duggon spoke about the worst of his injuries. One afternoon he had tried to lever up the cover himself, because the spoils would have been his ticket out of Ravencliff, but the priest had caught him. Never mind that the old drunk hadn't the strength to do it, the priest had cut off his right hand anyway.

"Damn near killed me," Duggon finished.

"So you won't be missing him now he's gone," observed the Inspector.

The old man laughed toothlessly. "Aye, that's a fact!"

"Did you know he was locking people in that hole and leaving them to die?"

"I suspected."

"Did he tell you that he wanted to kill the descendents of Angus Ashcroft?"

"Aye."

"Did you bring them to him?"

Duggon bit his lip. He looked away.

"No, OK," Greenwood decided abruptly. "There's no point going down that road."

"I was terrified of him, like I said."

"What about the others that he harmed?"

"They were my friends. McDougal and Shepherd. I know it's unlikely that drunks would save money, but they did, and thus they got out. I didn'e."

"Did they keep in contact with you? Letter? Telephone?"

"Would you?"

"No, probably not, but they were your friends."

"They must have needed to make a clean breast of it. At least one good thing came out of it. I had to give up smoking because I can'e light a cigarette!"

"Thank you, Mr Duggon. That's all."

"I can still take a drink..."

"Tell the landlady to give you a dram on me."

At half past ten, Greenwood and Garrick walked back to the rectory. They were tired when they arrived and the thermostat was up the creak. The house was as cold and damp as a greenhouse on the Arctic Circle. The forensics people had finished their investigation and transferred their equipment back to the city. Cobb was prepped to reveal the results. He had spent four years with the Coroner's Office and even had a degree in the field, but his findings were inconclusive initially. Garrick went to bed and the other two officers sat up to talk in the kitchen. Inspite of his pipe tobacco and a hot cup of tea, the Inspector was irritated by the jargon.

"Damn it Cobb, just tell me in plain English if there was an explosion!"

"An explosion took place. The lid weighed two stone and six ounces, and was broken into sixty eight pieces."

"Now *that's* English! What kind of explosives did you find?"

"None. No traces."

"So how did it happen?"

"The lads were confused, for a while."

"Confused? They're supposed to be scientists!"

"The force of the blast was concentrated vertically upwards through the lid, and we found ozone scratches on the chunks of the underside... indicating electrical activity."

"Like a bolt of lightning? Underground? That's impossible!"

"Then we started to bend towards an example of another phenomena. Igniting a flammable gas present known colloquially as 'marsh gas'."

"Methane."

"Aye – a reaction between funguses, the rock granite, and the decomposing bodies."

Greenwood puffed on his pipe. "That makes sense."

"But we found no charring on the dry clothing debris on the skeleton, nor any scorching on the walls or ceiling of the main chamber."

"Now I can see the confusion. The explosion was localised to the top of the stairs."

"Exactly, because methane is lighter than air. A large quantity of it had collected directly under the cover and was detonated by a spark from the action of the crow-bar we found this morning."

"So the Professor didn't do it?"

"Absolutely not. In these circumstances there is no way such an explosion can be engineered to cause, or conceal, a murder. And if it hadn't happened the Ashcrofts would have both died at the hands of Caine."

"Then they were lucky. It's the first example of accidental self-defence I've ever heard of!"

"I'm exhausted," said Cobb.

Greenwood started to tamp out his pipe. "Aye, me too. You've all done superbly."

They stood. "The lads moved your sleeping bag into the front lounge before they went. They thought the nice view would help you to think."

"Silly buggers."

"The ancient body is being released tomorrow so the Professor can make burial arrangements."

DCI Greenwood placed his pipe beside the kettle, ready for morning, and started toward the bathroom. Cobb had just one more thing to say before he went to bed himself.

"They say the Professor's ancestor may have frozen to death."

"Must have been a very harsh winter."

"No. According to the computer models, it happened in July."

*   *   *

McEnzie MG Classics phoned the Professor's mobile just after a hearty breakfast on Tuesday 24th June. They gave him directions to their Glasgow office. Miraculously they had found the necessary parts in stock and his car was ready to be picked up. The investigating police officers were also from the city and he hoped there was a chance they could cadge a lift. He just hoped he wasn't going to arrive there in handcuffs; a joke, to himself. DCI Greenwood and DC Garrick entered the pub while the Professor was having elevenses of a cup of coffee and two bars of chocolate. Stephanie was sitting beside him, eating yoghurt with a long spoon. The policemen were invited to sit down and the Inspector took his pipe out of a leather pouch. He frowned at their fresh clothes. Stephanie was in a dress of a thick blue material, and her father was wearing a shirt, slacks and a woollen sweater.

"You must have found your luggage."

"No, Mrs McTavish borrowed these from her customers. She told them that if Reverend Caine had been alive he would have forbidden it, and they couldn't give it away fast enough! Democracy strikes back!" She laughed.

"I've got two genuine Arran sweaters," said the Professor.

"I've got five!" exclaimed his daughter.

"Reverse sexism," said Garrick.

"OK, OK, let's get on with it," suggested the Inspector.

The DC opened his notebook and the Professor watched Greenwood fill his pipe. *These two must never learn of the Necronomicon* he thought, but lying to experienced detectives was risky. He wanted to tell part of the truth, if he couldn't lie outright; an axiom he had learned from mystery novels. When the questions began most were surprisingly benign. Greenwood seemed to know almost everything already and a lot of his inquiries were just fishing for verification. Others were like the point of a knife.

"I assume you did a lot of research into your ancestor?"

"Exhaustive, Inspector, both practical and academic."

"Take long?"

"Intermittently for thirty years."

Greenwood lit his pipe and pleasant scented smoke drifted over the table. "Did you know he worshipped the Devil?"

"Yes, I learned that."

"And you wanted the books and paraphernalia that were left after his occult experiment, which failed and killed him? It led you here?"

"That isn't the whole reason why we came. I guessed there may be some things remaining but I discovered nothing."

"If you had have done, they would be yours by right."

"I found nothing."

"So you knew the hole existed?"

"The last thing I discovered, believe it or not, was that it is one hundred and seventy years old."

"One hundred and sixty seven."

The Professor nodded, and smiled. "Remarkable. I suppose you got that from Duggon."

"Why did you *really* come here?"

"To move my ancestor's remains. When I was a boy..."

"- Go on."

"- Well, my father told me bedtime stories about Angus and I used to imagine his ghost was my guardian angel. I sensed sometimes that he was unhappy not to be buried in hallowed ground but I didn't know where he was, and later in life, after he stopped talking to me and left me, it became an obsession. A puzzle that took thirty years to solve."

The Inspector waited for Garrick to catch up with his short-hand, then he asked: "How did Caine die?"

The Professor told him of the dark and fearful path up the side of the cliff; and about the gas, the spark, and the explosion (an educated construction) but nothing about the *Necronomicon*.

"That ties up," said Greenwood, and the Professor could barely disguise his relief. "It matches our forensic findings. It actually took the lads over a whole day to work out how the explosion happened!"

"There aren't many perfect sciences," said the Professor happily. "When are you going back to Glasgow?"

"Tomorrow morning."

"Our car is there," said Stephanie. "Can we have a lift?" It was so blasé. She made her father proud!

"I don't see why not," said Greenwood. "DC Garrick will liaise between you and the mortuary. We can suggest a funeral service so you can make the final arrangements for your ancestor to rest peacefully. Now... who's ready for a drink?"

*   *   *

Stephanie fell asleep the worse for alcohol at half passed eleven pm. Abruptly, without even complaining the light was still on. Her father sat up in bed examining the wonderful pliant vellum pages of the *Necronomicon*. He flicked through it idly, staring at its continuous example of almost forgotten writing, and when he reached the end he made a discovery. He stumbled across a creased parchment folded tightly into the spine of the book. It shocked him with an affect similar to falling through thin ice into a frozen lake. Marvelling that he had missed it before, he carefully separated the page from the binding and opened it feeling like a little boy unwrapping the latest must-have kid's gadget at Christmas.

It was a map ten by twenty inches in size, and younger than the *Necronomicon* by many centuries. At the top was written 'DIMENSIONAL WINDOWS, *onto GEHENNA, HADES, CANDERRA, ACHERON, AND TARTEROUS'*, in illuminated gothic script. Beneath that title was drawn Britain... and cities spelled in old English. There were other sites, and dates in tiny numbers beside each landmark. The dates were dotted all over the map - some a history, some a prophesy - and particularly amazing since they spanned over three hundred years. They forecast 'Dimensional Windows' opening in the 21st Century, Stonehenge in 2031, Colchester Castle in 2052.

The Professor studied it for a length of time that passed by quickly. When he was tired he folded the page back into the *Necronomicon* and slid the book under his pillow. To anyone else it would have been an uncomfortable lump under the head, yet in himself he felt like a doctor resting on his bag of vital medical instruments. He knew himself well: the existence of this map was reinforcing his possessiveness of the grimoire. He would never give it up, not even when he was finished with it. He wondered what the hell Angus had been attempting one hundred and seventy years ago, and suspected that Hell was at the root of what had happened.

ZAXXON

CHAPTER-10

"Relation.ships"

Samantha's dad found the conference in Birmingham to be unexpectedly fulfilling. The hotel had been well furnished, the service exceptional. Mints on the pillow and satellite television to alleviate the occasional bouts of insomnia he suffered since the death of his wife. George had met some interesting people and enjoyed his weekend. "Selling city tours in the 2nd Millennium" had received a standing ovation that made him feel like a celebrity! He left Birmingham in the early hours of Monday morning, June 23rd, while it was still dark. He wanted to surprise his daughter with breakfast in bed, but he could never have anticipated the surprise that *she* had in store for *him*.

He let himself into the house at a quarter to eight and hung up his coat. He cut thick slices of brown bread for toasting, and started to prepare scrambled eggs for his 'little flower', moving quietly around the kitchen so as not to wake her. There was no evidence of two sharing dinner last night since Tony had washed up the plates and cutlery, and put them away. George filled a tall glass with cold orange juice, arranged her breakfast tray, and took it upstairs. He carried it to Samantha's bedroom but was disappointed the moment he opened the door. She wasn't there.

Her room was in a characteristically girlie mess but she must have stayed somewhere else last night and he wasn't pleased. Sam had been instructed to 'hold the fort' while he was away. She must let him know *at least three days* in advance if she intended to sleep somewhere else, always. That was a rule, amongst others, so he could keep a patriarchal eye on her. How would he be able ensure her safety if she didn't obey all the rules? Then he heard a noise from down the corridor, something between a cough and a snore in Beverley's old room, and he wondered why Samantha had spent the night in her sister's bed.

George balanced the rattling, tinkling, tray in one hand and opened the door with the other. He walked in and almost dropped the lot. Samantha was in the arms of a stranger, a boy, and they were obviously both naked. He was horrified and confused. He didn't want to see them scurry to put their clothes on, and he didn't need to shout the obvious question because the answer was as plain as a pikestaff. Sam had had sex. Confusion gave way to an emotion that he was utterly unfamiliar with - embarrassment, and that became an impotent anger. His brain seemed to seize up like an oilless clutch and he shifted his weight from foot to foot, unaware he was making puffing noises that woke her. Sam sat up, sharply, pulling the bed sheet up to her collarbone. The shock of seeing her father drove her heart so far into her mouth she could hardly talk.

"God! Dad, you're early!"
"I wanted to bring you breakfast."
"How did the conference go?"
"How could you do this to me? To yourself!"
It was a bloodless horror; one love betraying another love. "Please don't wake him up, OK?"
Her dad leaned forward, with his head tilted to one side, and his eyes focussed far off to the right. "Why did you do it?" he hissed, and then looked back at her. He arched his eyebrows.
"Because it was the right time."
"- And in Beverley's bed, to boot, that of your *own sister*."
"I would have told you but I wasn't ready to, because *you* are not ready."
"I can't believe you did it in here. Her room is positioned beside mine, it's right next door to where I sleep!"
"You weren't supposed to be back yet, frankly. I'm not going to apologise."
"You should be ashamed."
"No, I shouldn't. I said I'm not sorry." She felt angry. "How old am I, dad?"
"Eighteen."
"When?"
"Last November."

"Exactly - I've been an adult by law for over six months! You don't need to take responsibility for me anymore. I'm not a child."

"Just tell me that it won't happen again," he entreated.

She was filling with a strength that surprised her. "No. Because it *will* happen again." Tony softly jabbed her in the ribs. Her man was feigning sleep! "If you stop him visiting I'll go and stay at his. I make my own decisions."

"I just wanted to save you from harm."

"Your rules are an insult. They've not changed in four years. Do you actually want me to leave?"

"No, please Sam, but I think sex is a sordid thing before marriage."

"That is my personal private business. If you understood that you wouldn't be standing there as red as a beetroot with embarrassment holding a tray of cold food."

"It's your breakfast, Sam. I can heat it up for you, if you want."

She suddenly experienced a rush of sadness. "I do love you, you know?" Her anger was spent.

It seemed, also, that his was spent. "I'm glad," George said.

"But I love him too."

"I know that now," her dad whispered. "Is he that artful lad, Tony?"

"Yes, he is, and you'll like him a lot when you get to meet him."

"Are you two planning, to... I mean, well, are you wanting to, perhaps... you know?"

"Not at the moment."

"Good. I'll make you a new hot breakfast, and one for him as well. He's welcome to stay here in my house." He walked over to the window and opened the curtains with one hand. "You're my Flower now, not my Little Flower."

It was like the light from the window; a landmark. A new day. "Bless you, dad!"

He turned away, and carried the tray out of the room. Sam pulled the duvet off her boyfriend's face. Tony appeared puffed up and was squinting in the brightness. "That was spectacular," he exclaimed.

"My thoughts exactly. How much did you hear?"

"All of it."

"Kiss me!" demanded Sam.

They kissed.

"Who could have guessed anything good could come out of that situation?" he wondered.

"I can still hardly believe anything did. It's incredible!"

"I think he needs a girlfriend of his own."

"That would be super."

"Sam, I want you to know that I feel strongly towards you."

"You mean you love me?"

"On the way to, yes. You are my cuddler of great quality and greatness."

"I feel the same way."

"It's a big day for me today."

"You're going to phone Gillow's?"

"Absolutely." He pinched together his index finger near his thumb. "I'm *this close* to my big break. *This close* to being exhibited."

"I'm proud of you."

"I have to admit I'm proud of me too. Here, your dad's coming back in a minute. What am I supposed to say?"

"Just tell him I told you a few things about him you find interesting."

"Like what?"

"Like his tourism conference, his job. Say something like 'if you're away for a couple of months you can come back to the city with a tourist's perspective'. Tell him you think Bristol is a beautiful place. That kind of thing."

"You mean lie?!"

"Then talk about your paintings."

"I could talk about them until the cows come home."

She shifted her weight, in the bed, moved her face very close to his. "You are my favourite artist, Tony Newman," she said quietly. She placed a hand gently on his bare chest.

"You make me believe it," he exclaimed hoarsely.

They kissed until they heard footsteps on the stairs, and George Lingard walked into the room with a fully laden tray of breakfasts. He hoped that the youngsters wouldn't see he had been crying.

*   *   *

At twenty past nine Sam's father brought Tony an extension to the house phone and then went upstairs, leaving the couple sitting together at the kitchen table to call Gillow's.

"I wish I had my mobile with me." Tony felt scared. Like he was walking out onto the street after shoplifting. The phone felt heavy in his hand; he turned it over and looked at the buttons.

"Go on, go for it!" cried Sam.

He took a big breath and jabbed the number. It started ringing. He swallowed through a dry throat.

"Gillow's Gallery of Contemporary Art," answered a woman's polite voice, "Pamela speaking?"
Tony's Adam's apple bobbed up and down. "Pamela, I'm calling about some photos of my work that I dropped off to Mr Gillow last Saturday. I'd like to speak to him, please."
"I'm sorry, he's busy."
Samantha reached over the table and squeezed his hand. It gave him strength. "Well tell him it's Anthony Newman here. He'll want to talk to me, believe it."
"Please hold, sir..."
A crackly rendition of a folk song beeped into his ear.
"They've got me on hold," he hissed to his girlfriend. "And the music's crap!"
After a short pause, a deep voice with what some might call a 'BBC accent', said: "Arthur Gillow speaking. Is that Mr Newman?"
"Yes."
"I've been meaning to call you. May I call you Tony?"
"Yes!" Both were good indicators, of; something...
"I hope you didn't have to wait too long."

"I didn't - but your hold music is the worst noise I've ever heard... I'm trying to be amusing."

"How old are you, son?"

"Eighteen."

"I'm not going to exacerbate this. The A4 photo's of your paintings that you sent me reveal a skill far beyond your years. You have an understanding and a strong feeling for the use of colour that is simultaneously a highly commercial style. Have you exhibited before?" Tony said that he hadn't. "I'm pleased to tell you I would like to be the first."

"Fantastic," said Tony, but he couldn't quite grasp it; it was too sudden. He was sceptical.

"I want ten of the seventeen. Do you have a pen?"

Tony clicked his fingers at Sam, and he whispered the word. She passed him a piece of paper and a roller-ball pen. "Go on..."

"Are the dimensions of the canvases written on the back of the photographs all the same size?"

"Yes."

"Do the numbers on the rear of the photos correlate with the same numbers on the actual works?"

"Yes."

"In that case write this down: I want the paintings numbered # 1, 2, 4, 7, 9, 10, 11, 15, 16, 17, and I want them soon."

Tony had accepted it now, and felt a powerful rush of delight. He dropped the pen and ran a shuddering hand through his blonde crew-cut experiencing the happiness become stunned amazement. Chemicals seemed to be weighing down the frontal lobe of his brain that made him need to laugh hysterically or start shouting. "I... I'm... I don't know what to say... thank you, sir!"

"Call me Arthur. I've actually got the wall space already, believe it or not. Had a cancellation for this week that started today. Can you get them all here by half past eleven? I want to hang them immediately, this afternoon."

"Yes, I... of course. Arthur."

"That's good. Because we need to discuss terms and I thought we might do lunch."

"I'll be there."

ZAXXON

The older man replaced his receiver and Tony started to leap around the kitchen like a dervish, laughing and yelling: "They want ten paintings! They want ten paintings!" George walked in and gleaned what had transpired from his daughter, who was weeping with joy. He gathered that the situation was not being exaggerated and wanted to open a bottle of Champagne. He kept telling Tony that he was very proud of him, which made, if that were possible, Tony feel even more ecstatic. Eventually it was thoughts of a wage, of earning money, which calmed the two young people. They agreed to be paid for art was the ultimate compliment. They shared a cigarette and turned down the offer of a celebratory drink until later. Tony wanted to keep a clear head and his girlfriend needed to show up for college at ten o'clock.

"Right. Now then…" said Tony, thinking hard. "They want the paintings by half eleven. So… Sam, can you give me a lift to the flat when you go to college?"

"No problem. But we have to leave now. How will you carry the paintings to Gillows?"

"Demi could do it in his Honda. But I shouldn't assume he's in, so I may need to carry them in a taxi. Do you have any money?"

"Not a bean."

Tony tapped his fingers against his teeth and then turned to Sam's father. "I hate to have to ask for this Mr Lingard, but do you think you could see your way to lending me ten pounds?"

"Just the once," said the older man, rifling his wallet. He gave Tony the note.

"Thank you, very much. Now I don't need Demitrius. Let's go!"

*   *   *

Samantha dropped Tony off outside Launch Terrace and he climbed the stairs hoping Demitrius wouldn't be in. Although the black Honda Civic was outside, the wish may have been granted because in the summer Demitrius often used his mountain bike to get about. But at the apex of the stairs

Tony heard loud dance music through the jagged hole in the door. This indicated the Cypriot was in residence. Uncomfortable to know, like the appearance of the wooden splinters. He let himself into the flat and peeked around the next doorway. His mentor was sitting on the sofa reading 'Unexplained Magazine' with his feet up on the coffee table. He was so absorbed in the booklet that Tony could have used the cover of his music to creep up and make him jump out of his skin. It wasn't tactful, of course. He let himself be known from a respectful distance.

After Tony had made the obligatory mugs of coffee he sat on the floor. He didn't want to share the sofa with Demitrius when he was in this kind of a maudlin mood. The Cypriot turned down the output of his amplifier and started talking about psychic powers: telekinesis, accounts of poltergeist activity and bending spoons. Beneath this world he believed there was another, beyond the stink and steel of everyday reality, a place of magic and resolution. It revealed to Tony that his mentor might have gone as far as he could in his current life-style, that he was dissatisfied with the streets and was looking, now, to new (and perhaps dubious) horizons. The Cypriot read this understanding in his protégé's eyes and quickly shuffled the magazine back in with the others under the table. He changed the subject to sex, wanting a full report of Tony's exploits the night before.

Tony was reticent. When asked if he had taken Sam's virginity, Tony revealed he hadn't, but in a way he had lost his own since he hadn't come himself during the five-way romp, before Christmas. Demitrius said he knew that already. From the girl. He laughed uproariously because, as he said, Tony was the only man he had ever met to have faked an orgasm! Now it was Tony's turn to change the subject. He disclosed the phone conversation with Mr Gillow, and the need to order a taxi to get his paintings to the gallery by half eleven. Demitrius offered to give Tony a lift for the price of another mug of coffee. The younger man felt like a vending machine but he was pleased.

It took them a few minutes to load the 'Vampire'. Tony's excitement increased with every landscape they carried down the stairs, yet his sweat was cold. Demitrius put the split rear seats down. They stacked the ten canvases, plus an eleventh that was barely dry, which had not been requested, the blue and green portrait of Samantha. Tony was still wearing the suit he had undressed from last night before making love to her, his best wardrobe. Demitrius gunned the accelerator and they moved off. As he steered left, onto Gloucestor Road, he told Tony that he wanted him to paint his picture. A commission of £150 for a portrait of himself like the one of Sam, yet rendered all in red, and wished him to begin it after lunch that very afternoon! Tony readily agreed. They carried the paintings into an office at the rear of gallery that was white washed and full of potted plants and filing cabinets. His mind felt as sharp as a digital radio receiver. He did up his tie and was ready to talk, but, in the end, the quality of his paintings introduced themselves with a finer vocabulary.

"Not bad," said Arthur Gillow. He was well dressed, about sixty years old, and standing back to judge the canvas through half moon spectacles. "Not bad at all." He was tall and strong; essences of both physical and intellectual power. The picture was of the Clifton suspension bridge shining in the afternoon sun over the Avon Gorge. "And a subject I haven't seen for a while." He lifted it off the easel and leant it against the wall. He lifted the next picture off the workbench. "This is good also. You know if I had painted half as well as you do now when I was your age I would be celebrated!"

It was a rendering of an old burnt out manor house, in parkland called Ashton Court, a gaping grassy ruin of ivy covered beams. Mr Gillow moved his face very close to it and peered at the surface over the rims of his spidery spectacles.

"Extraordinary brush-work for oils," he opined. "Smooth. Is it from a photograph?"

"Actually, that one isn't. The three featuring the low sunrises originate from digital stills. The rest are live, except for one you didn't ask for, a portrait that I'd like to save 'til last."

"First hand interaction can produce the finest work," Mr Gillow said, lifting the next canvas onto the easel. It was a picture of fishing boats on the docks. "But in your example... well, I don't think I can tell the difference!" Tony frowned. "It's a compliment, son."

The proprietor liked every picture he had asked for. He was excited about the submissions, and then he saw the eleventh painting: the portrait of Sam in gouache and oils, and Tony heard him inhale sharply.

"You've saved the best," Mr Gillow murmured. "It's not quite dry, it's still a bit tacky, but this is high impact art. Your wash-through of her hair; the green highlights and the blue shadows blending into the rain, her firm jaw-line with a droplet of water falling into the sea, it's excellent. You clearly know her well."

"She's my girlfriend, Sam. You might meet her this afternoon."

"You are blessed."

"Actually it seems like a couple of the luckiest days I've ever had!"

"With experience you'll learn that luck has very little to do with it. Now we need to talk figures. I thought we might have an early lunch, next door. Do you like Italian?"

"I could murder a lasagne and chips!"

"Then follow me."

The men walked from the back office, onto the main exhibition floor. The spotlights were illuminated but nothing was hanging on the walls. Like a bright blank canvas, like white teeth in a mouth that could not yet talk. The receptionist was seated at the rear of the room under a black plastic sign that spelled: *'GILLOW'S GALLERY of CONTEMPOARY ART' Est: 1984'*.

"Pam," he said to the woman, shuffling Tony forward. "This is Tony Newman. He's a super artist and we're going to exhibit his work."

"Congratulations!" she said, with a happy lipstick smile.

"And I want them up by this afternoon. I need the whole crew."

"Who?"

"Everyone. And here by one o'clock!"

"Done," she said, picking up the phone.

"Come on, Tony, let's eat."

It was noon. Tony felt like he was on holiday. The sun made him sneeze, as usual. The world seemed to shine with deeper colours and more contrast. They walked out of the cool air-conditioning of the gallery into the sultry heat of the Watershed and it was like a foreign climate. The old man led him to the restaurant, where they sat at a table for two, by an open window, and requested drinks.

"Who are the 'crew'?" Tony asked.

"They're students. Mostly doing the Fine Art course at Bristol University, bright as buttons and hungry for work experience. Different people are available at different times but there is always a pool of at least five and they don't need to be paid much. And that brings me nicely to the subject of money, your money, namely how much you will be paid... oh, wait a moment..."

A moustachioed waiter appeared wearing a red waistcoat and an open shirt, placed a chilled pint by Tony's hand and a Bloody Mary infront of Arthur. Tony lifted his glass, scrutinising the bubbles, the golden colour of the lager, and then he took three huge mouthfuls and smacked his lips.

"Delicious!"

"What would you like to order, sirs?" asked the waiter. The legitimacy of his Italian accent was questionable. They told him what they wanted and he slipped away.

"Now let's discuss terms," suggested Arthur.

"I got a cash result!" Tony exclaimed.

"Son, *your paintings got the result.*"

"So how does it work?"

"In a public gallery you usually send e-mail images of your work to a selection panel and they can take several months to make a decision. In galleries such as mine, private businesses, we often prefer to make time to see them in the flesh, take a more 'hands on' approach. And the point is that we are *in business.* We work on a commission basis."

"How much?"

"Some London galleries take up to sixty percent of the net sales. We usually charge forty percent to an unestablished artist, but in your case I'm offering to take thirty five percent. I am confident we will shift them all, and quickly!" Tony couldn't help but ask what the cost of each painting would be to the public. "Six hundred pounds for the portrait," said Arthur, "four fifty for the landscapes; five hundred tops for the rest."

This was a revelation. It meant that Tony would pull in over two thousand pounds, more money than he had ever earned in his life, more than *he had ever even seen.* They ate their pastas dishes and the young man wondered whether or not to consume another eight pints of beer or drink a cup of coffee. He chose the caffeine. Because he had papers to sign and Demitrius's commission to begin this afternoon. The two men finished black espressos and Arthur paid for everything. Then they went back into the gallery's rear office.

"Let's start. What is your production rate?" the proprietor asked, picking up a pen from a jar on top of his huge desk.

"From a photograph I can do one landscape per week."

He wrote it down. "Same size as the others?"

"Identical. On 100% cotton duck gesso-primed stretched canvases."

"And the portraits?"

"That is a different. I could perhaps turn out those quicker, but I need to be... what? Fired-up."

"You mean your girlfriend is your 'muse'?"

"I suppose that's it. Exactly."

ZAXXON

"So paint her again from different angles, and again, in other lovely ways." He took a sheaf of papers from a drawer and pushed it across to the young artist. Tony started to read it. "As you can see, we have the first refusal on your next thirty works. We will also give you twenty percent of subsidiary rights of such as prints and post cards. You will be expected to do a reasonable amount of your own promotion, and your balance will be transferred to your bank at the end of every month, in arrears. It's that simple."

"I would rather my share be paid fortnightly."

"Bold as brass!" said Arthur, chuckling. "OK, pass the papers." He made the amendment, and pushed it back to Tony. "Now fill in your bank details, just there... Sort Code and Account Number... that's it. Now we both sign the last page at the bottom of page five."

They shook hands on it, and Tony joined the sweaty bustle of people on the promenade. He took off his jacket, undid his tie, and rolled up his sleeves. He pulled a cigarette out of his disintegrating packet feeling the heat caress his bare skin. And then he jumped in the air shouting with pure joy!

        *   *   *

Sam liked to drive her father about to demonstrate her skills and assertiveness behind the wheel. She parked in the NCP on Nelson Street and then they walked together at a leisurely pace towards the Watershed. Her meeting with Tony only two days ago in the June sunshine had been fateful. Kissing and holding his hands across the table by the canal had rekindled strong feelings in her, but she could not have known that they would become lovers so soon or that it would solve so many of her problems. She smiled and slipped her hand through her Dad's arm. They walked that way until they got to the gallery.

Eleven of her boyfriend's paintings were being exhibited. Each were widely spaced along the white washed walls and lit by individual spotlights in the ceiling. The halogen bulbs accented the use of the artist's fingertips in the texture of the paint and brought out the richness of the colours. George Lingard stared at one particular painting, the portrait of his daughter, stupefied by it for two full minutes, before he spoke.

"I didn't understand how he felt for you," he said, "until I saw this. Look at all the love in it!"

Sam was proud of her man, and said: "he's a brilliant painter isn't he?" And she realised that she was also proud of her dad's reaction to it. But she didn't anticipate what came next.

"I am going to buy it."

"Dad! It's six hundred and fifty pounds!"

"It is the most beautiful painting I have ever seen. This is perfect."

Her heart soared.

Yes, she thought, *this is perfect!*

ZAXXON

CHAPTER – 11

"In.quisition"

Several days of murder, magic, and mayhem had come to pass. Much had been easily and naturally absorbed by Thorn but he was still amazed by telepathy, the fruitless dream of many an imagination. He saw it as an intimate power, and revelled in it. Even without direct transmission from his loved one he could sometimes hear her thoughts, like browsing the FM dial on a radio and snatching words out of static, but for the last sixty miles he had heard nothing. She had been reticent in every way except empathy, the unconscious communication of emotion.

He wondered whether or not he had ever shared such feelings with his mother when he had been little, although that was long ago, before the Diazapam binges and the drinking. Another life that he could barely recall. His sweet self was gone, and irretrievable. Now his reality was his love of Lillith. She was sitting beside him in the driver's seat feeling an anxiety so intense he was certain his mother had never felt it or surely he would have remembered. She was taut as a shock absorber in a juggernaut. It was uncharacteristic, as amazing as the fact that she had referred to the map only twice in petrol stations in the many hours since they had fled Norfolk in the stolen Peugeot.

"I've got a photographic memory," she answered suddenly. "You know that."

Thorn was startled and he considered carefully what to say. "A map can't indicate where the traffic jams are. How could you have driven this far without using major roads?"

"The application of sub-reality subliminal messaging," she replied. "Kaos with a 'K'."

He had become accustomed to hearing her pretty voice again but he didn't know what she was talking about, and he asked to know.

"It is a channel of communication that advises using co-incidences. Directions, road hazards, timing, danger, all of

229

that. Information from a Lower Power that can multi-task thousands of dazzling messages in a single moment."

"But they are just co-incidences."

"And you would have found it amazing. But you will have to take my word for it."

"Why?"

"Your brain isn't sufficiently evolved. I made you an Incubus. Something else entirely made me."

"Then make me into a more powerful Incubus."

"Don't be so petulant," she snapped. She glared at him.

"Calm down. I'm OK about it."

"Good."

He looked out of the window, saying nothing, for a while. They were driving through geography that seemed as though it should be colder than it actually was: the Scottish Highlands, steel grey lakes and epic hills studded with early summer flowers. Thorn could see the beauty of it but then he found bloody murder beautiful also. Lillith could not register beauty at all. She was swearing inside, her viridian eyes darting restlessly over the barren landscape like a man looking for edible food in a landfill site.

"You're pissed off," he asked, "aren't you?"

"What?"

"You've been wound up for the last sixty miles."

"Yes, because of *this place*..." She pointed around them. "Look at it! I can't receive any 'K' link here at all, because of all this... damned *emptiness*!"

"Do you actually know where Ravencliff is located?"

"Of course I do."

"Even though it's not on the map?"

"I know where it is. We're close now."

"So what's the problem?"

"The problem is I have no indicators from 'K'. I can't reconnoitre the area. I don't know what's waiting for us."

"So let's just wing-it then, eh?"

She exhaled slowly, and then she actually smiled at him! "You're a lovely demon, Thorn."

"I love you, also," he said.

ZAXXON

It was half passed two in the afternoon of Wednesday 25th June. They were fifteen miles from Ravencliff.

*   *   *

"It's half passed two. Glasgow waits for no man; nor woman." said Chief Inspector Giles Greenwood. "We really must be leaving."

"Stephanie won't be much longer," said the Professor.

"She's a diamond."

"You have children?"

The policeman leant against the driver's side of his Ford almost as though he was too tired to support himself. "No bairns. I never married and it was'ne exactly a conscious decision. The job took all m' time and energy and before I knew it, I was forty. Och, I've got no one special."

"Stephanie is always telling me I should marry again."

"Divorced?"

"No. She died."

"I'm sorry. Look! Here comes the prodigal daughter now!"

Stephanie bobbed across the Tarmac towards them with a stride as joyful and as light as a girl half her age. They had never recovered their luggage so she was smuggling the *Necronomicon* out of the village in a plastic bag hanging from one hand. To protect her father she had pretended to leave it at the inn, feigning that it was *her* book to allay the suspicion of the Chief Inspector. That man actually asked her to sit next to him in the front seat with a bashfulness that was delightful. They moved off. Once or twice he glanced across at the bulky package on Stephanie's lap.

"So what's a nice girl like you doing with a mouldy old bible like that?"

"Well, in an amateur capacity, I'm studying Latin."

"Is it a family heirloom?"

"I know what you might be thinking, Vernon, but there are old books around both our households all the time."

The Professor leant forward. "That's correct, Chief Inspector. Continuously."

"Off the record, Professor?"

"Go on…"

"Was there any occult paraphernalia in that tomb?"

"Honestly? Yes, there was."

Greenwood glanced out of the window with his eyebrows arched, ruefully, for a moment. His Ford Orion approached Lillith's green Peugeot obliviously, like any other traffic. The man and the beast driving the vehicles did not know the other. The occupants of the first car had no idea how close they came to death and the demons in the other car had no idea how close they came to an early end to their quest. They swept passed each other, unnoticed, with a metre between them and were immediately forgotten. Greenwood was oddly satisfied with the Professor's answer. The case was closed now, but he could never have expected that he would have to return to Ravencliff only tomorrow morning to investigate further murders.

*　　　　　*　　　　　*

"Something about that car," the Succubus muttered. "Did you see its number plate?"

"No, I didn't."

"I neither."

"Shall we turn round and chase it?"

She tapped her fingernails on the steering wheel. Then said: "No, we're here."

The sun emerged from behind thin clouds and the vista appeared suddenly. Cliffs on either side and a track of stones and gravel leading down from the left of the summit. There was a car park that had an essence like a badly exposed photograph, as though age had wearied its contrasts into grey black asphalt and grey white lines. They turned in passed two sheds with *RAVENCLIFF FISHERIES* written on them, and parked. Lillith switched off the engine. Thorn felt her sense of achievement and he unintentionally made a mewling noise like a happy cat that seemed loud in the relative silence. They stretched their muscles in the fresh air.

He felt hungry. His beloved stood at the barrier looking out to sea with her black and silver hair bustling in the wind. The cliffs were shaped like lobster claws. The headland on the right was like a hand holding a speckle of monuments out to the ocean. What they sought was buried there, somewhere. A powerful knowing, but not like déjà vu, it was more an exaggerated recognition of the obvious. They started walking and the pleasure of it surprised her; the salty air, the grass flattened under her boots. Near three o'clock they crossed the scattered ruins of a church and happened upon a scribble of blue and white plastic tape on the ground with POLICE LINE – DO NOT CROSS written on it. Thorn squeezed it in his hands a few times then dropped it back to the heather.

"The police have been here," he said. "That's bad."
"We're worse," said the Succubus. "They've gone, don't worry."
"I'm not worried - I was just making an observation."

That the police had so recently swarmed over this place did not dent the sense of invincibility he always felt in his girlfriend's company. Although Thorn felt beyond their reach or judgement he didn't know that the 'law' had burnt his lovely Succubus at the stake in her last life. He absently kicked the bundle of plastic tape. The wind took it up, up, up, and off the edge of the cliff like an untethered balloon. He followed Lillith a few metres further on where they found a set of steps leading down into the ground. She leant over the gaping hole, with her hands on her knees, and closed her eyes briefly; then straightened.

"There's nothing down there."
"Why don't we go anyway?"
"Trust me. It's gone."
"I'll quickly have a look."

Thorn walked down the steps, quickly, and slipped and almost fell over. He regained his balance and saw nothing in the main chamber except a stone block that looked like an altar. He adjusted his sight but saw nothing on neither ultra-vision nor infra-ranging except a few spiders. He picked up one and brought it close to his eyes, wiggling between his index finger and thumb, and he ate it. Instead of the pleasant coppery taste he so craved it had a tang like acid rain soaked into a piece of mud. He spat it out and retracted his claws, feeling disappointed. He went back up the stairs.

"You're right. There's nothing there."

"But something *did* happen, here. The *Necronomicon* was deployed, I think, for the first time in two centuries, before it was taken. I can feel that like an echo in a cave."

"So what's next?"

"If anyone knows the story around here it will be the landlord of the local pubic house. Let's go deal with it."

They went back to the car park, and then joined the rough track leading down to the village. They brought death with them as they walked. They were hungry.

*   *   *

"We're closed now," shouted Ellen McTavish from her side of the studded oak door. "I'm sorry." More knocking. "Why don't you come back at half past six?" The knocking continued, with an urgency that seemed insolent. It occurred to her then that in spite of the fact that the Ashcrofts had left the village over an hour ago, Stephanie might have left something else behind. But she surely wouldn't be so *rude...* "Is that you, Stephie?"

A woman speaking with an accent Ellen didn't recognize answered. "Our car's broken down. Won't you help us?"

That same question had been asked three nights ago. Last time her husband had been behind the door, and Ellen had heard it spoken from outside in darkness and cold rain. Her instincts for danger would have been sharper if she had lived in a city before, but at this moment she thought it was just a co-incidence. She was not suspicious. It was in her nature to be kind. Ellen turned the key and unbolted the door top and bottom. There was a couple on the stoop, aged about nineteen, and her heart went out to these youngsters. They obviously had genuine difficulties. There was a strange look in their eyes, an intensity, like Ellen was the only person in the world that could help them.

"Please, do come in," she said.

They walked into the saloon. "Are you the proprietor?" asked the girl.

"Aye, myself and my husband William run the inn, here. Are you hungry?"

"We haven't eaten for a while."

"Car accident?"

"Yes, please!" exclaimed the young man, and he laughed. They looked at him. He said: "sorry, private joke," and it made him feel angry.

"I could heat up some chowder if you're really hungry."

"Yeah," he said, "I'm really hungry." He wanted to bite chunks out of this old woman.

Soon, Thorn, thought the Succubus.

"My name is Mrs McTavish," said the landlady, "but you can call me Ellen. If you want." She waited for the young couple to reciprocate her introduction but they said nothing. She lifted a flap in the bar and went behind the counter. "Would you like a drink, while you're waiting?"

"Snake Bite," asked Lillith. "Half lager, half cider. Make it as poisonous looking as you can."

Thorn sniggered, and said: "Bloody Mary, with as much blood in it as possible!"

"Och, now that *is* disgusting," said the landlady. She chuckled, punched a shot of vodka from the optic and poured tomato juice over ice.

Follow my lead, thought Lillith. "Does anything interesting ever happen around here?"

"Are you journalists?" Ellen asked.

"No. Holiday makers."

"What happened to your car?"

"We are supposed to be taking the scenic route to Stornoway but our clutch seized up about two miles down the road."

Ellen pumped lager into a glass of scrumpy, and looked disconcerted, for a moment, at the pint of opaque yellow goop she had created. "So what you're actually saying is... you didn't even *want* to come here?" She placed their drinks on the counter in front of them. "That *is* a new one!"

"Well, it's a pretty place," Thorn said. And he thought: *You can't withdraw her memory, can you? It's been under twenty-four hours since Arthur.*

"I'll go heat up your broths," said the landlady, and she disappeared through a small doorway at the back of the floor.

That's correct, no 're-collecting', now. It was tiring enough last time.

He held up his drink. *Look at this thing. A 'Bloody Mary' of fermented vegetables, a glass of cheap nonsense. Even its name is an empty promise!*

Pretend that you like it, for now, alright?

What are we going to do?

We will withdraw the information out of Ellen passively or torture her.

Thorn's mouth flooded with thin liquid. *Fresh blood!* He laughed skittishly aloud.

Ellen reappeared from her kitchen, smiling and rosy cheeked. "It's always nice to hear customers laughter in the Raven's Arms." The couple said nothing. The young man had a new look in his eyes that she didn't much care for. It was predatory, like one of the mousetraps that William sometimes put upstairs by the hole in the skirting board. Yes, just like that: a living mousetrap. She started chattering; she couldn't help it.

"We've had two other people staying over the last three days, a professor and his daughter, Stephen and Stephanie

Ashcroft, up from London. Lovely couple they are. Their car had broken down too!"

"Was this professor," asked Thorn slowly, "an expert in old books?"

Good, thought Lillith.

"No one told me." Ellen McTavish frowned about this. "Stephanie definitely had an old book."

The Incubus pushed his glass to one side. He was anticipating hot blood, wanted it so badly that he didn't care if his bestial appetite could one day reap their own undoing. He covered his mouth like a lying child, and gritted his teeth hoping they weren't altering into dripping irregular spikes. "Did they find a mechanic?"

"No, their car was towed away. I don't know where to but a policeman gave them a lift to go pick it up this afternoon. Och, there's been such a rumpus here over the last three days, I can tell you!"

"Go on," said Thorn, "tell us, then."

"The police corps?" prodded Lillith.

"Och, aye, loads o' them! Detectives, scientists, uniformed men. They were all practically living off of our hospitality, dozens o' them everywhere! They were investigating..." she leant forward and spoke the appropriate word with a conspiratorial stage-whisper: *"Murders!"* She nodded significantly.

"What?!" Thorn blurted out. "Murders? In *this* paltry place?!" He shook his head in wonderment.

Less of the 'paltry', thought his lover. *The Necronomicon has murdered, and it was hidden here for a very long time.* "What happened, Ellen?" she asked.

"The professor and his daughter got here late last Sunday night. They ate a hot supper and then the Professor went up to the crypt on the spit with Raul Caine, our village priest."

"The crypt on the spit?"

"Aye, it's a hole in the ground on the tip of the starboard headland. It's a strange niche nobody respectable has any business with; haunted, they say. The Professor and Reverend Caine went up there at the witching hour in cold fog with lamps and torches, and Reverend Caine never came back. My husband, William, says he died of a 'misadventure'. But there were other bodies in the hole."

"That's fascinating," said Lillith. She meant every word of it!

"The police were called in and they discovered an ancestor of the Professor had dug the hole himself in the first place and that the priest, for some reason, protected it by burying two people alive in it last autumn, and the summer before."

They were masquerading as Ashcroft, Lillith concluded.

"Apparently they licked the walls to get water, but they were found thin as twigs and dead as the morning after Hogmanay!"

"Hunger is a hard death," opined Thorn. *The priest was safeguarding the Necronomicon,* he thought. "Did the Reverend Cane try to kill the Professor too?"

"Apparently, he did, in exactly the same way."

The demons gazed at each other, quizzically. *Must have been a lunatic,* Thorn decided.

"And d'you know what?" Ellen continued, obliviously, "the police looked everywhere for a motive, asked every question, but they never recovered anything from the hole!"

They may have it.

No, Ashcroft has the book, determined Lillith. *He came here for it specifically. All we need now is some addresses.* "I know we are an inquisition, Ellen, but who did you think is the nicest out Stephanie and her father?"

"Och, I talked to Stephie a lot – you know, like an 'all girls together' kind of thing – thus I got to know her well, but they're both lovely people."

"So they're up from London," said Thorn. "Big place." *Now!!!*

"Do they share their accommodation?"

"Does he fancy her sexually? What kind of shit-box car does he drive?"

"Where does Stephanie work?"

"Does she like fucking?"

The landlady was seized by a rare terror. Adrenaline swept through her body like ice with a high electrical voltage running through it, freezing her to the spot. Her mouth felt as dry and as ashen as the bowl of a cold volcano. The blood drained from her face and her pulse-rate quickened by almost fifty beats per minute. "I... I'm so sorry... I'll just go fetch your broths, they'll be hot enough now."

Get her around this side of the bar and take her neck in the crook of your arm, Lillith thought, *but don't kill her until we know every location.*

Thorn moved with a fluid dexterity, reaching out and grasping the lapels of Ellen's housecoat. He hauled her bodily over the counter. She struggled and bumped about. Glass smashed and tomato juice splattered the floorboards. She fell to her knees and he pulled her upright. Her head was soon in Thorn's headlock and his teeth were just centimetres from her ear.

"Listen to me," said the Succubus, "and we might let you live."

"My husband will be... soon," wheezed Ellen, gasping for air, "in a minute; any time now!"

"We'll chop up that bridge when we come to it. Thorn, relax your arm a bit. Good; better now?"

"Yes," Ellen said, breathing easier, "no. I don't know."

"I need answers. If I think you are lying I will snap my fingers and my friend here will bite your ear off." Thorn was silent. "Some test questions: how old are you?"

"Fifty seven."

Lillith looked into her frightened eyes, and then said: "OK... How much does William weigh?"

"Fourteen stone of pure muscle."

"Really? Don't get quick-witted with me you bag-pipe. Where is he?"

"He went to buy some fish, half an hour ago."

"How long does that usually take?"

"Half an hour."

"Where did the police officer take the Ashcrofts to collect their car?"

"I don't know."

"- True. What time did they leave?"

"At thirty five past two."

Lillith stared at Ellen McTavish with a sudden interest. "Thirty five passed two: this afternoon?"

"Yes."

Son of a bitch, thought Thorn, *we drove straight passed them!*

"Now things get serious, and honesty will save you a lot of pain. Is the Professor a teacher?"

"He does lecture, but he also works at the British Museum."

"Good. Did Stephanie bring that old book with her?"

"No, I don't think so."

"How do you know?"

"It's been under the Professor's pillow since Monday night."

"Excellent. Did Stephanie tell you anything about her job? Like where, and what she does?"

Ellen hesitated, briefly, and said: "No."

Lillith snapped her fingers emotionlessly and the Incubus bit her ear off. There was noise, and blood, and Thorn lapped at the source making piglet noises.

"Tell us, NOW!" bellowed Lillith. "WHERE DOES SHE WORK?"

The landlady cried: "The tortoise, the silver tortoise!"

"What is that?"

"It's Stephie's shop, a jewellery shop in Covent Garden!"

Platch!

"You fucking *animals!*" a deep voice shouted suddenly. A burly Scotsman had appeared behind the bar that smelt of fish and could only be William McTavish. Thorn found himself being threatened with a firearm. Looking down the twin, tunnel-like, muzzles of a shotgun that appeared small in McTavish's hands. "Let my wife go – aye, you laddie - move away or you get both barrels!"

"Stand your ground, Thorn," said Lillith.

"You think I'm bluffing, mad woman?" He thumbed back the hammers.

"It can't kill you!"

At this moment Thorn was feeling the same helpless terror his victims experienced before he killed them. In this example, the sword had well and truly changed hands. Yet he didn't recognise it, knew only that he hadn't been this frightened since his nightmare of being poisoned in the Fire Exit on the first night of the solstice; just a scared teenaged boy, despite his highly evolved brain and physical capabilities. Yet that was the point. He wasn't human anymore. He was a demon, and loved another that said this weapon could not hurt him, and he was filled with renewed strength. He ran his tongue around his teeth and they started pushing out from his jaw-bone like enamel knives. His eyes became yellow with cat-like vertical pupils. His skeleton crackled into anatomical perfection and his skin became as pale as alabaster.

"Your wife tastes like a hot kettle," he growled gutterally, and licked his fingers.

"I see ye, Monster!" shouted William McTavish. "Get thee back to Hell!"

He fired his shotgun and the twin explosions were loud and hit Thorn in his lower rib cage. The savage kick hurled him fifteen feet across the room with a wisp of smoke trailing from the wound. His arms were pin-wheeling as he flew backwards and smashed into a table and two chairs, then rolled onto his back. He lay there blinking up at the ceiling through bright sunlight.

The landlord wanted to shoot again, fast. His next target was the mad woman, but he was feeling the euphoria of battle and his hands shuddered as he opened the breach of his gun. He reached for the ammunition in his pocket but fumbled with the cartridges. Three of them dropped on the counter and rolled onto the floor. The Succubus held razor fingernails to his wife's neck but she changed tactics. She wanted the gun rather than a micro-cosmic hostage event, so she thrust Ellen McTavish away from her and punched her so hard in the forehead that she died instantly.

The other demon was feeling a dull ache in his lower chest like severe bruising. Like he had been kicked in the sternum by a horse; but he knew the pain would come. The waistband of his jeans was soaked. It was a grievous bloody injury. *Lillith, I'm done for,* he thought. *Bastard shot me.* He squinted in the slanting late-afternoon sunlight and noticed a pot of fruit yoghurt on the windowsill. It was an empty 'Thornberry Yoghurt', of the strawberry variety, and he wanted to laugh, almost did. He coughed instead.

You said it couldn't hurt me, he gibbered silently.
I did not say it couldn't hurt you, I said it can't kill you.

She briefly grappled with McTavish, wrenching the 12-bore out of his hands violently. He broke most of the bones in his left wrist with a sound like snapping branches. She picked up two cartridges whilst Thorn was morphing back to normal physiology. *I'm coming undone!* He panicked, not recognizing the new sensation of his 'bestial deflector body' evaporating.

I'm still saying this, Thorn: it cannot kill you.
He rose onto his elbows, and saw the Scotsman holding his hands up. *Shoot him then.*
No, I want him to see you - look at yourself.

Thorn felt a stretching tickly feeling. His jeans were no longer wet. The spilt blood was actually running *backwards* in long trails. He watched, dumbfounded, as it slid back into his injury like a film played in reverse. The scorched ragged edges of the wound healed, new pink flesh spread inwards. He jumped onto his feet like an acrobat. Bird-shot was being rejected from his body, now. He laughed and shook the hem of his sweat-shirt as lead pellets rolled across the floorboards with a noise that seemed loud in its impossibility.

ZAXXON

"That's not possible," exclaimed McTavish: "No! Preposterous!"

Now rise, thought Lillith, still training the 12-bore on the Scotsman. *Rise and feel the invincibility of a Zaxxon warrior!*

Thorn growled triumphantly and started strutting towards the tableau in a satirical dance. He swept a chair leg off the floor and threw it at McTavish at thirty five miles an hour. The man managed to duck and it flew over his head and struck the mirror behind the bar, which exploded in a hail of glass. Shelves collapsed. Bottles shattered in cascades of alcohol and broken shards. McTavish stood up as the Succubus pulled back the right-hand hammer of the shotgun. He picked up a broken bottle-neck and lunged at her as she pulled the trigger. The single blast hit him in the left side of his chest and knocked him dead instantly head-over-heels against the back wall.

The door opened. Duggon looked around it, his face white. "Billy? Ellen? What in Gawd's name is going on?" he asked.

"Damn you!!" boomed the Succubus, in a bass inhuman voice.

Thorn 'whooped it up' at this next excitement. Lillith had altered during the fight into her 'feeder body', the beast Thorn loved so much to see, and she swung the 12-bore on Duggon in an arc and fired the other barrel and blew his head off. She dropped the gun, breathing hard. It clattered into a corner. The noise of the shot echoed away. Silence reigned except for the drip, drip, drip of liquids.

"Bloody hell!" exclaimed the Incubus.

"That would be accurate," said Lillith, changing back into her equally attractive façade of normality.

"There are people coming up the street."

"How many?"

"Probably all of them."

"We're leaving. We'll use the back way."

He picked up the shotgun. "Where are the bullets for this thing?"

"We don't need it."

"But I love it!"

"We already have total power without it."

"We took those knives, last time..."

"Stop mucking about, and follow me." She crossed to the counter. "If we're searched and caught in possession of a weapon like that we will be living in a Material Plane of hopeless disaster."

The shotgun was dropped. She opened the flap and he followed her behind the bar by the body of William McTavish. Glass crunched under their shoes. Near a beer pump that had somehow become bent at an angle Lillith saw seven or eight tiny boxes of wooden matches. She struck one alight and tossed it into the spilt alcohol on the floor, and the flame caught with sudden a *woomf* of air and heat. Thorn started laughing, bent double; laughing till tears came to his eyes, and the fire rose out of control. They escaped under cover of this arson. The smoke billowing from the coastal village could be seen for a hundred miles all around, but no one that saw it knew the name of the place it was coming from.

ZAXXON

CHAPTER -12

"Fix.ate"

Most large museums employ scholars proficient in ancient languages. Stephen Ashcroft had accompanied one such expert, Charles McDonald, to a burial site in Northern Iran ten years ago. These days McDonald was an Assyriologist based at the Royal Scottish Museum in Edinburgh. He was renowned in the four main forms of Cuneiform symbols: Old Persian, Sumerian, Babylonian, and Elamite.

The Professor always felt a tangle of emotion when he looked inside the *Necronomicon*. Awe, joy; a certain amount of dread, and respect; respect of the power he believed had created it. He loved the mystery and understood the grimoire even if he couldn't read it. The script he suspected was Sumerian, the first known form of writing, an archetypically bizarre choice for the *Necronomicon* because the language had been dead three thousand years *before* the book had even been conceived! The Mage of Renes, possessed (the Professor truly believed) to record the metaphysics of Satan, may have employed original stone tablets from Sumerian cities long gone to dust; or more likely as a method of encryption. Either way the Professor needed Charles McDonald's help. He wanted to start on a translation that very afternoon and needed it worse than a chocolate fix. He picked up his gleaming cherry red MG BGT from the garage, good as new, and told his daughter about his plans while they ate lunch at a delightful little bistro on the dockfront.

"I have to go to Edinburgh," he said, "to see a man about the *Necronomicon*." They tucked into chocolate fudge brownies.

"I want to stay here," said Stephanie.

"In Glasgow?"

"Yes. I've got an old friend living here that I went to college with."

"A girl? Or a man - hmm?"

"Nothing like that, you goat!" She laughed. "She used to live near us, in Walthamstow, up until six months ago. Do you remember her? We used to play squash together."

"Oh... the girl who takes six sugars in her coffee - Jane."

"- Jan actually, but close enough to prove you're not going senile."

"Now who's being rude!"

"She's invited me over and the way I see it is, we part company and you go on to Edinburgh and I'll stay at Jan's for a few days."

"Rent a car?"

"No, if Jan hasn't got her Toyota, I'll walk. Get a train back to London on Saturday."

Thus her father gave Stephanie a ride to her friend's flat, where they separated. The women went shopping. He drove off to pursue arcane knowledge unhindered by his daughter's anxiety that the *Necronomicon* was changing him. Apart from being more dedicated and focused he hadn't noticed any difference (and couldn't have cared less if he had) but Stephanie cared a lot, because rarely had he been this obsessed. He was distant, fidgety, and muttered to himself. He never let the book out of his sight - and when he had no option he kept it hidden under the spare wheel in the boot of the MG. He even dribbled a little, sometimes, when he talked about it.

Towards the end of a sunny Wednesday afternoon, the women bustled back indoors with heavy shopping bags from well-known High Street names. The bags had the weight and precious latency of baby elephants and they put them away with a tired interest. Jan was a beautiful blonde woman, with long legs and delicate hands, and she made tall glasses of Pimms with iced lemonade and slices of apple and fresh mint. They lounged around on the corner-suite sofa, talked about television stars and graphic design and gossiped. Soon the conversation turned to Stephanie's father.

"Totally obsessed?" echoed Jan, doubtfully. "That's a really extreme expression, Steph."

"I know, but the shoe fits. He's becoming unhinged."

"Sweetie, don't you remember the months of research he did into that Egyptian jar? He got reprimanded when he sent it back to Cairo because he believed it was cursed! And what about that powder he got from the bottom of a sarcophagus that he rubbed into your cat?"

"Tinky. He went nuts."

"That's right! *Tinky!* Fattest cat I ever saw!"

"He stopped eating as well."

Jan chuckled. "The point is you've been worrying about your father's sanity for years."

"It does seem to be worse than that this time though." Maybe the Pimms was getting to her head.

"Obsessive behaviour traits are at the core of your dad's personality, it's why he's made such a success of himself. What's he into now?"

"We came up to Scotland for an occult book. It's old, and it reeks of evil, believe me, I'm sensitive to these things. It's wrapped in human skin, you should see it!"

"I think I'll pass on that," said Jan glibly. "So now you're worrying because he's taken off on his own?"

"I'm worrying because he wants it translated, and it may have writing in it no one should read, knowledge no one should learn. At least two people have been killed in the last year and a half because of that book and who knows what other psychopaths may be out there that want it?"

"It's just an old book."

"Nothing is just 'old' and nothing just 'new', not to my Dad. It's a matter of perspective. Something becomes whatever a person truly believes it is, even if that thing is not what it really is."

"You said it. Belief is powerful. I, in my turn, believe that you're both overreacting to this thing and need to discuss it, to get a grip, temper your beliefs with rationalisation. It's that simple."

"I genuinely hope so," said Stephanie. She was not superstitious but she crossed her fingers for the first time in years.

*   *   *

"What the *hell* is this leather?" asked Charles McDonald, turning the heavy *Necronomicon* over and over in his strong golfer's hands.

"'Hell' is a clue," said the Professor. "You tell me the rest."

McDonald's fingertips experienced the wrinkled skulls and horror faces embossed on its front and rear covers, the scabby texture of its surfaces. "Human skin?"

"Yes."

"Approximately one millennia?"

"Yes, go on…"

"Esoteric and heretical?"

"Yes: possession would mean death."

"Vellum pages, gilt illuminations, hand scripted Latin text?"

"No."

"Hieroglyphics?"

"Earlier."

"I'm losing you."

"So, open it."

McDonald slid his thumbnail into the faded gilt edges in the middle of book and opened it as flat as he was able to. He stared at the writing, and he looked stupefied. "*Cuneiform?* I don't believe it!"

"Do you see the excellent condition of the binding?"

"Yes. Remarkable."

The Professor thought things were going well. He liked McDonald's study. It was dominated by an antique writing desk capped with a dyed green leather top that was scarred and worn. An untidy garden could be seen through the French windows. They were open, and offered a cool breeze and a marvellous view of the south side of the city. There were a few potted plants around the room and some archaeological ornaments that McDonald may have sneaked out of his work place. It was not an uncommon practise. The sides of the room were lined with shelves, books from wall to wall. The place had the smell of them, a library essence of dust jackets and warm carpets and concentration.

"Do you hear me?" McDonald asked.

The Professor looked up. "No. Sorry."

"I said I don't think I've ever seen a book after the First Crusade written in this language."

"Neither have I."

"But there's something wrong with it."

"What?"

"Do you know Cuneiform theory?"

"Yes."

"Then I'll test you. It's my turn."

"Can I come round the table?"

"Do..."

The Professor picked up a pencil and leant beside his friend over the open grimoire. "The symbols are almost exclusively created from three different kinds of wedges," he said, pointing with the pencil while he talked. "Vertical wedges have a triangular head at the top, with horizontal wedges having the head at the left, and the slanting wedges with the head - either in the central position - or at the upper left end."

"Good."

"The single diagonal slashes are word dividers, and the text is read from right to left."

"Yes!"

"And, I would hazard that this example is Sumerian."

"It isn't."

"Babylonian?"

"No, it's a mess, is what it is, a mish-mash of all four of the common forms. All of them, and none of them. It's some kind of code and most likely unbreakable."

"But you *can* de-cipher it?"

"No, I'm sorry, I can't."

"God, no!" The Professor clutched his head. Charles McDonald sat back in his chair and closed his eyes.

"Don't say that, Charles, please!"

"Just let me think, Stephen, OK? Go back to your side of the table." The Professor complied and sat on his smaller chair like a chastised child. McDonald steepled his fingers together. After a long moment he sat up and pulled open a drawer in his desk. He withdrew a small book with a ring-binder and a faded red cover, and said: "I may know a man who can."

"Thank God!"

McDonald flipped through the notebook and settled on a specific page. "Here we go. His name is Doctor Bryan Johnson and I have his address, here. Doctor Johnson's story is interesting. In 1835 an Englishman named Henry Rawlinson began deciphering the huge inscriptions of Darius on the side of a mountain in Behistan, and it was Johnson that de-coded the secrets of Rawlinson's diaries over a century later. He's done cuneiform translation all over the globe but what isn't quite so well known is that he also used to work for British Intelligence, during the Cold War, as a code-breaker."

"The perfect candidate!"

"You may remember him from your early days in Museum Street: a tall, gangly guy, long hair..."

"Oh. Ogry!"

"That's him. So named because of his aquiline nose."

"I remember the man. God, that was years ago. I was only a glorified office-boy at the time and he was middle aged even then."

"He was the oldest student on our course at Oxford, but many considered him a genius. He could de-cypher your book for you."

"Is he still alive?" Stephen Ashcroft was getting excited.

"The last time I saw the good Doctor, he was - at party last Christmas. He wife cuckolds him about everything but he can put whisky away like a magic trick. Yet he still has his mind."

"Fantastic!"

"He'll want money you know. Probably a lot."

"That's no problem. What's his address?"

McDonald referred to his notebook. "58 Keys Avenue, Horfield, Bristol, BP2 8CT."

"Phone number?"

"Just the land-line."

"Could we call him? Could you call him, and re-introduce me?"

ZAXXON

"Look, I have a lot of other things to do…"
"Please. I need this!"

McDonald pulled the old fashioned telephone towards him, and picked up the receiver. The Professor swallowed reflexively and tapped his fingers agitatedly on the arm rests of his chair. He badly needed chocolate. He was scared to talk to Bryan Johnson on a live-line because it was an inquiry of such momentous importance, the call may result in glory or failure. A beginning or an end, and nothing very much he could imagine in between. He stared at the *Necronomicon* and felt a deathly possessiveness like an arsonist staring at an un-primed parcel bomb. His friend stabbed out eleven numbers.

"Hello, Celia? Hi, Charles McDonald here… yes, I know… may I speak to Bryan, please? Thank you…" He cupped his hand over the mike and hissed to the Professor: "He's in the garden. She's going to fetch him!" Ashcroft gave him the thumbs-up. "Hello Bryan, it's Charles McDonald… thanks, great to talk to you too… yes, that was a super party… you're not wrong! Since I can remember what happened I must have been quite a lot soberer than you were… OK, I will: I've got a man here that needs assistance with a job which might get you a fat cheque… it's 'Chocolate Steve' from the museum, do you remember him? Yes, that's right - Stephen Ashcroft - he's head of the Adriatic Department now! Well, I think it would best if you were to speak to him personally…"

The Professor was panicking, shaking his head rapidly from side to side as McDonald gave him the receiver. When it was in his hand, he just got on with it. Undoubtedly it began as a nervous conversation on his side. His chest felt tense and hot, as if molten lead was solidifying under his ribcage, but he considered something that lent him dominance: he was the potential employer. He was not the man being interviewed for this job, he was offering it, and after rudimentary pleasantries had been exchanged he got to the point.

"Bryan, I've procured a book of cuneiform on vellum pages."

"Have you really? How old is it?"

"About one thousand years."

"That's most unusual. I'm afraid I haven't restored a book for anyone in a decade."

"It's strikingly well preserved."

"So what do you want me for?"

"Whoever wrote this used a melange of all four of the main cuneiform symbolic systems and I want you to break the encryption for me. Charles tells me you are the only man he knows in the world that can do it."

"You want me to transcribe the whole thing?"

"No, no, that would take far too long. What I'm asking for is a key, for the code in the text on a single document, so I can translate it at my leisure."

"It'll be two hundred pounds."

"That's very reasonable."

"Just courier the material to me and I'll have it ready for you in two or three weeks."

The Professor felt his anxiety return. "I want this as soon as possible, Bryan. Like tomorrow, but not like a Spaniard saying 'maniana', but tomorrow for real, actually tomorrow." He was embarrassed, and he looked up at the ceiling and wanted to kick himself.

"I don't need to work to deadlines, Stephen. It's one of the advantages of having a big pension."

The Professor thought of a plausible explanation. "You see I need to demonstrate a working version of this book for another commitment, which is coming up very soon, actually in two days."

"To be honest with you, the real problem is I have arthritis."

"- Three hundred and fifty pounds."

"For that I'll do it tonight. If you can get here!"

"I can."

"Where are you?"

"I'm in Edinburgh, but I have a car. I can be in Bristol by about ten o'clock tonight."

"It's a deal, but you're going to have to get an hotel room. My wife never allows anybody to stay over. It disturbs the cats."

"That's not a dilemma."

"She may still cook you a late supper. Do you have my address?"

"Yes, Charles gave it to me."

"Then leave now. I'll clear it with Celia. Somehow."

"Right, I'll see you tonight." He placed the retro receiver back in its cradle. "Thank you so much for all your help with my project, Charles, it may end up to be a life changing experience for me. There is just one more little thing..."

"What's that?"

"Can I have a cup of hot chocolate?"

The Professor withdrew six hundred pounds from his bank and bought two reasonably priced lightweight summer suits, as well as socks, pants, and toiletries. He then filled up the MG with fuel, and, on his way out of the city, stopped briefly at a large supermarket and emerged with a block of Dairy Milk. He also purchased, as a souvenir of his stay in Scotland, a large fresh haggis that he noticed had an appetising meaty smell even through its packaging. On the motorway just north of Carlyle he began the first leg of his journey, to follow the M6 to Birmingham. It was fraught with traffic jams. Accidents weren't always caused by fog or ice, people seem to think they can pay less attention to the road and drive faster just because the sun is shining. After a brief stop for coffee and doughnuts he took the M5 straight through to Bristol, marvelling over the co-incidence that he had stumbled across on the map hidden in the spine of his favourite book.

According to this map a 'Dimensional Window' was due to open at midnight on July 6th, this very year, in eleven days. But that was just a part of it. The real coincidence was the location: outside the front gate of the old manor house, in Ashton Court, near the centre of Bristol! He had to wonder if it was more than a mere accident of time and space. This 'window' was the first opening this century and to be the last for twenty-five years. He did not intend to miss it.

The Johnson's small semi-detached house at 58 Keys Avenue occupied a street of other small houses that were all exactly the same. Yet, if you were to investigate a little further, you might notice some subtle differences, minor points of individuality such as the colour of the paintwork and the state of the gardens. Even in the pools of yellow sodium streetlamps that barely staved off the night, the Professor could see that the Johnson's front garden was immaculate. Gardening was effective low-intensity exercise for anyone. They were both in their mid-seventies.

The Professor parked his lovely shiny MG in the road with its tyres brushing the curb then he carried his baggage to their door and rang the bell. Bryan's wife, Celia, answered. She was a feline woman with a sharp face and thin lips. She was wearing a listless housedress and her hair was scratched back in an uncompromising bun. She blocked his path, and looked him up and down.

"Are you Ashcroft?"
"Yes, Professor Ashcroft, at your service. I have a late appointment with your husband."
"Do you have the one hundred and fifty pounds, as agreed?"
"Oh; one hundred and fifty pounds... yes."
"In cash?"
"Yes, it's in my wallet."
"Good."

A ginger cat padded between his shoes into the house. It rubbed itself briefly on her ankle and looked up at him like he was a dish of mouldy teabags. So did Celia Johnson. She had a blunt yet pointed personality like a wheelbarrow made of carefully polished broken glass.

"What is that smell?"
"It's coming from this bag."

"What's in it?"

"I brought you a haggis, for dinner."

"You're not bringing offal into my house! Get that bloody horrible thing off my porch!"

The Professor walked down the road and found a dark green wheelie-bin outside number 56. He dropped the bag containing the haggis into it, unceremoniously, then went back to face Celia again.

"Take your shoes off," she demanded, next.

He did. Another cat walked past, a tabby this time, which didn't look at him at all.

"Now, let me see the state of your socks," she said. She bent at the waist, and sniffed at them. "Good," she decided. "Quite fresh."

"I only bought them today."

"Well, that's entirely your business." He suppressed his amusement, and she straightened up and sniffed at him again, non-specifically, then said: "I suppose you better come in."

They ate steak and eggs, and then the Professor and the Doctor escaped further lashings of his wife's tongue by scurrying into his study like rodents fleeing a tropical storm. It was full of space, and air: a pale cream minimalist room with simple pine furniture and a laminate floor. A ficus in one corner stood about as high as the ceiling, and on the desk was a printer and a powerful looking computer with a chrome finish. The Professor booked a room in a local hotel, using a telephone with oversized buttons because of the difficulty caused by Bryan's arthritis, and arranged to pick up his key from the night-staff. He guessed that using the computer keyboard would be difficult for the Doctor. Celia drank a cup of decaf tea then went up to bed.

Prior to beginning their business, Bryan magically produced a half-full bottle of 12 year-old Scotch and glass tumblers from beneath a false panel in the floorboards. He poured two large measures and Ashcroft found this hilarious but expressed it too loudly. His laughter had to be warned down, in volume, for fear of summoning the harridan back downstairs. He lightly patted the carrier bag on the table between them. It contained the *Necronomicon*. He swallowed a couple of mouthfuls of the strong liquor. Bryan's nose was red with bloodshot vessels, and he downed his tumbler without putting a strand of his long white hair out of place. The Professor was worried about it.

"If you carry on drinking like that I may have to call you Ogry."

"No one's called me that for twenty years." He poured another glass, looked at it cautiously and then pushed it away from him. "Alright, Stephen, what do you have for me?"

"The book I told you about. It's called the *Necronomicon*." He opened the top of the plastic bag and slid the book out of it delicately like it was made of crystal. "Allegedly it was written in coded cuneiform by a French monk, possessed by Satan, in about 1020 AD."

"I warn you I'm very superstitious." He massaged each of his hands, one at a time, with the other.

"It's safe. Honestly."

Bryan took hold of it. He lifted it up to his large nose and smelled it. "Harmless books aren't clad in human skin." He lowered it. "Tell me what you *really* think."

"I suspect it may contain new truth about individuality and evolution. A map of access points into multi-dimensional existence. That one can raise demons with it, and learn the secret facts of the afterlife. I suspect it."

"You actually believe that?" asked the older man.

The Professor answered carefully. "I said: *I suspect it.*"

"I'm not sure I want to be involved."

"It's basically just an old book that may lead one to a more spiritual way of life. Have a drink! I'm not asking you to read it, am I?"

The Doctor reached eagerly for his glass. "I do have an open mind, sometimes," he exclaimed, and drank the whisky like it was cold water in a desert. He smacked his lips and smacked the empty tumbler back to the tabletop. "You know my uncle was supposed to have been pushed down a flight of stairs by a poltergeist!"

"He probably just slipped."

"Probably."

"Have a look in the grimoire."

"That is just the *perfect application* of such an unusual noun!" Bryan flexed his fingers, carefully, then opened the book and looked down at a complex diagram. It was a black magic hex. "Oh, dear God, this really is very grim…"

The Professor chose that moment to play his ace. He slipped a hand into the breast pocket of his new jacket and withdrew a sheaf of money. Bryan's rheumy eyes followed the movement of the currency like a predator. It was placed on the table. "That is three hundred and fifty pounds, in cash," the Professor said, magnanimously. "Two hundred pounds *more* than your wife thinks you agreed to."

The old Doctor turned a page and stared down at the bizarre arrangement of symbols, then he looked at the money, then back to the page. "Am I selling my soul?"

"Don't so theatrical, Bryan, it's as harmless as an unloaded gun. I just need a key to transcribe it."

Bryan took a deep breath and picked up the cash. "Then, let us begin," he said. He opened a drawer in his desk. He dropped the money into it. "Pour me a Scotch would you, Stephen? It helps dull the pain. I think I must have cracked my knuckles too often in Oxford."

"You don't use pills?"

"I never use pills. Celia doesn't know how bad it is. She knows I drink a little, of course, but it's like a kind of game between us. She's my wife."

"I understand."

"I haven't had such an exciting commission in years!" He took out some fine-liner pens out of the drawer, and a pad of paper, and a magnifying glass. He re-opened the book, at the start, and leant over it studying the writing closely under the magnifying glass.

"Do you have a library?"

"Of course."

The Professor yawned. "Can I have a look at it?"

"It's on the computer," said Bryan, without looking up.

"You have to be joking!"

"No, I'm an OAP of the modern age. I've got three, 250 gig, parallel hard-drives under the desk! Most likely more than I'll ever need."

"How many books do you have on it?"

"Nine hundred and eighty five."

"Good Christ, that's amazing!" the Professor shook his head ruefully, and poured himself another drink. His friend took a large swig of his own, lowered his magnifier, and then said:

"No sub-page ink. First person initial impression. No subliminals."

"Is that good?"

"Not really, no. It means it's purely encrypted."

The Professor yawned again. "I have the utmost faith in you, Ogry."

"To be honest with you, Stephen, there is nothing you can do. You should get to your hotel. Get yourself some sleep, leave this with me."

"I can't drive. I'm over the limit."

"I'll order a cab."

The Doctor and his wife didn't own a car, they preferred to cycle short distances or use public transport. The Doctor tried four taxi services and learned they were all busy. It was nightclub rush-hour time. None could pick up for an hour and a half.

"You'll have to stay over."

"What about Celia?"

"What choice is there? The room's upstairs: second door on the left and straight on till morning!"

"Thanks. I think I will go up now. I'm a lightweight with the strong stuff."

"Sleep well," said Bryan.

Bryan's voice sounded kind.

"Good night," mumbled the Professor. He was asleep as soon as he relaxed under the soft sheets.

ZAXXON

On Thursday morning, the 26th June, he tore the curtains apart at half passed nine and squinted into the sunlight. He had a masochistically cold shower to relieve his hang-over and dressed in flimsy cotton trousers and an open shirt with the sleeves rolled up. He ate a small chocolate bar before he brushed his teeth, then went downstairs. He wanted to go have a look around the city after he'd eaten a proper breakfast. Celia Johnson insisted he eat some low-fat wholegrain muesli that tasted like a bowl of gravel.

While he was sitting in the kitchen, crunching this nonsense, he wondered why he hadn't seen Ogry yet this morning. Between mouthfuls he could detect, if he strained his ears, the sound of humming coming from the Doctor's study. He figured that Bryan must have made an early start on de-ciphering the Devil's book, and he crossed the hall and knocked politely on the door. He was invited in.

The printer was busy. It was making the traditional clunks and whining noises, but it was coughing up lines faster than any machine he had ever seen. Screwed-up paper littered the floor. Bryan was hunched over a note pad, glancing regularly at the flat screen of his computer, scribbling frantically, and apparently without pain. His hair was hanging into his eyes in lank ropes. There were strange things on the desk; a cut open lemon, a mirror, a small hair-dryer.

"Good morning to you, good Doctor," exclaimed Ashcroft in a very jovial mood.
Bryan glanced up, distractedly. "Oh, morning Stephen." He went back to his scribbles.
"And a fine morning it is too!"
The old man didn't reply.
"Have you breakfasted? I would avoid the muesli course if I were you…"
Bryan remained preoccupied.
"Oh, take a break Ogry, OK? Slap yourself!"
"I'm fine, I'm fine…" Bryan said.
"How long have you been working?"
"About three hours."

"Have you made any progress?"

"I have discovered an inversion." He put down his pen and flexed his fingers.

"What?"

"The text is a mirror image."

"Surely it can't be that simple!"

"It isn't. It's compound ciphered; pure Sumerian but coded, on top of, and after, that reflection."

"But you *can* break it?"

"I have serious news for you."

"What??"

"I can have it ready for you by seven o'clock this evening!"

"Fantastic!"

"The key will be user-friendly. I'll replace the symbols in S.N Kramer with the inverted code and bang it out on one page. It's a little more complicated than that to put together but the result will be a simple letter exchange solution." Johnson chortled at the younger man's expression of delight. "Fastest three hundred and fifty quid I ever earned!" he said, in a stage-whisper, but laughed harder.

"I'll leave it in your capable hands," said Ashcroft. The Doctor gave him a crisp business card and then he started walking in the direction of the door, his anxiety a giddy relief. "I'm off to have a look around the city," he said, and, just before he left the room, he added: "I'll see you at seven Bryan. Well done!"

The Professor went outside and walked around his MG admiring the fine job McEnzie Classics had made of the vehicle. Much of their work was hidden but he could see the new matching headlight, bumper, front wing, and white on black number plates. The body had been repainted a deeper cherry red colour that gleamed in the sun. It hadn't been cheap, but it had been worth it. If anything it might even look better now than it had before the accident! He unbuttoned the roof and folded up the black canvas and pushed it into the boot. With one hand gently but firmly holding the leather clad steering wheel, he started the car and gunned its powerful V8 engine. He moved off, the wide-bore exhaust burbling and grunting with potency, and followed Keys Avenue onto Gloucestor Road then downhill towards the city centre with the wind in his hair.

He drove around for a while looking at the sites until he found a sign that announced the close proximity of Ashton Court. This was an exciting new direction. The location of the impending 'Dimensional Window' and his first premeditated destination of the day. He drove between two squat little gate houses. The road was cracked like baked mud. It snaked through parkland of old trees and half-toasted grass, kicking up dust and bumping under his radial tyres. He knew that it was possible he might be expelled from the grounds, because it was private property, after-all, but he needn't have worried. At the end of the road he found the manor house and it was a burnt-out shell.

The Professor parked on a crescent-shaped driveway with fuzzy edges lost to nature years ago. His shoes crunched on gravel clumped together with wild weeds as he went in to investigate. He was accustomed to the exploration of ruins, and felt that familiar excitement that tourists experience, sometimes, but which an archaeologist feels with a more consuming passion. The house had burnt down about twenty years ago, he estimated, and it was a daunting sight. Grass had grown around what little was left of the Tudor building, and he pottered around the debris looking through window frames, and stepping over fallen gables covered in moss. The last embers of the fire had cooled long ago, but he fancied that he could smell the smoke of it billowing from the destruction. In his imagination, it was night. The roof was collapsing, beams come crashing to the ground with a sound of thunder and a billion sparks. A terrible heat sucking in air like a furnace: glass bubbling down burning walls and books dying. Crackling, snapping noises: the family silver melting and furniture burnt to charcoal. Like memory, itself, perhaps, becoming black.

Ashcroft shook himself like a wet dog to be rid of these images then he went back to the driveway. He stood opposite the gutted house, imagining some midnight to come when a glowing doorway may whisper open to a place that, as far as he knew, no living person had ever returned from alive to tell of what they had seen. Maybe it was a lunatic's mission. He climbed behind the steering wheel of his MG and thought he would decide nearer the moment. He left Ashton Court at 12:30pm.

He parked near the city centre and made a fruitless attempt to call his daughter from a payphone. Used the number she had given him, for Jan's flat in Edinburgh, which went unanswered. He decided to buy a new mobile phone, and call her on it later. He splashed out for a Pay-As-You-Go model and decided it was time for lunch. He wondered where he might buy a chocolate pudding that was as good as the entrée, and discovered a little Italian bistro out of the sun, in a place called the Watershed.

He took an inside table that had a pleasant breeze cooling his sweat, through large open windows, and opened his phone wrapping. He asked the restaurant staff if they wouldn't mind putting it on charge for him, and they agreed. He ordered a Ploughman's with extra tomatoes instead of pickle and after his empty plate was taken away it was quickly replaced with a large slab of Black Forest Gateau. He requested another portion of it, with cream. It was a good lunch, and, as he often did at times of gourmet satisfaction, he thanked his lucky stars that he had such a super-fast metabolism. He could eat tonnes of such food without putting on even an ounce of weight!

After he had paid his bill, he retrieved his phone half-charged and threw out its packaging. He slipped it into his pocket and roved amongst the students and tourists milling about the promenade to the far end of the shops, and back, brushing window displays with his eyes. One business he had overlooked was an art gallery called Gillow's, a tidy little place with a fine painting behind glass to attract customers. The room inside was cold, with that crisp electrical smell of air-conditioning.

ZAXXON

Rich colours were framed intermittently along a bright whiteness of spot lit walls. He walked around the exhibition and learned that the paintings were all by one man, named Tony Newman. The Professor was impressed with the quality of the work but thought purchasing anything was an extravagance he couldn't afford. Then one picture brought him to a complete standstill, with a gasp of serendipity. It was an image of Ashton Court Manor, which he had only left a few hours ago! The Professor's hand moved subconsciously towards his wallet. You rarely plan to buy art, it just happens, and if you don't grab the opportunity to own the thing you will probably kick yourself about it afterwards for a long time.

It was a stunning picture: early dawn, a cold fog. The gutted building was almost photographically rendered yet somehow also surreal in the artist's emotive understanding of the landscape. Ashcroft stood before it, loving it, and recalled the pleasure of clambering around the green wreckage within its ivy covered half-demolished walls. The artist may have used fog to create a visual echo of the smoke that had painted the sky all those years ago; the Professor liked to think so, but whether or not he had, Mr Newman had nevertheless truly captured the spirit of mystery of the ruined house. Outside which, Ashcroft knew, an enigma was due to unfold.

He paid for it with a credit card and declined having it bubble-wrapped because he was desperate for cold water and chocolate, and he wanted to call Bryan Johnson about the paperwork that might open the floodgates of the *Necronomicon*. He decided to carry it openly, and took it outside. Sweat jumped instantly to his brow as he stooped to adjust to the comparative temperature. It was like stepping off a cool aeroplane in a hot country, as humid as a steaming bed-sheet pressed into his face. He was about to return to the restaurant, for water, when a girl suddenly said: "My boyfriend painted that!" And the Professor turned. He saw a young blonde couple sitting on the outdoor garden furniture. They were smoking cigarettes, sitting either side of a table by railings erected to protect people from falling into the canal, although, in this heat, falling into the canal didn't seem like a bad idea.

"Don't do it again," pleaded the young man: "you said you wouldn't!"

"I can't help it, Tony. I'm so proud of you."

Ashcroft went to them, and held up the picture: "You painted this?"

The young man replied: "yes, I did." He looked just like a teenager; he couldn't be, surely?!

"You are Tony Newman?"

"I am, and this is my good friend Samantha."

"His *girlfriend*," she clarified.

Tony seemed to find the moment embarrassing so the Professor wanted to put them both at their ease. "You shouldn't feel awkward talking about your work. This is a truly masterful painting, Tony, I wouldn't have bought it otherwise. And I'm pleased to meet you, too, Samantha!"

She smiled happily, her eyes sparkling. "I'm Tony's cultural advisor, in all matters of culture, and you may call me Sam."

"I will, Sam," said Ashcroft. He was no longer in such a hurry, for a phone call, or a fix. He was extremely curious. "My name is Stephen Ashcroft. I'm Professor of Adriatic Studies at the British Museum, in London. May I sit?"

"Of course, Professor," said Tony.

Ashcroft was lucky to find a third chair. After placing his painting safely against the table leg, he sat between them.

"Are you talking to my man in your official capacity?" asked Sam.

"No, it's entirely random," he said. "You'd never believe how random."

"Isn't everything?" Tony asked.

"Do you mind if I ask how old you are?"

"Sure. I'm eighteen."

The Professor shook his head. Fond amusement brought water to his eyes. "That's amazing!"

"Thank you. It's my first exhibition."

An old man who was wearing an apron, and carrying a waiter's tray, came up to the table. "I bet you could both use a drink?" Ashcroft asked his young friends.

"Oh, thank you, I'll have pint of lager, please," said Tony. "Carlsberg Extra Cold."

"Same here," said Sam.

"You don't drink lager!"

"In this heat? I do now!"

Ashcroft decided to have a bottle of mineral water, and ordered the drinks for all of them. He watched Tony stroking his girlfriend's forearm, listened to them talking about a summer cinema block-buster. He saw their love. Judging by the quality of the artist's early works hanging in Gillow's, Ashcroft knew this teenaged *wunderkind* had a long, prosperous, and productive life ahead of him. He spoke of it.

"Don't ever stop painting."

"I won't."

"I can barely imagine the legacy you will leave behind in the world of Art."

"Thank you."

And Sam suddenly exclaimed: "Not to mention a jackpot of cash!"

"Spoken like a true agent," said the Professor.

She blinked at him. Then said: "*An agent?* Hey, that's a really good idea, isn't it Tony?"

The young man nodded and squeezed her hands across the table. Ashcroft fancied that he may have just improved the future. The old waiter arrived with two pints of lager and a bottle of Evian, and placed them on the table without a spill. Tony lifted his glass up to the light, peered into it at the bubbling golden liquid, then nodded. He chuffed down half the pint in one and smacked his lips appreciatively. Sam sipped her drink slower, with finesse. So did the Professor.

"How long have you been painting for, Tony?" he asked.

"Oh, about six years. I started when I was just thirteen. I went into the garden with a sheet of paper and a tin of water-soluble pencils that I borrowed from my older sister without asking. It was a hot day and I drank orange barley water. I put ice in it, and a slice of orange, and a straw, like a cocktail. I painted my parents house, and I loved doing it. Everyone said it was a stunning picture and my sister even let me keep the pencils! I suppose I haven't looked back."

"You are both students?"

"Sam is, but I'm not anymore. I was studying Art, at the college on Ashleigh Down Road, where we got off together, but I got kicked out."

"No qualifications?"

"Nothing to boast about. A few GCSEs. Nothing helpful." He drank.

"It shouldn't worry you."

"It's my parents that worry about it. They are traditionalists. They stifled me with the Old School Tie, and sometimes whacked me with it as well. There is no fun, no mystery under their roof, no room to imagine: just *"achieve, achieve!"* They brought us kids up by the book, with everything in its rightful place at the rightful time."

"But, Tony, your success is *living proof* that you *don't need* qualifications to get on in life," said the Professor.

"That's what I've been saying," said Sam. "Darling, you can rebel against all that upper-middle class moralistic crap and still end up getting paid *more* than they ever have!"

"In the long-run that's probably correct," said Ashcroft.

"Can I change the subject, please?"

"Of course."

Tony drank some of his beer. "What's it like being a professor?"

"It's not easy. I suppose you could say it's difficult but fulfilling. Working for a prestigious museum has a lot of responsibilities. The fun stuff is archaeological, digging holes in strange places, seeing things no man has seen for centuries, but I also catalogue and purchase antiquities, and teach at degree level. You get that far and people will respect you, seek your advice."

"Do you have qualifications for that?" Sam asked.

"Dozens! I studied for years at university and when I started working I found out that the studying never ends. But I like it. I think it's an important aspect of life that you do a job you actually like doing. You'll soon know exactly what I'm talking about, Tony."

"Maybe I already do. Do you live in London?" Ashcroft nodded. "What's it like?"

"It's busy there. You need a lot of stamina because it's a ceaseless barrage of audio and visual information, that never stops, and you need sufficient money to stay above the streets. On a lighter note there is a huge Art-scene in London and, if you get paid enough, there is a buzzing youth culture that offers lots of things to do, just about anything you can think of."

"Sounds brilliant."

"So what are you doing here, Professor?" asked Sam.

"I'm on sabbatical."

"What does that mean?"

"It means a working holiday," explained Tony. "Museum business?"

"No, quite private. I've got this fascinating occult book. A friend of mine is producing a way of translating it so I can read it myself. He lives here. Actually I might be staying in Bristol for a couple of weeks and I wonder if you can recommend an hotel?"

"How expensive?"

"Not too much."

"I know a good one," said Samantha. The old man suddenly recognised someone else sitting in Sam's chair. Her blonde hair shining in the sun, the way she tilted her head forward with that expression of eagerness in her bright eyes. She looked uncannily like Emily, his dead wife. "It's called The Three Cups," Sam continued, "a classy pub in Clifton that does bed and breakfast, and dinner, if you want it. I stayed there once with my dad. It's very nice."

Ashcroft was so taken aback by the resemblance that he felt choked. Tears came to his eyes and he totally forgot where he was. Tony became concerned by the tragic expression on his face.

"Are you feeling OK Professor?"

He looked up. Wiped his index finger unconsciously under his right eye, and said: "I'm fine." He took a shuddering breath. After a pregnant pause, he asked: "Did you say the 'Cups' public house, Sam?"

She drained her drink: "No, it's The *Three* Cups, actually."

"I ought to be going."

"Have another beer," suggested Tony. "My round."

"No, no, I have to go now, I've got a pressing engagement in Horfield."

Sam burst out laughing. The men looked at her quizzically. "Sorry, I jumbled it up in my head," she said. "Like being engaged in pressing a field of whores!"

Her boyfriend gasped: "Samantha! How could you say such a thing?"

The Professor smiled. "What made you think that?"

"I have absolutely no idea…"

Stephen Ashcroft stood up, stretching his muscles, and picked up the painting. "Well, it's been a real pleasure talking to you two. I didn't know the natives hereabouts could be so friendly."

"Look after the painting," said Tony.

"I will, son. Maybe we'll meet once more."

"Maybe."

The Professor turned on his heel, and the couple watched him go.

"I've got a really bad feeling," said Sam. "Strong déjà vu."

"Yes, I know," said her boyfriend. "I feel it too. Like we will meet him again, soon, and there won't be any choices, and it will be in desperate circumstances."

Ashcroft glanced back at them as he left the promenade, and smiled anew at their love. They seemed to be kissing as if their lives depended on it.

CHAPTER – 13

"Hypno.tic"

The demons arrived in London on the evening of Wednesday 25th June. It was wet. The side streets were like a blunt knife and humid and full of puddles. The sunset over the capital was bruised with rain clouds. They dumped the Peugeot at half past ten and spent the last of their money except for eleven pounds in coins on a cheap little B&B in Shepherds Bush, where they had an unexpected guest at dinner.

The room smelt rank. It had a grimy carpet and a thin layer of dust everywhere. Doubled-up shopping bags served to smuggle in cuttings from a destitute they had murdered in a near-by alley. They had slew him where he sat in the damp, stinking shadows. When he saw the Succubus's 3" long razor-sharp fingernails he had appeared almost relieved. It confused her in the killing stroke, a question raised simultaneously with the impossibility of an answer. She wanted to know why; too late. They left him with half a leg missing below the knee, and one arm with a bottle of dry white cider still clutched in his remaining hand.

Back in their room they tried to open the plastic bags carefully so as to spill as little blood as possible. They started consuming the meat. It tasted of copper soaked in red wine, and something like old short-bread. A few moments later they heard noises coming from the window, and looked up. Their guest had arrived. A thin black cat was tapping and scratching on the glass with one paw, its head tilted to one side and its fur soaked almost flat in the rain.

"It's a black cat," said the Incubus.
"I can see that, Thorn. But how did it get up here? We're three stories above the road!"
"Maybe it climbed up."
"Let it in."

Thorn opened the window, and he thought what followed was humorous. The cat padded over to the vagrant's arm with its pupils narrowing in the ceiling lights, its tail flicking from side to side, and licked it. Then it made snuffling noises as it ate, getting blood on its whiskers. When all three of them had finished eating she lifted up the cat's tail and opened its back legs, looked closely between them, and decided it was male.

"Let's call it Dracula," Thorn suggested.

"No, Vladimir was a personal friend of mine," said Lillith. A secret smile flitted across her face.

He noticed it. "Just how 'personal' a friend was he?"

She peered at him. "You're jealous!"

"No, I'm not... just tell me!"

"Let's say he impaled me also."

"Was he better than I am, in bed?"

"Drop it, alright?!"

The cat was stretched out on the dirty carpet, purring contentedly. Thorn wondered how to placate his loved one, and said, finally: "We've got to call this cat something."

"It won't live long enough to learn a name."

"Then let's call it 'Professor'."

"Hold that thought," she exclaimed, "that's good! Now, watch this!"

The Succubus held out her right hand, with her palm towards the animal, her fingers extended. The cat started levitating off the floor, slowly. It made mewling sounds with its moist black fur standing on end. Thorn started laughing. When it was three feet above the carpet it started doing lazy back-flips and summersaults in mid-air, a most un-catlike activity. "Now I will deploy a small 'air spike'," said Lillith. She changed her hand gesture, stretching her arms forward and back with an elegant movement like in Thai Chi, reigning in energy with one extended palm facing the other. Her eyes began to glow a pale blue. Thorn watched the cat's legs pin-wheeling crazily as it floated about, and laughed harder. Then the Succubus steepled her hands above her lips, and flicked her tongue across her teeth with a spitting noise like a silenced air pistol. The cat bucked once, went limp, and died before it hit the carpet.

"That's fucking amazing," said Thorn.
"I don't like foul language."
"What happened to him?"
"I fired an air bubble into its brain. It had an embolism."
"Can you do it to people?"
"Yes, and it is always fatal, but it takes more energy. Your target is broader and easier to punch through but you can only fire one 'spike' every twenty-four hours, like 're-collecting'. Examination of the body will always return a verdict of Death By Natural Causes, whatever that means. Now, drop the cat out of the window."

He picked it off the floor by its tail. A tiny part of him wondered why he wasn't sad. The thought was like a wisp of smoke that blew away on the night wind, leaving him emptier when he closed the window. Before he latched it he looked down. The cat was splayed out by a lamp post by some black railings. The Succubus almost understood what he was missing, almost, and felt unexpectedly tender towards him. She believed it was a hollowness that only she could fill, and took him to bed. They rutted until dawn. By the time they awoke the Professor was walking away with Anthony Newman's painting on Thursday 26th June and entering a boutique to buy sunglasses.

*   *   *

Lillith wrapped a mangy old towel around her and walked back into the bedroom. It had been a disappointing shower, the kind with an extended head that splits into rubber pipes stretched over the hot and cold bath taps. She began drying. She looked about. There was a splash of blood on the carpet shaped like Mickey Mouse, which they could not dare to leave behind. It wasn't much of a spill but it would attract the Law, and, if the police did manage to tie their acts together, they would probably be put on New Scotland Yard's MOST WANTED LIST and be hunted down like heretics in the 15th century. They needed to be very careful now. Conviction in a place of steel and concrete, from which there is no escape, was the worst possible scenario. They would have to fake eating prison food and without human meat they would slowly and painfully starve to death over a period of ten years. She did not want Thorn to know that. She smiled at him walking around, naked, putting the remains of the tramp into a plastic bag.

"You smell terrible," she said.
"It's these old bones that smell bad, not me."
"Take a shower."
"Our clothes are trashed, what difference does it make? Have you actually *seen* our clothes?"

She crossed to the bedspread and studied their garments. Her khaki combats were caked with dirt. The white tee shirt that she had swapped with Thorn for a sweatshirt, because she always wilted in the sun, was still damp from the rain. It had diluted the blood splats on it into pale blotches and runnels. The Incubus's jeans were crusty with grime, like an old unwashed oil rag, but luckily his sweatshirt was dark blue. It was fetid, but you wouldn't notice blood on it unless you were looking for it from under a few inches. Their underwear was unmentionable.

"We need new clothes," said the Succubus, simply.
"We haven't got enough money. We've got eleven pounds left."
"And hair-pieces, if we don't want to be noticed on a hundred cameras. How will we be able to infiltrate Covent Garden dressed like this?"
"We'll have to shop-lift."
"How? We need clothes to make clothes. We can't even walk out of this hostel onto the street without attracting unwanted attention!"
"There is no other way."
"Have you ever done it? Do you know modern security measures? Because I don't!"
"So let's wash them in the bath, scrub them with soap."

ZAXXON

"Excellent! We'll have to get the blood out of this carpet aswell, and wash the plastic bags so we can take the leftovers outside. Now let's see if we can't scrounge any cleaning materials."

Thorn found a nail-brush under the mirror in the bathroom, three bars of soap, and a floor brush in an empty bucket under the sink. They divided up the soap and started cleaning.

*   *   *

The Professor laid his painting on the passenger seat of the MG, and opened his new phone. He rang Stephanie with one hand, and used a handkerchief to dab the sweat from his brow with the other. He was pleased to make the connection. She said it was raining in Edinburgh, and that she had been worrying about him. It was evident in the tone of her voice. She was relieved to hear he was alright. He told her to go enjoy herself, and he would be staying in Bristol for at least another week. She said she would be back in London for cappuccinos with her staff by the weekend. He slipped the phone back into his pocket and started the car.

The exhaust grunted with torque as he moved off with the roof down, wearing Ray-Ban sunglasses, the coolest professor in town! He followed all the signs, but wished (not for the first time) that he had Satellite Navigation. He found Clifton but couldn't find the pub anywhere. About to use the mobile again, for a route, he came across a couple of locals walking a small dog. They explained the place was set back from the main road on the west side of the bridge over the Avon Gorge. He found the river, crossed the fantastic suspension bridge that Brunnel had engineered, and then made a left. Their directions were better than that of any computer. Half a mile down the road was a pretty hamlet of Tudor houses where he came across The Three Cups Inn.

*   *   *

"Lillith," said Thorn, "our clothes are all clean now except for your tee shirt."

"I got the blood off the windowpane, the sink, and the door-knob," reported the Succubus, "and I'll tell you about the carpet later, it's bad news. What's the matter with my tee shirt?"

"It's buggered. We don't have bleach. I could scrub at it for hours and hours and never get the stains out."

"So, now we only have one top between us. What else can go wrong?"

Thorn thought about this. His eyes wandered to the window. He registered the bright sunlight and had an equally bright idea. "I won't wear a top! It's hot enough! You have your sweatshirt back, and I'll go topless!"

"Won't that arouse attention?"

"Only from the ladies."

"So people will just assume you're a poseur?"

"Well, I wouldn't have put it quite that way..."

"You have a fine torso."

"I have! Now let's put the rest of the clothes on the windowsill to dry." He laid them out. "What's wrong with the carpet?"

"I scrubbed the bloodstain out of it but it was so dirty all over I've made a clean patch that stands out like a wound. It took me fifteen minutes to clean that one patch and now it looks like I'm going to have to shampoo the whole damn thing."

"The staff will notice that a whole carpet is clean just as much as a small part of it being clean."

"Yes, obviously, but a newly washed carpet isn't sufficient cause to call the police. I hope. If we don't, it will attract attention to that particular patch and who knows what police computers can do these days, with even just one drop of blood?"

"OK, so let's clean it."

"Yes!!"

At that moment Tony and Sam left the Watershed to go spend a pleasurable Thursday afternoon looking around estate agents. The sun made Tony sneeze. The young lovers were looking for their first flat while the demons continued cleaning with the tirelessness of production-line robots. Two and a half hours without breaking a sweat. At four o'clock the demons took their dry clothes off the windowsill, and dressed. It was time to bleed Stephanie Ashcroft.

*   *   *

The Professor turned the MG into the car-park of the inn and stretched his legs. The building had exposed beams and scented blooms; honeysuckle, pink and yellow roses and also flowerless climbing vines like ivy and wisteria. He guessed it was Grade-A Listed. There were small diamond-pane windows beneath a thatched roof, and most of them were open. It was cool inside.

He booked himself a single room using his credit card, and went to look around. It was like going back in time. There were period features such as flagstone floors and oak furniture, and pokey corners adorned with horse tackle and agricultural etchings of extinct equipment flanked by long dead farmers. It was beautiful. Yet the Professor's mind was always focused on the book, always theorising about Bryan's progress, thinking of it continuously. He sat in the garden and ordered a pot of tea with cream and scones. He had been told the key wouldn't be ready until seven pm, but by four o'clock he could wait no longer. He took Bryan's business card out of his wallet *(Book Restorer)* and pulled out his phone. He needed reassurance, even a few words. The call was answered quickly, which meant the Doctor was in.

"Hi, Bryan, it's me, Stephen Ashcroft!"
"This is Celia."
"Oh, sorry, Celia... is your husband in?"
"What in Heaven's name are you calling for?"
"Bryan and I still have some business to attend to. Is he there? I really must speak with him..."
"He's gone to get the lawn-mower mended."

"Wha...?!" It seemed as though he had been sucker-punched in the stomach. As if his tongue had been cut out and his brain had become incapacitated. "W... whe...

"Are you alright, Mr. Ashcroft? You're starting to sound like one of those phone-sex-perverts."

"Wh..."

"He promised me he'd do the lawn prior to nightfall, but he insisted it was broken. He went off with the mower in the back of a taxi-cab, if you can believe that!"

"Wh..."

"Speak up, man!"

"When will he be back?"

"He didn't say."

"I only bought this phone this afternoon. Thank God!"

"Excuse me?!"

"Take down this number, and tell him to call me."

"I'm sorry, Professor, but I won't be back till quite late tonight. I have bridge club."

"Please, Celia, take the number!"

There was silence, for a moment. Then Celia said: "Oh, where's the harm? Give me the number."

*   *   *

The demons moved out of the B&B after their massive bender of cleaning. It was too late to worry about the difference between the mess that the room had been in, when they had unlocked it, and the cleanliness they were leaving behind. They had completely worn through two and a half bars of soap! They handed in their keys to reception and carried one bag outside, intending to re-instate the dead tramp with his bones in the alley where they had killed him. The bag also contained the bloody and irretrievable 'T' shirt. Thorn looked for the cat by the railings as he walked passed them, but there was a bunch of flowers where it had lain, and the cat was gone.

On reaching the alley they found it was sealed off with blue and white plastic tape. Four uniformed officers and two plainclothes policemen were standing about, talking. Thorn had seen this kind of tape before, in more relaxed circumstances, but that memory didn't involve actual law-men! It was identical to the tape he had stumbled across in Scotland except for the words that were written along it: *'Metropolitan Police Line: DO NOT CROSS'* It had diagonal stripes and it was strung across the entrance of the alley to annex the crime-scene. Thorn took this in, and saw the police officers, and the bag of bones he was carrying abruptly felt very heavy. He couldn't tell whether the dread was coming from himself, only, or the both of them. Lillith's telepathy was like iced water.

Look away from them, she thought.
I'm scared, he returned.
A policeman cast a brief look at him, and seemed to see nothing. His eyes wandered off.
Keep walking!

They did. And the more distance they put between themselves and the police the stronger they became. They were Zaxxon demons, after-all, and started to remember themselves. Thorn threw the bag into a wheelie bin near Shepherds Bush Underground Station, where they bought two tickets with a gradually increasing optimism. Like the sun disappearing behind clouds, which they always enjoyed to watch, a comparative shadow that even in their love they would always carry around with them. Amongst the underground escalators and tunnels and platforms, Thorn experienced strong déjà vu and he could almost recognise why. It was like being teased by images of the past to be seen in a pool of still water, which always rippled and disappeared as if a stone had been tossed into it at the very moment he was about to witness the memory.

Dreams, thought his lover. *Rupert's dreams.*

Lillith tuned into the now, into Kaos, and started to learn about their target. She got amazing results. *The Silver Tortoise* jewellery store in Covent Garden closed at half passed five. It had old-fashioned blinds that could be drawn down the front door and all the windows, a silent alarm triggered by a button under the counter, and three cameras recording continuously onto a CCTV hard-drive. And it had an essence... of something, like... being in diamond mine. They would torment the woman into revealing her father's address and recover the Devil's book. They were close. What price, eternal life?

The train wobbled along the track, starting off with a rising whine heralding its acceleration, and pulling into platforms to pour out throngs of passengers like a huge slashed-open artery. The Succubus continued to learn, deploying extra-sensory information gathering, an enviable skill. Thorn watched her closely, as she was glancing around in the upheaval, tilting her head at different times to listen to different quarters; smiling occasionally, frowning at others, but always looking, and looking, and saying nothing.

When they stepped off the train he sensed she knew everything they needed to know. First and foremost she revealed that Stephanie Ashcroft was *not* in her shop, she wasn't even *in London*, but there were two staff running the place in her absence. A homosexual Frenchman, called Marcus, and a tall blonde woman who wanted to be an actress, with a name that rhymed with 'narrow line'. The demons followed small tourist signs into the main pedestrian area when Lillith's interior clock read 5:09 pm.

The place had risen to the sun like flowers in spring. Even in late afternoon it was a busy pageant of colour and noise. Most of the markets were still open; on outside stalls or in airy halls. Thorn followed his mistress through the dusty white contrast of hustling to and fro and felt a sense of purpose. *The Silver Tortoise* was down on the left, under fifty feet away. She revealed their new mission: to extract the addresses of Stephanie or her father from either of her staff using torture in broad daylight. It was the riskiest plan ever. The Incubus could not presently use 're-collection' nor 'air-spikes' because they were difficult to learn, but, since she had expended so little energy slaughtering the cat, Lillith could still use both. She called these capabilities 'hypnotics' and she had a full battery.

The demons walked passed the shop, very close to the window. They briefly glanced inside as they went by. It was dark, but they saw two older women gathered around a counter with a third person serving them. A girl with shoulder length blonde hair. The Succubus established they would wait until the place was empty before they made their move. Both were vibrating with cold rushes of anticipation. Caroline pushed her customer's debit card into the reader and wrapped the necklace carefully. The policy was pink and silver paper for women, and dark blue and silver paper for men. *The Silver Tortoise* had a lot more blue paper in stock than pink. Not nearly enough good-looking men came in, less than Caroline or her gay colleague, Marcel, would have preferred.

The dowagers said goodbye. The little silver bell tinkled above the door. A moment later it rang again and a young couple came in. The boy was in his late teens, and the woman had perfect skin, eerie green eyes, and premature silver streaks in her hair. Caroline coveted the woman's boyfriend. He had a proud back and a buff bare chest, and she decided to give Marcel an excuse to see him, and reached for the phone. The couple had already read Caroline's name-tag and looked around the shelves and cabinets. It was a hall of black velvet and reflections, and the Succubus saw her in a mirror pick up the receiver and punch the number '9'.

"Marcel? Could you come out here, please?" asked the assistant.
So his name is Marcel, thought the demon, *not Marcus.*
"The till receipt printer's got stuck, again... no, you should come out here... you really should. A – gain, you know what I mean? Alright, never mind." She replaced the phone.
The Succubus turned to her. "Excuse me, miss, I am interested in this silver dragon, here."

Caroline came around the counter to her side, unclipping a big bunch of keys from her belt. "Would you like to see it closer madam?"

"No, that's OK. I was just thinking it looks like it's for sale far cheaper than it's worth."

"That's because the eyes in this brooch aren't rubies, they're actually garnets."

The Succubus was momentarily disengaged by a connection. *Garnets,* she thought, *the stones that represent blood.* It focused her. "Right, then, I won't be buying it." *Thorn, take her by the throat when there is no one looking in.* She could sense his tension. *Be careful but do it soon.*

The Incubus crossed the shop floor and walked passed the windows acting casually. His hands were clasped behind his back in a fake essence of relaxation. He glanced through each window surreptitiously, like he was about to commit a crime, and that was a fact. There was no one looking in. In a section entitled: "Antique & Collectable" he noticed a knife in a glass corner-shelf, and the beauty of it captured his whole attention. It was five inches long and had that dull mysterious moon-shine glow of half-polished silver.

"Miss Caroline?"

"Yes, sir?"

"I'd like to have an intimate look at this knife," stated the Incubus.

"Yes, sir!" said Caroline. She started sorting through her keys.

I can't hear you very clearly, thought Lillith, *I'm collecting energy to attack, but I do know that we are not here for the shopping.*

Bear with me, he responded. *You watch the windows.* "Is it solid silver?"

Caroline prised open the cabinet. "Yes sir, thirty-five ounces of the purest," she replied, and reached out her hand to the shelf.

"Is it sharp?"

ZAXXON

She picked up the knife, carefully, and handed it to him haft first. "Let's just say that it wasn't intended to be a paper-knife."

The Incubus examined the scrollwork of the handle. Felt the reassuring weight of it. The smoothness of the blade. "So, what was it intended for?"

"Some say it was used during black magic rituals." Caroline looked a little embarrassed.

That is correct, thought the Succubus. *It's called a Vorpal Blade.*

Thorn ran his right thumb along the edge of the dagger, and cut himself. The wound sealed up spontaneously with a pleasant little tingle that Caroline didn't notice. This was his wake-up call.

Windows!? he thought suddenly.

Lillith responded like a distress flare in his dark mind: *Clear!*

He took the assistant from one side, and immobilised her by the neck. "Keep still. Keep quiet."

Lillith twisted the door sign to CLOSED and pulled down the blind. Then she ran from one side to the other, pulling down the blinds over all the windows. This needed to be done quickly because Marcel might be watching the whole event on CCTV at this exact moment and may have already phoned the police. She intended to wipe the cameras' disc-drive when it was over. She ran behind the counter, picked up the telephone receiver and dialled '9'. Caroline struggled every few seconds until Thorn held up the tip of the blade near her left eye. She froze.

"Would you like to have an intimate look at this knife too?"

He detected that she wanted to shake her head, but she overcame the instinct, and remained still. "Please! No!" she exclaimed. She was buzzing like a live wire.

So was he. Fear, excitement; it was the same. "Keep still. Keep quiet. I won't tell you again."

*   *   *

Marcel ran a hand through his greased-back hair and pinched the bridge of his nose. He was trying to manipulate the calculator with a worsening headache, and regretted volunteering to carry out the daily takings. Caroline was perfectly capable of it, but he had complied so he could sit in Stephanie's cool spacious office, and because she was his boss. Perhaps he had also agreed because she was his friend. Unfortunately he was not mathematically minded and it usually caused a right thumper of a migraine. There was neither Paracetamol nor his homespun remedy of elderflower tea to hand. The phone rang, and he jerked, surprised.

He picked it up with no idea of how his head was going to feel within the next ten minutes. He heard an hysterical woman, with an unrecognisable accent, saying that Caroline was having some sort of epileptic seizure. He said he would be right out. The Frenchman opened Stephanie's office door; hurried across the back room and pushed through the bead curtain into the front of the shop.

It was dim in there. All the blinds were drawn. It was also hot, and had a feeling of latent violence, and a smell like insufficiently deodorised sweat. The room had the essences of a boxing ring, and no one was having a fit. A woman, who looked completely unaffected by this underlying excitement, and who obviously wasn't a customer, was facing the counter. Her arms were crossed over her chest and she was staring at him with strange coloured eyes. His own eyes moved on, and his breath caught in his throat like sawdust. A pretty boy was half strangling Caroline from behind and threatening her neck with that cursed knife from 'Antique & Collectable'. They were being robbed! Marcel took a step forward, and reached, tentatively, under the counter.

"Don't even *think* about it!" said the woman. Although she appeared to be unarmed, her nonchalance suggested otherwise. "Take your hand out from under there or I'll have it cut off!"

"And I will eat it," said the boy.

"Good. That's better."

"We'll co-operate," the Frenchman grovelled, "just take the money, oui?"

"Take the money? That's a good idea. We'll take it after we've got what we came for. Do you have a code to blank the disc-drive?"

"No, no! Just press DELETE three times."

"Then let's see if you've told the truth." She opened her arms. "Come here, Marcel."

Marcel didn't want to, but he didn't want anything to awful to happen to Caroline. He came out from behind the counter, and walked to the woman feeling a deep terror. She took his hands. They felt soft and smooth and thrummed with energy. She pulled him towards her into the middle of the room. "Look into my eyes," she said. He could hardly do anything else. He started to feel sleepy and there was something like fingertips shuffling about in his brain, flash visions of disorganised memory. She rested her hands on his shoulders and her eyes started to glow bright green. Then the whole lot started to come up: all his memory-cards. The last two mature thoughts Marcel ever had were his headache had gone, and that this woman was an alien.

She took all of it. A montage of everything he had seen and done, every skill, every experience. Afterwards the Frenchman gagged and fell back against the counter. He didn't know what was happening, and blood was leaking from his ears. He didn't know who he was, where he was, or why he existed. No memory, no identity. He fell to the floor, and dribbled. *I can speak fluent French*, Lillith thought wistfully, *and suck cock like a pro, and ice skate!*

"What have you done to him?!" screamed Caroline tearfully.

"Shut up!"

Did you get the information? asked the Incubus.
There's a wall safe in Stephanie's office behind the mirror.
It's full of money and the combination is 7 4 2 8.
What about the addresses?
He never knew either of them.
Why the Hell not?
Because just over a year ago a man from her staff who had professed to be Stephanie's friend burgled her home twice. Marcel was jealous of Caroline because he thought she had been privy to the address, but he never knew for sure. Let's finish this.

"Caroline, Marcel has the mental age of a two year-old. I will now ask you a series of questions and if you lie, or withhold any of the answers, my friend here will see you cut so badly you'll wish that you were equally brainless."

The assistant nodded with the eagerness of dread, her eyes streaming.

"I want the key that locks the front door. Now."

Caroline sorted through her ring, pulled off the required key with her hands trembling, and gave it to the demon.

"Good." Lillith closed her left hand over the key making a fist. Re-collecting Marcel had taken more energy than she had anticipated. Her levels were low - insufficient for either an 'Air Spike' or her empathic-tracking array. She would have to try to spot the lies the old-fashioned way, with body language. "Do you work for Stephanie Ashcroft?"
"Yes."
"Does she pay you enough money?"
"Yes."
"Tell me her father's address."
This was unexpected. Caroline was so nonplussed she almost forgot her situation. "I don't know."
Thorn brought up the dagger under her chin. "Tell us or bleed!"
"I don't know it!" Caroline cried out, "I swear I don't!"

"Tell us Stephanie's address."

The assistant hesitated. She looked up and to the left, accessing the creative side of her brain: "I don't know, for sure, but I think she may live somewhere in Greenwich."

"You brave fool," *Stab your dagger into her left leg.*

The assistant screamed and Thorn clamped a hand over her mouth. He pulled out the knife, slowly, and the blue denim soaked up the spreading stain like blotting paper. Caroline bucked and struggled until her noises became a whimper, and then the Incubus removed his hand.

"Stephanie's address," prompted the Succubus.

"I don't want to say it!"

"Stab her other leg."

"No, no! Please! Number 81, Tall Cedar Avenue, Hammersmith. That's it. That's all!"

The Succubus looked over Caroline's shoulder and thought: *Don't get blood on you.* She drew the underside of her hand across her neck in an abrupt cutting motion. Thorn raised his knife and realised the gesture. His victim fell to the floor. Lillith found CCTV equipment in the back room. A vision-mixer, from three cameras, attached to a hard-drive recorder. One of them was currently displaying the tight butt of her loved one as he worked on the safe! The security 'feed' was colour and divided into boxes on a flat screen monitor. The screen read 5:43 pm. It was exactly the same time as Lillith's interior clock.

She reached for the DELETE button and pressed it three times. The monitor went black and somewhere inside the hardware she heard the disc drive making quiet squealing noises. Now she used Marcel's little secret, the sequence of buttons engaging the *Recycle / Recovery* mode. To beat it she stuck the sharp end of a pencil into the factory-reset switch. The image returned. The word S T O P was prominently displayed and all the digital counters had reset to zero. It was done. The demons locked the door on their way out. They left with £860, a *Vorpal Blade*, and Stephanie Ashcroft's address.

"D'you fancy going shopping tomorrow?" asked Thorn.
"Yes, alright."

ZAXXON

CHAPTER – 14

"Auto.mobile"

Tony went into the kitchen and washed mugs. There was a bad smell in there. It was a hot Thursday night, and at least one of the three milk cartons standing beside the toaster had gone sour. The sink was full of dishes that seemed to be growing like a fungus that can only be observed. He filled the kettle and hoped that this night would see his last crime. It was half passed nine. The Dreyer brothers were due at the flat soon. 'Purple Rain' by Prince was playing through the arch from Demi's room. He looked a little like Prince did. Tony spooned coffee granules and then sugar into the mugs. Again, he asked:

"Did you hear me?"

"Speak up," demanded the Cypriot.

"Sam knows I'm going with you after the MG and she's fine about it."

"Women should keep out of men's business. I told you that before."

Tony wanted his mentor to ask *why* she didn't mind, but he didn't, so the artist answered anyway: "Because if I go out with you tonight you'll never ask me to again."

"I said that?"

Tony didn't fancy playing three-bullet Russian Roulette with the milk on the counter and was relieved to find a fresh carton on the bottom shelf of the fridge. He poured some into the mugs and added boiling water. "That is right, isn't it?" He stirred them.

"Did I *really really* say that?"

"You swore it!" Tony walked through. He placed the drinks on the glass coffee table.

"That's the point, Tony. You didn't need to mention it," said Demitrius. "You have my oath on it, and also the promise you can have anything you want from inside the car. I rarely give my word but if I do, it's written in stone. Alright?"

"OK."

"And I'll tell you something else. If we *do* manage to get this car tonight we'll have a party tomorrow like you've never seen before."

Tony sat on the smallest chair of the suite opposite his mentor. There were stereo parts and sticky cups on the table. The Cypriot's futon was half made with puffs of duvet poking out of the side cushions. Clothes and copies of *Unexplained Magazine* were tossed haphazardly around the floor along with a litter of CD covers and DVD boxes. The mess made Tony think of the place which he would share with Samantha, and keep very clean. They had already perused a few properties today. He would go soon. All he would leave behind was the red portrait of Demitrius that was hanging over the mantle-piece. He had so far accumulated over two thousand pounds from the sale of his art and that was easily enough to rent a flat, even with sufficient space for a studio. He picked up a magazine. A man with a moustache and wires coming out of his head was squinting into a glass jar containing a paperclip. TELEKINESIS A REALITY was splashed across the cover. He chuckled.

"What's so funny?" asked Demitrius.
"Do you actually believe this stuff?"
"What stuff?"
"About psychic powers. And aliens."
The Cypriot appeared to be pleased with this subject. He put down his mug. "If you're asking me if I believe in UFOs, I say – yes, I do. The universe is so big there has to be extra-terrestrial life."
"Like pod-people?"
"Call them what you want."
"You know, you used to be able to tell a Pod-person because they wore white headphones."
Demitrius thought about this, blinking at him, and then he exclaimed: "You cheeky bastard!"
"What about psychic powers. Do you believe in that?"
"Look, if you're just going to take the piss out of me I'm not going to talk about it."

"Seriously."

"OK. There has to be because the human mind has so much potential. That's basically it. We only use a quarter of our brain in a life-time and it wouldn't surprise me that if, after thousands more years of evolution, we will have developed abilities those magazine writers couldn't even imagine. Maybe some people have those abilities already."

Tony had discussed this as a boy with his mother. He had been an angel, then, but she had never truly believed this to be a fact. The Cypriot's interest in the paranormal had been hidden until recently, like an embarrassing habit. Tony couldn't recall exactly *when* these publications had started laying around in the open. The man had always been so stoical and materialistic in the past. Now it seemed he was changing, breaking the mould, admitting belief in bizarre things that revealed dissatisfaction with his own life-style. A hole in himself, perhaps, which needed to be filled even with the intangible. The buzzer attached to the front door vibrated in the corridor, a relic of 40's cutting-edge technology.

"Ten o'clock," said the Cypriot. "Right on time. Go and let them in, Tony."

The kid left the room. Demitrius stooped to collect his magazines off the carpet and his back creaked. In secret moments to himself he sometimes attempted to move objects on the coffee table with his mind, hoping he could awaken some hidden part of his brain, but he had never succeeded. If he had telepathy, if he had heard Tony's thought that he was undergoing a crisis, he would have told the guy he had hit the nail on the head - and would simultaneously hate to admit it and want to hit Tony on the head with the same accuracy. It may have begun last winter, with Tony himself, with his creativity putting Demitrius's own lack of it into stark relief. The problem had worsened since.

The Cypriot was bored of cars, sex, and money. He had gorged himself on these and was now suffering what you might call a 'life question'. He had a lovely car, but nowhere to go. Drugs weren't the answer; neither was drinking. He wasn't an escapist. Demitrius dabbled in both but never habitually. What he needed was a more spiritual attitude but he didn't know what it was. He could not define it, nor knew how to begin building it. So he waited. Waited for his Playboy mug to shift just those few telltale millimetres across the tabletop, when the hole would be filled. It was a fine answer, just a solution most people would consider impossible.

He looked up at his portrait. It was still moist with expertly applied shades of red, but he was seeing it with different eyes. Noticing characteristics that he did not want to see. It was undoubtedly brilliant, yet it seemed to emphasise his inadequacies and although that made him angry, there was no point taking it out on Tony. The artist had kept true to the work. He had painted a kind of mask, yes, but only what he had seen. If Demitrius had changed so much he could no longer see the power and poise he had seen in it before, he would want the picture gone. Except he knew he would keep it because he was wise to the fact that it was all a matter of perception. The man staring out of this painting would alter with all his moods, and it was that mirror-like mechanism, of Tony's portraits, which revealed his true genius.

The door in the corridor BANGED against the wall, and Demitrius smiled with the surprise. It was his chemical of choice, always had been – adrenaline. Raised voices were approaching, friends, people that respected and admired him. The rush of that old excitement was enough to lift him out of the grave of a (possibly) uncharacteristic and a (certainly) useless depression. He looked up at the painting. It seemed to be winking at him with secretive amusement!

He stood facing the door and cracked his knuckles. He was going to arrange a tournament around this MG tonight, and he felt good. He loaded a CD into his player, dance music at a low volume to be unobtrusive yet encourage excitement. The brothers came in, followed by Tony. Jason Dreyer looked subdued and envious. Demitrius guessed Tony had just told him he had sold almost half of his paintings. Patrick placed a canvas gym bag on the coffee table.

"What is that smell?" he asked.

"A carton of milk's gone off in the kitchen," said Tony. "And all the plates are a mess."

"Why didn't you do something about it then?" Demitrius demanded.

"It's your mess," said Tony, defensively. "I haven't slept here for a couple of days."

"Do it later. Just make the coffee now, alright?"

"Yeah. Make the coffee," Jason patronised.

While engineering everybody's drinks, again, Tony heard Jason make a tactless inquiry. Heard him ask the Cypriot if that "pompous public school twat" had painted the portrait over the mantle-piece.

"Yes, it's good, isn't it?" Demitrius asked him, his voice hard.

"I don't…"

"Isn't it good?"

"Well, I suppose…"

"Tony is an excellent artist. And if you call him a 'twat' again you're going to be making the coffee for the rest of your life."

Tony felt warm inside. He chuckled.

"I was just…"

"- And that life may not be very long."

"I'll apologise to him."

"No, no. Just respect him, Jason. There is business to attend to."

The kettle was boiling. Tony tipped away the old milk cartons into a gap in the tottering pile of crockery. Two of the three were almost solid and he had to shake them out in thick smelly clots of white muck, and then he sluiced them under the tap. The bin was almost full. He figured Demitrius didn't know his way around his own kitchen and went to pieces whenever Tony was away. Tony didn't like it but soon he would be gone - permanently. He carried the four steaming mugs next door and placed them on the table, as safely as possible, yet quickly to avoid getting a scald on the outside of his fists.

"Thank you, very much, Tony," said Jason deferentially.
"It's alright, Jay. We're all good at something. Remember when you said I can't wire a plug? Well, it's true!"

Jason's older brother coughed awkwardly.

Demitrius stood. "As you all know, tonight we are after a classic MG. That means a late 60's or early 70's MG: B, A, Midget or BGT, and since there are two seats in the car I have decided to make it into a competition. Patrick has brought some retro tools that I would like him to explain to Tony." Demitrius sat down. Patrick stood.
"Classic tools for a classic car," said Patrick. He unzipped the bag and announced each object as he laid it on the table. "We have the bar, the crate tie, the slide, the ratchet, a couple of screwdrivers, a spanner, and the keys. Do remember, Tony: *none of these tools* will open a modern car."
Jason said: "Demitrius, we're cold-calling tonight. Have we got time for this?"
"We do," said the Cypriot expansively. "Let me explain the tools." He shoved past Patrick and sat on the sofa. He picked up the thin strip of reinforced nylon and pressed it in half, with the fold pointing towards the tabletop. "This is a crate tie and it's used for opening doors. You slip it between the glass and the rubber seal, push it downwards until you hook the lock plunger in the loop and then just pull it up. Bingo! The driver-side door is always the easiest because it's used the most. You can't reach far enough into some cars that have mechanisms nearer the armrests." He put down the tie and picked up the biggest screwdriver. "This is used for 'popping' quarter-panes."
"I know about that," said Tony. *"Remember?"*
"I don't like irony - unless it's my own," the Cypriot ascertained menacingly.

ZAXXON

"I'm sorry."
Jason sipped his drink.

The Cypriot put down the screwdriver and hefted a steel pipe. It appeared to be a piece of scaffolding pole that was about sixteen inches long and sawn off at both ends. "This is the bar. It's used particularly on classic cars to break off the ignition barrel once you are inside. Push the end of the bar over the top of the lock, lever it off, then fire her up with a screwdriver. It's considered risky because of its bulk. It's difficult to conceal and if it's found on you it could be classed as a concealed weapon."

Against Tony's better judgement he was actually beginning to find this stuff interesting. He pointed to a metal ruler with numbers embossed along its edge. "What's that for?"

"We call this the 'slide'," said Demitrius. He picked it up and he turned his other hand over horizontally with his knuckles pointing at the ceiling. "This is used for opening doors, too, and it's applied the same way as the tie." He pushed one end of the ruler between his fingers. "Push it under the seal and when you feel a resistance, that's a little bouncy, you smack the slide on the top." He clamped the slide in his fingers vertically and made a hammering motion with his free hand. "Done hard enough it will snap the rod between the lock and door-handle."

He put down the slide. He picked up a small metal tube that had nuts and bolts on one end and a thick screw emerging from the other. "This is called the ratchet. You twist the business end of it into the keyhole, and then turn the bolt at the top with a spanner. It pulls out the whole ignition assembly like a corkscrew."

"It's also particularly effective on bikes," said Jason.

"That's right, Jay. Now, lastly the keys." Demitrius held up a bunch of them on a large metal ring. "The only keys you'll ever use, Tony, will be your own. These are for experts. They are collected and adapted by the crème del a crème of car thieves. Men like Patrick can 'jiggle' a key from one vehicle to unlock a completely different one. It causes no damage, and it is believed to be the height of the art."

Demitrius chucked the bunch on the coffee table. "That's it. What's the time?"

"Nearly a quarter past ten," said Tony.

"How will this competition work?" asked Jason.

"Since our target is a two-seater and there are four of us, we will split into two teams. We will go equipped. Each pair takes it in turn to select three tools. We will divide the proceedings equally and have a monster party tomorrow night. The first team to hide an MG around the back of Launch Terrace, and phone it in, to the others, wins. It's the losers that pay for the party!"

"Excellent!" Patrick exclaimed.

"I'll go with my brother," said Jason.

"That's fine with me," said Tony. "Who chooses first?"

"You do. Greenest first."

Tony carefully studied the items on the table. "I choose the keys, so Patrick can't have them."

"Son of a bitch!"

Demitrius laughed raucously. "I can use them too! Alright, Jay, you're next."

It took no longer than a minute to divide up the remaining tools. Jason and Patrick selected the slide, the bar, and the screwdrivers. Demitrius and Tony chose the keys, the tie, and the ratchet (with its associated spanner). They left the flat dressed to blend in. It was warm outside, and they wore the same simple summer clothes they had worn all day to avoid suspicion. The teams split up at the intersection with Gloucestor Road. The Dreyer brother's turned left, and headed down hill towards the city centre. It was their style to work electronically, to disengage the surveillance in car parks, so they headed to whatever Aladdin's Cave of a multi-story was the nearest. Demitrius and Tony turned the other way, to the right, and started up the hill, out of Montpelier.

The young artist accepted the Cypriot's offer to carry the tools. He was comfortable with that, but he also felt a little cowardly. Most likely Demitrius was going to prison in under a month. If they were caught in a T.W.O.C (standing for Taken Without Owner's Consent) it could go worse for him during his court appearance, because 'going equipped' proved that the crime was pre-meditated. Yet it wasn't worth dwelling on what hadn't happened. They cruised the dark pavements with an up-beat feeling of excitement and sensed a heaviness in the night air that signalled rain. It was like the city was an old wreck uncovered by a spent hurricane, and they were night diving on it for treasure in shark-infested waters.

*   *   *

Ashcroft arranged to meet his retainer at nine pm, and arrived ahead of time because of his obsessive anticipation for the key to translate the *Necronomicon*. He was surprised at Bryan's choice of meeting place. It was an Art-deco wine bar, as opposed to a traditional pub, and even at this early hour it was a hive of activity. He bought himself a half pint and looked around while he was waiting. There were Grecian statues between the booths at the back, mirrors, spherical lampshades, marble columns rising from a laminate flooring to a pale blue sculptured plaster ceiling, and many pot plants that looked healthy and huge. Overhead fans comprised of wooden blades and brass fittings spun up a cool breeze.

He could smell ales and spirits, and the perfumes and aftershave of the youthful people that frequented the place. They stood in tight groups; tall, and sociable, their summer clothes adding vitality to a décor of space and sophistication. Bryan arrived at half past nine. He purchased two drinks then walked unsteadily between the youngsters to the Professor's table.

 "You're late," stated Ashcroft.
 "I'm sorry about that, old man," Bryan said. He placed a pint and a large glass of Scotch near to his hand.
 "It's nice of you, but I won't drink and drive."
 "They're both mine."
 "Oh. This place, it makes me feel geriatric. Why did you arrange to meet here?"

"I like to look at the ladies," Bryan confided. "You wouldn't see totty like this in the Dog and Pheasant, and that's a fact!" He burped. Even before he arrived Bryan was obviously well on the way to being drunk.

"I can't believe you just said 'totty'!"

"This place doesn't seem the same without the pleasing aroma of cigarette smoke."

"Do you smoke?"

"No."

They sat together, quietly, looking around the bar.

Bryan asked: "Did I tell you the story of my first girlfriend?"

The Professor said that he hadn't. So the small talk began. He tried to nudge the conversation toward the grimoire, but the Doctor drank five more pints with whisky chasers, and avoided the subject. He blathered trivialities for almost forty-five minutes. Ashcroft got so frustrated he almost wished he *could* drink. He knew Bryan had decrypted a key, and envied the man because he maybe the first person to have read some of the book in 167 years, but he had to bide his time; bite his tongue. Once every slurred and slurping detail of his first five relationships had been discussed, the Doctor finally relented and began to talk about what they truly had in common. The book.

"It's profound," he revealed. "Very scary material."

"How much of it have you read?"

"One section. That was enough. The prologue spells out its purpose to illuminate the true nature of man, and to raise the human brain to a radically higher state, using magic. I use the word 'spell' as a pun but, also, with the utmost seriousness. The grimoire refers to these as 'conjurations'."

"What kind of magic?" Ashcroft asked. His pulse was beginning to race. Johnson took a long, slow, pull on his pint and the Professor resisted the urge to reach across and shake him. "You mean it physically transforms?"

"Yes, magic that accelerates evolution, one ability at a time. If you read enough of it, it will induce metamorphosis of your neural nets into an advanced brain more akin to alien than human."

"So, the dormant mind awakens."

"Exactly. Telekinesis, pyrokinesis, telepathy; all these abilities, and more, inherent in each of us, become usable. And when the transformation happens you really know about it. I read the first chapter on moving objects with the mind alone, and I felt a rush of pleasure that I imagine is similar to that experienced by users of narcotics. Oh, yes."

"You actually think it's addictive?"

"Absolutely. I'm trying to get drunk enough now to forget about it!"

"Presumably you now have telekinetic abilities." Ashcroft leaned forward, and placed a slab of Galaxy milk chocolate on the table. "Try moving this."

"I will not." The Doctor rubbed his nose.

"Go on. Try it."

"I don't want to even *attempt* to." Now he was touching his mouth, like a bird pecking for food.

"Where's the harm?"

"I told you last night, Stephen, I will not get involved in matters of the occult."

"It's a tiny paranormal experiment!"

The Doctor pushed the chocolate bar off the table. "I told you, no! Forget it!"

"You chatter nonsense for over an hour; and then, when you finally start talking about my book, which is very important to me, you duck out of verifying what you've discovered at the last moment! What a bloody wind-up!"

"You'll be able to read the whole damn thing yourself soon, Professor. For all I care you can read all of it, and go to Hell in a hand-basket!"

"Alright, alright." Ashcroft exhaled wearily. He reached down, picked the chocolate bar off the floor, and ripped open its wrapper. He chewed off a soft sweet chunk.

"Damn and blast it!" exclaimed the Doctor.

"What is it now?"

"I didn't take the washing in while Celia was at Bridge Club. We really must get going."

"Just one more question."

"Oh, for goodness sake!"

"It's important."

"OK. But make certain this is the last one."

"Do you know what happens at the end of the book?"

"No, I never read it, of course. But if I had to hazard a guess I would say its purpose is to alter everyone into that advanced mental state I told you about. To change us into aliens, overnight - the whole human race. God alone knows what would happen!"

The Professor thought about it, chewing more chocolate. A new Golden Age of enlightenment through the brotherhood of an advanced species. He could rule this next era himself.

"Don't concern yourself Ogry, I won't try that," he lied.

Bryan looked at his watch. "I'm worried about something else, actually."

"What?"

"I didn't mow the lawn."

Ashcroft finished his chocolate fix. They stood. "Is that bad?"

"It's not good. I had to leave the mower at the shop because it's faulty. When I went home to tell Celia about it, when she gave me the number of your new phone, she told me to borrow next door's and cut it before nightfall. But I had to take a drink, I *had* to. D'you understand what that's like?"

Ashcroft glanced at the chocolate wrapper in the ashtray. "I do, sort of. Now finish your scotch, Bryan, and we'll go sort it out."

The Doctor looked back briefly at the women, with a rapturous expression of regret, guilt, and lust. They walked to Keys Avenue through heavy rain for about five minutes. Bryan stumbled most of the way. He unlocked his front door and fell onto the mat in the hallway dripping wet and laughing. The Professor hauled him up. And realised in the same moment that Celia was watching them, standing in the kitchen doorway with her arms crossed and her face angry under her wild mop of grey hair. The verbal assault began.

"I haven't seen you since you left with the mower," she said. "If you couldn't mend it you were supposed to borrow the Flymow from the Jones's."

"My darling, I was unavoidably detained on business," he hiccupped.

"You're drunk!"

"So I am, so what?"

Celia looked flustered. She went into the kitchen and started chopping onions. "I just got back from Bridge Club and nothing has been done. The washing is soaked because you left the line out in the rain, you stupid old man. Have you been back since I let you out this afternoon?"

"No, I needed to get away. Because... because..."

"Because you have no sense of responsibility," she exclaimed. The Doctor's face was blotchy. Now it reddened with anger. His back straightened. "You're a useless good for nothing old soak," she continued, the knife slicing through the onion, "a fool with no self-control."

"Stop it." The Doctor's hands were fists; clenching and unclenching.

"You're sleeping in the spare bedroom tonight, I can tell you. I won't have your stinky beer fumes in my face and put up with your snoring all night, you blithering idiot!"

"Please. Not in front of a stranger."

"You'll have to wear dirty 'Y' Fronts in the morning but you probably prefer to do that anyway!"

And the knife suddenly jumped. Nudged into the side of her left index finger. Blood speckled the chopping board and dripped to the green linoleum floor. Celia held up her hand with an appearance equally pained and shocked. "What happened?" she asked dazedly. Bryan rushed to her side.

"Oh, my darling," he said, holding the finger under the tap, "it'll be alright in a minute. Don't worry."

The Professor stepped forward, but he felt awkward. "Is there anything I can do?"

"Yes," the Doctor spat, "you can fuck off! You and your book caused this to happen, you witch!"

"Are you mad?"

"Oh, you bastard, you know *full well* it did." Bryan started pulling off sheets of kitchen paper from the roll. Celia whimpered. "Take your paper-work, and your precious hideous *thing*, and leave."

"Where is it?"

"On the table in my office."

Ashcroft went in there and found the *Necronomicon* with the key to translate it. He folded them together and returned to the hallway with the book in its usual place, tucked under his arm. He realised he had just witnessed actual telekinesis, however terrible an example. He stopped in the kitchen doorway and watched Bryan wrapping paper towels around his wife's injury.

"I'm sorry," he said to them. He almost meant it.

"Just leave this house."

"OK. Thanks for everything Mrs Johnson."

It was a crazy place. Ashcroft was pleased to get out of it with what he had come for. He figured it was time to retire to his hotel for a little bit of heavy reading. He took some deep breaths of the cold moist air and unlocked the MG. He hid the book in the boot, slammed it shut, and drove off in search of a 24hr shop to buy chocolate. In his need of it, his whole body quaked. He couldn't get away fast enough.

*   *   *

Demitrius and Tony got off to a poor start in the tournament. Neither of them particularly liked rain and both were disheartened by the weather, trudging through streets as dimly lit and as wet as a candlelit shower curtain. The rain came. It soaked them, and went. Even after an hour they had still found no MGs that fitted the order. They saw lots of roadsters and Metros, but nothing classic. Tony felt as though he was in another reality, risking his sanity and perhaps his freedom in a waking dream. They entered Horfield and he saw a little blue sports car by a garden gate, which gave him a rush of excitement like a key unlocking his chest. But Demitrius said it wasn't an MG. It was a Triumph 'Spitfire' that had more alarms on it than the Bank Of England.

It started to rain again on Demitrius and Tony with renewed vigour. Water poured down the gradient of the street like a fishless river. The Cypriot kicked an empty beer can into a puddle. He imagined Jason and Patrick Dreyer in some warm dry car park, somewhere, like a showroom. His trainers squelched, his feet wet to the core, and at eleven o'clock he finally told his protégé that he had had enough of it. They turned on their heels and headed back. For them the tournament was over and Tony was not exactly upset about the decision. The artist wanted water of the drinkable variety, and Demi wanted crisps. There was an all-night Spar shop a third of the way along Gloucestor Road. They made their way there for these simple things. But what happened as they neared the door was sudden and astonishing.

A bright red MG pulled up to the shop, and stopped with a tiny squeal of rubber against the kerb. It gleamed in the fluorescent lights. An old bearded man got out and walked into the shop leaving his keys in the ignition and the engine burbling through a huge bore exhaust.

   "I don't believe it!" whispered Demitrius. "Bloody hell, it's perfect!"

Ashcroft studied the confectionary shelf like a child at Christmas. His mouth was flooding with saliva and he chose a big tablet of Dairy Milk, two Kit Kats, and a Mars Bar. He laid them on the counter for the shop-keeper (who sounded like a Hungarian) to scan, and was just pulling out his wallet when he noticed movement out in the road, on the periphery of his vision. He understood his mistake - and understood, also, what was about to happen – and felt dread. Through the window he saw two people getting into his car, but not for a length of time sufficient to describe them later. He barged through the other customers, almost knocking over two girls with a basket of wine, and ran outside. He was too late. The engine roared as the MG ran a red light and took off down the hill. The Professor howled with despair. The *Necronomicon* was gone, and so was the solution to unlock its awesome power.

*   *   *

"You must be kidding!" said Jason on the other end of the mobile phone.

"No, I'm serious: a cherry red 1974 MG BGT in mint condition. We're sitting in it now."

"Well, I guess that unless someone else steals it off you before we get back, you guys have won."

"Yeah - you're paying for the party!" exclaimed Demitrius. He lowered the phone and told Tony. The younger man chuckled.

"OK," said Jason, "we'll be there in twenty minutes."

"Sweet."

"Is she kitted out?"

"To the nines."

"Do us one favour, yeah?"

"What?"

"Don't look under the bonnet until we get there, OK? It'll be a lot of fun."

"Fine."

The Dreyers arrived twenty minutes later. They trudged around the back of Launch Terrace to where the MG was hidden: parked by some abandoned allotments behind two large plastic oil tanks.

"Stainless steel straight-through pipe," Jason muttered. "Such beautiful paintwork!" He leaned under the dash and popped the bonnet catch.

Demitrius lifted it and Patrick shone a torch over the engine. "Good Christ!" he exclaimed.

They crowded round.

ZAXXON

"It's a 2.5 litre, V.8!"
"About 220 brake horse power," confirmed his brother.

Tony didn't understand the discussion that followed. The words floated over his head, but did sound interesting.

"Chrome plated engine block."
"Twin over-head cam with veneer pullies…"
"Webber side-draft carburettors…"
"We could get ten grand for this."
"At least!"
Jason looked inside at the interior. "Hand-stitched calf skin. Plush upholstery, but a bit wet. I think the roof is going to need replacing."
"That's not our responsibility."
"Is there anything in the boot?" Tony suddenly asked.
Jason suggested they look. He opened it up and pulled the carpet off the wheel-well. "Demi? There's a book in here. It looks really old."
The Cypriot came around to the back of the car and took it from Jason. He held it briefly, his features clouding in the torchlight, and then he shook himself. "Tony takes anything found inside the car. That was the deal." He handed it to the artist. "Take it, if you want it."

Tony took it from him and held it in both hands. And he knew, somehow, that he had seen this book before. He felt a powerful déjà vu coalescing this moment with epiphanies in the histories of many passed lives. It seemed to be thrumming under his fingers. He smiled, exploring the cover with his fingers. "Thank you very much!" he said. He sniffed the leather, and felt the reassuring weight of the book. "I'll take it, Demi. It's marvellous and beautiful!"

CHAPTER – 15

"Demons.trate"

Thorn remained capable of questioning his own existence. He didn't hate himself, or his lover, for what he had become. He couldn't remember the circumstances other than when he had understood the cost to his soul, but had still elected to become a demon. If he had made different choices they would have changed nothing, except perhaps the timing of it. His was an inexorable destiny. As unavoidable as a caterpillar facing its cocoon. A metamorphosis from boy to monster like walking down a street and stepping on a loose paving stone that vanishes immediately from memory, long before you unlock your door. The taste of a child's food, the softness of a child's bed; gone.

Now he ate human meat, and drank human blood. Nothing else. He was a blight upon the Earth; his lover with him. Indeed, in the old language, 'Blight' was, for the most part, the epithet of all demons that roamed the Material Plane. Their love was paradoxical because they were truly terrible, yet they were like any other carnivorous animals. They killed to survive. The only force on the food-chain above them (metaphorically speaking) was The Law, but the creatures were somehow ephemeral on camera footage and protected by warped DNA and changeling teeth. Lillith's hair had been dyed completely black. They were just another couple of predators in the concrete jungle. Thorn could live with that. It wasn't such a high price to pay for eternal life, but 'forever' was a long time and it didn't occur to him that at some point in the future there might not be any human beings left to eat, maybe because of the *Necronomicon* itself. This was another of Lillith's motivations to recover it. She suspected that the hand of the Lord of all Zaxxon had been forced, the latent danger of the book ordered out of the Material Plane. And Angels were watching.

At half passed one pm, on Friday 27th June, the demons parked opposite Stephanie's little semi-detached house on

Tall Cedar Avenue and awaited her return. It was a nice summer afternoon, on a quiet street, lined with trees with lush canopies of green leaves. The sky changed from blue to grey to blue. Sometimes it rained; they were prepared to wait for a long time. In that respect their quest was like a war of short battles, between periods of often boring readiness, they sat through together. Lillith gave Thorn the occasional blow-job and they pondered the meanings of important things.

"I like shopping," Thorn stated.

"I know."

"I liked buying these clothes this morning."

"I know, but I can't see why you bothered buying two suits," retorted his loved one, "when you have to throw out your garments every time you eat, anyway."

"While you were busy at the Yves Saint Lauren counter, I bought six sets of cheap black tee shirts and black cloth trousers, for feeding. So I can chuck them out."

"Oh, so that's what you were thinking!"

"It was supposed to be a surprise. I'll never get blood on this fine suit, I swear it. What's the point in having all this power if you don't look good with it?"

"It's an irrelevant connection."

"I'm the best dressed demon on the planet!"

"Actually there are at least 26 other Blight better attired than you in London alone."

"Yeah, but I liked to buy them." He sat quietly; then he asked her: "Did you like shopping too?"

"I went because I had to," she replied.

"But what about your new bag? Every woman needs a nice hand-bag!"

"It's just a satchel, Thorn."

"It's made of antique snake's skin, for God's sake. You smiled when you bought it, I saw you!"

"Maybe I did."

"Yes!!" He smacked his hands together gleefully. "You know we should take more money."

"For the last time, Thorn, keep such stupid ideas to yourself. We're not Bonnie & Clyde, were on a crucial mission for the dark forces of our Zaxxon leader."

"But –"

"No buts!"

So they sat there, for a while, saying nothing.

An image of the knife he had taken from Stephanie Ashcroft's jewellery shop yesterday popped up and wavered in his mind, again; sharp and silver. Lillith had pondered it many times and the thought was always accompanied by a 'pushed sub-thought' that made him think about throwing it away. But it was not his thought. He liked the knife very much. For some reason he couldn't understand, which went beyond the aesthetic, it felt absolutely lethal.

"That's because opposites attract," said Lillith.

"What, this?" He decided to brandish the knife and plucked it from out of his jacket pocket.

"Keep away!!"

"Why?" Its edge gleamed, a razor of silver.

"It's a *Vorpal* blade, Thorn, deadly to us."

"What are you talking about?"

"It was forged to kill demons."

"What?" He was astounded. "*Kill us?*"

"Yes."

He lowered it.

"Only seven were made, smelted from a cross taken from a church in Palestine during the Crusades in the Middle Ages. I have felt the pull of them. In past lives I managed to destroy the other six. It's a sub-plot in our story, if you like."

He waved it in the sunlight. He wanted to stab someone, wanted to cut the Air-bag out of the dash-board. "But, how did you... have the strength, to do it?"

"I pitched myself against their power, and overcame the addiction that could have damaged my destiny-line. Now you must reject yours."

"How? Melt it?"

ZAXXON

"No, it's easier than that, you use dirty water. It is *the spirit* of this knife that must be destroyed. Dirty water saps its purity, and strength, and eventually leaves behind a lifeless husk. You need to drop it into the sewers."

He switched the *Vorpal* blade from his right hand, to his left, and back with fluid ease. His mind seemed to be stuttering on the brink of something he couldn't cope with.

"Get a grip on yourself!" the Succubus demanded. She gave him an empathic slap on his brain and it was a shock.

"OK! I'll do it!"

"So do. Get out of the car."

Before the knife could influence him otherwise, he tugged open his door and stumbled out onto the pavement. He didn't know whether the thing was blessed or cursed, and tried not to think about it. He walked down the street in a daze to a storm drain by the kerb, an iron grill open to the troubled sky. He knelt by it. In his hands was the knife, everything he had ever wanted, as warned. He didn't notice that Lillith was nearby, watching.

He stared at the engraving and the beautiful scrollwork, but the moment to be rid of it was now. Thorn didn't think he'd have the strength to try doing it again another time. He exhaled in a rush, loosened his fingers, and dropped it through the grate... a single second passed... and then it plopped into the shitty water and sank into obscurity. He straightened up.

"Platch, sweet Thorn!" Lillith exclaimed, and hugged him. "No one will find it for a hundred years, and if they do it will be a vacuous rind of silver. For you this was another Uxbridge."

"I seem to remember that word."

"It means no return from a pivotal choice."

"Where did I hear it?"

"From the dreams of Rupert."

"Oh, *him*..."

"Come, we should get back in the car."

The demons returned to the dirty hatch-back. To unwind they fumbled with each other's clothes and had sex that was physically awkward in the circumstances. Thorn's orgasm faded quickly. When they returned to their vigil, so did the rest of his excitement. Compared to the rejection of his knife, sitting in the cramped Peugeot was a magnified boredom, but they didn't have to wait long. Thirty-six minutes later, at 5:55 pm, a tall woman wearing a white sundress with long curly hair appeared round the corner. She walked towards them on the edge of the other side of the road.

"It's her!" said Thorn.
"That is correct," said Lillith.

Stephanie Ashcroft walked with confident strides along the sun-dappled pavement carrying a shoulder purse and a small grey flight bag. As they watched her go up the porch steps of Number 81, the demons became suddenly cold, as normal people also do in the last second before a fight. They watched the Professor's daughter take out keys.

"Let's run across the road and grab her."
"Wait."
"I've been waiting all day!"
"We must take her in the house: this street is too exposed." The tall woman went inside and closed the door behind her. "Let's allow her time to get comfortable."

Thorn swore, and resigned himself to thinking about Stephanie's long smooth legs. "I'm hungry," he said. Although in this example he didn't know whether he was hungry for meat or for sex. He was frequently insatiable for both.

"You know how we do things, Thorn. We feed only after 11pm."

"No one would see. The woman is indoors; a scream is just a scream, whatever the time, isn't it?"

"Those are the rules. It's safer in every way. Darkness is our friend." The Succubus said nothing else, for a while. Then she pointed to the second floor: "You see that frosted glass window?"

He craned his neck to look up at it. "Yeah, what about it?"
"It's been steaming up for a couple minutes."
"She's taking a bath."
"Yes."
"And vulnerable?!"
"Exactly. Now let's engage her to mortal combat in the Material Plane."

The demons cranked open the car doors and alighted eagerly; closed the doors definitively, yet quietly, behind them, and crossed the road. Looking left and right - for more than traffic, they mounted the porch steps with brisk energetic bounds. A shiny brass Chub lock dominated the green paintwork of Stephanie's front door. Thorn gave it an experimental push. It was locked.

Shall I kick it through? He thought to Lillith, feeling a rush of excitement.
No. I have the 'Touch', replied the Succubus.

She felt the lock with two fingers of her right hand. *Just don't interrupt.* She closed her eyes and tilted her head down: frowned, drew the tip of her middle finger around the keyhole and there was a brief crackle of sparks. The bolt moved back in with a quiet 'click' and she pushed on the door. It whispered open across a deep-pile beige carpet that led onto a tidy hallway. They could smell perfume, and the musk beneath. They could hear the sound of water running upstairs. Sliding their hands sensuously along the glossy white banisters, they crept up the steps.

When they were half way up, before emerging onto the brightly lit top landing, they could see three open doors. Their eye-line was level with the floor, at head height. The middle room was dominated by computer equipment, the bathroom was to their left, and the main bedroom was on their far right. They couldn't see into that because they were looking at it from the wrong angle but they could see shadows dancing over the visible carpet as Stephanie busied herself for her bath. The demons were about to continue up when she suddenly emerged from the bedroom wearing a short silky cream dressing gown. She padded across the landing - right beside them - her eyes fixed ahead. She did not see what she didn't expect to see.

The monsters gazed under the hem of her robe, as she passed, each feeling a delicious sexual *frisson*.

They waited for a moment. Heard the sound of the taps being shut off and finished the remaining steps. They followed her into the steamy bathroom and crowded into the doorway. Stephanie was standing in front of a mirrored cabinet, with her left side profile to them, tying up her hair. She sensed their proximity, looked round and gawped at them. There was a strange woman in a blouse and a short skirt, and a teenaged boy well dressed in a fine cream suit - in her bathroom!

"Who are you?"
Make a joke, challenged the Succubus, feeling most relaxed.
Stephanie's voice quaked as she spoke: "What are you doing in my house?"
"We're from the Government," said Thorn. "There's drought on and we've come to make sure you haven't filled up your tub too much."
Lillith guffawed. Thorn briefly fantasized about opening Stephanie's robe. He felt embarrassed, and guilty, and tried to smother the thought. *Go on then, do it...* Lillith prodded.

He reached out and tugged apart the tie, and the robe fell open. Stephanie felt a flash of embarrassment more powerful than any Thorn (or Rupert) had ever experienced. She re-tied it quickly, but not before the strangers had gotten a good gape at her underwear.

Worth waiting for, Thorn mused. *I want to have sex with her.*
So do I, thought Lillith.
Can I watch?
The Succubus spoke. "We want your father's present address."

This didn't surprise Stephanie at all. "He lives in Great Russell Street," she answered. "He has a flat opposite the British Museum."

It was incredible how quickly she had concocted this lie. No such flats existed, yet the trespassers seemed to swallow it. Stephanie could see from a mile off that her dad's precious book was at the core of this crisis. Her mind was considering her own defence. There was a gun. She hadn't thought about it for years, but it was hidden in her bedroom in the bottom drawer of her bureau, a box of bullets with it. But how could she get enough time, unobserved, to get her hands on it?

"Does your father have an ancient book in his possession?"

Stephanie almost laughed, skittishly. She had been right. The consequences of her father's demonic book had finally arrived on her own doorstep. Clenching the ends of the tie around her waist, as tightly as possible to stop her hands shaking, she acted enthusiastic: "Is it smelly, and heavy, and covered in crusty leather?"

The trespasser's eyes opened wider. "It is here?"

"Yes, it's in my bedroom. If you wait here I'll go and get it for you."

"Why should we wait?" asked the boy.

Stephanie patently ignored him and looked directly into the strange eyes of his companion.
"I want to put some clothes on."

"That's acceptable," said Lillith. "You've got four minutes." *We'll clean our teeth.*

I haven't cleaned mine for a week, thought Thorn, and marked the time on his digital watch.

Stephanie padded out of the room and the succubus flipped open the mirrored cabinet and found a chipped cup containing two tooth brushes, one old and one unused, and a tube of Colgate.

If she doesn't actually have the book you can rape her.

311

I want the old brush.
There, take it.

They squeezed out a portion of paste, each. They started scrubbing in front of the mirror. Thorn found himself becoming aroused by the soft worn-down bristles. Lillith feigned amazement. She looked at him with her eyebrows raised and chuckled.

Are you erecting because that brush has been in her mouth?
No! Alright; yes. Give me a break, OK, Lillith? She's good looking meat. I'm only human.
He carried on cleaning.
That's always my point, you aren't human at all. You're an Incubus - the most highly sexed male Blight in any world!
He looked at his watch. *Do you fancy a quick one? We've got just over two minutes.*

The Succubus smiled. He closed the bathroom door.

*   *   *

Stephanie Ashcroft knew that she would have to fight alone. She could scream from a window but she would most likely be dead before anyone came to her aid. She couldn't call the police either. Her mobile phone charger had disappeared in Scotland along with the rest of her luggage, and its battery had been dead itself long before her flight to Gatwick. She had no land-line extension in the room and cursed the lack of it. Crossing to her bureau like a piece of lint on a strong breeze, she wondered if there was sufficient time to throw on some clothes, as well as procure the gun from amongst the cold weather wear in her bottom drawer. She opened the middle drawer. Snatched up a pair of jeans and a 'T' shirt. She had never dressed so quickly!

Her father had brought back the pistol from South America several years ago. He had given it to her for 'home defence' but, of course, she had never expected to use it. It was a Webley. She knew that because it was written along both sides of the barrel. It was bigger than she remembered; and blacker, and it felt reassuringly heavy. Rifling the tweed skirts and cashmere sweaters for the ammunition, she wondered how he had managed to bring it into the country. Had she ever asked how he had beaten Customs? She could not remember. Her exploring fingers turned up the box of shells. She swallowed several times, her mouth dry, and ripped the cardboard lid off it. The bullets looked powerful and shiny, and were in a block as neat as new batteries on a factory conveyer belt.

Fiddling with the gun, trying to open the damned breach with her breath catching in her throat, she noticed something wrong with those bullets. They had holes in them. All the lead points were hollowed out! Stephanie could only hope they would do the job, if the situation passed critical and she actually had to pull the trigger. She was full of dread and curiosity, about everything, particularly the time. There were sex noises coming from the bathroom, now. That was good, but after their coitus things were probably going to get violent. The trespassers aspired to acquire something she did not have. How many minutes, how many precious *seconds,* did she have left?

Frustrated with the Webley's idiotic catches, she pressed something else and suddenly opened a pivot in front of the trigger guard. The whole barrel assembly dropped forward. It startled her. The empty drum was exposed, and her hands shook as she fumbled to load the six chambers. She dropped a few shells on the floor but it was done faster than she could have hoped. She snapped the gun back together, and stood with her feet apart. Thumbed back the hammer, and raised the weapon with both hands like she had seen done on TV. Stephanie waited. Her back was against the wall.

The sound of sex soon diminished until all was quiet. The bathroom door opened and the trespassers crossed the landing and walked into plain sight. The boy registered the threat. He halted warily in the doorway, but his companion walked forward a few steps. She grinned and opened her arms, but the gesture was not friendly, it was suicidal. Stephanie re-discovered her voice.

"Don't come any closer!"

The woman said nothing. The boy drew up behind her and stood at her left shoulder. Their smiles were the same; they shared the same secrets. It was as if the couple were communicating telepathically. Stephanie found herself getting really wound up by the silence - it was heightening all her senses. She could have heard a bead of sweat drop onto the carpet; could have smelt the scent of their rut from a hundred yards; could feel the wood in the butt of the pistol as though it was still part of a living tree. And abruptly they screamed, from the tops their lungs, a nonsensical word like "Meeaeet!" with a long 'E'.

Stephanie jumped with shock and pulled the trigger. The affects were incredibly immediate. The pistol kicked into the palms of her hands, there was a muzzle flash in the afternoon light, smoke, and a detonation. It was awful. The woman took the bullet in the lower chest and was thrown against the wall in a spray of blood. The vessels carrying Stephanie's own seemed to shrink deeper beneath her skin, she could physically feel herself going white. She dropped the pistol and hurried over to kneel by the wounded woman. The movement may have saved her from fainting.

"I didn't mean it!" she cried, "I didn't!" she said, through her fingers. Then: "God, I'm sorry!"

The woman was laying on her front, facing the wall, her features hidden. Arms and legs akimbo like a casually discarded child's doll. She looked totally dead. Most of the blood was rushing from a wound in her lower back, partially concealed by a tatter of singed clothing. The boy knelt beside Stephanie and spoke.

"Her name is Lillith," he said. "Now, watch closely. This is the best bit."

"What is?" She had forgotten all about him.

"The power of our union." He carefully peeled back the ripped, wet, cloth. "She is Zaxxon."

The bullet had torn through the woman's stomach and passed out of the other side, smashing the vertebrae about two thirds of the way down her spine. "We are both demons." The exit wound was the size of a fist and it was the reddest thing Stephanie had ever seen. "You don't believe me?" Something really strange was happening. "Witness the miracle of your own doom!"

The blood was...moving. Stephanie blinked. It was sliding down the spray pattern on the wall, diagonally in the direction of Lillith's body leaving white wallpaper in its wake. Like it was alive. Dribbling back to the source with the effect of a film in reverse. Pieces of bone were being recycled into the wound. It was healing itself. Muscle covered cartilage, skin covered blood vessels, and Lillith abruptly animated, raised herself on her fingertips, twisted towards Stephanie with her raven hair hanging over her face, and hissed like a feral cat. Stephanie's mind was having a kind of seizure. The scent of cordite from her first shot was still in the air and all she could think of was the gun. She was about to leap backwards and grab it when an arm slipped around her neck. The boy was standing behind her. His arm was very strong.

"Be careful with her, Thorn!" said Lillith.

Lillith stood, stretched happily, and raked her raven hair back with her fingertips. She walked a few steps further into the room and scooped up the Webley. Stephanie struggled towards it making small noises of desire.

"You want this sword?"
"Yes! Yes!"

Lillith nodded to Thorn, who released her. "Have it then." She returned the pistol to Stephanie, who stepped backwards towards her bed, aiming it at them.

"Now I've got you!" Stephanie exclaimed.

"It won't do you any good," Thorn pointed out.

Lillith stepped towards her. "Did you not see what just happened?"

"Stop it, or I'll shoot, I swear it!"

"You've got a really short memory," commented her companion. "I used have the same problem when I was a boy. I couldn't remember a damned thing!"

"That sword is useless."

"No, no, impossible," Stephanie whimpered.

"Accept it!"

Stephanie lowered the muzzle. Her blood filled with ice.

"We cannot be killed," stated Thorn.

"But the same thing cannot be said about you," said his lover. "Now give me back the sword, answer a few simple questions, and we may not use it on you." Then she added: "I may demonstrate mercy." It was a lie. She opened her hand to Stephanie, who hesitated. She noticed the crumpled up projectile on the floor. "Monsters!" she whispered.

"That's a matter of opinion. Don't screw this up, Miss Ashcroft," advised Thorn.

"You've given us enough trouble. Now give me back the sword!" shouted Lillith.

Stephanie shuddered. "OK, OK," and passed it over butt first into the monster's palm.

"Good." Lillith aimed it at her casually. "You don't have our book do you?"

"No."

"Your father has it." It was a statement, not a question. "When did you last talk to your father?"

"Yesterday."

"He is in the South West, presently, is he not? Avon? Somerset?"

"Bristol."

"Good. Furnish us with his address there."

ZAXXON

"It's in my note book, in my handbag." Stephanie glanced left, at her dressing table.

Lillith's eyes followed. There was a shoulder bag by the mirror, like a prize in an expensive lucky-dip. "Fetch it."

"- And I suggest no tricks, this time," said Thorn.

Stephanie had never seriously contemplated her own death. Before this it had always seemed to be something that was kind of preposterous, but now everything had changed. She had witnessed an abomination, had seen the impossible made possible, and she would call in that 'demonstration of mercy' because without it she would surely die. She picked up the bag.

"Turn it upside down on your bed," ordered Lillith.

Stephanie did. Amongst the litter of cosmetics, coins, shop receipts, and bits of tissue that showered onto her continental quilt, was her Lloyds address book. It was slim, black, and well thumbed, and a small part of her could not touch it. It reeked of betrayal. But the part which was not afraid didn't last more than a few heart beats. The bravery was dissolved by a memory, in a vision of blood spilt and unspilt, by the undoing of a wound she had personally inflicted that should have been terminal. So she picked up the booklet. She could not fight these creatures.

"Open it," ordered Lillith. "And tell me where your father is staying in Bristol."

Stephanie flicked through to the last entry. "The last known address I have is where he was staying last night. Number 58, Keys Avenue, in Horfield, with the Doctor and Mrs Bryan Johnson."

"Thank you," said Lillith, and raised the pistol. She thumbed back the hammer.

Stephanie gaped down the barrel, momentarily unable to comprehend the turn of events. Her hair prickled with sudden deep-seated terror. She was about to cry out Lillith's own expression, "demonstrate mercy!" when the succubus fired a fatal shot before she could say more than half of the first word. Sufficient time to say "demon-s" only, before the bullet pierced her heart. The Zaxxon locked the front door behind them, and crossed the street.

They climbed into the grimy car. The Succubus examined the AA map until the route was adhered to her memory, which took under three seconds, and then she started the engine telekinetically, without using a key. She guided the vehicle onto the road. They were going to track down Stephanie's father, now. They didn't take the actual address book, which was an over-sight, but they did take the gun and its ammunition with them, as if they weren't venomous enough already.

CHAPTER – 16

"Arm.it.age"

Tony experienced a vision during the night after the crime, a dream so vivid he could not forget it after he awoke even if he wanted to. The old book was under his bed. He liked it. He had been worried he would have trouble getting to sleep after all the excitement but the book seemed to take him there like magic. It fatigued him with a silent essence, powerful and reassuring, like the engine of an ocean liner pushing through a moonlit sea at the beginning of a long journey. He slipped into REM easily. From there, more poignant dreams swam up from his unconscious depths to envelop him like bubbles. The artist fidgeted in his sleep, sufficiently to have woken up Samantha had she had been lying beside him. Indeed, if their bodies had been touching in their slumber, she may not have been the victim inside his nightmare.

In Tony's dream they were sitting alone, outside the Watershed, on a cool windless day. He was passing his share of the spoils across the table into his girlfriend's hands. He wanted her approval but as she grasped the book her curiosity evolved into an expression of disgust. She would not open it, and he retrieved it, angered. Sam would not give it a chance because she obviously didn't trust his judgement. If she would just look at it, see that ancient text even briefly, he was sure that she would love it as he did. So he turned the front cover of the book toward her, reached around and opened it in her face. The leather shuddered in his hands, and a surprise took hold of the exposed vellum that was as far from what he wanted as the sea is from the summit of a mountain. It started crumbling, with a noise like fine art on fire, and became dust pouring onto the table in a small avalanche of black powder.

He returned the tome to himself, alarmed and desperate to halt the erosion, feeling an increasing rage focussing on Sam because it was all her fault. She had hated it from the start! He ran his fingers over the disintegrating text and saw that this was more than a metaphorical illusion; it was the symbols themselves that were crumbling, not the paper. His fingertips looked sooty and he licked the powder off one of them without thinking. The affect was almost instantaneous. Joy swept through his mind in a happy explosion. His features became numb. His lips stretched into a mindless rubbery smile and his brain filled with brilliant ideas like fluffy clouds. Everything was alright, now, but he couldn't tell this to Sam because for some Hollywood reason beyond his control he found himself leaning over the table and snorting the stuff up his nostrils like a vacuum cleaner.

"I'm growing into a flower," he managed to say.

"Stop it Tony," Sam cried. "It's addictive!"

He looked up at her. "It's just seeds. Billions of seeds."

"It's cocaine!"

He raised one eyebrow theatrically, something he had never been able to do whilst sober. "I never heard of black cocaine before." He snorted more.

"That's because you don't know anything about it."

"This powder...it's just words, Sam, words written long ago from which great flowers grow. My body is the water and my spirit is the light and I'm growing -" He tapped his heart: "...here." He slid the ancient book across to her. "You must join me."

"I won't!"

"If we are not unified, from this day and this hour, we may never understand each other again."

"Don't say that."

"Grow with me, my darling, stem to stem."

"I don't want it!"

"Be a beautiful flower too. It's white, you know."

She saw the dust in the cleft of the pages. Although she didn't want to think about it, she guessed there was enough left for her. "Don't make me," she moaned. "Don't make me do it, Tony!"

"If you do love me, truly, you will."

ZAXXON

He smiled at this, nodding, and watched her face gradually lean toward the open pages. Her nostrils flaring, getting closer and closer to the powder. From now on he knew they would live together in the same garden. The tip of her nose touched the black seeds like a kiss, and jagged teeth sprang from the edges of the book, like a classique man-trap. Razor sharp iron jaws swung closed and clamped through her neck and took off her whole head in one huge mechanical bite. He sat there, traumatised. Unable to do, or move, or think of anything except the wilted white flower inside him. He needed more powder. None remained. There was nothing left on the table but blood and the machine that spilt it. And engraved on the rear of the trap were words that finally galvanized him to scream:

WITH LOVE FROM DEMITRIUS x

Under his sweaty duvet Tony awoke instantly, shaking, reaching for Sam. The scream on his lips connected his dream-world to his bedroom. He sat upright as fast as the trap which had sprung closed over his girlfriend's neck, and the residue of the nightmare stank of selfishness and cowardice.

It was so vivid he knew two things for certain. Not only would he have to be rid of the old book, but also that the dream would take a long time to fade. It was six o'clock in the morning. The thing under his bed was his prize in the ancient cat-and-mouse game of crime, Demitrius's game, yet later this morning Tony would sell it for as much cash as he could get. He lowered his head to the pillow. The book seemed to radiate the opposite elixir to the engine that had helped to drowse him last night. A noiseless desperate essence like blood falling onto the road from the undercarriage of a speeding ambulance. He fell asleep anyway.

*   *   *

It was Friday 27th June. That afternoon, after a tasteless platter of cod and chips, Tony found the shop he had been looking for. It was behind the main pedestrian precinct. Carrying the book under his arm, where for some reason it felt the most comfortable, he walked up to the place, sneezing in the sun. It looked exactly like the cliché he had imagined it to be. The facade was an anachronism. It would have looked more at home in Victorian times, and the window display was a grey disorganised clutter but, on the inside, Tony sensed wisdom and secrets. The sign read: 'Andrew Armitage: Antiquarian book dealer' and on the grimy door glass was written: 'Books bought FOR CASH!' Tony could almost smell the currency. The last word was 'CLOSED' but he could see a man leaning over his counter with a pen. So Tony tested the door. And to his relief, it opened.

Tony entered the shop to the accompaniment of a small clanging bell. The dusty interior was the same, straight out of 19th century England, like he had travelled in time to a simpler age. The shop keeper was old, about fifty, and looked much like a ghost: grey hair, a grey moustache, thin spectacles. He was wearing a linen suit of a colour that blended into the books around him like camouflage. His face crinkled and Tony realised he was smiling.

"Are you open?" the young artist asked him.

"Of course we are, sir," replied the man. "My name is Andrew Armitage. I am the Proprietor."

"I've got this book I want you to take a look at." He walked up to the counter holding the thing in both hands. "It's really old."

"Well, I'll have a look at it for you," said the shop keeper, and chuckled. "Just how 'old' is it?"

Tony placed it on the worn varnished counter but for some reason his hands seemed to be paralysed. "I don't know - very old." He couldn't let go of it. *Seeds, billions of seeds...*

"Is it your intention to sell it?"

"Yes."

"May I look at it?"

"Yes." Tony forced his fingers to open, and pushed the book across to the shop keeper.

Mr Armitage took hold of it by the edges of its leather cover, opened it, and suddenly appeared horrified. He looked like he was about to be sick and snapped it shut. "I'm sorry. We don't deal in foreign works, only English or Latin." He pushed it back to Tony.

"But it's hundreds and hundreds of years old!"

"Undoubtedly."

"Maybe a thousand, and in the back are the papers to translate it."

"That's not the kind of Note of Provenance I would ask for. Why don't you sell it on *e-bay*?"

"I'm not on the Web at the moment," said Tony. He wouldn't have known what to do even if he had been. "Three hundred pounds!" he blurted out.

"Offer it to a museum."

"Fifty pounds!"

"I'm sorry. You'll have to leave."

"I'm sorry too," said the young artist. He picked it up. Turned and left the shop.

*   *   *

Tony had amassed such wages from the sale of his paintings that now he had more money in the bank than ever before. He didn't know his copy of the *Necronomicon* was the only one that existed. To someone who knew what it was, at auction, on a good day, it could have fetched around thirty million pounds! Tony Newman held it over a dustbin in a hot street. He had hoped to raise a few hundred quid to add to his growing fortune but he had just wasted the bus fare. He thought about flowers, and drew the book back to himself. Disposing of it was too much of a waste. He hugged it. If he couldn't sell it, he would read it, and start this afternoon...

He got back home at half past three and found he was alone in the flat. That was good. Demitrius had tacked a message to the bottom of his wide LCD TV saying 'working on the new ride - see you at about half passed seven - PARTY TONIGHT!!' Tony walked into his bedroom feeling as thrilled about the book as a kid about to open the biggest birthday present of his life. The room was baking. He pulled apart the curtains for light and opened the windows for cooler air. He cleared the desk that his Dad had bought from MFI last year with one sweep of his arm.

Brushes, pens, pencils, sketches, and note paper were knocked off it onto the grimy carpet like a matchstick house demolished by a strong breath. He pulled up a chair. Unfolded the translation papers, laid the ancient book beside them; and although he was thirsty he was too excited to fetch water. There was a brief confusion when he realised that he had nothing to write with. He leaned over and picked a sheet of paper and a pencil off the floor, and started the task. The pencil was a '3B' and the blackness of its soft lead seemed appropriate, as was 'Launch Terrace', the name of the building where this transcription was about to take place. He wrote down his first words, which he knew must be the title:

'NECRONOMICON GALAXION: ENVISAGE OF THE FOUR FLOWERS.'

There was a précis written in Old English inside the front cover. According to that, and the adjusted Pagan calendar it utilized, the *Necronomicon* had been constructed at the very beginning of the first millennium. The writer was a Frenchman named Thadeus, a magi in an order of witch monks called the *Sect of the Blight*. They lived in a priory, in Renes, surrounded by reversed religious symbols. Thadeus had been inducted into this environment at the age of twelve, traded against some of his mother's more popular improprieties, and had lived there until he died at the age of thirty. A servant, at first, then up the levels of the Black Robes.

ZAXXON

'Home' had been a sleepless grey place of whispers and cold stone, hidden deep in the countryside near the town. According to the notation, the head of their order gave Thadeus a simple choice on his thirtieth birthday. To be re-incarnated as a lowly beast, or become a Stygian demon, by offering himself to the force that resided in the lowest vicinity of the world. To be possessed by Him that they worshipped, as His writer. Thadeus had chosen the latter, deploying what is known today, to some, as 'automatic writing'.

He was used like a marionette. Blacked out at his desk, on a regular basis. He illustrated anatomy, prophetic machinations, conjuration, symbolic magics, and traversed page after page of arcane knowledge from beyond this world into a form of writing previously unknown. Much effort was made to conceal this legendary work but it was a secret that could not be kept. Eventually it was alleged the Devil had driven his pen. This was true; but even if it had not been, it would have made no difference. In those days a simple allegation like that was all it took to have you killed. He was accused of keeping a mouse as a 'familiar' (which was actually his pet rodent Gypswick), raising the dead, invoking goblins and other devices of Pandemonium, and conspiring with the Devil. These charges were overstated, of course, but that made no difference either. Three days after he had completed the book, passing it into safe hands - and into obscurity, for many decades - Thadeus was burnt at the stake alongside everyone else in his sect.

Here the notation ended and the cuneiform code began. The reading would be more difficult, now, but Tony soon familiarised himself with the method of decryption, and was well ready. He picked up his pencil and began the translation. He worked from right to left, from the bottom up. Looked back and forth, from the wedges and slashes of the bizarre language, into letters and words, and word dividers, in plain English. It was a slow process but it was magical; and Tony wanted to know it all.

The four sides involved, at the most excellent beginning, had agreed our planet exhibited great potential. So they moved it closer to the Sun by space-tug, eons ago, and injected it with a micro-cosmic catalyst of life as an experiment to avoid a war that could have laid waste the entire galaxy. Demitrius had been right about the existence of aliens. Life on Earth had been due to their intervention and Tony himself wasn't very surprised.

This ambitious venture had been instigated by four matriarchal societies living and dying around four thousand other stars. They were named after flowers, and there was an illustration of these at the bottom of the page in coloured inks and fine gold leaf. The two small red and blue blooms like chrysanthemums were called the *Luminon* and the *Plexity*: and the two giant black and white blooms, like roses with huge spikes, were called the *Zaxxon* and the *Pleiads*. These flowers grew most prominently on Planet Galaxion, which was the Seat of Interstellar Government.

Before the war these great nations had viewed themselves as perfectly balanced. A Yin Yang configuration had been drawn on the next page. The names of the four alien races were indicated to their allied colours. A little red in the white (a little *Plexity* in the *Pleiads*) and a little blue in the black (a little *Luminon* in the *Zaxxon*). And all were contained within the Milky Way Eternity Circle and rotated by the 'S' shaped curve (a 'mirror', which divided them) called The Propeller, which was driven by a black hole in the centre of the galaxy. They had lived in peace since time out of mind, until evolution itself made them telepathic - and destroyed it.

Terrible weapons were created: plasma smart bombs, ion canons, lasers. They marched against each other in new battleships. The police fought the army, and where the two largest sides met, the black and white didn't make any kind of shade of grey, it made the green colour of blood. Whole planets were broken up and scattered into asteroids, and trillions were dying. So, in the hope it wasn't already too late, the four sides agreed to hold talks on Galaxion, where they re-formed the Interstellar Government and began their visionary quest.

Under the perfumed purple sky of that planet, The Most Respected Lady ordered the manufacturing of a computer program called The Book of the Dead (which almost converts, sardonically, into Latin as *The Necronomicon*) and on it were recorded the names of the victims of all that had died during the conflict. It took two standard years. One of the data-processors hypothesized that if it was printed on hardcopy the length of the paper would be 95 kilometres. During the conception of this tribute, the great nations conversed. Their armadas were ready to attack but they envisaged a way to create a lasting peace. The envoys knew of a primordial planet in a remote district that merely needed to be moved. It already had a lovely small moon, and it didn't need to be 'terra-formed' because its atmosphere had been calculated to be perfect for carbon-based life. They called it Eden. That's how Chapter One ended.

Tony's pencil was blunt to the wood. He went into the kitchenette for refreshment, and drank a lot of water. It cooled down his brain and he returned to his desk feeling healthier, and discovered something else in the *Necronomicon* that was amazing. The chapters ended with magical rites to invoke paranormal ability. Thadeus's quill had recorded these as 'conjurations' that offered to cheat the evolutionary process. There was such a rite at the end of every chapter in the book, and, in this first example, it generated the power of telekinesis. The instructions stated the faculty could only be unconsciously applied, like moving a hand or a foot. Tony's perspective had changed suddenly from abstract theory to intimate biological fact, but his hesitation lasted a few seconds, only. He re-sharpened his pencil.

The translation looked slightly inane but the *Necronomicon* needed to be taken seriously, the power of its knowledge accepted with the utmost respect. The text asked on behalf of the reader for what was called the 'Touch', the word for telekinesis in the ancient parlance, and the conjuration was a curious blend of poetry and mathematics. The tribute was to the spirits of the *Luminon*; the application, to their goddess Tanith. Part of the decryption needed to be read aloud, and that would deliver the conjuration in any language. Engineer an ability beyond imagining. There was no need for 'fetishes', as the book called them; cauldrons or potions or hexes, they were superfluous to requirements. Tony took a deep breath. The last instruction explained the numbers were neural nets (very advanced science) and the *magic* was what awoke and connected them.

He started to read it aloud. Immediately felt a narcotic-like 'high' before the last word was even out of his mouth. A wonderful head-rush, pleasure the like of which he had never hitherto experienced. He looked around his room with a confused smile, shivering with joy, and chuckled. It was a sound that sounded distant and hollow to his own ears, but somewhere in the deep recesses of his metamorphosing brain, where his future and his sanity were being changed forever, Tony could hear Tanith's song. The sweet music of the *Luminon* sung in a soul-stirring language he had never heard before, nor could have imagined. The wonder of it made him think of rivers, and starlight, and it was accompanied by the deft fingers of an alien picking harp strings. He was alone in his room. Rocking backwards and forwards, with tears of ecstasy pouring down his face.

Eventually he opened his eyes. There was no indication as to whether this magic had taken a few seconds, or a few minutes, because his watch had been long forgotten. He ached for the return of that feeling, worse than a person with influenza getting out of hot relaxing bath in a freezing bathroom and wishing to get back in the tub. His chin rested on his chest until he had his breathing under control. It had been the most amazing thing. Like a flower during a drought filling from the root with the strength of cool fresh rain. Tony flexed his hands over his desk, and tried to flip over the next page of the *Necronomicon* with his mind alone. It didn't work.

He experimented with moving something smaller, his pencil, but that didn't work either. He picked it up, recalling the instructions had said the capability was directed sub-consciously, but he didn't really care right now. He looked at his watch. There as about an hour before Demi returned home at 7:30, there was a pencil in his hand, and secrets to uncover!

*   *   *

The four great nations prepared Planet Eden for their experiment to stop galactic war and prevent their own annihilation. They tugged the little world to the correct distance from its star, altered its tilt and rotation, created multiple-layer atmospheres, adjusted electro-magnetic fields. And, at last, after a thousand forecasts, primitive cellular life was catalyzed. The four sides dismantled their arsenals and decommissioned their gun-ships. They left the rest to evolution. Stability was restored to the galaxy and the fauna of the planet ultimately became sufficiently advanced to populate with the souls of their own races on (what they hoped) was a re-incarnation basis. They were advanced races, and sent envoys. They knew a lot about the After-life.

They continued waiting. The planet was re-named The Earth by its own people. There was no war, except that which they had inadvertently started themselves, which had been hidden from them. A conflict beyond the Material Plane fought by the Gods and Goddesses of the *Zaxxon* and the *Pleiads* for human souls. The aliens waited, eons, for the Answer. A time passed that was so long the young artist figured they had probably worked it out on their own. Supposedly the aliens are out there, still, looking down at us. Waiting to see how the people of Earth may live with telepathy, if that were possible, or if it would cause an apocalypse.

The *Necronomicon* surmised that such destruction may have already happened - six times – but the Devil was a crook. Tony had already out-guessed the purpose of this book. At some point, probably at the end, the *Necronomicon* would be capable of creating mass mind-to-mind communication overnight. It would be a disaster, a cheat. People needed to be acclimatized to telepathy, slowly and carefully. The book instilled undeserved power in individuals, upset the balance of the learning curve of life, and ultimately may ruin our planet's natural right to the opportunity to progress. Yes, *damned* was the operative word.

'THE IDENTIFICATION OF ORIGINS'

This page was faded. It was a sepia colour, like most of the rest of them, but the illustration showed as clearly as the nose on your face that we are not quite as individual as we thought we were. Tony squinted down at the revelations and learned that all Earth people are allied to the four nations, everyone is spiritually connected to and, to some extent, *physically*, part alien! The evidence can be used to identify a person's true origins, through the creases of an adult's forehead, in the markings of what some call the 'third eye'. A distinction to be seen in the pattern of the skin above the nose and between the eyebrows in the act of frowning.

People whose skin made an upside down 'box' formation (known as *The Gate*) were of the *Plexity*. Those whose skin scrunched into a shallow angled 'V' shape (known as *Angry Water*) were of the *Pleiads*. People with a few vertical lines (known the *Little Flame*) were from the *Luminon*, and those with horizontal lines (the more bars, the higher the ranking) were of the *Zaxxon*.

Tony tried to light a cigarette but his lighter was out of fuel, and his hands were shaking. It was the greatest conspiracy of all time. Taken from the end of Chapter Two, in the Devil's own words:

ZAXXON

The Earth people will not know until the hour of their doom that in the short future it is Art that kept them alive. Not love, nor money, nor the politics of kings or princes. Art keeps their world turning. Their society will scorn Art, but they will not be able to live without it, and they will not understand why.

Emissaries from the Four Tribes have been incarnated among them for three millennia. Infiltrated their civilization as Artists, connected to the Outer Forces via synchronicity. They are guardians, to develop the race and keep its secrets. The facts will be hidden in the writing and music, on the stage, or on canvas, of these Artists, and they will be celebrated. They are like the wheels of The Experiment. They are made of stars, and they will control the people with their creative process: cloaked in metaphors, but for those with eyes to see, who will awaken. Necessarily, I may also incarnate purer demons called Blight to counter Angelic movement in the future of their Material Plane.

There can be no argument that Eden ensured an age of peace within the Galactic Plate. The problem is the experiment's unrealistically long duration. Much intrigue has disappeared into myth down the long light-years; some has been remembered in testaments the like of this, mine own. Now all eyes are upon the Earth. Yet what, wonder ye, of the fate of the people of that planet? I say all will fail. Their souls will not always be returned from whence they came. Brother will kill brother, and their spirits will join the Tribe they deserve to according to their behaviour during life. I have seen this before. Here, below, is the conjuration to raise fire at will without flint or tinderbox. No fetishes are required. Take It, and light yourself!

Tony's pencil had teeth marks on the stem but he couldn't recall biting it. His chest felt tight. His tongue flicked continuously over his lips in body-language that was typical of want, because it was truly like a narcotic. That's how he compared the conjurations of the *Necronomicon* - to heroin – and he needed its magic so badly it was the perfect

331

comparison. He had refused to take such a hard drug all his life but he physically needed this head-rush, now, and he didn't care about the paradox. A dribble of spit dangled from his mouth and dropped onto the page as he translated the tribute. It was to the *Zaxxon*, yet it was not evil, per se. The application was for the 'Flare', old parlance for an oil lamp or a phosphorus torpedo, and it was offered up to *Yogsothoth*: the Lord of Fire. Tony stood, and raised one hand.

He spoke the numbers, and the poetry, unselfconsciously aloud in the commanding voice of an orator. The pleasure took him immediately. He fell to his knees in a state of rapture; shaking, teetering. The experience was as beautiful as last time. The music of aliens was drawing nearer, so he struggled back to his feet. He could hear bells approaching, and drums, and wood-wind instruments; with a bass-line so powerful he became captivated. And then it took him: he danced. His arms shaped sunrays in the air, his body swaying like reeds in limbs flowing with dark resonances that only he could hear, and he danced around his room. It was his *right* to, and it was also just... *right*. Ignorant of time passing, the conjuration left him spread-eagled on his bed shuddering and bewildered. The front door banged open. People bustled into the hallway.

Demitrius shouted: "Rock this funky house!" and Tony leapt off his mattress and snatched up the *Necronomicon* and the paper-work, re-crossed the room quickly on the tips of his toes, and lobbed it deep under his bed. So hard, and so lackadaisically, he wondered if he may have damaged it. But at least it was hidden before the Cypriot poked his head around the doorway. The man's moustached face shone with an unusually winning smile, and he tossed Tony a can of beer. The artist cracked open the Jamaican 'Red-Stripe' and it was so cold droplets of condensation had formed around the outside of the tin. What he really wanted was a glass, so he could hold it up to the light and check the quality of the lager. He drank several big swigs and found that it was heavy to his taste, and chilled, and delicious. He figured it might even take his mind off his high, if he drank enough of it.

"Thank you very much," Tony exclaimed.

"Don't mention it," said Demitrius. "We've another two cases of that stuff. The Dreyer Brothers are paying for it. Come through and see them. It's paaarty tiiime!"

Tony rubbed the sweat off his face with his right forearm: "I'm right with you!"

He followed the Cypriot through the corridor to the living-room. It was west-facing, quiet, and full of light shining through the window. It emphasised dust particles and streamers of smoke, and it had that elongated orangey/yellow quality that heralds sunset. The young artist found a place to sit near the glass topped coffee table, on the carpet. He didn't mind. The table had party and drug paraphernalia on it in a neat row like a parade of plastic soldiers. A box of matches, Rizla papers, two bottles of Jack Daniels, a bag of grass, a small pipe and a lump of resin to smoke in it. Jason was rolling a joint. There were also two small bottles of Amyl Nitrate and a baggie of white powder, which captured Tony's attention. "What's that stuff?" he asked Jason.

"Nothing too heavy, just a bit of Speed."

"We've got enough drink and drugs here to sink a ship."

"Yeah, man, we is goin' to the *moon!*"

Tony had travelled further than the moon, already - twice that day. Patrick Dreyer was desperately pushing buttons on the stereo system. He was one of those people that didn't like to be in a room with others in the absence of music. Demitrius helped him; opened a CD case, placed the disc onto the drawer and sent it sliding back into the machine. A drum loop started. It was simple, at first, then the song began to build with a melody that was trancelike and uplifting. Demitrius twisted the volume control upwards. Tony took a puff of marijuana, aware that the hot end was like a tiny forest fire, near his face. He thought the music that

Demitrius had chosen had a style that was allegorically slightly beyond this world, but it lacked depth. It was not even close to the purple velvety power of a song composed by aliens of the *Zaxxon*. He passed the joint to Demitrius then chugged down half a can of lager.

In one afternoon he had learnt some things uncloaked, and without metaphors, so revealing they could influence everything. Undermine political power, destroy the church, even cause the entropy of society. 'The Alien Source of Man, fact and myth': he thought - that would make a great book title. He had become aware of the nature of Art. He wanted to celebrate that, but was it right? The book was like rocks on a railway line. There was a little tear in his left eye, which was banished by a mouthful of whisky that burned down his throat and heated his stomach. He didn't want his life to be different, but maybe it was already over, and too late to weep about. If he so chose he could be an angel, again, like when he was a little boy. He could undertake the responsibilities of a true Artist and incorporate the secret into his work, coalesce the origins of frowning skin into his paintings, maybe, hiding them in trees or water or sky. But he wasn't excited about it. He wasn't interested in painting at all.

The *Necronomicon* was causing a weight of guilt. Stealing his ambition like burning his clothes and leaving him naked and cold. He didn't want to lose his painting. It was his self-esteem, his job, but there was more, and it was worse. When he thought about his girlfriend he felt dirty inside like the aftermath of a terrible lie. He didn't want to face it, but his passion for Sam may have become diluted in the conjurations of the book. It was under his bed, now, and always in the back of his mind. The thinking behind it was the mechanism of a Venus fly-trap. It manipulated its reader with sweet nectar to create an addiction in which the reader loses themselves, designed to suck them past the last chapter and to read the final conjuration - and lose everyone else. The book was against love. Considering who had written it, this shouldn't have been a surprise. Jason passed

ZAXXON

Tony the joint, and poured more sour-mash whisky into his glass.

Tony did not want to have his whole life turned upside down by an inanimate object. He didn't want to be a victim. Most poignantly, he didn't want to be a bad person, because he really wasn't. Action needed to be taken, so he raised his glass, to himself, in a silent oath. He would fight his addiction. He would mend his love for Samantha, and he would never read the *Necronomicon* again. In fact he was going to try to find the strength to destroy it. Now *that* was worth celebrating! He took a deep drag of the joint, finished his whisky, and cracked open another beer. Tomorrow, after getting back from the moon, he would use Interflora to send his beloved some beautiful flowers.

"Oi, Jason!" Demitrius was exasperated. "I already told you, don't roach your spliffs with my Unexplained Magazines!"

"It's an unexplainable roach, Demi."

Patrick was chopping and shaping lines of white powder on the glass. "If you guys make me laugh I'm gonna end up blowing this stuff all over the floor. Do you want to snort a line of Speed, Tone?"

"No! Thanks, but no."

Night had fallen, and the music had become loud. It thumped and rippled through the walls and ceiling and rattled the electric bar fire in the grate. Demitrius had a reputation amongst the other tenants: none would complain. An hour or so went by. The second bottle of whisky was cracked open and the little hash pipe was passed about. Tony noticed the Cypriot hardly inhale it, probably because the man was a control freak. Occasionally the hashish appeared in Tony's own hands and the hot smoke was oily and affective. He felt happier, but more importantly he felt *clean*, and that had nothing to do with the pipe.

Time seemed to move at different speeds. Tony felt like he was on a funfair ride on a summer night: tilting, spinning.

Patrick suddenly ran out of the room with a hand over his mouth. Jason was having trouble focusing, his eyes looked drooped. The table was littered with spent matches, bits of tobacco, a couple of busted cigarette lighters, an overflowing ashtray, and beer cans. There were empty cans around the floor, also. The room smelt like an illegal rave party. Demi seemed to be guzzling what remained of the second bottle of Jack Daniels, holding the bottle base up in the smoky air. Tony could hardly believe his eyes but he never saw the man put the bottle down. Everything was phasing in and out, becoming a blur. Jason fell over sideways with a bottle of Amyl under his nose. He had taken a huge sniff of it and fainted dead away. It spilt over his sleeping brother's trousers with a smell like a swimming pool. He didn't get up. Demitrius passed Tony a beer and the artist opened it blearily. He was seeing double; the table was tilting diagonally but somehow nothing was falling off.

"So what have you been up to today?" slurred Demitrius, sitting on the sofa like a Buddha.
"Oh, I was jus' readin'."
"That old book?"
"Yeah, it really screwed with my head, y'know?"
"What's it about?"
"Magic spells, and stuff about aliens." Tony swallowed half the can of beer. "I don't even wanna *talk* about it, fuckin' thing's *evil*." His head fell forward onto the table with an audible bump. His consciousness was slipping away. "Demi, can you hand me a cigarette?"

The white and gold packet started moving by itself. Sliding along the table into Tony's hand like a car with an empty fuel tank rolling up a hill. Demitrius gaped, and observed this impossibility with an excitement almost akin to terror, as one of the cigarettes floated out of the box with no strings attached and up into Tony's half open mouth. The young artist's face was to one side, his eyes closed. "Thanks, Demi," he muttered. "Got a light?" A lime-tinted fire-work sprouted on the tip of the exposed tobacco. A green flame that changed into the usual crusty orange colour once Tony had taken a couple of puffs.

It was pivotal. Maybe because of the whisky, the Cypriot adapted quickly. He didn't question the miracle because he didn't need to. It was an act of the paranormal spawned by Tony's book, genuine magic, and tomorrow morning he would kick out the others and take it for himself. He considered taking it now, but it wasn't the time. He needed to be sober. He wanted space and light, and to be alone with it.

The young artist was snoring. Demitrius plucked the burning cigarette out of Tony's moist mouth and stubbed it out in the ashtray. Then he pushed Tony's forehead until he slid off the table onto the floor. The Cypriot intended to read this thing from cover to cover. He had been waiting for this all his whole adult life. He would read it all.

CHAPTER – 17

"Motives in.augur.ated"

Two days had passed since the theft of the MG. It was Saturday 28th June, eleven AM, and the sun was shining through a gap in the curtains onto Stephen Ashcroft's face. His eyelids twitched and he got out of bed slowly. He had slept longer than usual because things weren't going well. For most sleep is the healthiest and most reliable escape from uncomfortable reality. A few minutes before the theft he had been expelled from Bryan Johnson's house for being a 'witch'. He couldn't afford to stay anywhere except the Three Cups, but it was a perfectly satisfactory Inn, and pleasantly appointed. The guest's bathroom had a power-shower. Stepping into the narrow cubical he turned the temperature control dial to blue, and gasped at the cold. It was refreshing. He washed uncommonly thoroughly as if to rid himself of pessimism, slough the skin of recent bad luck that had grown so tightly around him. He dressed in cream cotton slacks and jacket, clothes he had bought recently, and went downstairs to eat a hearty breakfast.

Powerful forces were arrayed against him. Nothing could express how badly he wanted the *Necronomicon* back. So close to discovering the secrets of the universe, and taken at the last instant! He had an appointment with the police, at midday today. After learning what there was to know in that place he would find his need of the book had become so desperate that he would be willing to kill for it. To occupy himself, in the back of a taxi, he combed his hair and his beard. He put on his re-production RayBan sunglasses and figured he looked quite dapper for a man of his age.

At five to twelve he paid the cab driver and pushed through the doors into the police station. He was feeling anxious. There was a constable behind the shatterproof glass at the reception desk. She was leaning over a clip board with a Biro, wearing summer-time 'short sleeve order' uniform and she was a good looking brunette. She had a nice chest and an intelligent face. Feeling more at ease at the sight of her, he walked up to the window folding up his sunglasses and sliding them flirtatiously into the breast pocket of his jacket.

"Can I help you, sir?" the constable asked him.

"For a certainty," he said. "My car was stolen two nights ago. I reported it yesterday and I was told to come back at midday, today, for an appointment with an Officer Grey. He is expecting me - or she," he quickly added, "of course, she."

The officer picked up her clip board and flipped through a few pages. "Oh, yes. You are Professor Ashcroft?"

"Yes, for my sins, I am a Professor."

She didn't crack a smile. She frowned. "I have a new emphasis here, some kind of complication. It seems that you are going to be seeing Detective Sergeant Auger, of the C. I. D. Please wait a moment." She turned away to use a phone. He could only catch a few of her words: Know. Take. Terrible. The police woman replaced the receiver, and said: "The detective will see you shortly, sir."

About a minute passed. Ashcroft heard the entrance beside the reception being unlocked with a metallic clunk. The door swung open and a man of about forty came into the foyer wearing a well-cut blue suit. The man was obviously a veteran. He introduced himself with a gaze that made the Professor feel perturbed. He was trying to smile, but he looked more accustomed to being sad.

"I am Detective Inspector Auger, of Avon and Somerset C.I.D," he said with a strained voice.

"Professor Stephen Ashcroft, victim of crime in Avon and Somerset."

The detective reacted with a dutiful chuckle that was utterly humourless. "Please, follow me."

They passed through a linoleum tiled corridor, which had over-head fluorescent lights, and a unique mixture of smells. The odour of emulsion paint, and a softer scent like sweat and deodorant brewed with coffee. Ashcroft was led through a doorway into 'Interview Room 4'. There were three chairs covered in red vinyl, an intercom and a tape deck on a battered pine table. A few Neighbourhood Watch posters were all that diminished the banality of the new paint work. It was a garish yellow that completely failed to be cheerful. The Professor sat at the table and wondered what manner of people had been questioned here. What chaotic scenes the room had been host to over the years. DS Auger sat opposite Ashcroft and he looked like a man with a heavy burden. He peered at Ashcroft almost tenderly, and the older man was beginning to grasp that this was about more than his car.

"I take it you've found my car?"

"Professor, do you smoke?"

"No. I eat chocolate."

"Then I suggest you eat some now. I have bad news for you. I'm sorry we couldn't have done this in a more pleasant room."

Ashcroft took out a Twix bar and ripped it open. "Is this about Stephanie?" but he already knew the answer. Of course it was.

"Two members of staff at her jewellery shop in Covent Garden were assaulted last week. The mind of one of them was completely broken, and the other was murdered. Our London colleagues went to her house when she was due back from holiday, and found an address book at the scene with Mr and Mrs Bryan Johnson of Bristol written at the back, as being where you yourself were at the time she wrote it. The Met thought you maybe in danger, so they communicated this to us. We took a statement from the Johnson's and they told us you left their house, by car, on the night of Thursday 26th. We ascertained you are a Professor, but we didn't know where you were staying after you left their property. We tied it up when you came in yesterday to report your vehicle stolen."

"What do you mean by 'at the scene?' What do you mean 'you *were* Stephanie's father?' What do you mean '*were?*'"

"Stephanie was pronounced dead from a single gunshot to the heart at her London address, fired at approximately twenty past six pm, yesterday."

ZAXXON

Ashcroft's fists clenched as he wondered how he would begin to cope with this, squeezing the horror out of it until his knuckles went white. He did not want this to be because of the *Necronomicon*. He bit his lip. "I knew it," he murmured, sounding lost, but he was damned if he was going to cry here. No. He would save that for the lonely darkness and weep until the sun rose or sleep took him, as he had grieved for his late wife Emily. He pressed the palms of his hands to the tabletop, and began to regain his composure, get himself under control. "Was it quick?"

"Instantaneous."

"Do you think she was murdered by the same people that attacked her staff?"

"That is very likely. It would have been how they obtained her address."

The Professor unconsciously rubbed the underside of his eyelids with a finger, although his eyes were dry. He found he could think again. "What about CCTV?"

"Nothing - they erased the hard-drive, but we know there are two of them."

"What about the survivor, the guy who's mind is broken? Just what exactly the hell does that mean, anyway?"

"The man has suffered an irretrievable mental collapse. The doctors think it was triggered by something he saw. Blood was missing at the scene, which we think was cannibalised, and that is why the perpetrators maybe what the Press have dubbed the 'Private School Savages'. Two young people attributed with at least twenty killings, as far away as Norfolk and Scotland."

The professor's heart began thumping. "What was the name of the place, in Scotland?" he asked.

DS Auger took a black notebook out of his jacket pocket, flipped through to a specific page. He told the Professor it was a village called Ravencliff. "Why? Is that where you and Stephanie stayed on holiday? Were you there?"

"We left four days ago."

DS Auger began writing in his book, smiling a little for the first time from one side of his mouth. "Did you witness the fire?"

"No."

"Strange..."

"What fire? What was it that burned?"

"A little public house called the Raven's Arms."

"That's a pity. We liked that place... what time did it happen?"

"Late afternoon of Wednesday 25th," said the policeman. "'Arson, to conceal cannibalism and three murders, which was set at around four o'clock'. That's what my notebook says, anyway...but I don't understand why we didn't know you were there," he muttered that to himself.

"That's because we weren't," said the Professor.

Auger looked up. "What do you mean?"

"We left the village on the Wednesday, yes, we even got a ride with a policeman who had been there concluding another matter, but we actually left *on the late morning – hours before* when you say the new murders happened."

"Now we have a motive for the killings in the village *and* in the jewellery shop," said the detective. "They are searching for you. Christ, but they've been tracking you ever since!"

"That's exactly what I was thinking."

"Do you know of any reason why they might be looking for you?"

"No idea," the Professor lied. "Best get a patrolman to guard the Johnson's."

"Yes." Auger jotted this down. "Where are you staying at present, Professor?"

"The Three Cups Inn, in Clifton."

"Would you like an officer to protect you?"

"No, I have to go London."

"Do you have a mobile phone?"

"Yes, I bought one last Tuesday... so I... so that I could..."

"It's OK, just give me your contact details and you can go." It was written down.

"Detective, just one more thing... about my daughter... did these 'school savages'... did they..."

"No. Absolutely not, she was untouched." The professor said nothing. "I will escort you outside."

The officer led him out and through into the foyer, where they appraised each other awkwardly.

"Charing Cross Hospital, Pathology Department," said DS Auger. "Take these cards, because if you are staying in Bristol they could be useful. They're for bereavement counselling, and victim support. And this one," he added darkly, "is for contacting *me*."

"I might do that."

"In the circumstances, I think it's a question of 'when' rather than 'if'."

"Will you call me about my car?"

"The moment we find it. You know, Stephen, we can't raise the dead, but life goes on."

"I know," Ashcroft replied tiredly. "Thank you, you've been very tactful."

"I have?!" The policeman looked surprised.

"Goodbye Detective."

"Farewell, Professor. *Be on your guard.*"

They shook hands. Then the old man pushed his way out through the double doors into the street busy with people in the white sunlight. People with no problems except the noise and the traffic fumes. He began to sweat. He found he had a concept forming in his reeling brain, an idea for life. For the policeman was wrong. Ashcroft believed that the dead *could be* raised – using the *Necronomicon*. And, as his only daughter had probably died because of that book, he intended to recover it. He would not go through the Dimensional Window, he would use the grimoire to resurrect Stephanie, or die trying.

CHAPTER – 18

"Dis.appear"

The two demons spent the night of Stephanie's murder, Friday 27th June, sleeping in the Peugeot. They pulled into Bristol at 7:30 the next morning, and they had a long wait ahead of them. They hadn't successfully hunted for food for three days. Key's Avenue was a residential street and Thorn agreed to wait until dark before making any move on the Johnson's. His stomach felt like a hole in a lightning-blasted tree. The succubus was starving also, and they were both dribbling guilelessly into their laps. Two hours after Stephen Ashcroft changed the status quo at the police station, there was a disturbing new development. They had driven passed the house, many times, but now a tall law officer was standing on the front porch. He took up his position there at three o'clock. Thorn wondered how the police had anticipated their next move so quickly.

"It was the address book" said Lillith.
"Yes, we should have taken it with us." He thought about this. Then asked: "Why didn't we?"
"It seems that having a photographic memory can be an oversight."
His innards growled loudly. "I don't know how much longer I can wait, Lillith."
"We should have supped on the Ashcroft woman," she observed disgustedly.

At nine o'clock, with the sun become long and red, Thorn changed his suit. He had six sets of disposable black cloth trousers and black tee shirts, for feeding. Looking at himself in the rear-view mirror, he ran his hands through his hair, and wiped the spit off his mouth. "Let's shoot the copper and pull him into the house before anyone sees," he suggested.

She raised her eyebrows and pondered this again; for the first time seriously. You can't just stroll down to the local corner shop and buy a human pie and a side of pickled elbows. If they killed a law officer the heat for their capture would be stepped up to boiling point, but if they didn't eat soon their judgment would gradually become impaired. Their stomachs would start to eat themselves. Although they could barely exist for a decade without eating, it would be ten years of indescribable pain. The Succubus could multi-task many problems simultaneously. A portion of her brain was dedicated to acquiring the *Necronomicon,* another to solving the food shortage, and the rest she used to take their minds off their hunger. She welded their memories together, to share, as a couple, more pleasant experiences.

They had not made love in a real bed since the room in Shepherds Bush. That had been slow and wet and luxurious. They saw the room again now, in the shared eye of their one mind; the soft bed, the dead cat, all the loving. For Lillith rutting was a great escape from the tribulations of her duty to the *Zaxxon.* For her voracious cocks-man, it was a 'natural' part of his being. Their need was worth the finding of a decent bed and calling an end to the sweaty acrobatics in the car. The Johnson's own bedroom at # 58 was just around the corner, sixty yards up the road. They could make love there, find the whereabouts of Stephen Ashcroft, and eat. Satiate all their appetites in one foul swoop. Was that worth slaying a policeman? She laughed.

"Bring out the sword!"

"It's about bloody time," said Thorn, pulling the revolver and its ammunition out of the glove compartment. He grappled with a small handful of the shiny cartridges, tipped them from the box and shoved them into his pocket. He checked the load and snapped the pistol shut.

"We'll need something to muffle the noise. See what you can find."

Thorn twisted round in his seat and looked down into the rear foot-wells. Unexpectedly, he saw the blood-stained sweatshirt he thought he had left behind in Scotland. "This is perfect."

They kissed like only humans can, but with the lust of beasts. She started the engine. The cloth was wrapped around the muzzle of the gun. They drove slowly around the corner and approached # 58. *Use mind-life from here-on in,* thought Lillith. The Incubus rolled down his window. He took aim. The sun had almost set and the policeman was standing in a pool of light from a lamp above the porch.

He was a bull of a man, at least six foot five inches, his back straight, his hands clasped behind his back. The Succubus slowed down to fifteen miles per hour. He looked at the approaching Peugeot with suspicion. When the car was directly level with the front of the house, it almost came to a complete stop, and the policeman strode out to investigate. He was just reaching for the radio-mike attached to his left shoulder when Thorn shot him in the lower chest - twice. The report was muffled by the sweatshirt into thudding noises that seemed louder than they were in fact. The man staggered back and went down like a felled tree. He passed out, bleeding, onto a mat with the word *WELCOME* woven into the fibre.

Lillith parked the car in the next available space, outside the neighbours' house at # 60. It was close by, good for a rapid escape. It was not yet full dark and she was thrilled and terrified. They shared that perception. This latest attack had achieved a new standard of blatancy. They walked over the policeman's prostrate body and they were either too famished or excited to confirm that he was actually dead. His breathing was so shallow it was not discernible. Thorn reached up and twisted the porch light bulb until it blinked out. He didn't think the shots had been *heard*, nevertheless someone could have *seen* what had been done. He glanced around constantly in the twilight as his loved one applied her slim fingers to the lock. She closed her eyes. Three seconds later she pushed the door open.

Thorn went in behind her, and took hold of the policeman by his boots. A television was on in a nearby room. *Stay absolutely silent,* thought Lillith. It sounded bizarrely to him like the whisper she would have used if she had said it aloud. *We must not disturb them.* Thorn dropped the stinking sweat shirt and pulled the sixteen stone dead-weight of the policeman into the house, with one hand. In the other he held the pistol. He closed the front door and said, with telepathy: *I think we may have gotten away with it so far.* There was a phone on an antique mahogany stand by the stairs. The Succubus picked up the receiver and snapped the cable connecting it to the cradle. She put the pieces gently back on the table-top. Beside the table was a framed painting of a burnt-out house that she stared at curiously for a long second. Directly ahead of them was a brightly lit kitchen.

Get a blade, ordered Lillith.
I've got the gun.
A knife is a longer threat, and quieter.

Thorn went in to investigate and found a selection of knives on a magnetic rack over the stove. He took a carving knife and rejoined his lover. They moved together to the door of the living-room, from which was emanating the noise of the TV. They nodded to each other and walked in.

The Doctor and Mrs Bryan Johnson looked round at them with an expression of such profound shock Thorn wanted to laugh. He opened his arms in a gesture of greeting with a gun in one hand and a knife in the other. The room was plush. It smelt of flowers and furniture polish; there was a 'standard' lamp behind the sofa, a large screen TV in the corner, and in the rear were glass doors giving access to a garden.

"Where is Constable Graham?" asked the Doctor.
"Constable Graham is dead," stated the Succubus.
Thorn raised the pistol, to shoulder height, and turned it back and forth. "I shot him."
"And he'll shoot you also if you don't answer our questions with truthful clarity."
"Yes, I will," mollified Bryan. "Of course I will!"

She gestured to the television. "Then turn that off, and come here." The Doctor did as he was told. He stood in front of the succubus. "Where is Stephen Ashcroft?" she asked him.

"I don't know."

"He stayed here, with you, on the night of Wednesday 25th. Where is he now?"

"I swear it, I don't know."

The Succubus was having difficulty reading this old man's body language. He wasn't using his hands, his face was deeply wrinkled, and his eyes never left hers. "Are you protecting Professor Ashcroft because he is your friend?"

"He's no friend of mine," Johnson claimed. "When you catch up with that bastard, tell him he's left a painting here and I want it out of my house!"

This took her by surprise. "Are you referring to the picture in the hall?" Bryan nodded. "Did he paint it?"

"Humbug! He couldn't paint a wall!"

"Did he... meet the *artist*?" Her forehead and her armpits were becoming clammy at the mention of that word. Her skin crawled. Artists with a capital 'A' had hunted and killed *Zaxxon* with blade, bow, and blaze, on a regular basis, for 3000 years. She knew their devious ways of old. They never lit the fires themselves, they manipulated superstition. They had no arsenal the like of Lillith's but they did have a feeble form of short range telepathy and controlled 92% of the entire world's money. That this painting belonged to the Professor himself was too coincidental to *be* a coincidence. "Did he say where he purchased this painting?"

"No. I mean... I don't remember."

"Then, come closer, Bryan."

He did.

"Don't hurt him!" cried Celia Johnson from her perch on the edge of the sofa.

"Shut up!" bellowed Thorn.

"Don't worry, Doctor Johnson," crooned Lillith. "It will all be over soon."

Bryan took two steps forward until his face was half an arm's length away from hers. It was a beautiful and flawless face, he mused, as pale as fine porcelain. Her eyes captured his like a cobra charming a rodent, and they began to glow a bright green colour with the radiance of LEDs.

"What? What?" repeated Celia Johnson, stubbornly disbelieving her own perception of this reality. "What's happening?"

Her husband shuddered as if electricity had been shot through his spine. He muttered unintelligible words and a ribbon of saliva dripped from the corner of his lips. The Succubus raped his mind.

She plucked up his memory on little slides the size of postage stamps, which had virtually no existence in the Material Plane. He moaned. Then he was silent. She absorbed and filed away these 'memory cards', wiped him clean of his every experience like a bottle of Champagne emptied into an eager mouth. He smiled, with false teeth like a skull, shuddered, and then collapsed. The demon left him crawling along the carpet towards his wife with only the sensuous instincts of an infant.

"Platch!" said Lillith.
"What have you done to him?" Celia blubbered.
"He's got something precious," Lillith replied. "Something that everybody wants, deep down. He has gone back to his beginnings. He has a clean slate."

On the inside the Succubus was in turmoil. Her lover was amazed by her thoughts. Bryan Johnson had read the first chapter of the *Necronomicon* and gained 'The Touch'. It was a development she could never have accounted for. He had applied it accidentally to interfere with a knife being used by his wife while she was cuckolding him. He had also created a solution to decrypt the *Necronomicon* for the Professor, who had driven off after that argument resulted in a tablespoonful of blood. Lillith visualised the rest of Bryan Johnson's database. Apart from cosmic mythology that she already knew, which nobody else should, there was nothing else. *The police came here to question them early this morning*, she thought. *Neither of them know where Ashcroft is. Kill them.*

Thorn smothered the gun muzzle with a cushion, and shot them in the head. The Doctor fell on his face with a dark stain forming around his head like a halo on the pale carpet. His wife flopped back into the sofa looking sightlessly at some point beyond the ceiling with an essence of complete relaxation. Thorn used the knife. He cut the cloth of the Doctor's trousers from ankle to groin, and Lillith joined him for the sustenance. Afterwards she felt stronger than she had for days, and more powerful. She left Thorn like a mammal over-feeding before hibernation and walked into the hall.

When she held the painting out in front of her she had a frisson of recognition. It was a moody rendering in rich oil colours of the ruins of Ashton Court Manor. This was where she was due to deliver the *Necronomicon*. The exact location of the Dimensional Window that was going to open on the gravel outside the gutted house on the night of Sunday 6th July. She smiled ruefully, without surprise. What everyone else in the world believed (except Artists) as 'possible' and 'impossible' she defined differently. Her life was full of black miracles. And it happened, yet again, when she saw the signature in the bottom right hand corner of the piece that cemented the connection with Ashcroft.

The undeniable instinct of hers was that the artist, a man named Anthony Newman, had either lost grip on the *Necronomicon,* or he still had it. Knew this like it was written on a silvery piece of paper shining in a coal cellar, and, when she turned it over, she saw an identical silvery label stuck on the rear of the canvas advertising the address of the gallery which sold it: *Gillow's Gallery of Contemporary Art, # 4 Watershed Parade, BR4 8NG* and she laughed. Their next manoeuvre had been summoned out of thin air! She hooted, with glee, laughed so heartily that she didn't see the eyelids of Constable Will Graham flicker with tiny desperate sparks of life.

Thorn was washing the blood off his hands in the kitchen sink. He couldn't detect what she was laughing about, because (like all paranormal ability) telepathy had a fixed wavelength that required conscious control quite different from normal biological perception, but he smiled to hear her good humour. She came into the kitchen and told him what it was about.

"I don't see what's so funny," he complained.

"Trust me, it is amusing."

"I wish I had remembered my suit. I wore this stuff to throw out after dinner but I forgot my suit."

"Don't worry about that, my lovely. Come upstairs to bed..."

She led the way up. He followed her, looking up at her swinging bottom clad in tight khaki linen, so close he could have nodded his forehead into her rounded buttocks. They used the bathroom then found a room which was dominated by a huge bed covered with a pale blue quilt embroidered with purple flowers. They dimmed the lights, and closed the curtains.

"The link between Ashcroft and this artist is undeniable," stated the Succubus, unbuckling her jeans and pushing them over her hips. "We'll go to the gallery to get Anthony Newman's address and then we'll be almost done." She peeled back the bedcovers and pressed the springy mattress with one hand. "That's nice," she murmured. She took off her underwear.

"You said we would be 'done' after this place," he complained, stripping himself. "I thought it would be over by now."

"Not until the delivery. We've got eight days," the Succubus said, and she moved to him, and kissed him. She lay back on the bed.

"This old book is being passed about like a football. There'll be a penalty kick soon, mark my words," he said, joining her, and stretching out, and loving her.

"Darling," she explained: "*We are the penalty.*"

Constable Graham climbed back to consciousness through a haze of pain. He was freezing and felt as though his abdominal muscles had been kicked by a horse. Dimly he realised that the perpetrators of his wounds were having sex upstairs. He reached for his radio mike, and it took him all his strength to rotate the volume dial, down, down... He thumbed the transmit button.

"Base, this is seven four," Graham wheezed. The carpet under him was soaking wet.

"Roger, seven four," said the controller. "A situation report was requested every thirty minutes, haven't heard from you since 2100 hours. What is your status, over?"

"I've been shot," said Graham, releasing the button.

"Can you repeat that, Will, over?"

"I said I've been shot." He spat blood on the banisters. "The two School Savages are here and one of them is armed. They may have killed the Johnson's." He was assaulted by shivering, in a world of ice. "Send a tac team, and medical assistance, Ov – o – o..."

"Roger that, Will, hold on!"

The constable let go of the mike, whispered the word "over", and died.

A few minutes after his last exhalation, the demons experienced a mutual orgasm rippling through their unique bodies. They lay back against the pillows, relaxing in each other's arms. Their breathing slowed. They listened to the sirens of emergency vehicles wailing in the distance and started going to sleep, not because they needed to, but because it seemed like a pleasant idea. Sirens that were getting closer. And closer... and now, coming down the street like klaxons before a war.

"Damn it!" said Thorn mildly, raising himself onto his elbows.

"Get dressed. Quickly," hissed the Succubus, jumping off the bed and pulling on her clothes. She grabbed Thorn's shirt and trousers and chucked them at him. "Do you feel strong?" she demanded. While he was dressing there were tires screeching, and shouting and slamming doors. "Come on, do you feel strong?"

"I feel strong!" he cried, pulling on his trainers and lacing them up.

"Good!" She turned the lights off. She parted the curtains and looked out. There were several police cars parked in a semi-circle on the opposite side of the road, three vans, two ambulances and: "I don't believe it. They've got a *fire engine!*"

"What do they need it for? Is that bad?"

"I don't know."

The scene was flickering with a confusion of blue and red flashers. Officers were crouching behind the lead cars and some of them were aiming hand-swords at exactly where she was standing. It was a hell, of reflections and yellow fluorescent jackets, running about in the strobe-lights.

"Let's go downstairs. Switch to *infra-ranging...* do you have it?"

"Yeah..."

"Grey on grey?"

"Yes!!"

"Well come on, then!"

The Succubus went downstairs and moved from room to room switching all the lights off. Thorn loaded his pistol with rounds from his cheap blood-stained trousers. The dining-room window faced the blockade and Lillith stood carefully to the left-hand side and peeked through the drapes at the Peugeot. They hadn't clamped the wheels yet, nor let the tyres down. So far it had been ignored.

"THIS IS THE POLICE!" bellowed their representative through an amplifier. "YOU ARE SURROUNDED. RELEASE THE JOHNSONS." There was a whistle of feedback. "PUT YOUR WEAPONS DOWN AND COME OUT WITH YOUR HANDS RAISED ABOVE YOUR HEADS!"

Thorn's face went white.

"Don't worry," said Lillith. She tilted her head, and exclaimed: "Listen - there's no helicopter!"
"How do you know? I can't hear it."
"Exactly." She was trying to calm him. "If they had one available it would be above us by now."
"That's good," he said doubtfully, crossing the gun from hand to hand.
"It is very good!"

The Peugeot was a small car. If they could reach it without being shot in the head they could drive it straight down the pavement and passed the road-block. They could make their getaway with no 'eye in the sky'. In fact, she had taken both the memory and the car from the same man, and he had been a rally driver for England!

"Change to telepathy," she ordered. *We're going to make a dash for the Peugeot.*

Thorn looked away from the window, away from the policemen he had just seen arrive wearing black Kevlar jackets and riot helmets. They had utility belts plump with ammunition and grenades, and were carrying MP5s. *Now they've got machine guns,* he thought hurriedly.

Our bodies aren't normal, Thorn. We can take a lot of stick.
Sometimes I feel normal.
Only when you're afraid.
You're hiding something. He reached into her mind.
Stop fishing.
Tell me!
OK, I don't know if we can survive a bullet in the head.

What?!
As far as I know it's never happened before.
That's it, we're screwed!
Calm yourself, Thorn. They will aim to disable us, not kill us.
You hope!
Are you ready?

She looked out of the window and saw a man running away from the Peugeot back to the other side of the street. Now it had three flat tyres.

Shit!
What's wrong?
She told him.

"PLEASE ALLOW CONSTABLE GRAHAM TO HAVE MEDICAL ASSISTANCE," trumpeted the man with the megaphone. "THERE IS AN AMBULANCE STANDING BY!"

Lillith drew the palm of her hand from her fringe down to her chin, in an expression of alarm and exasperation, simultaneously wiping the sweat from her face. *We're running out of options.*

"Don't say that!"
She raised a finger to her lips. "Ssshh…"
"WE WILL PHONE YOU ON THE HOUSE LANDLINE IN THE HALL IN TWO MINUTES!"
You broke that phone, the Incubus thought.
Yes, I know. And I don't Reach that there are any others. Go look through the patio doors.
That's a great idea - we could go out the back way!

Thorn left the room and Lillith stood to one side of the curtains again. If they ran straight at the police directly across the road and through the cordon, it would narrow their field of fire in seconds. Now she was looking at the houses *behind* the blockade, and the germ of an idea was growing in her mind. If the facades of the residences on the other side of the road were identical on the outside to #58, they may be arranged exactly the same *on the inside*. The demons would have a kind of 'map', be able to storm through a building across the road much quicker. Lillith accessed her visual memory and pulled a card featuring the outside of #58. She compared its appearance to the houses opposite, and swore graphically. They were different. But the principal was the same.

A powerful emotion like iced water rushed through her tense body. It was terror, although she recognized it was not her own. It was Thorn's, and it had hit her as suddenly as a distress flare. She mind-melted with his imager. Through his eyes she saw the grey heat signatures of armed men coming up the garden.

Get back to the front door, she thought loudly, *I think they are about to make a breach.*

He ran up to her, sweating, and breathing hard. "They were lying about the telephone."

"I know. Listen, we're going to run out of this door and cross the road, jumping over the police cars, and batter through the bay window of the house opposite."

"That's crazy!"

"We can't give ourselves up, Thorn, we cannot."

"It's suicidal!"

"It isn't. Listen, if we charge the cordon their angle of attack will narrow very quickly until after a couple of seconds they will be aiming at each other and will have to cease-fire. In the meantime we'll be through the other house, over the back-garden fence, and gone. I doubt there's even anyone in there. They probably evacuated it."

"I'm really scared..."

She held his face in her hands. "I know, my love, is your sword loaded?" He nodded. "Then I'll go first. We will shed their blood thrice that which they spill of ours!"

"Let's do this!" cried Thorn.

He thumbed back the hammer of his gun and the Succubus unbolted the mortise-lock. There was a huge crashing noise of glass breaking, from behind them, from deeper in the house. She kicked open the front door and the two of them burst out of #58 and started running towards the police at a 90' degree angle to the pavement. Thorn was shooting on foot, with his arm extended, the pistol waving about randomly. His first bullet shattered a windscreen. The second ricocheted off the bonnet of the car behind which was crouching the man with the bullhorn, who ducked and raised the microphone to his mouth and shouted: "OPEN FIRE!"

Two dozen pistols and automatic rifles crackled almost in unison with a huge noise. The tranquil street of Keys Avenue had never seen so much violence; shouting, and smoke. Thorn was hit in the belly and Lillith took two bullets in her legs, but they could still run, and run she did – right at the police howling like Boudica going into battle against the Romans! They were both armed with sharp claws and lengthening teeth, now, for they were changing into their 'feeder bodies'. They couldn't help themselves. The sum of all the excitement was that it catalyzed their torsos to fill with extra muscle and their eyes to glow yellow. Nevertheless, they did not 'turn' completely. They became half the beasts they could have been, yet it was enough to confuse witnesses and to create the dexterity to leap over cars.

Lillith went first. Ran up to the front grill of the first car like a long jumper, launching herself into the mad nightclub effect of stroboscopic confusion and deafening muzzle flashes. Thorn was hit in the hip, fired his gun until it was empty and emulated her leap. She was shot just under the clavicle and landed on the nearest police car with its red and blue lights flashing beside her footwear. Both of them trampled dents into the roof for three or four steps, and then jumped onto the roof of the next. More bullets whipped passed them. When the police found themselves about to shoot each other, a shout went up to stop firing from both sides.

The demons stamped across the bonnet of the last vehicle and over the garden wall, then took long strides towards the bay window. The relative silence was broken as they crashed through the glass, landing half way across an unlit room. Lillith smashed a dining table, fracturing her arm, but she was instantly on her feet. All injuries from the glass disappeared with a tickly sensation as they moved into the lounge. The family smell in there made the Succubus feel inadequate and sick. It was thick with warmth and smiley gloom, but unlike #58 there were no patio doors. Even with light intensifying sight it was hard to judge a path through those little windows, so Thorn followed her to the kitchen, where they discovered that the back-door was unlocked.

They walked into a garden. It was cool and fresh. They were halfway to freedom yet here the night had essences of anticipation and danger. Like waiting for a gunpowder squib jabbed into the moist grass to ignite and light up the undersides of tree branches and shrubs with crackling white fire. They moved down the garden and Thorn recognized the mastery of her plan. How lucky it was they didn't have armed police coming up at them from the other direction. Shouts could be heard from Keys Avenue. They peered over the back fence and saw a lampless cul-de-sac, a side road lined with parking garages.

One of them was open. The door was folded up under the roof and its interior was lit up like a cruise ship sinking in a dark sea. The *Zaxxon* could see a man getting into a car and climbed wordlessly over the fence. They approached him as he started his vehicle, a new model Volkswagon Golf. By the time he had shifted the gear into reverse the Succubus was tapping on his side window. He looked at her, and saw something he didn't like. Maybe her teeth were too big, or her clothes too bloody. The garage smelt like an unlit funeral pyre. He reached around and pushed the locking knob in the corner of the window. When he released the clutch, the 'rev' counter climbed and the engine roared but the car did not move. Thorn had taken hold of the back of the vehicle and was lifting its spinning wheels off the ground.

Lillith experienced the urge to punch her fist through this idiot's window, but she used her brain instead. She deployed kinetics to disengage the central-locking, opening the door with the 'Touch', and wrenched the driver out of his bucket seat. She took him by the nape of his neck, and his chin, then twisted his head around with a crunch until it was facing the wrong way. She dropped him onto the concrete. There was no shoe pressing on the accelerator pedal, but the VW was still in reverse. She shouted to Thorn over the engine noise to keep the car up so that she could put it into neutral, and he nodded. She climbed in. When the car was idling they engaged telepathy.

Find the remote door switch, she ordered, *quickly.* For some reason telepathy always seemed to be faster than talking aloud.
Why don't you use the Touch?
I can't grasp the mechanism.

Lillith got out and tipped the driver onto his back, his hair facing upwards and his nose pressing into the floor, and started searching his clothes. Thorn got into the vehicle, looking for a relevant button on the dash.

I can't see anything even 'remotely' like it, he thought, *if you'll pardon the pun!* He laughed skittishly.
Look properly. If we can't shut the room there's no point to any of this.
Take his wallet.

They had been lucky, so far, but Thorn didn't seem to fully comprehend the need to close the garage door. If they did the Volkswagon would remain unknown to the police for sufficient time to escape. And stay gone, far away from here.

We were almost killed and all you can think about is shopping! She rifled deeper into his pockets. *He doesn't have the device.*
I've found something. There's a button on his key-ring.
Is it actually on *the key?*
No, it's on a little box with a picture of a door opening!
Let's get out of here, Lillith thought.

She grabbed the dead man's wallet and hit the light switch. The room was plunged into comparative blackness and Thorn climbed across into the passenger seat. The succubus got into the driver's seat and reversed the VW out of the garage. She pressed the button Thorn had found and the door slid down with a rumbling whine. For a second Lillith wondered which way to drive. Whether to go left, or right, and then instantaneously she saw a lamp switched on in an upstairs window - to the right.

She switched on the car's low-beams and steered in that direction at a sedate pace. Two police cars entered the road at the other end. So it was not a cul-de-sac, after all. They were cruising along slowly, shining spot-lamps in their search for the Private School Savages. Once passed the last garage, Lillith turned out of the Horfield district. Three more police cars went screaming passed them, in the other direction. Their blue lights were flashing and their sirens were wailing, and Lillith turned left towards the centre, and then drove east out of the city. The two demons found that they could breathe again, now, and they relaxed back into the car's sporty bucket seats. On the motorway to Bath they turned off an exit ramp and drove into the countryside. A helicopter flew by above them.

"They're too late to catch us with that thing," stated Thorn.
"Absolutely correct, my darling." She looked up and out of her side window. "We are driving due east and that machine is flying southwest!"

The VW's headlights picked out a sign that indicated the direction of a campsite. "Platch!" said Lillith, and adhered to that route. They had stayed in such a place before. It would be busy with summer people, but the demons could see through empty caravans for the lack of heat in them, so it was a classic place to hide. She was confident. It felt good to be away from the city, out here amongst this barren darkness.

"I wish I hadn't left behind my two new suits," said Thorn, examining the scorched holes in his shirt.

"Did you manage to hit any of them?"

"No. Maybe one. I lost the gun, too."

"Don't worry about it. How many shots did you take?"

"Three; how many for you?"

"Six!"

They turned off the road through an open gate into the camping area. The Succubus plucked a bullet out of the cleavage of her blouse. She tossed it to Thorn. He caught it almost magically, and looked closely at the crumpled lump, and exclaimed:

"This has been inside you!"

"Yes. So have you."

She stopped the car in a safe corner of the field, switched off the head lamps, and then cut the engine. Not much time would pass before they understood how close they had come to dying.

CHAPTER – 19

"L.ear.n"

Demitrius had seized control of the flat at eight o'clock in the morning after the party. That had been two days ago. The others had been sleeping and he had awoken them with a blunt instrument in his right hand. Forced them to get their coats and leave, in a ruthless coup d'etat. They had been shell-shocked and complied with neither question nor explanation.

Patrick Dreyer had been so hung over he could hardly see. His brother had fallen down the stairs and been lucky to get away with just a sprained wrist. Tony had been the last out, forced to pack a bag feeling cowardly as he went about it, torn between wanting to keep the *Necronomicon* and relief that he was finally leaving this apartment, a place in which he had never truly belonged. He left in a cab to see his girlfriend. He would send for the rest of his stuff at a later date, though he would be surprised if he ever saw any of it again.

Demitrius had found the *Necronomicon* beneath Tony's bed. It looked as though it had been tossed there in a hurry. Some kind of map had become dislodged from where it had been folded flush with the spine. By the afternoon of Sunday 29th June he had gained his third kinetic power. Translation was a long-suffering process because he didn't have the right kind of brain for it. His skills lay in other forms of competence. Turning that bizarre sprawl of long forgotten writing into English took up to ten minutes to do just one sentence, but he was getting faster and the effort was profitable beyond his wildest dreams. At half passed two on the second afternoon, Monday 30th, Demitrius realised that he had been so engrossed in the work he hadn't eaten since yesterday morning. His lips were cracked and his tongue was sore from lack of water. He went into his kitchen.

ZAXXON

He opened the fridge using his mind. Telekinesis was a dream come true and he thought it was wonderfully lazy ability. The fridge contained shrivelled apples, half a tub of course pate, some pizza bases and a lump of cucumber. He drank a lot of cold water, with the spout of the tap in his mouth, then started putting together lunch. He spread pate over the dough bread, thinking about what it meant to be one of the *Zaxxon*. He had looked into his bathroom mirror this morning and wrinkled his forehead into the signature of that darkest tribe. Although they were supposed to be the bad lads, he wasn't concerned about that aspect within himself. There were many levels of existence.

The most powerful presences upon the Earth were the angels, and the almost insignificant number of *Blight*. Down the ladder, becoming increasingly more diluted towards the bottom rung, were just about everybody else. The more diluted the bond a person had with the nation they were born to, the more of an individual they are, and the easier it is to change that affiliation by deeds done. And somewhere in between were the Artists. People that inspired such emotion that everyone wanted to be one of them, *or be with them*, who apparently had all the secret power in the world. Demitrius reacted badly to that. Jealousy was a cheap emotion in the beginning, but it could cost dearly later.

He had awoken at the desk this morning with a head-ache. He had found himself slumped in the chair with his forehead pressing onto an exposed page of the open grimoire, having had strange dreams. After washing down three Aspirin with coffee, he had destroyed the portrait Tony had painted of him. Had smashed it over a chair because the man was an artist. Tony had read some of the *Necronomicon* and knew his place in the world. That meant he could no longer be trusted, assuming he had ever really been trustworthy in the first place. Demitrius needed to know how to deal with these amazing things, to discover his own path through this new world scenario.

The book was all truth. Every statement in it was verified by a musical head-rush of pure joy and the consequential parapsychological powers he now commanded. Down-loaded to either very new neural nets, or very old ones, and lined up in his advanced brain like weapons: Telekinesis *(The Touch)*, Extra Sensory Perception (which the book called *'Reaching'*), then Pyrokinesis *(The Flare)*. He had experimented with that latter ability today and almost burned down the building. The Cypriot had exerted a fire in Tony's waste basket and, when the flames had evolved from a lurid green colour to yellow, it had begun to catch the curtains and climb. Demitrius had grabbed the fire-extinguisher and put the fire out with gushing powdery white blasts of CO_2, all the while imagining setting alight to a person, and laughing, and laughing.

The stink of the fire took a long time to disappear. After he finished eating his pate and cucumber breads, with the *Necronomicon* open infront of him, he threw his plate and cutlery onto Tony's mattress then picked up a black fine-liner pen. He had no interest in the map at this time. He wanted another 'fix' and settled down to transcribe the next chapter. Ambient trance music was playing on the stereo next door, to help him concentrate, but not loudly. It took him almost four hours to write more esoteric knowledge. In the Dark Lord's own words:

The environment of Planet Earth is a meaningless vellum paste beneath the common senses of perception, inane to the human soul, which aspires to greater things. The shallower society becomes the more people will sense the uncomfortable truth of the world around them, which is merely a vehicle for the evolution of the soul. It will spawn paranoia, *a word composed of the most telling of all symbols in a Cuneiform alphabet. The more people are programmed to obtain goods and chattels, the more they will sense that paranoia from which life revolves for a changeling soul. Like a game to cancel re-incarnation, with paranoia as the obstacle, philosophy as the tool, and Heaven as the prize.*

ZAXXON

New explorers usually discover the source of this knowing in pairs. They cannot be told what to think. There are countless trails of thought, but there will usually be two friends to share the journey. Two individuals that grow and exchange ideas until their mutual draw-back is overcome. And when their paranoia is white they will be free to go their separate ways and experience the freedom to achieve any goal in life. To seek each other out and kiss each other's souls across the world. Here is the conjuration to enable short range variable wave-band telepathy. As a fetish, after the words are spoken, spit with hatred upon a pared apple.

Demitrius fetched an apple from the fridge. He peeled it at the table using a stiletto switch-blade, then spoke aloud the verbal components of the magic. As usual he thought it wouldn't take, doubted his pronunciation of the strange words, but the head-rush came. After he spat venomously on the skinless fruit he abandoned any attempt to think straight. His senses took him through exquisitely warm clouds of fluffy toffee. Everywhere he looked appeared to be the same pale yellow colour of a peeled apple, but he refrained from laughing because part of him guessed it would sound like the strangled gargle of a madman.

A song of the *Plexity* began. It was the ultimate personal stereo. He worried he might float out of the window like a puff of candy-floss to the sound of that piano. A virtuoso alien, playing in the middle of his head from inside a glass bubble under a waterfall. He felt that he would blast off into space. Then, gradually, the song peaked... and he came down, and the true colour of reality returned. The Cypriot immediately needed to transcribe the next conjuration. He was dribbling with desire for it, but he didn't like losing control. That was why he had avoided drugs in his life, and the *Necronomicon* was a dangerously powerful high. He closed it.

The idea that life revolved around paranoia didn't really surprise him. Until the dawning of the 21st century paranoia seemed to have been a taboo subject, although everyone suffered it, to an extent. Just because the word began with 'para' did not mean it is supernatural, or psychotic. Some may even consider it to be a defence mechanism, a black or white aspect of the human condition. Since it doesn't manifest itself in shades of grey it could become extreme and personal. The worst possible example of it in Demitrius's opinion was that experienced through the circumstances of a person's surroundings. Like a homeless man walking through a shopping centre at Christmas. Feeling removed from all those smiling people buying presents for each other. The sense that society is a pointless sham, just beneath the surface, with carols playing onto the pavement telling of warm firesides and snow that never came. Trying to ignore a lost childhood, and smoking a marijuana joint to celebrate, which would just make it all worse.

This was the kind of environmental paranoia that Demitrius called a 'life question'. Bad television had made his front lounge feel like a flimsy post card in the past, with "suffer alone" written on it. As if part of him was no longer there, an uncomfortable flash-thought he had never discussed with anyone that his whole life was a lie. That if he could look beyond his room he would see the camera-man and the director waiting behind the propped up card-board walls for the next take of a film that would never be shown because of its unadulterated sarcasm. And if this happened too often it would make life hardly worth living. L.S.D is the most powerful catalyst of such horror. Those curious or stupid enough to take it could find themselves at the heart of the sham, feeling spontaneously worthless. Have a bad trip and you won't be able to escape into sleep, for at least seven hours, with every aspect of your life in question and terrified you will feel like it for the rest of your existence.

Demitrius wondered if his embryonic knowledge may initiate a learning curve, and lead him onto the true path to reversing his limitations. To make the secret moments of his inferiority complex that made him so violent, into the permanent superiority complex that everyone thought he already had! If the opportunity arose he might bring up the subject with his peers, but he didn't fully comprehend the problem. Why couldn't such a rare and temporary feeling be ignored? Was it because the scars ran too deep? Thinking about his lost friends, those he had evicted over his possession of the *Necronomicon*, the Cypriot realised that he hadn't left the flat, since - for two days! Cool rain was falling outside. He needed fresh air with a similar desperation to when he had needed water, and pulled on his black leather jacket.

The strip of brain tissue at the back of his head was twitching as he walked under the grey sky. It felt very weird. He could hear an imperative, hissing and whispering noise, which became louder on the outskirts of the city centre. Once amongst the busy shoppers the volume increased into an overwhelming hysterical babble. On his mind was a common phrase: "Be careful what you wish for in case you get it."

But he could hardly hear himself think. The highs of elation and the lows of terror that he had experienced this day, had been extreme. He pressed his hands to his ears, but of course that changed nothing. He couldn't block it out and it sounded like twisting a radio tuning dial through random chatter. The world had become a stage inside his own head. He stopped walking.

Across the street he saw a woman with heavy bags who was realising she had lost her purse. A pink teenaged girl was choosing a watch for her boyfriend. An old man was silently swearing to himself because he couldn't light his pipe in the rain. Even children, most wanting sweets and toys, one thinking she was too old to be in a pram, was pushed passed where he was leaning against the window of a Blockbuster DVD store like a man drowning. He tried to build a dam against this senseless rush of telepathy, imagined he was a sonar operator on a submarine because he wanted that essence of sound-control, but the image was too complicated. He thought about his own existence, instead, re-affirming his position as a unique character amongst all these people. Everyone had their own self-contained private agenda. He accepted that, and it made their thoughts quieter... and quiet... and then almost completely gone!

He tried to listen directly to the thoughts of a specific person, focussing on a pretty woman who had given him an appreciative look. He was alarmed at her silence. Now everything seemed to have become a matter of emotion, only. The unnatural onslaught had ended, and he was relieved about that, but not for long. His anxiety attack faded quickly. Left him sitting on the fence between telepathy and empathy, feeling disappointed. Which was the most powerful? Which was the most useful? Did he even have a choice?

These questions were answered when two tall men wearing belted trench-coats swept passed where he was standing. Telepathy was the best. They were both communicating with their minds with consummate ease. Not the sub-conscious babble of the multitudes, but genuine telepathy.

The point you won't accept is that all of those paintings are a blatant allegory of mind-life.
How can they paint about something they don't know? They're non-receivers!

The Cypriot stepped out onto the cobbled street. He followed them, a few paces behind. Their wave-length was functional and very wide. He got the idea that they were discussing the Royal Academy Summer Exhibition. Their phantom voices had educated accents. Demitrius could tell who was speaking because of an almost three-dimensional sense of direction unexpectedly like using his ears. Their boots rippled through the warm puddles.

All those painters have been pre-prepped, by our metaphors, and the very best will become Artists - it's part of our purpose, and their destinies.
You think I don't know that?

The symbolism is all over the place, it's thinner than ever, it's never been closer to the surface.
And construed as schizophrenia.
Oh, pardon me, Doctor! How long do you think that magic net will protect us?
It doesn't matter. It is not possible for a sane person to accept telepathy.
Not according to my fan mail.
That's because the shadows in your songs tally too closely with other people's music. They aren't segregated, they're too easily verifiable.
That's the way forward.
No. It's too fast. There is too much to lose.
It won't be long before society understands.
Artists are supposed to keep the world safe, not devastate it. You came to Bristol today to help me scout locations for a documentary, not talk about this shit. Let's do some work.
I want to win.
Don't start with that again. The 'glittering prize' is just one of Gabriel's myths. He wants to destroy absolutely everything. There is nothing to 'win'. Surely you don't believe anything he writes?
Armageddon cannot be avoided.
I've had enough of this. Believe me, if we take care it can be avoided. You need to think about that, my friend.

They were walking out of the precinct, now, in 'silence', heading for a car-park. Demitrius knew that was their destination because the bad guy was thinking about getting into his new Jaguar, and was worried about the safety of some expensive audio visual equipment. The kinder of the two was thinking about his young wife and children. Demitrius broke into their conversation. He thought the following to the pro-apocalyptic 'friend':

How does a monster like you get to dominate so many people? Where does your over-sized influence leave the common man?

The pair turned their heads and looked at him over their shoulders. Their world-weary faces paled with shock. The good telepath answered.

You can hardly be a 'common man' if you can talk like this to us.
Fuck off! I'm common as muck, Demitrius thought. *You play with billions of souls like it's a game of cards! What is this 'us' thing, anyway? What gives you the right to all this power and money?*
Do you want money?
No, I'd like to kick ten bags of shit out of both of you!
You can try, threatened the dark Artist.
You've got a selfish death-wish, pal, in every respect.

The three of them crossed the road into the car-park.

He's Zaxxon, thought the other.
- But not Blight.
Let's just get into the Jag.
I want some answers! demanded the Cypriot.

The dark man unlocked his car. They opened the doors, and climbed in. *We don't have any answers that you would understand,* he replied, and started the huge engine. He put the gear stick into reverse.

The only telepaths Demitrius had ever met, or were ever likely to meet, were actually amazing people that were about to drive away. He abruptly felt lonely. He tapped on the driver's side window and it rolled down with a hum like unwrapping a gift. The dark man looked up at him and asked what he wanted. Demitrius let slip a question that made him blush. It caused the first embarrassment he had experienced in over a decade:

Will I see you again?
Only on television.
What am I supposed to do?
Paint. Write. Make music.

ZAXXON

It wasn't really the answer that Demitrius needed. *I suppose your documentary is secretly about the end of the world*, he mused bitterly.

There aren't many secrets left, thought the dark man, rolling up his window. *And they are all about the end of the world, haven't you noticed?*

He reversed the car out of its space. Demitrius didn't know what to say.

They drove away.

On his way back to Launch Terrace the sun came out. It evaporated the rain water and thickened the humidity on the streets. The Cypriot felt sweaty and regretful, matters somehow interrelated. The conversation he had shared with the Artists was going round and round and round in his head. It was easy to judge them from the annexe of your own home; simple to collate and generalize, like a video game from your favourite chair, but he had actually met two of these 'gods' in person. Before he had imagined them to be war-lords and power-mongers, now his opinion had altered completely. They had problems beyond his comprehension, global responsibilities, and in spite of all that power he would be willing to bet that most of them were uncorrupted, decent, and gentle people. For a turn-around it was a real mind-bender!

The Cypriot was relatively untalented. He was one of the best 'wheel-men' in the Southwest, but he had no credibility left within himself. He was just an adrenaline junkie. The *Necronomicon* had come into his life so recently, and it had just as quickly ravaged his routine into a mere existence. Now the book was all he had left. Because there could be an apocalypse; because he was going to prison and because he would lose his driver's license, but mostly because the prestige he had been building up for so many years now seemed comparatively worthless.

On his way home he went into a super-market. He was hoping that the mundane task of shopping would take his mind off these thoughts, which were at best functionless and, at worst, spiritually depressing. He crossed from isle to isle, putting products into a hand-basket, trying to focus on what little was left unchanged in his fruitless life. He needed a more optimistic attitude. He didn't want to include paranoia theory or the power of the *Necronomicon* in the equation, but that was impossible. He was super-human, now. He would just have to adapt, re-invent himself. It was that simple. But he had never felt so alone.

Back at the flat, he dropped the shopping bags, and went into his kitchen to exercise restraint before continuing his work on the book. He diverted his own attention using hot coffee, made in his old Playboy mug. Seeing it caused him a pang of sadness. He had a collection of girlfriend's phone numbers in a little black book but he might as well throw it out, or practise 'The Flare' on it, because the numbers were redundant now. He had always preferred weak-willed women. No one on that list would be able to cope with what had happened to him. So he sat at the table, accepting that the *Necronomicon* was his only refuge. He held it to his chest, inhaling its unique smell, like the odour of a leather interior in a car that had been under a tarp for a few years. He associated the smell with drug-rushes and domination. He extracted the map he was using as a bookmark, and opened the book at chapter five. He had been treading water for days. Now it was time to let himself sink.

Before he uncapped his pen he paused, to think about what he wanted. Characteristic of the man he had been, his shallowness remained and was a wonder to him. Fame, money, respect. He wanted all that stuff, and he wanted to brag about his capabilities without changing the world too much. He might have made a brilliant magician. Unfortunately he was due to be 'sent down' within a month. At Her Majesty's Pleasure, to use the traditional colloquialism. He would be inside for about two and a half years and it was going to require a monumental effort of restraint <u>not</u> to exercise his psychic powers. Using them in prison could be a logistical disaster, and entail an unknown quantity of repercussions. He wondered what would happen to him if he got caught, and he closed his eyes. What if the government incarcerated him for experimentation? What if they drugged him in an underground laboratory somewhere with electrodes stuck to his head? What if they put him in a white room - and he was never seen again?

The Cypriot knew he ought to be enjoying a golden ticket to an elevated sense of self, but he wasn't privileged. He was trapped. He looked down, and discovered the old map was in his hands. He had never really been interested in it until now, and decided to look at it. He opened it on the desk. Squinting down at the tiny words and numbers, a sudden and almost comical expression of surprise crossed his face. It was a map of Britain, and it was written in Old English, not Cuneiform!

'Dimensional Windows' were described on it, which opened onto different vicinities of Hell; or, perhaps, Heaven. Pain, pleasure, dates, places. And always at midnight. He paid particular attention to the notation written over his home city of Bristol, and it dawned on him that there maybe another way out. In an amazing co-incidence, a Dimensional Window was due to open (on what he knew already, from his Unexplained Magazines, was an intersection of 'Ley Lines') outside Ashton Court Manor on Sunday 6th July. That was in six days, and Demitrius needed to think carefully.

If he was actually going to 'throw in the towel' he needed to ensure the decision wasn't made with his archetypical impulsiveness. Nevertheless he chose quickly. There was probably no such thing as co-incidence, and there was nothing left for him here. He would take the escape route, migrate between dimensions and experience undreamt of worlds. He didn't care if the physical part of him lived or died.

He had never been so dangerous.

CHAPTER – 20

"Heart.ache re.solution"

Ashcroft had always hated funerals. Before the illness that had taken Emily, funerals had always seemed to be too much information at once. He supposed everybody felt the same, particularly once they were 'well matured'. When he bid farewell to old friends only a small part of his attention was ever on the service, and this had remained true, until today, because today it was his only child being buried. Nigel Hawthorne had helped him choose the hymns and handle the arrangements. A short service was held on the afternoon of Sunday 29th June inside St. Mary's Church, Hammersmith, and then the mourners had moved to the graveside. The sun shone down impassively from a blue sky that somehow seemed unsuitably beautiful for the occasion. Grief bore down on Stephen Ashcroft like the increasing weight that gets heaviest in the back of your neck just before you faint. He let his mind wander. He thought of Stephanie's apparent objection to being born, and the vicar's droning voice faded from his regard.

Hospitals had been more primitive in those days. Although Emily had been in labour for about ten hours and had almost lost the battle, seeing their cute wrinkly little baby the couple had agreed that the mother's supreme effort had been well worth it. Stephanie had been difficult to feed as a little girl, hiding parts of her unwanted dinners in odd places. She used to climb the kitchen counters where she accumulated a hoard of mouldy green bread crusts on top of a cupboard. As calcium is good for bones, Emily believed, so Omega was considered good for a child's brain development. But Stephanie didn't like fish. She only ever ate it in the form of fingers, occasionally, and never without complaint.

As a toddler who had only just begun to process memories properly, Stephanie had been bitten badly by a rabbit. It had taken years of coaching to reverse her aversion to animals afterwards, to encourage her to get along with them. When the family were living In Lewisham, at the age of five, she used to ride around the garden on the family dog like he was a donkey, a fat yellow Labrador called Wellington. Before him they had kept a cat called Spike. Spike's cat-flap had remained in the kitchen door until they moved house two decades later, and as a puppy Wellington had used the flap all the time. One day he discovered, of course, that he had outgrown it. While on a weekend break in the Lake District, the old lady responsible for feeding the dog had taken ill and forgotten about him.

Wellington had got stuck in the cat flap, half-in and half-out of the kitchen for two days, and no one had paid any attention to his barking. They found him looking distressed, but slimmer for the accident!

At the age of seven Stephanie had been cooked some fish fingers and she had accepted them without protest. Even more unusual was that when Emily came back downstairs after washing her hair, with a towel wrapped around her head, Stephanie had finished them and was actually asking for more. Her mother cooked another three and went up to blow-dry her hair. She came back and found her daughter was licking her empty plate clean and asking for more. Captain Bird's Eye would have been proud! Emily thought, but she was suspicious. She grilled the last four in the box, handed them over, then hid behind the side door to the kitchen.

Stephanie waited, as though to ensure the coast was clear, then took her plate and fed the fingers to Wellington through the cat flap! Emily had jumped out, trying not to smile, and Stephanie had cried for so long that her mother had had to placate her with a steaming bowl of Noodle Doodles normally reserved for Saturdays. When her husband had got back that night he'd laughed about it till his sides ached!

The vicar closed his book. One of the undertakers threw a handful of earth onto the coffin and it landed on the wood with a hollow crumpling noise like one of Ashcroft's sobs. He had arranged a wake at his house in Shepherd's Bush and about twenty people showed up after the service. It was a sombre occasion. They stood about in tight groups talking about Stephanie's life and the tricks she had pulled with hushed voices. The Professor had laid on a spread of red and white wines, juice, canapés and sandwiches. He played a classic Dave Brubeck CD, quietly, and suggested that if anyone wanted to imbibe something stronger to let him know. The vicar was drinking screw-drivers. Ashcroft made sure he drank no more than two glasses of Cabernet. He worked the room, and Stephanie's university friends said how "very nice" it was to see him again but he didn't know them and he didn't say much. He just felt old and tired, and continued to suppress his secrets.

Hawthorne came up to him later. His tailored woollen suit smelt of the mints he always crunched. His bushy eyebrows and his handlebar moustache made him look like a retired Spitfire pilot. The thing with the mints allegedly originated when he gave up smoking, but now it served another purpose. To disguise the drink on his breath. He looked like an alcoholic RAF man, always with a story ready in exchange for a double shot of anything from the back of the bar. He was nursing a large Brandy and a fistful of vol-au-vents, and he asked Ashcroft how he was baring up.

"Not well, Nigel, I'm afraid."
"Shall we retire to the study?"
"That's a good idea. The others are treating me like they're afraid I might burst into tears at any moment."
"It isn't surprising."

Hawthorne took the Professor's elbow and propelled him into the adjacent room. He closed the door. They sat by mahogany occasional tables on comfortable, leather upholstered, armchairs.

"We need to discus the future of Stephanie's shop," Hawthorne stated.
"I don't think I'm ready to deal with that right now."

"Do you want to sell it?"

"I don't know if it's what she would have wanted. You are the major share-holder. Can I leave that with you and the others to decide, according to her Will?"

"Yes, if that's what you want."

"It is." The Professor finished the last drop of wine in his glass and placed it on the side table. "Her staff were assaulted by killers that are still looking for me at this moment, did you know that?"

Hawthorne put down his tumbler. He steepled his fingertips, thought for a moment, and then asked: "How much antagonism do you feel towards Stephanie's murderers?"

"Don't try to psychoanalyse me Nigel."

"I'm just checking that you aren't harbouring any desire to go vigilante."

"No, I'm too old for that. That's for the police."

"Good." Hawthorne pushed a prawn cocktail pastry between his lips. "How is the investigation proceeding?" he asked, his mouth muffled.

"They have pictures of the two killers. They know who did it, and they damn nearly caught them two days ago, in Bristol."

"So? Who are they?"

"They have been dubbed the 'Private School Savages' because some kids attacked each other in a school on the outskirts of Norwich. There were some fatalities, but no probable cause. No one knows why it happened. The press say they're a couple of gypsy drug fiends. That may be true, now, but I don't think it started out that way. One of them was a harmless GCSE pupil. Now he and his girlfriend, cannibalizing along the way, have been tracking me down since the beginning. But somehow I'm always one step ahead of them."

"Why are they looking for you?"

"I'll explain that later."

"Cannibalizing what?" Hawthorne blinked at him. "Oh. You mean... actually *cannibalizing*?"

"Exactly so. They killed and partially ate a friend of mine and his wife in Bristol last night. They also shot a policeman and the Law came down on them hard."

"But they escaped?"

"Apparently they were shot several times, but they just disappeared."

"Any hospital reports?"

"None that I've heard of."

"Well, there you go then. They've most likely curled up somewhere and died of their injuries."

"I want them brought to justice."

"Of course you do. But they will be, either way. They will be brought to justice whether they be alive or dead."

"My daughter was shot with a pistol that I had given her illegally."

"Don't you *dare* go down that path, Stephen! It's wrong!"

"I'm going to bring her back, Nigel," he muttered softly. He couldn't retain his secret any longer. He had to unburden himself and to Hell with the consequences.

Hawthorne raised his bushy grey eyebrows. "Pardon?"

"I said I'm going to bring her back."

"That's what I thought you said. Are you referring to Stephanie?"

"Two weeks ago I found an archaic grimoire in Scotland. It is called the *Necronomicon* and it was written in the Middle Ages by a monk possessed by Satan himself, and that is a *fact*."

"The only fact is that you've swallowed too much claret."

"I've had two glasses. This book has the power to raise the dead, I'm certain of it."

"You cannot be serious…"

"When I was in Scotland this homicidal priest locked me in a crypt and left me to starve to death. The *Necronomicon* sent out a stream of energy that smashed through the cover-stone and saved my life, and killed him, plain as I sit here." The Professor realised that he may be babbling. "This book has the ancient rites to powers science cannot imagine."

"May I look at it?"

Ashcroft realised that the man was humouring him. Should have known he would before he ever got into this conversation. Hawthorne had been humouring him for years. Ashcroft was too tired to feel irritated, but neither could he put a stop to his tongue.

"I haven't got it right now. It was in my MG when it was stolen last Thursday night, but I'll place an advert in the local newspaper offering a reward for the book. A big reward. I'll even let them keep the car!"

"So, you are suggesting bringing Stephanie back from the dead?"

"Yes, I can do it."

"Drop this crusade before you do something really crazy."

"I cannot."

Hawthorn was quaking with anger. "I loved Stephanie too you know, like a daughter. I felt like a father to her, myself, and I think you may have totally lost your mind!"

"Why would the Public School Savages be pursuing me if the power of the *Necronomicon* is an illusion?"

"It's not an illusion, Stephen, it's a *psychosis!* Let me spell it out to you. Just once. If I hear evidence that you've been tampering with her grave I will have you Sectioned under the Mental Health Act in a blind instant! What kind of state would she be in, if you did bring her back? Have you not read 'The Monkey's Paw?"

"Yes, I've read it, but that was fiction. This is real life," Ashcroft replied.

"And real death," Hawthorne pointed out. "And in reality, people who have died stay that way. You need to accept that she's gone."

Ashcroft clenched the armrests of his chair. "Leave my house!" he shouted, "and take that fawning rabble of parasites with you!"

"I am leaving, Stephen. But I will be watching you." He stormed out.

Ashcroft broke the seal on a fresh bottle of London Dry gin. By the time he had finished his first glass, he was sitting alone in an empty house.

CHAPTER – 21

"Blood.y bound.less"

Tony awoke from his nightmare shouting unintelligible words with his heart thudding quickly under his ribs. He was sweating with terror from every pore. The moon shone through the open window and a blessed night-wind was billowing the bedroom curtains, cooling his brow. Sam was awake, also. Her face seemed to be floating above him like an mirage in the Sahara. She smelt of musk and wild flowers, and her features were fragile in the semi-darkness, beautiful as fine crystal. Tony's slowing heart ached with unquestioning love. She propped herself up on one elbow and looked down at him.

"Was it the same dream?" she asked.
"Yes," Tony replied. "Demitrius exploiting magic to rule a planet tearing itself to pieces."

Three days ago, before this conversation, Sam's father had allowed Tony to stay at the house after his abrupt eviction. It was against his paternal instincts but during dinner that night, Saturday 28th, Sam had summarised the cause and affect of Tony falling out with Demitrius. Tony had been kicked out so dramatically he had desperately needed to be with her. He took up the flag: told of his terror, and spoke candidly of not wanting to be alone in some strange hotel bed that night. Sam's dad had accepted this, but what she did not reveal to him was that Tony had arrived on their doorstep in an almost senseless state of withdrawal. He seemed to have developed a drug habit. This had amazed her, but what else was she supposed to think? What other explanation could there be for his warped dreams, the night sweats, the sudden bouts of shaking and shivering?

She could not accept the truth. Not at first. That was understandable. Yet Sam believed it all after one demonstration of his new powers, and went on to learn about the *Necronomicon,* and the two conjurations that had caused his spontaneous addiction. Magic was real, and Sam guessed that the status quo of their relationship was inevitably going to change. She had nursed him through his 'cold turkey' as best she could. As far as her father was concerned Tony was incapacitated upstairs with influenza. He tossed and turned, muttering strange words, and sometimes objects floated around the room like a menagerie of weird birds. Luckily nothing caught fire. She had tended to him with water and a cold cloth, and had tried not to treat him like an alien from a space-ship that had just touched down in their front garden. He was still her Tony, her man. Through his confusion and aimless appetite, she could still see the love in his eyes, and she dared hope that maybe their relationship wouldn't change too much after-all.

His fever-like symptoms broke on the afternoon of Monday 30th June. That night his delirium was gone and he slept easily. Only the dreams remained: the figure of Demitrius as sovereign over a world of zombies and mass telepathy and unquenchable flames; standing on top of a hill at night, wearing a purple velvet dressing gown with his fist raised in the smoke, and his insane eyes lit by blazing orange fire. Tony confirmed it was the same dream, and took an unsteady breath. He offered a weary smile up to his girlfriend in the dimly lit bedroom.

"He's just sitting there, isn't he, reading it all the time?" asked Sam.

"Yeah, I think so. Maybe day and night. God alone knows what powers he has collected already."

"We have to stop him."

"How? He is totally addicted and quite capable of murder, I'm sure."

"We must get it back because your nightmare cannot be allowed to happen."

"Yes, I agree..." He inadvertently imagined the sweetest bliss of reading a conjuration.

"I can see you, Tony, even in moonlight. I've seen that look on your face many times in the last few days. I bet the *Necronomicon* has caused nothing but misery and death for a thousand years. The book must be destroyed. Can you do it?"

"I don't know."

"Can you gain strength from our love?"

"I can."

"That's lovely!"

"Tomorrow is July 1st. Like a new beginning. I'll do it then."

"We can drive to his flat in the afternoon, if you like. That'll give you time to work up a full steam."

"OK, I'll do it, if I can get my hands on it."

"Let's tell him we need your clothes and your art materials. You know Mr Gillow wants more paintings out of you!"

"Demi is tough, Sam. He won't give it up without a fight unless I can trick him, I know it."

"Snatch the thing the moment his back is turned. Or fight. You can use your secret powers."

"They're not secret to him. I'll probably wind up in A&E... and what powers will he use?"

"You have to try."

"We'll go at midday tomorrow."

"Then, sleep well, my lovely brave man," crooned Sam.

He tried to sit up. "I'll have a nightmare!"

"No, no, you won't," she pushed him gently down into the soft bed clothes. "It's alright, because I'll be holding you." She snuggled down beside him. "There, that's better isn't it?"

"Yes." He sighed, and was quiet for a moment. Then he said: "Sam, I love you."

"I love you too, very much," she affirmed.

They both fell asleep.

Shortly after eleven o'clock the following morning, July 1st, the couple dressed and went down to the kitchen. The family's middle-aged Spaniel, Winston, gave her a toothy grin when Sam gave him a tummy-rub. George had cooked a brunch of bacon and eggs and poured glasses of orange juice. A weight like a rock was clogging Tony's chest because of the fruitless discussion about Demitrius fighting with telekinetic abilities. The truth was that he would use his fists, also, and they both believed it was likely the Cypriot would beat the shit out of him. Neither wanted to daunt the other's courage, so neither spoke of it. Conversation around the breakfast bar was subdued. The food seemed tasteless. Tony owed it to the keepers of The Great Secret to try to remove the latent horrors of the *Necronomicon* from the equation. Although taking the book was as foolhardy as trying to give a manicure to a werewolf, these Artists had tended the Earth and he was an artist too. His blood felt like ice in his veins but they had kept the world safe for so long he felt he had to try, at least.

After the plates and cutlery were stowed away, in the dishwasher, Tony and Sam went outside. They sat on white-washed wrought iron garden furniture. Tony sneezed in the sunlight. They wanted to enjoy the heat, but they were nervous, fidgety, glancing often at their wristwatches, so they decided to share a Marlboro.

"Sam, wouldn't it be safer if we phone him first?"

"You can't arrange an appointment with that man, Tony, he won't see you."

"But we could kind of 'prepare' him, rather than have him react violently to a cold call."

She took a puff of the cigarette. "If we give him any warning we're coming round to collect your things he'll probably just leave them outside his front door. We need the element of surprise, Tony, because we need to *get in there*." She passed the cigarette back to him. "Understand me? We need to *get in there*." She was saying it like a football hooligan. "Say it with me, the same way:"

"Get in there!"

"Yes! That's it!"

"GET *IN* THERE!" cried Tony, swinging his fist in the air, and taking to his feet.

She fished the car keys out of the tight back pocket of her jeans. "Ready?"

"Absolutely yes!"

"Then let's do it."

The Volkswagen was like a sauna so they rolled the windows down to the seals. They talked intermittently, and Sam agreed to enter the flat also. The presence of a woman might be a calming influence on a pig-headed chauvinist like Demitrius. She drove to Launch Terrace at a leisurely pace. Tony figured she wasn't in a hurry to get there either, and she parked behind the MG that Tony had taken with a man that had then been his friend, stolen in the heady days before either of them had read the *Necronomicon* and been changed forever. It was blue now, tagged with number plates Tony didn't recognize. He wondered how angry the owner had been to lose his car. Then considered, for the first time, where the man had obtained the *Necronomicon* in the first place? And how much of it he had read? Thanks to Samantha he had beaten his withdrawal and felt no regret that the book had to be destroyed. But actually getting hold of it would be very difficult.

The couple got out of the car and kissed. Sam whispered a few words of encouragement and Tony unlocked the street door to #21. He led the way into the cool hallway. They mounted decaying carpets up the three flights of narrow, dark, stairs. At the top he decided to knock on the door instead of using his key, and he hoped he wouldn't associate the odour of the place with the ecstasy of accelerated evolution. Smell could beget memory and, in this example, also a powerful deja vu. Tony's heart was trip-hammering in his chest, when he realised how afraid of Demitrius he had always been. He sensed his girlfriend's breath quicken on the nape of his neck as they heard soft footsteps approach the door. He zipped his black leather jacket up to the neck. Sam had asked why he had chosen to dress in such clothing on such a hot day, and Tony had told her it was to look cool in front of the Cypriot. In fact it was to cushion the blows if things turned nasty.

The door opened. Demitrius looked out at them. His hair was wet, hanging around his head in lank black ropes, and he was resplendent in a purple velvet dressing gown. Tony had a feeling he had seen it somewhere before. The flash of serendipity on the Cypriot's face quickly changed into an expression of paranoid suspicion.

"I can read your mind, Tony," he said, with his curious accent. "I can feel the fear in you. I know what you want." Tony tried not to think about anything connected with the *Necronomicon*. The Cypriot leaned forward, and peered at them closely. "You want *my secrets...*"

"We want the rest of Tony's clothes and his art materials," Sam exclaimed boldly.

Demitrius frowned. "That's it?"

"Yes!" said Tony brightly. "I'll even make you one of my special coffees in your Playboy mug!"

"You come in," the Cypriot declared. "She stays outside."

"It's alright I'll be fine here, Tony. Just get what we came for."

"Are you coming in or what?"

Tony was led through his old bedroom into the kitchen. He saw the *Necronomicon* lying open on his MFI desk. It was grabbing his attention like a magnate as he walked passed, and it looked like it had been read about one third of the way through. He hardly dared to imagine what powers the Cypriot had gleaned from between its ancient sepia coloured pages. Did Demitrius really have as much ambition as Tony's nightmares suggested? Not yet, perhaps, but he would if left unchecked. Tony put the kettle on and was surprised to find milk in the fridge that wasn't sour. The older man watched him like a hawk from the doorway.

"I saw the MG," said Tony, to break the silence.

"The buyer went legit," Demitrius replied absently. "Bought himself a Triumph instead."

"You'll keep it then?"

"I don't care. I sold the black Honda Civic. I'm not really into that stuff anymore."

Tony stirred sugar into their drinks and passed Demi his, in his favourite mug.

"Delicious," the Cypriot said. "Now drink your coffee, get your stuff, and fuck off!"

"Move out completely?"

"Yes. I need to be alone while I'm studying shamanism."

"Is that what you call it now? Getting high?"

"It's not just about getting high." Demitrius sipped his drink delicately. "Oh yes, I remember. You've read some of my book too."

Tony gripped his mug harder. "That book was mine Demi. You gave it to me yourself!"

"So, I've taken it back, so what? You don't have the brains to appreciate it anyway."

"Oh, bullshit! You don't need intelligence to read that book, you just need an addictive personality and the curiosity of a lunatic!" *And a taste for power,* Tony thought.

"Power beyond imagining," said the other.

Shocked how easily the Cypriot had read his mind, Tony vowed to re-double his efforts to tread carefully, from now on, with his words and thoughts. He drank some coffee, and said:

"The *Necronomicon* is a drug. I've spent the last three days shivering and sweating and shaking because it's addictive. You know that, Demi, and I only read two chapters!"

"I'm not addicted to anything. I could stop reading it tomorrow."

"So stop then. Destroy it."

"It's more important than the Bible! Get your shit together and leave."

Tony was wasting his time... and now he would have to divert the Cypriot's attention, somehow. He put his empty cup on the draining board, and said: "Alright, I'm going in a minute. You can keep your cursed book, but I warn you it will change you so much you may as well commit suicide now."

ZAXXON

He walked into his room. He started putting clothes into a bin-liner. His easel was leaning against the mantle-piece over the cold decommissioned fireplace. He could feel the other man's gaze burning into his back as he folded it up and carried the things into the corridor.

Sam took delivery of the easel and the bag. "Are you OK?" she asked breathlessly. "Is it there?"

"The book's in my old room."

"Get it as soon as he so much as looks the other way."

"I'll try." He kissed her furtively and walked back into the flat. He came back a minute later with a second bag of clothes, and his paint box.

"Still not got it?" Sam asked.

"That bastard never stops watching." Tony gave her the wooden box and the second bag. "Take this lot. I'm going back in."

Tony rolled his duvet and pillows into another refuse sack. After that he leant six gesso-primed stretched canvases against the door. He opened the battered wardrobe and started to load the remainder of his clothes, pushing them into the last bag slowly because he was running out of time. His hands were shaking, yet Demitrius appeared to be more relaxed, perhaps believing what Tony had told him about keeping the 'cursed book'. The younger man folded each garment, with exaggerated care, knowing the other would become impatient. And it worked.

"OK, don't try anything," said the Cypriot. "I'm going to get dressed."

He walked out of the room, and all was quiet. Tony felt fear and relief, powerfully, in equal measures. He let go of the bin liner he had been holding in his right hand with a muffled thump. He moved to his desk and paused, looking down at the book, waited to ensure Demitrius wouldn't trick him in return and jump out of a doorway. He didn't, so Tony picked up the heavy tome feeling a little light-headed as his fingers touched the leather, and closed it. He carried it horizontally across the room in both hands like a tray balancing tall expensive Champagne flutes. He pushed through the door - and the Cypriot was waiting on the other side.

Tony's heart seemed to fall through his body, and into his feet, like a large dead battery.

Although the older man had a smaller build, he was effectively blocking access to the landing outside. He was dressed in torn jeans and his Slush Puppy tee shirt, clothes he claimed to wear for business, only. His face looked paradoxically grim yet gleeful. He barked like a dog and attacked Tony with the speed of a striking viper. Took the young artist by the neck and shoved him back into the bedroom. The *Necronomicon* was dropped onto the dirty floor. It lay in the middle of the carpet between them.

"I knew you were after it all along," hissed Demitrius. "I told you I can read your mind. That's why I had to get dressed. I never fight in my bath robe."

Now Tony was experiencing more determination than terror. *So it's to be a fight then,* he projected, and summoned his telekinetic ability, 'The Touch'.

The Cypriot was knocked off his feet with a supernatural ripple in the dusty air, thrown backwards with the energy of a train. He went sprawling down the wall and banged his head on the edge of the fireplace. Tony took two steps up and kicked him in the genitals, then stepped back, breathing hard. The book was on the floor in front of his Reeboks. He imagined heat and burning smoke, and flames, and he was rewarded with pyrokinesis that he hoped would be as flammable as the girl in the book *'Firestarter'* by Stephen King. Green flames blossomed around the *Necronomicon* and enveloped it quickly. He channelled all of his power into the base of it, the carpet charring around the book like a blackening picture frame. Nevertheless, for some reason, the book itself was not burning. Its ancient cover of human skin remained completely unaffected.

Tony stared down at his failure with confusion. The next thing he knew was a fist looping into his chin. He suffered a huge thump and an astonishment of red stars. Then he was punched in the stomach, which felt like being impaled on a fence post. He glanced up blearily.

"What are you looking so surprised about?" asked the Cypriot, and barked like a dog, again, dancing from foot to foot. "You know you can't destroy the book using its own magic." He punched Tony in the face and the young man almost had a white-out and began to bleed from a cut above his left eyebrow. "And you can't kick a man effectively with soft shoes. Next time try wearing hobnail boots. Like these!" He pulled back his heavy right-hand boot and then swung it vengefully towards the younger man's groin.

Tony protected himself by swerving instinctively sideways. The boot swept through the air, and missed him completely, and Tony smacked Demitrius in the face with his arm extended. The man looked stunned and Tony hit him again, in the teeth. Demitrius went off balance, but all too briefly. He bounced back grasping Tony by the neck and squeezed hard, immediately, literally spitting blood. Tony shuddered and started going crazy in his own head. He felt faint, he could feel the lack of air to his lungs and the lack of blood to his brain, and blackness was creeping into the periphery of his vision. The Cypriot barked, and pushed Tony back until he bumped into his bed frame and collapsed onto the mattress.

"No," he said, releasing Tony's neck. "That let's you off too easily." Tony gasped in air. The relief was unparalleled: the darkness, receding. "I'm not going to kill you. I want you to *suffer*."

The artist stared at the Cypriot's right hand, at the coin ring on his index finger. A gold sovereign embossed in drying blood, the first blood Tony had ever shed in a fight.

"I sucked the memories out of a dog in the flat downstairs this morning," Demitrius continued happily. "And I learnt all its secrets. Subsequently the little fella couldn't even walk. Do you know, for ten minutes I actually thought I was a dog?" Tony looked up at his face. The man was mad. "Now I'm gonna take your experiences and make you into a mindless vegetable, and afterwards I may even paint a landscape. I'm going to be an artist and I'll work ten times harder at it than you ever did." His eyes lit up with a green glow the colour of emeralds, Tony's favourite stone.

He liked looking at it, and started to feel sleepy. He saw flash visions of muddled memory, felt something shuffling around in his brain. Somewhere through the feeling of cushiony soft feathers, a silent alarm was warning him to prevent this. To stop the fingertips digging any deeper. So he raised the meat of his left hand to his mouth and bit down on it until blood welled from the imprint of his teeth. That broke the hypnotics. Tony stood up and swung his fist into the Cypriot's face, whose nose crunched under the impact. The man was knocked back onto the floor, in the centre of the room, with blood pouring down his chin. He collapsed blindly on top of the *Necronomicon* and grabbed it into his arms.

"I've had by dose smashed before, dony. It wone stop me for long."

"I broke my addiction to the conjurations Demi. I really did. And you can too." Tony moved towards him, hesitantly.

"If you make un more step in the direction ob dis book, I'll kill you. I swear it."

"I'll risk that."

"And then I'll kill your girlfriend, and I'll kill your family, and I'll get away with it. You know I can do it."

Tony straightened up. "That's it, then," he said. "I'm done."

The artist walked back to the doorway and picked up his blank canvases. Demitrius was kissing the *Necronomicon* and making pig noises. He was a bloody, sordid, little man, crawling around on a dirty carpet, but he was also the most terrifying monster Tony had ever met. Outside, Sam was waiting for him by the street door in the car. She saw the blood on his face, and his desperate, stricken expression, and she knew all was lost.

"It's not bad," she murmured, examining his eyebrow. "You don't need stitches."

"I tried," he moaned. "Sam, I really wanted to, but he cheated. I couldn't get it."

"I know that my sweet. It's in God's hands now."

She started the Beetle and they drove away without looking back, except into their own minds – where there resided a strong suspicion that everything that had happened had taken place before.

CHAPTER – 22

"Des.pair"

After escaping the gun battle on the night of 28th the demons had driven into a camping site. It was far enough away from the city, and the police, to experience blasé relief. They had reached a point of safety in the night and felt skittish with humorous shudders. The adrenaline was short lived. Powerful as they were, the memory of being struck by so many bullets and the likelihood they had almost been shot in the head was a continuous and terrifying regret. A shadow had been cast over their inviolability.

They were confused by this new question of their own mortality. Terror, and post trauma stress, kept them cowering in their caravan hideout for five nights. They spent the time re-living moments from past lives, talking about the *Necronomicon*, and welding their imaginations together on trips to places that were bizarre and inhuman. They needed to re-build their courage. Only seventy-four hours remained until they had to deliver the grimoire through the Dimensional Window outside Ashton Court. Sex helped, but it was hunger that drove them outside.

The door to the trailer squeaked open at midnight and the two demons crept out of the sweaty darkness and dropped onto the grass, stark naked, in the fresh night air. The metamorphosis took them. Fed by the need to feed, they stared with wonder up at the firmament of stars above until their sight went red, and blood was all they could think of.

Their fingernails became claws, their teeth grew into knives, and every muscle and sinew in their bodies became the mechanics of killing machines. The Succubus led the way like a lioness smelling her prey before she sees it. She caught the scent of sex from a caravan on the edge of the field, and bloody murder followed. They tore a young couple out of bed then limb from limb with a razor sharpness so swift it was uncannily quiet. They ate until their bodies returned to normal: plump and satiated and tired. After they took a shower they found a set of keys for a Ford Focus.

"That's a fine vehicle," Lillith observed.
"I saw it outside," said Thorn. "Have they got any money?"

The succubus looked inside the dead woman's purse, for money, and found sixty pounds. She took one hundred and thirty pounds from the man's wallet and subsequently discovered he had been a Metropolitan Police Officer. The woman had been his young wife.

"Something's turned against us," said Lillith. "This is bad."
"What does it mean?" asked the Incubus.
"It means the police now have an added reason to bring us down, perhaps the most powerful of all motives - revenge. We've already killed at least one officer and now we've killed another and his wife! We must cover our tracks very carefully. We'll wrap the bodies in sheets or towels - anything that's clean, and bury them in the middle of nowhere."
"Where?"
"I don't know. Anywhere. An Earth version of 'the back of Beyond'."
Thorn thought about it, for a moment, then said: "We can't take their car. They'll trace it."
"We can't leave it for the same reason."
"It'll be sad to lose the Golf."
"We need to change transport more regularly anyway. Now we have to eradicate the left-overs of our supper."
"There's blood everywhere, Lillith. We'll have to bury the duvet and bed things with them."
"Pay attention. All fabric with blood on it gets squeezed out in the shower cubicle. We wash it away, then carry the bodies out to the Ford without shedding a single drop on the grass. We take their food, their toiletries, and their garments. And after we've scrubbed the rest of the caravan, we will burn it."

"When the coppers see the fire they'll be here within half an hour."

"Actually they will be here in under twenty minutes, but even with the fire brigade in tow they won't be able to extinguish the flames in time. There will be no trace of the people left."

"I think their clothes may fit us."

"So do I."

"I want some blue jeans. Levis, or Wranglers."

"Concentrate, Thorn, get a hold on yourself. We cannot make a single mistake."

"So let's do it."

"Alright, but no lights. We use Ultra-vision."

They crept around the caravan like moles in an earthen tunnel, communicating with telepathy. To normal sight the blood was as black as oil on the white sheets, in the moonlight. Seen in ultraviolet everything was grey. The look in each other's eyes was weird and reflective. Thorn liked it. What they saw had less contrast. Seemed to be smaller, closer to them. The place was humid with the scent of blood, and claustrophobic. They bumped into each other carrying wet bundles from the bedroom to the shower cubicle, and back and forth; rinsed, squeezed them dry, washing the stains down the plug hole. They tore up the carpet tiles, with their fingernails, and carried everything outside. The bodies were wrapped in a duvet and placed together in the boot of the Ford. Every incriminating component was pushed into the car. Finally they dressed, pulled on leather sandals that almost fit, and Lillith lit a candle and twisted the taps on the stove. The caravan began to fill up with flammable gas, with a hissing sound. She left the candle burning at the opposite end of the lounge area under the window.

They switched their optics to normal sight. The job was over. The Incubus made certain the door and windows were closed then climbed into the Ford with Lillith. The engine turned over with a somnolent rumbling noise from under the bonnet. She drove across the field, slowly, without lights. Trailers and recreational vehicles with tungsten bulbs in small windows seemed to hover above the grass like ships passing in the night. When she turned onto the road she switched on the headlights and steered away from the city, hunting for sanctuary in farmland.

Far behind them there was a sudden flash, and a crumpling vibration like the car had been driven over a narrow cattle grid. Lillith watched a balloon of fire rising above the countryside in her rear-view mirror. Thorn watched it from over the split rear seats. It disappeared, quickly, leaving a temporary and colourful imprint on their retinas.

"So that's that, then," exclaimed Thorn.
"We did it, my love," said the Succubus. "Now we just need a safe place to bury the detritus and find the tools to do it with."

There were many signposts around the crossroads and intersections for small villages. Lillith usually drove the other way. There were closed gates, and signs such as: 'NO TRESSPASSING', 'KEEP OUT' or 'PRIVATE PROPERTY' that were becoming increasingly irritating. Thorn yawned often.

"How are we doing for fuel?" he asked tiredly.
"Loads of it."
"Do you mind if I sleep?"
"Alright... No! Wait!"
"What is it?"

Another sign, illuminated by their high-beams, loomed out of the darkness in front of them. The sight of it drove Lillith to a sudden and reflexive halt. There were two lines. The top half read: 'HAVEN FARM' and on the bottom was: *'BUILDING CONDEMNED'*.

"Platch, be upon me, Thorn! This is the place!"

She turned left, into a gateless entrance and proceeded down the driveway. The succubus hadn't been outside for many days, and was experiencing a fear of the unknown, but she also had a contagious enthusiasm that made Thorn smile. They were like a couple of kids embarking on a Ghost Train ride at a seaside amusement park. Dry mud bumped under the tyres. Further up the road, on the left, she saw a large barn and immediately to their right was a sprawling Edwardian house, which looked mostly intact from this distance. They parked and went to explore the edifice, leaving the headlights on.

The leaded windows were all smashed. Half of its roof had collapsed. Broken grey slates littered the ground around the exterior walls, which had been rendered with cream plasterwork that was now crumbled across the ground in many patches like powdered eggs. The front door was lying on the porch. They proceeded carefully through the doorway and the site smelt of dry rot and restless spirits. Floor boards creaked with weakness and uncertainly. Exposed beams had fallen out of the ceilings and through walls, demolishing everything in the way. The demons weren't concerned about cutting themselves, or getting bruises, or even broken bones; because, of course, they could heal spontaneously. The problem was the extent of the destruction.

"We can't stay in here," the Incubus stated simply.
Lillith agreed with him. "It's uninhabitable. Let's go."

They re-traced their steps with care, and, when they were back outside, Thorn asked her about the next plan. Lillith stood there, considering this, and abruptly her face lit up as brightly as the headlights of the Ford.

"Let's look at the barn!" she exclaimed.
"What barn?"
"It's over there," she said, pointing with one finger. "Up the path on the left. Walk with me."
"I can't see it."
"Use your Ultra-vision."
"Oh, bloody hell, *that!* I see it. It's huge!"

ZAXXON

There was a tractor with three wheels missing, and a Land Rover, which had been abandoned by the outer wall. Those walls were hewn of beech and appeared to be sound and strong. There was a pile of old tyres by the double front doors, which they opened with a slight difficulty, and went in to investigate the place. It had a tall vaulted ceiling, a dirt floor, and it was as warm and dry as a new cardboard box. They found a hurricane lamp with some oil left in it, and a gasless Clipper that looked like it had been squashed by a block of concrete, but they only needed a spark. The flint was intact and Lillith lit the wick. The building filled with light. There was a rusty yellow Mini Cooper in one corner, farming implements and gardening tools in the other, and by the far wall there was a scattering of sweet scented straw that made Thorn want to climb onto and have a rest.

"We can't sleep yet," indicated the Succubus. "We have to hide the car."

Thorn lowered his arse to the floor like an old man, slowly, the joints in his knees popping. "Can't you do it yourself? I've eaten too much and I'm dog-tired!"

Lillith stared at him, reached into his mind and empathised with the cloying extent of his fatigue. Apparently morphing in and out of his Bestial Feeder Body exhausted him. "Alright, I'll do it," she decided. "Just make sure you save me a warm pile of hay."

He lay back. "No problem." He closed his eyes.

The Succubus dimmed the brightness of the oil lamp and the opened the barn doors. She walked down the path wondering how they would dispose of the Ford. The headlights were still on and the front of the condemned house was lit like a stage set in a dim auditorium. She was worried the battery might be too sapped for the starter motor to operate because that would cause a lot of extra work. She took the keys out of the tight pocket of her stolen jeans and opened the driver's side door.

The interior had a powerful smell of blood that she found sexually arousing. Lillith twisted the key in the ignition. The starter motor whirred several times like an old computer hard-drive that couldn't process the recipe for a cucumber sandwich. She swore, but when she turned the key a second time the car started. She turned the steering wheel tiredly and drove it up the path. When it was parked, she switched off the engine, yawning whilst she closed the doors. She went to lay with her Incubus in the soft straw. Thorn opened his eyes, briefly, and smiled at her. They were asleep by 3 am.

*   *   *

The next morning in North London was Friday 4th July, and Stephen Ashcroft awoke at eight o'clock with a real bitch of a hang-over. He had been rushing about on the business of his dead daughter and had been afflicted with drunkenness every night since last Sunday. He was still dressed in the clothes he had flopped into bed wearing the night before. He had watched a reality television show on Sky drinking Gordon's Dry gin until he didn't know whether the people on the television were watching him or if he was one of the people on the screen and he was watching himself. He started talking to the TV. When someone on the screen shouted "fuck off!" he got frightened and went up to bed.

He didn't really want to surface yet but he was heading back to Bristol this morning. It was to be an important day, today. What actually forced him out of bed was a mad craving for orange juice. He opened all the curtains on the floor and padded down to the kitchen in his socks, drank half a carton of Tropicana and switched off the television in the sitting-room. He went back upstairs. He was shocked by the bedraggled grey beard and the haggard look of his own face in the bathroom mirror. He took a cold shower.

Once he was dried and brushed, he selected his clothing carefully because he required an imposing impression. He dressed in an open necked shirt of white Egyptian cotton, a lightweight cream jacket, pressed Chinos, and a pair of tan Hush Puppies. As usual, given the chance, he had a tall mug of tea and a bar of chocolate for breakfast. After packing a small bag with two changes of clothes and overnight toiletries, he ordered a cab to take him to Paddington Station. There was just one thing left to do before he left. He looked around, with great but quite unexaggerated care, and prised open the Armenian vase on his bedroom windowsill. He delved into it with one hand then extracted a bundle of fifty pound notes, a thick roll of £5,000 bound in an elastic band. It made a small bulge in his jacket pocket that he patted often whilst on his trek to Bristol.

He had no car but with the exception of being squeezed together with commuters, Ashcroft enjoyed train journeys. He relished being carried, liked to sit by the window rocking gently from side to side to the somnolent rumble of the wheels clack-clack-clacking along the tracks. Trains had a warm and friendly plastic scent which was relaxing to him, like the smell of the rubber dinosaur he had cuddled in bed as a little boy. The ceaseless montage of the countryside was also a pleasure. Many shades of green so different from London, rushing by with that deep 3D effect that only a passenger can see, and only when travelling at high speed. It was agreeable but it didn't take his mind off his problems.

Stephanie had been interned in the ground last Sunday 29th June. The Professor intended to raise her from that grave, and he needed the *Necronomicon* to do it. He had never read any of the book but he had faith in it, and faith was vital. He needed to believe that in spite of the fact his daughter had been buried for five days, the book would restore her to full health. He would not consider any worse possibilities. People typically don't recall bad moments in order to carry on with their lives. The Professor had forgotten the morals of the famous stage play *"The Monkey's Paw"* and the tale of his ancestor, Angus McLoughlan Ashcroft, being driven mad by the sight of his long-dead wife shambling towards him, grey green, and putrefying. That his only child was becoming more irretrievable with every passing hour was simply unacceptable.

The threat Nigel Hawthorne had made at the wake, to have him Sectioned if he tampered with her grave, would become irrelevant when he saw her. Magic would resurrect her, and Nigel's old heart would melt. He would be joyful to see the miracle, and what stories would Stephanie have to tell of the next world?! The risk Stephen Ashcroft now faced was a matter of time. If he didn't recover the *Necronomicon* soon it may disappear with whoever held it into the Dimensional Window at Ashton Court at midnight on Sunday 6th. Shortly after his train left Paddington he used his mobile phone to call the Three Cups Inn, and managed to book the room he had occupied before. The train pulled into Bristol Temple Meads station at half passed eleven.

He took a cab to the hotel to collect his key and drop off his luggage. He took the same car straight back into the city and ate lunch by the canal. Seeing the Watershed again reminded him of his lost painting, and the young artist and his attractive girlfriend he had met there last time, when life had been simpler. He paid the café bill, checked the roll of notes in his pocket, again, and then walked through Greyfriars through a hot dry dusty wind, to the offices of The Bristol Evening Post.

In the foyer his manner was frantic. He was sweating and his hair was in disarray. The receptionist looked like she was readying herself for him to gabble off in some insane language at any moment. Politeness won her over. She directed him up to the second floor, to the Classified Ads Department. He told the young man behind the desk he wanted thirty five words to say the following:

To the thieves of the red MG BGT stolen from Gloucestor Road on June 26th: You may keep the car, but I want the old book that was in it returned. Reward of £5000. Call Stephen Ashcroft on 07444917898.

The Professor wanted this in the motoring sales section of the paper, emphasised, and in a box. The youthful advertising man typed it up then stared at his monitor as if it was a dubious request. He tapped his black Biro against his mint white teeth then offered to place a small 'social interest article' in the newspaper, for nothing. Ashcroft turned this down. The thieves would be more likely to read the car advertising section of the paper than any other pages. The clerk charged Ashcroft £18 for three days, muttering something about the rarity of the petition, but the Professor wasn't really listening. His wristwatch said it was 2:45pm. He had pitched his best shot. The little statement would start in tonight's edition, Friday 4th July. He prayed it would bear fruit.

*   *   *

The demons were digging a hole. They were using shovels to scoop loamy soil onto a growing pile beside the excavation at the far end of the barn. It was hot in there, but Zaxxon did not require as much water as a human being. They had a unique biology and metabolism, and they processed different electrolytes because the necessity for water could be a disadvantage in combat conditions. Blood contains minerals they refined, instead, and they could pass it to each other through a small wound in times of comparable drought.

When the hole was deep enough to fulfil its function they lifted the bodies out of the Ford and buried them in it. They also put in the blood soaked sheets and duvet, and clothes they didn't want to adopt. They patted flat the earth that concealed this damning evidence and tossed away the shovels. Lillith led the way outside to look at the Land Rover because they needed to replace the Ford. It was a 'Defender' model, dirty with dust. Dried mud was splashed up the wheel arches, but the tyres were intact. Lillith opened the driver's door with a squeak of rusty hinges.

"I can't find any keys," she said.
"Couldn't you hot-wire it?" Thorn asked.

"I never learnt how." She thought about it. "I have re-collected a few scenes from victims into popular cinema but the memory-cards are faint. I suppose I could give it a try…"

Thorn lifted the bonnet. "I wouldn't bother if I was you."

"Don't be so pessimistic."

He dropped it with a loud bang. "There's no engine in it."

She chuckled about this and led the way into the barn to look at their last chance for an easy escape.

The Mini had been yellow once but now the extensive rust made it appear both yellow and sienna, like a bruised pear. They found the keys in the glove department. The tyres were solid and the engine was cleaner than either demon could have rightly expected. Nevertheless, it would not start.

"The battery must be flat," said the Succubus. "Maybe we can jump-start it."

She walked to the Ford Focus on the other side of the barn and opened the boot. She rummaged under the hatch for a while. Her mind smiled when she was rewarded with a thick wire that had two sets of crocodile clips at either end.

"I thought you didn't know how it was done," the Incubus observed.

"This is a different thing. This cable passes electricity from a charged battery to an empty battery so we can start the engine of the car with the empty battery."

"We can't do that every time."

"Running the motor charges the battery also."

"How?"

"We can't get into these details, right now, it's nearly four o'clock."

"You don't know do you?"

"No." She climbed into the Ford and reversed it up to the Mini.

After connecting the leads, Lillith successfully jump-started the smaller car. It made grunting noises, coughing dirt from the exhaust, however it soon stabilized. She gazed at the dashboard display and started jumping up and down, repeating herself with excitement:

"There's half a tank of fuel! There's half a tank of fuel!"

"That's brilliant," said Thorn. "Can we have sex, now, please?"

They left the Mini's engine running and shared each other. Afterwards the Succubus felt very relaxed, and seemed optimistic. Lying back comfortably on the bed of straw, breathing in the pleasant sleepy smell of carbon monoxide. Their luck appeared to have turned.

"We can be rid of the Ford, now. But we have to do it properly," she said.

"It's covered in blood. We can't leave it in here."

"That's my point exactly." The succubus was thinking aloud, pinching her fine chin between forefinger and thumb. "We can't dump it in the city, or on a country road. Or even on the edge of a field. And we can't burn it."

"Why not?"

"During the day there would be column of black smoke a hundred feet high, and at night it would light up the countryside from miles around." Thorn watched her face, and witnessed the solution occur to her like the relief of starvation with bloody food. "I know! We'll ram it into the house!"

"That's crazy," he said. "Isn't it?" She looked at him levelly. "You're not joking are you?"

"No. We take it round the side of the farmhouse hidden from the driveway, and drive it straight into the middle of the ruins." She opened the barn doors. "It won't be uncovered for weeks!"

"You mean 'you' rather than 'we', of course. I'm an observer."

"Then observe," Lillith said, feeling a flash of anger as she climbed into the Ford that she didn't know was justified. The engine rumbled to life.

After checking the warning lights to ascertain the SRS Airbag system was functional, she exited the outbuilding and drove down the path. A third of the way along it Lillith turned the steering wheel to the left and guided the car onto the field. She was soon positioned behind the farmhouse at ninety degrees to the wall, but too near. She fastened her seat belt. The farmhouse was so dilapidated she estimated that hitting it any faster than thirty and the car would probably go straight through it and out of the other side. Her adrenaline was beginning to flow: pulse, heart rate, skin temperature, all increasing. Her visual processing was accelerating into tunnel vision.

She shifted the gear stick into reverse and backed up about sixty feet, then thrust the Ford into first and stamped on the gas peddle. The rear wheels spun up a cloud of soil. The car leapt forwards and she briefly saw Thorn, standing on the path to the right, appearing flushed with excitement. The acceleration seemed too rapid. With the exciting stench of blood in her nostrils and screaming words that she didn't recognize herself, the Ford hit the wall of the house at 27 mph.

The Air-bags inflated. All went dark. There was a huge crashing noise. The windscreen cracked. The front wheels bucked like a wild horse then something bigger went through the screen completely and Lillith was showered with pieces of glass. Beams were falling like the matchsticks of a giant. Tiles and bricks were hitting the roof with random thumping sounds and a chunk smashed the rear window. Then, after one final judder, the car came to a halt. The succubus pushed the expended Air-bag out of the way and stared out of the glassless window at the muted confusion of debris.

"Platch," she muttered.
"Are you OK?" Thorn shouted from somewhere else.
"Yes," she replied, with a shaky voice. "I'm... fine."
"I asked if you were OK!"
"YES! JUST LET ME GET ON WITH IT!"
"Alright, there's no need to shout."

She could smell her own sweat. After disconnecting the seat belt she tried to open the driver's side door, but it was stuck. She manoeuvred herself through the broken glass into the other seat, wounding the palms of her hands in the process with painful little cuts that healed spontaneously. She cranked open the passenger door and paused for a moment, squinting up at the ceiling, as dust filtered down. It stopped with a hollow rattle. The Succubus stepped very carefully out of the car. It looked like a bomb had exploded. The room was an assault course of broken wood and plaster and rubble, and she crossed it contorting herself at different angles with her back hunched. Like a moth to the light she eventually ducked through a small hole in the wall, on her hands and knees, and emerged into the fresh air and the blazing early evening sun. Thorn walked around the corner.

"There you are!" he exclaimed. "Truly awesome!"
"I thought so also," said Lillith. She made a circuit of the ruins to ensure the car was completely concealed. "It can't be seen. It worked Thorn!"
"I know, you're a genius my love."
She sniffed down her cleavage, pulling a sour face, and started trying to brush herself off with dusty little pats. She accidentally stroked the dirt deeper into her clothes. "I need clean garments."
"In the barn," said the succubus. "Let's get naked again!"

Lillith didn't want to drive into Bristol before dark. They rutted in the straw, until the shafts of sunlight shining like lasers thought the cracks and holes in the outbuilding had an orange red quality. The sun had set. Night was beginning. They rubbed down the windows and the rusty paint of the Mini with a cloth, then Lillith drove it out of the barn. They made for the city, saying nothing. The signs they followed became bigger and more clarified as they went along. When approaching the on-ramp onto the motorway the succubus finally spoke:

"Any sign of the police force and we're turning back."
"I vote we keep going."

"They have our descriptions; and they have guns too, sometimes. Anyway I am the driver, so it's my decision". She pressed on the gas peddle and pushed the Mini up to sixty five. The car was burping and shuddering like a drunk. "We need another vehicle. This is not suitable."

"Like a Ferrari!"

"You've been watching too much hotel television."

"I have to, Lillith. My education was cut short."

"I don't want you to know what a mess it is out there."

"Out where?"

"- In the world."

"It's nothing we can't handle, together. We can cope. Ducks to water - Zaxxon to blood!"

She sighed heavily. "You must understand something, Thorn. Even if we do succeed in delivering the *Necronomicon,* to the Dark Lord, we will never be accepted in this world. We will always be hunted, and have to live in the shadows as renegades for the rest of time."

"I have an idea about that," Thorn expressed, blocking his thoughts by pulling an imaginary blanket over his brain.

"What idea?" she asked, reaching into his mind.

"No, don't go fishing, I'll tell you later."

"Tell me now!"

"It's a surprise." Then he leaned forward, peering into the distance. "Shit, it's the police!"

Blue lights were winking on the motorway approximately one mile ahead. Lots of police cars, and figures in yellow fluorescent jackets halting vehicles and talking to the drivers.

"It's a road-block," moaned Lillith.

Thorn could feel her panic. There was lorry on its side blocking almost the whole width of the road. "No, no, it's an accident."

The officers were directing cars in single file by what looked like huge rolls of paper that had been scattered across the Tarmac. They were about to join the traffic queue when Lillith noticed an escape route. A hole had been ripped through the metal barrier of the central reservation. She immediately took the opportunity for a U-turn. She switched off the headlights and brakelights, and drove through the gap entering the carriageway travelling in the opposite direction. She switched the lights back on and accelerated to a sedate pace.

Thorn ran his hands down his face and the Succubus realised she had been holding her breath for about three minutes. They smiled all the way back into the bleak countryside, but shared a cold sweat. They had waited too long. Destiny was reaching towards them, now, rather than the other way around. Fear still stopped them, and they concealed it from each other because neither would admit it.

The journey ended where it had begun. The Succubus bumped and wobbled the old Mini back up the path and parked it in the barn. Thorn closed the doors and lit the hurricane lamp. They relaxed on the straw, talking about interesting things. Discussed how rally cars could be made to appear unremarkable; told stories of the couple buried under their feet returning revengefully to life; and considered the link between the age of a man and the varying taste of his meat and blood. They obviously didn't need sleep. They had sex several times and stabbed each other with a screwdriver, for fun.

"What did you mean when you said you have an idea about our future?" asked Lillith.

The Incubus rolled over to look at her beautiful face. "I mean why don't you convert other people like you did to me?"

"I hadn't thought about it…"

"If there were enough of us, if we were an army, we could take over the whole world."

"It's an attractive idea."

"Rest, my sweet. Think about it."

She shut down the present tense of her own bodily system. Thorn followed suit and their minds drifted like the dust particles which swayed to and fro in the unknown tides of air through the barn. The lantern ran out of oil during the night.

CHAPTER – 23

"Marri.age"

Stephen Ashcroft had placed a desperate bulletin in the local evening newspaper. He felt anxious, continuously, because nobody answered it. In spite of eating a lot of chocolate he slept only five hours that first night. On the morning of Saturday 5th he decided to take a hike along the edge of the River Avon as an antidote to the interminable waiting. Later, he ate an early supper and watched banal television. His mobile phone was always ready in his right hand. At the same time, 7:38pm, Patrick and Jason Dreyer were sitting in their unkempt lounge, in their dirty two bed flat, sitting in front of their own television. Patrick finished rolling a joint of 'skunk weed' and puffed on it several times like a man lighting a cigar. He settled back into the old threadbare sofa to watch *Eastenders* on the BBC. His younger brother Jason was reading The Bristol Evening Post and the paper was rattling noisily every time he turned a page.

"Can't you read that quietly, bruv?"
"How?" Jason asked, loudly turning another page.
"Just pack it in will you - I'm tryin' to watch the telly!"
"Pass that spliff in my direction and I might consider it."

Jason laid the paper on the table. He took several large puffs of the drug, then perched the joint on the edge of the ashtray, and retrieved his newspaper. He opened it and turned a few pages with a loud crackle.

"Shut up! Shut up!" Patrick shouted, pressing the button on the TV remote to turn up the volume.
"I'm just reading the jalopies, alright? Chill out, man!"
There were no further interruptions for a while, and Patrick was pleased about this. Suddenly Jason was jumping to his feet enthusiastically: "I don't bloody believe it!"
Patrick was intrigued; the TV temporarily forgotten. "What is it?"

"You remember that MG Tony and Demitrius swiped the night we did that competition thing?"

"What about it?"

"Well there's a box about it, right here, from the owner. You're not gonna believe this!"

"Just read it, OK?"

"To the thieves of the red MG BGT stolen from Gloucestor Road on June 26th: You may keep the car, but I want the old book that was in it returned. Reward of £5000! Call Stephen Ashcroft on 07444917898.

Did you hear that, bruv? Five thousand quid! Five!"

Patrick's excitement now matched his brother's. "I remember that book. Tony had it, didn't he?"

"I'm pretty sure Demitrius took it off him the morning after the party, but I'm going over there."

"The man threatened us with a piece of scaffolding pole, and you fell down the stairs and sprained your wrist. Don't forget that." Patrick stubbed out the remains of the joint in the ashtray.

"So now it's time for us to get back into his good books. A few thousand is a hell of a sweetener."

"No doubt about it. What if this Ashcroft has offered the reward as a trap?"

Jason started tearing the little notice out of the page. "I don't smell pork."

"Alright, I'll trust your instincts. Let's go to Launch Terrace."

They tied up their grimy trendsetting trainers then pulled on track-suit tops from which they had cut the hoods when 'hoodies' had become unfashionable. Jason Dreyer tucked the cutting from the newspaper into his pocket. "Demi's gonna love this!" he exclaimed. They turned off the TV and locked the dank flat behind them, narrowing their eyes in the low sunshine. "It's lucky we didn't get too stoned, isn't it Pat. Isn't it?"

"You're kidding, bruv." His head was swimming. "Why do I always seem to be wasted whenever something important happens?"

ZAXXON

Ten minutes later they were standing by the street door to #21, buzzing the top flat. Jason pressed the button again. There was still no answer, no noise of any kind from the other side, so he held his finger down on the doorbell until they were graced with a reaction. They heard someone coming down the stairs.

"Let me do the talking," whispered Patrick.
"But you're stoned," Jason said quietly.
"I'm sobering up."

They heard clunking and rattling sounds emanating from behind the door. A mortise being unlocked. A dead-bolt slid aside. A security chain being unfastened. The door swung open and Demi stepped onto the porch. He was barely recognizable. His long hair was greasy, his nose was black and blue, and he had a fuzz of beard sticky with old food. He was wearing a disgusting 'Slush Puppy' tee shirt sweat-stained at the armpits, and a foul smelling pair of jeans that appeared to be stained at the groin. What was even more bizarre was the glass jar of spiders he clutched close to his chest like a marsupial with a baby.

"What are those for?" Jason couldn't help asking, looking with distaste at the little creatures.
"They are my pets. Like you two used to be." Demi squinted down at the older brother, his dark eyes smouldering with suspicion. "What do you want, Patrick?"
Patrick was experiencing a paranoid head-rush. His hands were numb, his tongue felt dry and swollen. "We want to... we err... that is to say, we..."
"We've come to see you about Tony," Jason stated.
"Oh, that feisty little trickster!"
"Yes."
"OK, you can come in."

Mounting the damp flights of stairs Patrick lagged behind the others. His brain felt like a sponge pudding. On the way up the steps he pinched his cheek and slapped himself hard in the face, to stimulate clearer thinking. In the stench of the

Cypriot's front room, the man put the jar of arachnids on the coffee table amongst the rubbish. Patrick found him staring at both himself and his brother like they were no better than the landfill of milk cartons and fast-food boxes and filthy mugs and cutlery that littered the bed-sit. Patrick had been friends with him for a long time, but the unwashed and intense Demi standing before him, now, was not the man he had known.

"What have you been doing?" he asked them.

Patrick took deep breaths, steadying himself further. "Oh, the usual. You know; getting stoned."

"Yes, I can see that."

Patrick was ready to pitch his plan to secure Tony's address, in the event that Demitrius refused to give up the book. He didn't mention it. Or the reward. Not yet. "We have a bone to pick with that twit, Tony."

"Twat - not twit," said the Cypriot. "I've picked many bones with him."

"See, we lent him some money about four months ago to purchase paint and canvases and that stuff, and, I'm sorry, but we didn't want you to know."

"Why?"

"Because Jason wanted to be top-dog in front of you."

"That was foolish. I could have enforced the repayments. How much did he take you for?"

"Four hundred pounds. He swore in the event of his being exhibited he would pay us back ten percent of the net receipts on the first twenty paintings sold."

"A sound investment," observed the Cypriot.

"Word is, he's flogged the lot."

"- And we haven't seen a single coin," added Jason.

"We want to go pay Tony a little visit, to indicate our annoyance. Do you know where he is?"

Demitrius smiled under his blotchy painful-looking nose. "You need the address of his bitch. Wait here. And don't touch the spiders." He walked into the corridor.

Jason leaned his mouth towards Patrick's ear. "You know, bruv, you can't divvy up £5000 very easily between three people."

"Are you saying we should jump him?"

"Yes. I'm sure he's got the book, and he's completely out of his tree!"

"Let's try the normal channels, first. See if we can't get him on-side."

The Cypriot came back into the room holding a small ledger. "This is Tony's address book. All his contact points are in it." He handed it to Patrick, who slipped it into his back pocket. "Promise me one thing: when you bust his nose, tell him it's a gift from me."

"No problem," said Patrick.

"There is one more thing, Demi," Jason said, hesitantly. "If Tony has that crusty old book he got from the MG we would like to have it in lieu of payment."

"It's not Tony's book. It's mine. Understand?"

"We've just learned something about it you probably don't know."

"I know everything! *EVERYTHING!!*"

Demitrius was suddenly in a rage. The younger brother tried to tell him about the reward. He was just pulling out the newspaper clipping when the Cypriot struck him in the jaw so quickly Jason never saw it coming. There was a loud thump and the piece of paper floated down from side to side like a feather to the carpet.

Patrick stepped in front of his reeling brother and swung a hay-maker that completely missed his assailant's face. The other man dodged it like a pugilist and retaliated with both fists. He bruised Patrick's chin, cut his cheekbone, and split his lower lip. Patrick's skull was whining and felt heavy. Jason stepped in from the right-hand side as Patrick stumbled backwards, bleeding. He observed Jason get the Cypriot with a lucky strike, as if from a long distance away, that connected with the man's weakest point – his nose. The Cypriot made a growl of pain. Patrick managed to pull himself back onto his feet. He was not a natural fighter, but as his brother moved in, he dared to believe they could win.

He thought about the five grand. And that was when everything went really... bizarre. Demitrius laughed as if he'd heard the thought, stepped back and swivelled sideways on his left foot, and extended one fist forward and the other back, in the gesture of a martial artist. His face was a mask of blood, and concentration. Jason was not even within reach, but suddenly he flew backwards and hit the corner of the room with a noise like a brick hitting the wall. He went sliding down to the floor. Patrick's mind couldn't understand it. He charged blindly at the Cypriot and found himself treading on air. Reality wobbled, and he was crashing into the door of the bed-sit as if he'd been thrown by a windless hurricane.

Demitrius stepped up to his younger brother and swung a kick at his head.

By a stroke of fluke Jason caught the heavy boot in both hands, and twisted it just shy of breaking the ankle. Put the man off balance so he collapsed over the coffee table. Both brothers were on their feet, quickly, but they were certain of nothing. The Cypriot laughed at them, again, as they advanced. He jumped upright, and casually swept a hand palm-down from the left and to the right. Patrick saw the atmosphere in the room change again like a distorted reflection. He blinked, but it was still happening. As the air in front of the brothers was rippling, like some unseen engine dropped into a clear sea, suddenly they were kicked backwards as if by an invisible horse.

It was much worse than last time. The energy propelled Jason against the paintwork. Patrick hit the doorway leading to the kitchen, after actually turning sideways in mid-air, landing upside down in a confused heap with one of his arms broken. He propped himself up on the other arm, moaning with concussion. Everything seemed to be red and grey, swishing about and stinking of electricity.

He wondered how his brother was faring. His own forehead was cut and livid and his nose was out of joint. He spat a gobbet of blood on the floor. And his eyes met the piece of paper that Jason had torn from the Post. It was the wrong way up, near his battered face. On the reverse side of the clipping he saw a jumble of letters, emphasised by a power he didn't understand: *"u canot win, get out,"* Patrick read. He got the message - but, impossibly - it was made out of... completely *different words*. He felt re-invigorated as if by a bolt of lightning. He retrieved the scrap of newsprint and pushed it into his pocket, then scrambled over to his brother and got the younger man onto his feet and hauled him out into the corridor. "Come on, Jay, we're leaving."

"Yeah, push off you pussies!" Demitrius shouted.

The brothers hurried down the steps. The door to the flat slammed shut behind them so hard it rattled the banisters at the bottom of the stairs. They ran onto the street, and they kept running until they collapsed on the pavement in total exhaustion.

"What the hell was all that about?" gasped Jason, sweat pouring down his bruised features.
"Some kind of voodoo shit," said Patrick, breathing hard. "I think I may have broken my arm."
"Which one?"
"The left – here - halfway between my hand and my elbow. It's really painful."
Jason moved nearer to him, on the kerb, and took the appendage gently. He squeezed it at both ends. "How does this feel?"
It didn't hurt anywhere near as much as Patrick had expected. "Not too bad..."
"Can you wave your hand?"
He did. Patrick was further surprised. "This is right weird," he said, "I could have sworn I heard it snap like a popped window." He snorted blood into the back of his mouth and spat it on the road.
"One last thing," ordered his brother. "Hold your hand up and try to wiggle your fingers." Patrick concentrated hard and discovered that he could move them all. "Your arm isn't broken, bruv, it's just badly bruised."

"What about my nose?"

"Well that's a different matter. Looks like you put it on the wrong way this morning."

"What does 'morning' mean? I've always wondered…"

Jason grasped his brother's nose, took it vertically in the knuckles of one hand. "Grit your teeth, and don't worry, I've done this before…"

He abruptly yanked it straight into conformity. Patrick jumped upright, stamping his feet and swearing graphically, gouting fresh blood. An old lady walked past them pushing a tartan covered hand-trolley with a French loaf sticking out of the top. Her expression was a mixture of disapproval and abject terror. Peeking at them, from around the corner, she took out a mobile phone.

"We have to get out of here," said Patrick. "Now."

They started walking. "Let's go round the back of Montpelier Hill. There'll be a lot less people."

"That's thinking on your feet. First thing tomorrow we'll call Tony and sort this thing out."

"Sort what out? Are you joking? You saw what Demi did to us. There's no way in hell we're going to get that book off him."

"I want the money, Jay. We'll get it even if we have to fight him again."

"And how d'you propose to do *that?*"

"We'll use Tony. Because he may have some of the same powers as Demi."

Jason stopped walking and gazed at his brother with admiration. "That's genius!"

"Keep moving. I could murder a spliff."

"So could I, bruv. Let's get stoned!"

"Just as soon as we've phoned Tony."

The brothers double-locked the front door when they got in. Jason played drum & bass music on the lounge stereo and rolled a joint of marijuana sitting on the sofa. The table was a scatty clutter of matches, ripped cardboard, and empty beer cans. It didn't occur to them that the mess was similar to the shambles in Demitrius's flat, the result of lazy neglect. The joint was huge. Patrick found Sam's location in Tony's address book, and her mobile number, and also the 01173 coded number of her dad's house in Cherry Garden Hill. Patrick flipped open his own phone and dialled hers. Since the service provider's answering service kicked in immediately it indicated her phone was switched off. Next he dialled the land-line number of her dad.

Mr Lingard eventually answered, and he sounded suspicious. He asked if the man calling him was named Demitrius. Patrick reassured him that he was definitely not a friend of the Cypriot's, then regaled him with a couple of bullshit stories about the adventures he had shared with Tony, and how chummy they were. Sam's dad revealed the couple had gone camping at the Cheddar Gorge and said they would be back in Cherry Garden Hill tomorrow at about 5:30pm.

Patrick took the scrap of newspaper he had managed to evacuate from Demi's flat out of his pocket. He double checked Ashcroft's contact number, and wrote it down (near a nipple on the cover of Penthouse magazine, and on the back of a cigarette packet) in case he lost it. He considered calling the man, there and then, but he didn't have the book yet, and, if he was honest with himself, he might never have it. He glanced at his wrist watch. It was showing 9:20pm. He looked again at the four digit cash reward printed on the scrap of paper and noticed there were droplets of dried blood soaked into it.

*   *   *

"You'll have to pack up your art things soon," said Samantha, her voice echoing delightfully, as usual, around the cave. "There's hardly any light left."
"What's the time?" Tony wondered aloud.
"Twenty passed nine."
"I think I'll just do a *little bit* more..."

He applied further umber and raw sienna on the canvas in stylised rectangles. The brush strokes were differing sizes and slanted like shadows at different gradients. It brought out the depth of the rocks in the foreground, but there were no highlights left in the scenery before the artist's eyes. In the sky, the bruised purple of sunset was giving way to the Prussian blue of star studded night. He could do no more painting for the moment.

"You're right, it's too dark." He popped his brushes into a cup of white spirit, and carried his easel over to the side of the cave. "I'll finish it in the morning. Let's light a fire."

They laid down dried grass, small twigs then larger sticks; and set it up just beyond the mouth of the cave so it wouldn't fill with smoke. Tony squashed the pile, to make it denser, and struck a flame with his Zippo.

The couple had arrived at the Gorge just after lunch, and climbed into a cave Sam had played in as a little girl on picnics with her parents. They had no tent and the cave was to be their home for the night. It was wide but not particularly deep, and the incline was long and therefore easy to walk up even carrying boxes and bags. Tony arranged his art equipment.

It was a good position and an excellent subject. The view was a geological marvel of sedimentary stacks and buttresses and cliffs shaped by forces Tony guessed he would never understand. While Sam read a Harry Potter novel, he set about enthusiastically capturing the essences of the ancient rocks, using oil pigments between dark earth and pale sandstone. They had a break in the afternoon to eat and collect wood. They shared pork pies with tomatoes and cheese coleslaw, and spent almost an hour collecting sufficient wood to last the night. They stored it in a pile at the back of the cave.

Tony reached into the heap with his lighter. The dried grass caught immediately. The small twigs flared up, and the flames spread quickly through the larger sticks. Crackling sounds echoed through the cave, which was filled with glistering light. Tony pulled the cork from a bottle of Sam's favourite red wine, and cracked open a beer for himself. The couple shuffled up to get closer to the heat. They both liked fire and stared into the flames as if mesmerised.

"You know," said Tony, "there's a prophesy in the *Necronomicon* that the world will end soon."

Sam raised her eyebrows briefly. "A lot of people believe that. How does the book say it's supposed to happen?"

"It says that eons ago the Earth was created as an experiment, to survive the evolution which was the ruination of all other races in the galaxy. It says that Artists are telepathic with each other and they have been keeping this conspiracy for thousands of years. They are filtering fragments of this secret back into society, and when everyone in the world becomes telepathic it will end in disaster."

"You believe that?" Sam asked

"No," he said. "I can't."

"Do you believe the book was written by the Devil?"

"All the evidence indicates it."

"Well, the Devil *lies* Tony, remember that." She felt déjà vu.

"It's a good point." Tony lit a cigarette using a twig from the fire. "Artists have families just like everyone else. I don't believe they will intentionally destroy that. In fact, I think they are protecting us."

"Unless the destruction happens because of another possible future. Like Demitrius using magic to take over the world."

He felt chilled just hearing the man's name. "I don't want to think about him."

"You can't ignore it."

"He beat me up, Sam, and it wasn't just that. It was like he cheated. He threatened to kill me - and you - and our parents." Tony took a puff of the cigarette.

Sam drank some wine. "He might have been lying, also."

"It wasn't worth the risk. He's got nothing to lose. He's going to prison in a few weeks."

"Do you really see bars holding him back?"

"Yes."

"And what about *after* he's read the book? The whole book? What then?"

"I don't know."

"I've seen you wake up in the middle of the night, sweating and terrified. We're going to have to try to get it back, again. Your visions must not be realised."

"We cannot physically overpower him. You said: 'It's in God's hands now' after last time."

"So try to think of a way of trapping him, a con, anything..."

"We need other people on our side. The Dreyer brothers are completely loyal to Demitrius...but I have some absolutely massive friends in the college rugby team that I could pay to get it for us! For enough cash, that would work!"

Sam felt such relief, like a woman dry and dirty, and dying of thirst, stepping under the heavy sheets of a fresh cold waterfall. "My darling, if you do this I'll marry you now."

"Right this moment?!"

"Under the stars."

"Like getting engaged?"

"No, we are beyond that. We can't know what tomorrow brings because we are fighters in a war against evil. Take off your signet ring."

He did. His passion was making him shudder. "This feels right..."

"Let me see it." She reached out her slim hand and tried it on. Slipped it easily onto her marriage finger. She withdrew it and gave it back to him. "This silver band on my thumb was a gift from my first love, now forgotten." She gave it to him.

"It fits," said Tony.

"Pass it back. Stand up."

She put her wine glass aside and they stood opposite one another, holding hands in the flickering light from the fire. It felt like they were medieval lovers on an illicit rendezvous in a lonely castle. They made their vows. The whole world was their cave, now, and they were the only people in it. After they ceremoniously exchanged rings, he looked down at Sam with such love that he suddenly understood, briefly yet with an undeniable certainty, that they would live to see the end of this conflict. Many would die, but they would live.

"You may kiss the bride," said Sam.

CHAPTER – 24

"Pro.vision"

Thorn walked up to the rusty Mini, again, and swung a boot at the front wing. The noise of it echoed around the barn.

"Can't you stop kicking that vehicle?"

"I hate this vehicle! I'm frustrated, Lill. We need something with more 'oomph' but we won't find anything around here because it's the middle of nowhere. The Dimensional Window opens tonight and we're stuck in this boring old place. I want to do something other than chew my fingernails."

Lillith took her own fingers out of her mouth, and looked with surprise at her ragged nails. They were strong enough to engrave rock, yet her teeth were stronger. "Be patient, Thorn."

"Can't you feel it?" he continued.

"What?"

"It's like our future is a big empty hole."

"I sense that too, but relax. I have a plan. Come sit with me on the hay."

He did. "What's the plan?"

"We don't have Ashcroft's address, but we do have the address of the gallery from the canvas we found the night of the gunfight. We couldn't take it with us, but it was painted by a man named Anthony Newman, and the scene is the facade of Ashton Court Manor from the courtyard. Exactly where the Dimensional Window is due to open tonight, at midnight. Trust me: the artist is either aware of who has the *Necronomicon,* or he has it himself. And the owner of Gillow's Contemporary Art has his address."

"How do you know all this?"

"I said trust me. We may just have enough time to pull this off."

"Is this another one of your weird 'Reaches'?"

"It is called prognostication. All my feelings are weird - I'm Blight."

"How do we approach the gallery?"

"I deploy 'the Touch' to open the front door of the place fifteen minutes after it closes, at a quarter to six. We take Gillow around the back of the shop and I 're-collect' his memories. We learn where the artist lives then go there."

"What if Gillow isn't there?"

"Then you will have to use the ability to tap whoever is."

"Me?!"

"I can only do it once every 23 to 24 hours, Thorn, remember that."

"I can't forget anything even if I wanted to. So, you're saying we do one each?"

"Exactly. This is a more intricate scenario: You re-collect Gillow's address from whoever is in the shop. We go there, and I tap his memory-cards to find Anthony Newman. Then we take Gillow's car and drive straight to the artist."

"I've never done it."

"Listen carefully, Thorn: The triggers are located on opposite ends of your conjuration drive, second to the left and second to the right. Do you feel them?"

"I think so."

"To 're-collect' you hypnotize your crop at close range and picture yourself reaching into his fore-brain. Your eyes will glow bright green as you extract his experiences in what is known as a block of 'memory-cards' and merge them with your own brain, which has many hundred times the capacity of a mortal, and which will automatically sort the memories in date order. You will know everything he learnt, feel what he felt, and be able to do anything he could do."

"I'll know how to drive, finally!" exclaimed the Incubus. He was peering at her. "I can do it." His eyes started to glow.

"Hey, have a care!" They looked away from each other, briefly. "Once we re-possess the book we hide out in the country park near the ruins of the manor, until midnight."

"Can we dump that horrible old Mini?"

"Yes. Nothing we have done will be discovered for many days. The important thing is to deliver the book to the Prince of Darkness, tonight. After that we can do what we want. We should get as far away from here as possible. Travel around Europe, perhaps, to start with."

"Yeah. That's a good idea."

"You mean 'that's a *great* idea'."

'That's a *great* idea." He looked at her. "Why can't I say 'good'?"

"Partly, because I am great. Mostly because none of my ideas are actually good."

*   *   *

Chapter Sixteen of the *Necronomicon* was regarding the summoning of demons, the largest section of the book so far. Demitrius learnt *Zaxxon* was a generic term for all of them, particularly those that wander the Earth dressed in human form, which were also known as 'Blight'. There are many hells and heavens, the book postulated. Not only actual dimensions for receiving souls, but also present on the Earth now as emotional experience. The easy way; the hard way. There were five vicinities functioning as 'holding cells' for demons in their true form, never walking the Material Plane unless called, which hardly ever happened. The usual result, when it did, was a couple of dubious articles and an unfathomable photograph in the more leery of the tabloid newspapers. The Cypriot found a succulent number of creatures to choose from, all illustrated in the chapter. The price for each summoned was a small reduction in the potency of the soul.

He would start with a 'Tarteran Snarler' to guard the flat. It was about the size of a large dog and it could be easily harnessed with a chain. He had a collar and a lead ready. The conjuration required spider blood on the hands, and a 'taste of lead' on the tongue. According to the *Necronomicon* those in the cold, blue, hell called Tarterous were first incarnated in ancient Rome as they were adept in their attraction to warmth and violence. The smaller were the lions and tigers of the Colussium, and the larger were political figures. These monsters, in their original hideousness, needed 'a taste of lead' to summon them because many centuries ago Rome was contaminated with the latent madness of that metal. The water was carried by lead pipes, and some archaeologists have speculated the poisoned supply may have contributed to the fall of the city.

Demitrius took a wiggling spider out of the dusty old jam jar and smeared it over his hands. He licked the tip of a dark pencil that he had found under Tony's desk, and read the words aloud. The flat was a mess. He didn't realise it. If he had he might have known that a Tarteran Snarler would feel quite at home in the stink of it. He specified his choice of creature and finished the conjuration with a tribute to The Custodian, as the book called the holder of the keys to that Hell. But nothing happened. No tiny piece of his soul was taken, no glorious head-rush was experienced, and no creature appeared.

The Cypriot needed to make progress, in spite of shuddering with withdrawal and disappointment. He started opening drawers in Tony's desk, searching for something that could clarify if a mistake had been made. The boy must have left some pencils behind. He found what he was looking for, a tin box containing an assortment of Rowney pencils. Written on the lid was one word for what they were made of, and it wasn't lead - it was graphite!

Demitrius wondered how to deal with this, but he didn't need to think for long. He recalled that somewhere in the flat there was a set of lead chess pieces his father had given him. Not exactly a commendation. The set hadn't seen the light of day since he had moved in. He eventually found it in a cupboard that hid access to the plumbing behind the toilet. The box was bent, the board was broken, and most of the pieces had fallen down the back of the prehistoric insulation behind the wall tiles, but he managed to get a handful of lead.

After attaching the dog's collar, to the chain, he scraped the flaky enamel paint off the Black King with his thumbnail. He licked the lead, and said the words that might successfully summoned the demon. This conjuration felt different. There was no 'high', it was the reverse. It was not accelerated evolution since something was taken from him, instead of given. It was magic, nevertheless it induced none of the euphoria he so craved.

The room became as cold as a freezer and the creature materialized after a wobble in the questionable reality of Tony's room. It was now sitting on the carpet in front of him growling and dribbling. Demitrius sat at Tony's desk trying to assess whether his soul felt smaller, but he didn't know what he was supposed to be feeling. Inside, he felt about the same. The room was getting warmer.

The Snarler was a maniac's masterpiece. It had more teeth than an adult Rottweiler, stronger jaws, and it was the same height, but there the canine similarities ended. It actually looked more reptilian than mammal. It had a green skin like the armour of a dinosaur, and lumpy scales like the metal studs on a biker's jacket. Its powerful neck and shoulders had hinges that looked like the gills of a shark, to allow flexibility for its stinking maw. It had six insectile legs, rigid except for eight joints, and the top pair featured sharp blades like lobster claws. Its eyes were shining, bright blue, and they indicated an intelligence that was somehow out of kilter with its physique. Demitrius walked over to it with the dog chain.

"That is unnecessary," growled the creature. Its voice was as alien as a dragon from the bed of the ocean, and quiet. "You are my master until the moon sets two nights hence. At that time I will fade through the Veil."

"Two nights," said the Cypriot, and raised his eyebrows. "Yes. Yes, that is good."

"Yet I must stay out of the sun. The light burns me."

Demitrius wondered if the thing was telepathic. That could be useful. He sensed mortal danger when he began to reach into its mind. His skin prickled with terror, and he went no further, stopped on the edge of unnameable offensive possibilities.

"What would you have me do?" it hissed.

Demitrius could barely think after feeling such intrinsic terror, and a part of him wondered if he had bitten off more than he could chew. He suppressed the thought. "I want to see how you move," he decided. "Just... run around in a circle."

The demon turned on the spot using its bottom four legs. Crossing and uncrossing them with the chittering noise of a roach. It wasn't graceful, but it was quick.

"Now, fetch this," ordered Demitrius, and threw the dog chain against the wall.

The monster coiled up all of its legs and sprung from the middle of the room, jumped to the wall in one apparently easy leap. Demitrius began to understand its anatomy. It had a flexibility and balance appropriate to jumping accurately over long distances. The Snarler picked up the dog lead in its mouth and started chewing through the chain. Demitrius watched it swallow the masticated steel and wondered what else it could eat. He picked a plate off the floor. He tossed it to the creature. It caught the plate in its teeth and crunched the china like a biscuit.

"How sharp are your claws?" he asked it.
"They can cut stone. Am I satisfactory?" the thing whispered.
"Yes, quite satisfactory," said the Cypriot. "I need you to stop anyone coming into this place."
"Are you expecting your enemies to storm the ramparts?"
"The ram... the what? Oh, yes. A few people, sometime tonight."
"Do I guard the castle with lethal force?"
"Keep them out. Kill them only if you are in danger."
"That is not likely."

He left the creature at the top of the steps sitting outside the front door. He went into the kitchen and made black coffee, thinking about the future. Things had got weird lately. His intentions needed to be considered carefully. He had enough lead to lick a thousand times, to raise a legion of monsters into the world - an army, if he was willing to pay for it. Deploying such a force and using the *Necronomicon* he could take over the whole planet. He looked down at his old Playboy mug and he knew that he couldn't live with the consequences. It would undoubtedly cause an Armageddon. He had no desire to go to prison, of course; but then neither did he want to be responsible for the deaths of millions. So he decided to take the only other available way out. He would go through the Dimensional Window, tonight. It would be his last opportunity for escape and adventure. He would go through it in a few hours and take the book with him. Wherever he went he would surely be rewarded for his restraint and humility.

*   *   *

Patrick and Jason arrived at Cherry Garden Hill in a stolen Vauxhall. They arrived at Sam's dad's house at 5:45pm with a boot load of make-shift weapons. There was no noise from inside the big house. No cars in the driveway. No one answered the door bell. The brothers couldn't raise Sam's mobile either, so they did what they could do. They sat on the porch, and waited. At exactly the same time the demons were standing under the extended roof of the Watershed. Not many people were walking along the promenade and no one paid any attention to a young couple looking into an art gallery.

Most of the lights inside were switched off. Although the CLOSED sign was hanging on the inside of the door, they could see a small woman in the dim interior. She was 'power-dressed' in a grey suit jacket, a white blouse, and a knee-length grey skirt. She was busy dusting the exhibits, and she was blatantly alone.

Gillow isn't here, Thorn stated silently.
Agreed, thought the succubus. *It's to be Plan 'B' then. You tap this woman for Gillow's address. We drive there, then I tap Gillow for Anthony Newman's address.*

ZAXXON

I know what Plan 'B' is, thank you. Thorn pushed experimentally on the door.
I sense your anxiety. Can you do it?
What's more to the point is can you open this door?
I think so. Let's see.

She applied her slim fingers to the lock, unconsciously pursing her tongue between her full lips. The woman inside the shop was moving from picture to picture, using her feather duster with such care it was almost as though she was re-painting them herself, and was completely absorbed. Lillith slid her fingertips to left-hand rim of the keyhole face-plate. She closed her eyes and probed the mechanism with kinetics.

Thorn was embarrassed about the accusation of 'anxiety', so he meditated upon darkness and moonlight. He recalled sweet blood in the mouth of his 'other self' and the bestial freedom of the hunt. Lillith noticed this new determination. He was becoming colder. She could physically feel his body temperature dropping and his heart-rate slowing. She couldn't concentrate on the door.

I can't do it, she admitted.
You have to. I need to kill.
Are you hungry?
No. I just need to kill. Now.
His mouth was dripping onto his tee shirt. This was not acting. He was morphing into his 'feeder-body' at this very moment! *Get a hold of yourself,* Lillith thought quickly. *This is neither the time nor the place for that, understand? Rein it in!*
???
Think of a bright sunrise. She projected an image into his imagination drive of a sun blazing with red and gold fire, emerging over the summits of mountains.
He lowered his hands. *I think I feel better now, Lillith.*
Yes? She looked at him and laughed wryly. *That was close! Bugger me!*
I have, many times. What were we doing?
Plan 'B'.

Oh, yes. I can do it. Open the door, then.

The woman inside had stopped cleaning the exhibition. She was now sitting at the back of the shop behind a large rounded reception desk, doing something else, and paying absolutely no attention to the Blight outside her own front window. Lillith raised her hands to the lock again. She tried hard to understand the mechanism: nevertheless, it would not yield. She created a mental map of the springs and pivots, releasing her pent-up breath, and then both their faces broke into huge smiles. She began to manipulate it successfully. The complicated lock clunked open.

Gentleman, before ladies, thought Lillith happily, standing to one side and gesturing with the sweep of an open palm for him to enter.
Why, thank you ma'am, he thought. He pushed through the door.

They walked into the cool interior and locked eyes with the smartly dressed woman. She was in her mid-thirties and appeared surprised and perplexed; to Thorn, almost comically so. She didn't seem to know what to say. Eventually she told them that the gallery was closed. Her voice had no accent, unless speaking in an educated and cultivated manner could be termed an accent in itself.

"We're here to collect your memory cards," said the Succubus.
"We don't sell postcards. How did you get in?"
"The door was open," Thorn stated.
"I'm certain I locked it."
"In a life like yours, nothing is certain." *When she comes round this side go up to her and take her cheeks in your hands, at the right moment, like you are going to kiss her,* ordered Lillith. "For example, you can kiss my friend here, or you can die. You didn't expect that did you? Come out from behind that table."

ZAXXON

The woman stood up and crossed to their side. Her shoulders and neck were hunched up, but not with fear. Had any of the trio been able to make the comparison they would have opined it was more like the coiled legs of a Snarler about to leap. She had survived three armed robberies and was feeling an anger and a bravery, so unknown to the demons, that neither could decipher it.

"Is Mr Gillow due back here tonight?" asked Lillith.
"No. He's playing poker with seven police officers."
"Really?" asked Thorn.
"No, of course not!"
"What is your relationship to him?"
"He is my husband."
"Where do you live? What is your address?"
"I wouldn't tell you in a thousand years."
"Not voluntarily you wouldn't," said Thorn.
"Hurt me all you want. I won't tell you anything." She crossed her arms.
"My friend here just needs a kiss."
"You're both insane."
"We have had a row, and he needs a small sign of affection… if you kiss him we'll let you go."
Mrs Gillow popped her eyelids open and nodded briefly. "Just a kiss? Really?"
"A long, intimate, moist kiss," said Thorn.
She was looking at him. "That's all?"
"A hot, lingering, wet French kiss."
She exclaimed, "yes! I'll do that!"
So the incubus walked up to Mrs Gillow and slid his hands around her waist. "Your perfume smells nice," he said, starting to rub noses.
"It's by Christian D'ior," the woman said, breathlessly, pressing herself against him. "It's called 'Poison'."
"I'll bet that it is," said Thorn.

She looked up at him to see if he was joking - and he had her. The eyes which carried the theft of her life gone and her life to come, was a bright green that transported her to a soft place where nothing mattered and left her bereft of all experience. Thorn let go of the woman, and she dropped to the white tiled floor. She crawled about.

"I've never done it so quickly myself," said the Succubus. "Let me guess: she wasn't getting along very well with her husband."

Thorn laughed. "Her name is Mary and the other day she threw a computer keyboard in his face. She was having affairs with *three other men!*"

"Did she know Anthony Newman's address?"

"She knew two things that matter: one, that there is a folder on the artist in the filing cabinet. Two, that the file says his address is 'pending' because he is moving house, soon. But she never knew *where* he is moving *from.*"

"Damn it! What else have you learnt?"

"I can paint a passable watercolour, but I still can't drive. Mary didn't know how."

"Grip! I mean what have you learnt *about Gillow?* What is his address?"

"29, Flare Close, Clifton."

"Excellent." Her back straightened. "Is he there, now?"

"No, he's gone to an Art's Council meeting. After that he's going to an up-market restaurant called the Embassy Suite. He'll be home at about eleven o'clock tonight. That's too late, isn't it?"

"Maybe. What is his Christian name?"

"Eugene."

The Succubus looked around the dimly lit room as though the paintings intimidated her. She looked back at Thorn. "We cannot crash the meeting. There will be security measures, and too many people present. We'll have to re-collect him afterwards. When he is at home preparing for his meal. We'll stake out the house and wait for his car."

"A red Saab 9000E, registration B49 XLE," clarified Thorn. "But there is no gap in his schedule between the meeting and the restaurant. Mary is supposed to be shagging a croupier, but her husband is going directly to dinner with the people from the meeting."

"Then, we wait."

"Until eleven o'clock?"

"Yes - it'll be close. We drive to Flare Close. We wait till he gets back from his dinner, and then we tap him. Somewhere in Eugene's memory is the address of the artist."

"Who either has the *Necronomicon*, or knows who has it."

"That's what I said. I'm certain of it."

Thorn pointed out: "You told Mary nothing is certain in life."

"I said nothing is certain in a life like *her's.*"

"Nothing is definite in ours either."

"I admit it," Lillith muttered. "We had better pray I'm right."

"*Pray?* Who to?"

"I don't know."

CHAPTER – 25

"C.ash"

On their second day in the Cheddar Gorge, Sunday July 6th, the sun was cooled by the wind direction swinging to the north. It blew into the shade of the cave, pleasantly cooling the lovers. Tony finished his landscape and found he had an excess of orange and yellow pigments in his paint box. One of the best pictures he had ever produced was the portrait of his girlfriend using the mixed mediums of blue gouache and oils. Tony had just begun to understand Sam then, and interpret his feelings toward her, which had lent the painting a powerful love. Her father had bought it, contributing to the relaxation of his over-protective hold over his daughter.

They ate prawn pasta salad for lunch and afterwards Tony decided to paint a nude of Sam using the spare pigments from the landscape because he had an additional canvas. She sat inside the mouth of the cave wearing just a pair of knickers. He used sable brushes to apply his love, and worked his lust into the work with his fingers in the raw paint. Earthy shades of cream conveyed the immortality of the surroundings. Red was a suggestion of arousal at breast and groin. Bright yellow was for the sun-kissed contrasts. They talked a lot about sex while he was working, and wound each other up exquisitely for many hours. He finished at 7:30pm after adding an invented tattoo onto her right shoulder. They couldn't help but make hard, passionate, and satisfying love; deep inside the cave. What he had added to the portrait he believed was his responsibility, as an Artist, to reduce the possibility of world destruction. It was a figure eight on its side, his subliminal from the Great Secret expressing the attainability of a woman to love for all infinity. They got into her Volkswagon.

In Cherry Garden Hill, Sam pulled up the gravel drive in her old car, arriving at her dad's house at 8:40pm. She noticed that his Mercedes wasn't there, then saw two dubious looking men sitting on the front porch. Tony told her they were old associates, Patrick and Jason Dreyer. She parked beside a Vauxhall Astra, and, as the couple got out of the car, the brothers' tired and irritated countenance became expressions of joyful relief. Sam called out:

"Hey, there! My dad isn't back yet, is he?"

"No, we haven't seen anyone for three hours," exclaimed Patrick. "You were supposed to be back here at half passed five. What happened?"

"Something came up."

"Yeah," said Jason, "Tony's brush!"

"Must be important," the Artist muttered, thinking of the Cypriot. His skin prickled with goose bumps from sharp memories. "What are you two tea leafs doing out here, in the sticks?"

Jason was never one to waste words. "We need your help to fight Demitrius."

"Gladly," said Sam. To Tony, she murmured: "I guess we don't need the college rugby team."

They moved the art equipment and the picnic basket inside the Edwardian building to the foot of the staircase. Sam invited Tony and the brothers into the heart of the house, the kitchen. While she fed Winston the Spaniel, she was intrigued by their unsuppressed excitement. They sat round the kitchen table in the light of a stained glass lamp shade, drinking mugs of coffee. Jason gave a summary of their side of the war against the Cypriot. He told of the huge reward for the book, and of his own and his brother's disastrous attempt to take it. They all scrutinised Patrick's bruised purple nose, solemnly, and with respect. His younger brother finished the story with a renewed enthusiasm:

"So when we couldn't get you on the phone we decided to come here and wait. Your old man said you would be back by 5:30pm. That time came and went, but we knew that if you were definitely coming back tonight, you would have to be here by sundown, at least. And here you are! Now we have Tony on-side we should be able to get the book off

Demi and claim the reward. We'll be prepared this time. I'll use the bar on the bastard."

"We're going to need more than a piece of scaffolding pole to get passed Demitrius," opined Tony. "He could bend it into a horse shoe with his mind alone."

"You can also, sweet-heart," said Sam. She looked at the Dreyer brothers, significantly. "Tony has the power!"

"That's what we were counting on," said Patrick.

"Did I ever tell you he is my favourite artist?" she added.

Jason chuckled. "We kind of guessed."

Patrick requested a demonstration. Tony frowned at the half-full cafetiere of coffee in the middle of the table, and it started to float. He raised it about seven inches above the tiled surface.

"Does anyone need a refill?" he asked.

"Yes, me, me!" cried Sam, rapturous with excitement.

Tony moved it towards her, holding out his right hand with his fingers splayed to aid concentration.

He levitated the jug over Sam's cup and his audience gasped as the cafetiere tilted in mid air. Tony poured a generous measure of coffee into the cup, then floated the jug once around the table and lowered it back to the surface. He finished his display by saying:

"You'll have to get your own milk and sugar..."

"That was absolutely brilliant!" cried Jason, taking out a pack of cigarettes. "I'm feeling a little freaked out, do you mind if I smoke, Sam?"

Sam said it was OK and took a china ashtray off a shelf. She pushed it to him like a barman in the American Old West sliding a glass of Bourbon along the counter. Jason grabbed the tray and took a lighter out of his pocket.

"Allow me to light that for you," offered Tony.

"How? Is this another of your abilities?"

"Yes. Hold it out."

Jason grasped the cigarette, back to front, in three fingers of one hand. He observed the exposed tip catch fire with a lurid green flame. When it was burning normally he took a puff.

"These are incredible powers, Tony," he said. "We'll beat that son of a bitch for sure."

"You don't seem to understand," replied the artist bitterly. "I've already used these capabilities to confront Demitrius and failed miserably. He damn near killed me."

"Yeah, same with us," said Patrick.

Sam retorted, to all of them: "So you teamwork both muscle and magic, at the same time. You have to go back there and get that book!"

"For the money?" Patrick asked her.

"No."

"Maybe you want to read it yourself?"

"No. It's because the book must be destroyed."

"It's worth £5000!" exclaimed Jason.

"Tony, explain it to them."

"I might have gained some sort of... potential for premonition. Just a little bit. I've been having these nightmares, more like visions really, of Demitrius taking over the world. Everything is burning and Artists are being executed, and there are gargoyles living amongst the horror. It is like Hell."

"And we think it could happen if we don't destroy the book," Sam finished. "Which is called the *Necronomicon Galaxion*, by the way. It is the root cause of that possible future. If not in the hands of Demitrius, then somebody else. I've said it before and I'll say it again, it's caused nothing but misery for a thousand years."

Patrick wondered aloud: "Is there some way we could claim the reward *and* trash it?"

"The money is important to us," said his brother. "We phoned the Professor earlier. He has it *in cash*."

"What is this man's name?" Tony asked.

"Professor Stephen Ashcroft. He says he's staying at an inn called The Three Cups on the south side of the Avon Gorge."

Sam couldn't seem to believe her ears. "We've met him!"

"That's right," exclaimed her man. "A couple of weeks ago outside the Watershed. He bought one of my paintings!"

"Are you sure?"

"It was us that advised him to stay at The Three Cups in the first place."

"How the hell did that happen?"

"OK, OK," muttered Patrick, drumming his fingertips on the tabletop. "We clobber Demi and take the book to Ashcroft. We offer it to him for the five 'G's, but conditionally. We need to convince him to destroy it after he's put it to whatever use he wants."

"Or maybe," Tony continued for him, "we find out what he wants it for and then decide whether we want to give it to him or not. Get the information *before* we go up against Demitrius so we know what we're fighting for."

"That seems right," said Sam. "We'll do it tomorrow."

"Why don't we do it *tonight*," suggested Jason.

"It's only half passed nine," Patrick indicated. "I'm for doing it tonight."

"Let's get it over with," said Tony. "Are we all agreed?"

They all looked at Sam. "I suppose so," she said. "I'll call him and tell him to expect us by a quarter to ten. We'll meet him in the bar and down some Dutch courage first. Does anyone have a phone?"

Patrick passed her his, and Ashcroft's number scribbled on a scrap of paper. She licked her lips and prodded the digits. Her call was answered immediately by a man who identified himself as Professor Stephen Ashcroft. In his cultured voice, excitement was evident. It was a voice she recognized. Her throat constricted and her pulse began to race. It was her moment to take direct action for the first time regarding the terrible book, but she was scared. A thing that felt like a boulder was clogging the underside of her ribs with unwelcome adrenaline.

"Professor, my husb – I mean my boyfriend – and I, we met you outside the Watershed a couple of weeks ago. You bought one of his paintings, a picture of that weird old place at Ashton Court?"

"Yes, I remember. What is the nature of your call?"

"We know the location of the *Necronomicon Galaxion*."

"I've never heard its full name before."

"A friend of mine rang you about the reward."

"Yes, tell Mr Dreyer again that I have the full amount, here. Can he bring it to me tonight?" The pitch of his voice sounded strained.

"What's the rush?"

The line crackled for a moment.

"That's confidential."

"We want to discuss it with you before we recover the book."

"You don't have it?"

"No. Not yet. The man that stole your car has it, and he's very dangerous."

There was a pause. "How much of it has he read?"

"We don't know. A lot."

"That's not good."

"We can be at the Three Cups in twenty minutes. Will you meet us?"

"I'll be in the Saloon Bar."

"OK, we'll see you there."

She jabbed the red 'end call' button and slid the phone back to Patrick.

"It's all set up. Whose car shall we use?"

"Ours was stolen," said Jason, amiably.

"Surprise me!" exclaimed Tony.

Sam smiled. "We'll take my VW."

"Do you want us to dump the Vauxhall before your dad gets back?"

"There's no time."

"The boot of our car has some improvised weapons in it that need to be transferred to yours," Patrick explained.

"What kind of weapons?"

"Two huge spanners, a steel bar, and a baseball bat."
"Scary, but useful. We'll move them now."

Sam stood up and crossed the kitchen to a set of drawers beside the Aga oven. She took out a pad of yellow Post-It notes and a Biro. "Can someone put the coffee cups in the sink, please?" She scribbled a message to her father. It said she and Tony had gone out to have some Friday-night fun and they would return before two am. Writing it helped her to believe that they *would* come back. She pressed the sticky piece of paper onto the side of the kettle. Her Spaniel sat panting in front of her, agitatedly. She ruffled his ears. "It's OK Winston, darling puppy. I'll be back soon. Yes, I will! *Yes!*" She straightened up. "Alright lads, let's go."

The quartet paced through the house in single file. Their shoes crunched on the gravel as they walked up to the back of the Vauxhall and transferred the collection of weapons from there into the compartment under the bonnet of Sam's Beetle. Dusk had fallen over the land, with a summer enchantment. Stars were discernable in the darkening heavens. It was warm yet they wore jackets and coats knowing they might be out late this night. Sam started the engine, headed up the drive and turned left in the direction of the bridge. They all knew how dangerous it was to go up against Demitrius, but this time they were armed with both blunt instruments *and* sorcery. Patrick wondered if he was the only one who actually felt sad about the way things had turned out.

*   *   *

Sam parked at the inn. The four of them stepped out of the car feeling mutual determination. They each knew in their own way that they were warriors living in a real mystery, and they could influence events other people never experienced. A few young people were smoking on the outdoor furniture as they went through the front door, and they brushed passed other customers in the main bar area. They found the saloon bar on the far side of the Tudor building. The dismal view of the car-park to be seen through the diamond-pane windows was enervated by a pleasing scent of ale. There were three old customers in the small room. One of them was the Professor.

They walked up to him and names were exchanged, but Tony needed no introduction. He asked what they all wanted to drink and purchased the round. He carried the drinks to where they had gathered around a small oak table. Ashcroft asked Jason if he had stolen the MG, earnestly, then asked Patrick the same question. They both said they hadn't. He seemed to assume the young Artist and his girlfriend would never have done such a thing. Tony would have told the truth, if he had been asked, and he was sure the Professor would have been suitably shocked. Patrick completed his answer by revealing that he knew who had.

"Is there any chance I can get it back?"

"There is every chance. But the chassis number and VIN number have been changed, the plates are 'ringers', and the log book and service history have been altered. The new re-spray is a kind of light blue metallic paint. You wouldn't recognize it yourself."

Ashcroft's posture straightened, bristled like an offended puffer fish. "I'd like to call the police!"

"There's no point getting angry."

"Your advert said we could keep the car," Jason pointed out.

"We may be thieves," said Patrick, "but we have ethics, and that includes never calling the law on an associate. They'll be no police. Not unless one of us is seriously hurt in the fight to recover your precious book."

"And that's the point, frankly," said Sam. "We're here to talk about the *Necronomicon Galaxion*."

The Professor appeared to be enchanted by those two words. "You're going to recover it yourselves?"

"You sound like you know our enemy."

"Maybe I do, in a way..."

Jason joked: "You're welcome to come along for the fight!"

Sam re-asserted herself, as leader. "Gentlemen, can we focus, please?"

Tony swallowed a drought of his lager, and then spoke up. "Professor, we're here to ask you why you want the book back so desperately."

"To you, that is an irrelevance. It is my personal business."

"It's relevant to us," Sam exclaimed, "because we believe the book should be destroyed." Ashcroft appeared startled. "And if you don't tell us why you want it - you'll never get it."

Tony saw Patrick Dreyer restrain his younger brother, briefly, with a hand to the forearm. Jason quietened and relaxed back in his chair. He drank a little Tequila. All eyes turned to the Professor.

"You wouldn't believe me if I told you," he said. "Not a single word of it."

Sam crossed her arms. "I've seen a lot of bizarre things recently. Try me."

"My daughter was murdered a few days ago..."

Her expression softened. "Oh, I'm sorry." The others concurred.

"Yes, well, it was very quick. But there is hope, because –
"

"- excuse me," interrupted Tony: "how can there still be 'hope'?"

"The *Necronomicon* is many hundreds of years old, and it has many esoteric powers. I think you know you believe it, and it is a fact. One of the rites can restore life to the newly deceased. About two centuries ago my ancestor used that magic to raise his wife from the dead, nevertheless he was too late. She was so decomposed he had to kill her again."

"That's disgusting!" cried Tony.

"My daughter is called Stephanie," Ashcroft continued, "and she has only been in her temporary box for one week. I intend to deploy the *Necronomicon* to resurrect her."

"It's not really any of my business, Professor," said Patrick solemnly, "but I think you're as mad as bat-shit!"

"Crazy as a loon," agreed Jason.

"You're right," he snapped, "it is none of your business. My destiny is to be with Stephanie again, to be a better father towards her than I ever was before. This magic will work and it will be my second chance. Since it makes such a difference to you, you'll get the £5,000 and when I'm done with the book I'll burn it myself." He took a bar of Dairy Milk out of the inside pocket of his jacket, and ripped it open. "You have my oath on it!"

Everyone looked to Tony's girlfriend, again, for a decision. There was a dramatic pause as she delicately sipped a mouthful of wine, staring at the Professor over the rim of her glass. His face was a mask. His neutral expression was hiding a powerful underlying passion but who was she to deny him the opportunity of resurrecting his daughter, in these strange days? She knew the power that lay between the witch-skin covers of the *Necronomicon* and she didn't doubt he could do it. If he brought back a zombie, it wouldn't be her fault. But maybe she was avoiding taking that responsibility, was being biased in her rationalisation. What she knew for certain was that he had promised to destroy the book afterwards, and she believed him.

"OK, Professor, we'll get your book back for you."
"Bless you young lady," he said, relaxing with joy. "Bless all of you!"
"Drink up everyone," exclaimed Jason in a business-like tone of voice.
"There is just one more thing," Ashcroft said. "I want to go with you."
"No way," said Patrick.
He ate a piece of chocolate. "I want to be there when you emerge triumphant."
"We may not – and you may not. This man is lethal and he's holed up in a top floor flat that's difficult to access, particularly at night."
"In that case let's do it tomorrow," suggested Sam.
"Midnight is the beginning of tomorrow," said the Professor. "I have something else to reveal to you."
"Then tell us. And be quick."

"Today is the 6th of July and, at midnight tonight, a 'Dimensional Window' is going to open in the courtyard outside the ruined manor house at Ashton Court. It is a gateway to another reality."

Tony was intrigued. "How do you know that?"

"From a secret map folded into the spine of the *Necronomicon.*"

"A map? I never saw any map."

"It is there, and believe me when I say that your 'dangerous associate' will be going through that door if you don't stop him, and he'll take the book with him."

"But this could be good," exclaimed Patrick. They all looked at him.

"Somebody disappearing with my book isn't 'good'," stated Ashcroft.

"We need the money, bruv," Jason murmured.

"No!" said Patrick. "I'm talking about creating an *ambush*. If he intends to go through this window thing he'll leave the flat at about a quarter passed eleven and we can clobber him when he comes out!"

"Now we have a plan," said Sam, "and a very real chance." She finished her wine and placed the glass on the table. "Professor, do you have transport?"

"I hired a car from Avis yesterday."

"Good. Do you have a pen?"

"I'm never without one." He handed her a Parker roller-ball.

She wrote Demitrius's address down on a beer mat. "Meet us here, at half past eleven."

"It'll all be over by then," said Jason, "and after that we do the deal. You use the book, burn it, but first you give us the money."

"I fully intend to do all of that."

"What are we waiting for?"

They lit cigarettes as soon as they got into the car park. Samantha drove onto the main road in her VW. Silence descended over the quartet like a wet blanket over a fire. She selected a disc from the CD multi-changer, an old rock album called *'Hysteria'* by Def Leopard. The brothers sitting in the back appeared more relaxed with the up-beat noise. They started talking. She noticed that Tony was looking at the gold signet ring on her marriage finger, and used the 'fade' control to move the music into the rear of the car. She fervently took his hand, in her left, and they spoke in hushed tones.

"If we do have to go into the building, you can't come with us," said Tony.

"It's OK. I'll wait in the car."

"Oh, good." He looked relieved.

"I don't expect that Patrick would have allowed me to anyway. You will be careful, won't you?"

He seemed to be bolstering both their courage when he said: "We'll win through. Our love for each other is like an engraving of the name 'De Beers' on a diamond to identify it isn't a conflict stone. Do you believe that?""

"Yes. I love you, very much."

"Then, that may be enough."

"Except that I think it is a conflict stone."

"The hardest ever cut."

CHAPTER – 26

"War"

Sam parked her Beetle on the opposite side to Launch Terrace. She locked the doors nervously and switched off the stereo. She waited with a First Aid kit open on her lap and a baseball bat in the passenger seat foot-well. The three young men stood outside the front door of #21 with their makeshift armaments. The Dreyer brothers were brandishing heavy spanners and Tony held a steel bar, and every time someone walked past they had to turn away to conceal these weapons.

They waited for Demitrius to come out for twenty-five minutes and then had to accept the ambush could fail. They had been ready to hit him for a period of time that seemed much longer than it actually was, and their nerves were frayed to the bone. They all looked at each other in the pool of light cast from a street lamp. There was nothing to discuss. At 11:06pm Tony unlocked the door and Jason led the way in.

They entered the blackness of the ground-floor hallway in single file. Jason pressed a switch on the wall. The dank place was lit by a dusty low-wattage bulb dangling from the ceiling. Patrick went inside next, followed by Tony. Jason raised his fingers like a soldier with the back of his hand facing them over his shoulder. They stopped. Jason tilted his head slightly. Tony could hear no noise coming from the other two flats on that floor. The man in front gestured to move on. They mounted the stairwell and Tony's adrenaline started to rush through him like electricity. The light became dimmer. Shadows danced through the banisters and over the mouldy carpet. They held their tools out before them as though they were fire torches and they were attempting to escape along forbidden passages of a mediaeval dungeon.

Jason secured the middle floor by hitting the next light switch. Once again they could hear no sounds from the other flats. He waved at the others to move on. The boards creaked as they mounted the last flight of steps, which went up and snaked around the corner to the mystery of the Cypriot's door. Tony realised something was different. He had the sense of an animal-like evil at the top of the stairs that he thought must be Demitrius, and he could detect an odour he had never smelt before. Like sulphur. Jason Dreyer was about to lead them round the topmost corner when Tony hissed, as quietly as he could manage: "The bastard's right outside his door!" And then the lights went out.

Jason struck a flame with a Clipper lighter. "It's okay," he said. "It happens all the time."

"He's right," said Tony. "They should come back on in a few seconds." He bumped into Patrick.

"Look, just nobody move, alright?!"

The bulbs remained cold. "The lights aren't coming back on, Jay. What do you want to do?"

"We go on. And we need to do it before this lighter melts."

He held the huge spanner out in one hand and the Clipper up in the other. Lit only by the tiny flickering flame the cramped space had taken on a terrifying new aspect. Tony's skin felt clammy and all of them were panting like race horses after thirteen furlongs. The temperature started rapidly falling at the apex of the stairs. When Jason rounded the corner he saw something crouched by the Cypriot's door which threw him into a panic. During the brief moment before his thumb left the gas of their only, and almost insignificant, source of light, Tony glimpsed a hideous monster over Patrick's shoulder. It was a dog lobster thing, with green scaly skin, and frozen blue eyes. It opened its mouth and hissed and dribbled through its teeth. As soon as it saw them its jaws began to clack open and shut like a riot policeman banging a baton against a shield.

"Christ!" Jason shouted: "Demi has turned into a demon!"

He thrust passed the others and bolted downstairs. The artist had the impression that his hearing was comparatively magnified in the blackness. The creature stopped banging its teeth together and Tony could hear a new noise, now, like a high tension cable being stretched as if it was coiling itself up to spring. And within a split second the demon did pounce, with the essence of a *Ballista*, a gigantic crossbow, being fired. The rest of the fight was a confusion in the darkness. Patrick knocked Tony down the steps where he hit the carpet on his back, and was winded at the foot of the riser on the middle floor hallway. The piece of scaffolding pole fell out of his hand. He began to haul himself up, breathing raggedly, reaching around blindly for his weapon.

Patrick loosed a hoarse battle-cry. Tony heard scuffling sounds, and then the noise of the man's spanner thumping the monster with a sound much like whacking a leather boot with a hammer. Patrick and the demon then fell grunting and bumping headlong down the stairs and landed on top of Tony, whose lungs expelled a whoosh of air. He was trapped under the weight of writhing limbs. Patrick screamed and blood poured into Tony's face, whose flailing hand connected with the steel pipe. The blood stinging Tony's eyes was impenetrable and the cold blue glow of the demon's gaze was barely bright enough to pierce the darkness. Tony could smell the putrid stench of its maw. He started to wriggle back and forth, under the stage where this battle was set, to be able to breathe again, and to fight.

He was halfway out from under them when Patrick gurgled and a glut of blood soaked Tony's jeans. The older man twitched a few times then ceased struggling. He lay still but Tony had no time for remorse. The demon was already goring its claws into Patrick's body to move it out of the way to gain access to its next target. This actually helped Tony to escape the rest of the way.

He stood up and backed off with the steel pipe held out in his right hand. The monster's merciless blue eyes locked with Tony's and the artist glimpsed somewhere else. A dimension of daggers of ice, frost-bite gone mad, and upside down castles of frozen blood. It was too much. He chucked the bar in its face and sprinted down the steps, almost turning an ankle, stumbling downwards in the blackness. On the ground floor he pushed through the front door and emerged into the lights of the cool street, trying to wipe Patrick's sticky blood from his face and out of his eyes. When Sam saw him she left Jason's side and ran to him, her hands roving over him hysterically.

"Are you cut? Are you hurt?"

"I'm OK," he said breathlessly. "It's not my blood. It's Patrick's."

Jason walked over to them, and his face was as pale as snow. "Is he still fighting the thing?"

"No. He didn't make it." Tony watched the man sit forcefully on the pavement. "I'm so sorry. I tried to help him out but I got trapped, and I couldn't see. There was no hope. The thing is from another planet."

Jason held his head in his hands. "Oh no, no. Shit!"

Sam knelt beside him. "It's not your fault."

"I *ran*, woman, don't you understand?"

"But she's right," said Tony. "If you had stayed in there you would most likely be dead too."

"I'm going back," Jason decided. He stood up and made moves for the door.

Tony reached out, grabbing his arm. "No, you aren't, Jay. Sam's calling the police. If one of us gets hurt we call the police. That was the deal."

"But he's not *hurt*, is he?" cried Jason tearfully, "he's fucking *dead*! And I'm going to kill it!"

He struggled wildly, and it took Tony all the strength he had left in his body to haul him away from the door, and slap him hard in the face. He stopped straining and glared at Tony sullenly.

"Alright. Call them."

Sam said: "I'll tell them there's a wild leopard loose in there. They'll bring guns." She patted her pockets for a moment, then she asked, apologetically: "Does either of you have a phone?"

"I've got a Pay-as-you-Go Nokia," said Jason, "but there's no credit left."

"You don't need credit to call the emergency services."

He gave her the phone. "Then be my guest. And I hope they do bring guns. Very big guns."

Sam dialled three 9s.

*   *   *

The two Blight had been waiting for two hours outside #29, Flare Close, Clifton, both continually on edge. At 10:45pm Gillow's red Saab finally pulled up the driveway and parked outside the impressive house. Lillith and Thorn exited the Mini as the diminutive art dealer stepped down from his car. They ran up behind him as he walked up to his door. The Incubus poked a slim painting trowel that he had taken from the gallery against the small of his back. The man froze.

"Turn around slowly," ordered a young woman that sounded Irish.

Gillow did. He had an extensive art collection in the house and assumed he was being robbed. The bandits looked like they were in their late teens, probably strung-out on drugs. Their youth irritated him more than anything else. He was not afraid. The boy's weapon was a joke.

"What do you want?"

"Open the door," ordered the boy, prodding him in the lower chest with the tool.

"Are you going to stab me with a palette knife?"

The boy raised the knife to the corner of Gillow's left eye. "I said open the door."

Gillow experienced fear for the first time. "Yes, OK." He turned his key in the lock and the three of them moved into the house.

ZAXXON

The hall area had a high ceiling of oak beams and magnolia plaster. There were deep pile carpets, in shades of scarlet, and antique furniture. The place had a warm clean smell like a child's chinchilla. Paintings adorned the walls and were arranged up either side of the stairs. So much art. The woman was pretty and she moved unexpectedly and gracefully up to him. She slipped her soft slim arms around his shoulders.

"Do you like me, Eugene?"
"How do you know my name?"
"Kiss me," she murmured.
He protested, half-heartedly. "I have a wife!"
"Are you sure about that?" asked Thorn. "I bet you haven't kissed a girl for a month. Kiss her, Eugene!"
"Oh, what the heck," Gillow exclaimed, putting his arms around the Succubus. "This is *pleasant* burglary!"

He didn't know that one of his wife's last, mature, thoughts had been something similar. He started kissing her, so expertly that the Incubus got jealous. Thorn unconsciously clamped the palette knife until it cut into the underside of his fingers. He looked down at the wound, surprised, and watched the blood run back into his body and the skin seal up. The injury disappeared. Then he observed Gillow's body sag in Lillith's embrace, like a sack of grain, like a punch-bag that had been battered until it had broken from its anchor. She dropped him onto the Turkish rug, where he gurgled and squirmed about on all fours.

"Where does Newman live?" Thorn wanted to know.
"Top flat, 21 Launch Terrace, Montpelier."
"We'll take his car."
"Definitely. Eugene thought it was the best executive car he ever had..."
He stared at her. "Are you feeling regret?"
"No, Thorn. That is impossible. I just learnt something about art."
"What?"

"That most people are impressionists, in the worst definition of the word. They paint any manure that looks good. There are fewer Artists with a capital 'A' in the world than I thought. It's not a bad thing."

The Incubus didn't fully comprehend this, so he moved on. "I'll get his keys," he said. He riffled Gillow's pockets and found the keys to the Saab. After that he stuck the palette knife into his neck, again, and again, until he died.

The succubus was soon laughing with her whole body. "How bloody obstinate you are, Thorn!" she proclaimed, tears rolling down her face. "What a good choice of colour, it really brings out the red in the carpet! Let's get out of here!"

They closed the front door behind them. Thorn unlocked the Saab.

"What is the time?" he asked.

"11:07pm, 52 seconds," she replied promptly, without looking at a watch. She took the keys off him. She started the engine. "We should be there in fifteen minutes."

*   *   *

Hearing the ruckus outside the flat, Demitrius knew that they had come for the book, and to try to kill him. They had obviously been no match for the Tarteran Snarler. During the pregnant silence after the fight he assessed that his old friends were probably dead. The police would soon follow, nevertheless he knew what to do. Demitrius brushed his hair and changed his clothes for a clean white tee shirt, black jeans, and a black leather jacket. This was the final battle, just beginning, and it was essential to be well dressed. He slipped a chess piece into his pocket for a multiple conjuration from Chapter Sixteen. He intended to raise a mass metaphorical 'lead poisoning' by summoning many demons to his banner. His clock indicated it was a quarter passed eleven. It was almost time to leave.

He was not disappointed to have left the last chapter unrealised. He had glanced at it. The magic had many passages, a complex rite involving blood sacrifice and the preparation of rare roots and herbs, which would have been difficult to obtain even if he had wanted to. He had rejected the concept of total power because of his unwillingness to cause an Armageddon. Mass telepathy might eventually happen, anyway, but he did not want to be the catalyst. He knew that he had done good.

The Cypriot spent his last few minutes looking around the flat, trying to commit all his lovely things to memory, before he left it forever. His Technics stack stereo, silent, in the corner. His favourite mug, stuck once more to the glass-topped coffee table. The sofa-bed he had made love on, and slept in, for so many years. He would never see this place again, yet he was surprised by what little the things meant to him. It was time to drive to Ashton Court and take the Last Train To The Other Side, twenty passed eleven PM. He wiped a spider on his hands and leaned over the *Necronomicon* open at Chapter Sixteen. He verbally applied a part of the conjuration which was called a *'multiplier'*. It gave him the power to transfer many demons directly into the Material Plane. The book had been designed to raise Hell at every opportunity! He had committed the names and attributes of twenty-seven terrible creatures to memory, and he merely needed to name them with a lick of lead. He called them as he went down. After a delay of a few minutes they would be unleashed in the street
to cover his escape.

"Ronove, Skin Monkey, Cinnamon Stripper!" he said, with a loud, bold, voice. "Pranzible, Sinistar, Demon Calamari, Batgoil, Oriaxx!!"

He summoned one after the other, with every downward step. Soon his tongue felt grey with a taste in his mouth like biting silver foil. He spat a lot on the mildewed carpet. He never thought he would have children but soon he would be the father to many. The *multiplier* needed time to arrange a queue and thus was slow to traverse them through The Veil. He was beginning to feel kind of 'thin' inside.

The dim lights illuminated one casualty on the middle floor, the hacked-up mess of Patrick Dreyer. There was a smell of copper and dirt in the air like an old penny. There were no other corpses. They others must have escaped, or been completely eaten. The monster that killed Patrick was staring at Demitrius from amongst a gargle of frozen secrets.

"Tarteran Snarler," said the Cypriot. "Go outside and be furious."

The thing banged its teeth together, once, then turned awkwardly on its insectile legs and grappled down the steps with its joints clacking. Raising Hell, Demitrius followed it, but he could detect the cost, as something fundamental was shrivelling inside him.

The Scott, DI Higgins, was co-ordinating the action against the animal alongside DC Johnson and DS Augur, and a representative of the Zoo. An armed tactical team had arrived with two ambulances. The Gloucester Road entrance to Launch Terrace was cordoned off.

In spite of the fact that the boy was covered in blood, Higgins had recognized Tony immediately. The officer recalled the lad's association with the known felon Demitrius Kiriacou and a quick radio check confirmed that this drama was, indeed, centred around Kiriacou's address. Sam held her stricken boyfriend's hand during questioning. Tony told the officers that although he hadn't seen the man for several days, the beast almost certainly belonged to the Cypriot. He described the roar of a large cat in the darkness. The Zoo curator was informed of the difficulty of the confined space of the staircase, and decided not to dart it. He recommended that the animal be put down, with extreme prejudice.

"We will," Higgins assured him. He raised a loudhailer to his mouth and thumbed the transmit button. "Tactical Team, move in!" he announced.

ZAXXON

Six men in black uniforms, who had been hanging around the back of a white riot van, ran across the road with their shiny boots clumping on the Tarmac. They took up positions around the door to #21. They wore riot helmets, and body armour, and carried fully automatic MP5 assault rifles. Four men waited either side of the entrance. The other two slung their machineguns, and swung a small but heavy battering ram at the door. Once, twice, then it burst inwards. A dog-shaped creature leapt out of the house and it jumped accurately up at one of the men standing in front.

It was a scaly muddle of legs as it clamped its teeth round his throat. The battering ram dropped on to the cement with a clank. Red splashed green. The man to the left of the door was so stupified that his finger came down reflexively on the trigger of his weapon and he accidentally fired five rounds into his colleague's shoulders and the nape of his neck. The officer died spontaneously but the creature did not let go. Its claws sliced through his steel-plated Kevlar vest like it was made of pastry. His severed head flew off and went bouncing down the edge of the road. The others fell back, and lowered the muzzles of their rifles at the monster as it veered to one side and homed on another victim. They opened fire almost simultaneously with a noise like a thousand thunderstorms. Spent cartridge cases went tumbling over the pavement where they lay inert, smoking, and shining, like brass nuggets in the lamplight.

Stephen Ashcroft could hear this battle from a distance as he went down Montpelier Hill. He was driving an Avis rental, a Ford Mondeo Zetec, and the sound was getting louder as he approached the place where he had arranged to meet the others. Launch Terrace was not cordoned off on this side, maybe because it was an insignificant minor road. The Professor arrived on the opposite side of the street behind Sam's Beetle, well back from the stroboscopic flashes of gunfire. He saw Tony and Sam and Jason were sitting in the rusty old car. There were lots of people running about. He switched off his headlights but not before DS Auger had noticed him park. The policeman ran down the pavement towards the Ford with his body hunched up as if stepping down from a helicopter. Ashcroft depressed the button to lower his window and DS Augur looked in at him.

"What are you doing here?" he asked, appearing to be surprised and suspicious at the same time.

"I arranged to meet someone." There was a loud burst of gunfire.

"Speak up!"

"Those people in the Beetle are my friends."

"Do they know the Private School Savages?"

"No, they stole my car, and I've come to get it back."

"I have good news for you," said the police officer. "Listen, I have to be very quick. The couple suspected of killing your daughter were caught on CCTV breaking into an art gallery just a few hours ago. The resolution is very poor but we have accurate descriptions from three eye-witnesses. Does what's happening here have anything to do with them?"

"No. Of course not! How could it?"

The ground trembled in the lamplight, a minor tremor. Guns were fired. A man started screaming.

"Stay in your car."

"Have they murdered anyone else? What the hell is going on here?"

"I can't talk about it any longer. Wait in your vehicle until I tell you it's safe to get out."

He ran back to the action. The screaming man was a member of the response unit who had lost both his legs to the teeth of the beast. His confederates were running out of ammunition. The rounds they fired slowed it down not a jot and every hit deflected off the demon's scaly carapace causing bursts of sparks. Bullets were ricocheting in every direction, striking wood, and bricks, and glass. Opening its dribbling jaws wide, the thing charged at another man who managed to shove the barrel of his MP5 into its throat. He adjusted the rate-of-fire-selector to single shot then pulled the trigger and blew the demon's guts out of its tail. It collapsed, convulsing, then lay still in a spreading pool of stinking yellow pus. The rest of them carried the legless man to an ambulance.

The street rumbled, again, with a more sustained intensity. An earth-quake of about level two on the Richter Scale. Windows shattered and sheets of glass fell and crashed over the pavement. The road was actually starting to break up. People were shouting as much with incredulity as terror, as rancid steam erupted from cracks in the Tarmac. Reality wobbled, like hail stones falling into a lake, and incomparable things rose from the ground. In the surrounding houses, friends and neighbours stared with eyes like saucers as the street outside their homes went to Hell.

'Skin Monkeys' were headless ape-shaped creatures with a gormless face gazing out of the middle of their chests. The *'Demon Calimari'* were gigantic fungal infections with tentacles that secreted powerful corrosive acid. *'Pranzibles'* were visceral bags, with teeth, strutting about on eight lower limbs that had the crushing strength of titanium hydraulics. *'Ronoves'* were human sized ears, directed by sonar, on little legs that were scuttling around people's feet trying to jab them with poison stingers. *'Batgoils'* were flying rats with a wing-span of over two feet of stretched pink skin. *'Sinistars'* were the front line in any invasion, atmosphere processors shaped like star-fish crustaceans that breathed oxygen and exhaled sulphur-dioxide. *'Oriaxx'* were powerful bovine animals that were somehow organically-inverted, a bull that made a slippery buffer of its interior organs on the outside.

Other nightmares were appearing that defied cognition, as Demitrius could have testified from the illustrations he had misinterpreted in the *Necronomicon*. Demons everywhere. Realizations of the unimaginable, leaping and jumping and so appallingly *real*. With his face lit by flashing strobe lights, DI Higgins got on the radio and asked for the Fire

Department and five ambulances. He also requested (although he didn't much care for ricocheting bullets) another armed tactical unit to come to Launch Terrace immediately. One response officer, who had run out of ammunition, was running about stamping on *ronoves* with his heavy boots, and laughing and laughing, as one of his friends was swept off his feet by a charging *oriaxx* and smashed against a wall. A paramedic found himself holding his end of a stretcher alone, while his colleague was slain of a cracked skull by a scampering *pranzible* that had jumped onto his head and squeezed its legs like a vice.

Demitrius emerged from the twisted door-frame of #21. He stared at the inert Tarteran Snarler. His first child was now dead. Standing on the broken door, with the *Necronomicon* tucked under one arm, he muttered a couple of words and licked something, then transferred whatever it was back to his jacket pocket. He gazed along the confusion and carnage and locked eyes with Jason Dreyer, who was sitting in the back of a Volkswagon. The Cypriot smiled at him. Jason got out of the car in a flying rage.

Another quake shook the scene as the dead man's brother ran blindly across the road spitting and shouting. A chunk of cement about the size of a common bus veered up and cracked off at one end like a huge crumbling biscuit. It knocked Jason off his feet. He was attempting to climb out of the hole, yelling obscenities, when a thick orange tentacle whipped out and adhered to his face. It burnt him as it dragged him down, screaming, into the chasm.

The wheels of the empty riot van were rolling backwards into the same fissure. The vehicle fell halfway into the hole. It began tilting sideways, with the corner of its roof pointing up at the black sky. A *skin monkey* jumped playfully out of the hole and scrambled up the side of the van and perched on its roof, as the bonnet became trapped between two slabs of paving. The engine was crunched and petrol gushed out and ignited. The van exploded with a gigantic din, and red hot shrapnel and shards of Tarmac flew in every direction.

ZAXXON

Members of the public were roaming the street, unchecked, as if dreaming. The blazing *skin monkey* leapt off the van onto a woman whose dressing-gown caught fire. Subsequently, it jumped into the treatment bay in the back of an ambulance where a constable was being treated for toxic shock. It clambered around the interior of the vehicle and set that on fire, also, squealing like a piglet. Two paramedics in burning jackets fell out of the back and rolled around in an act of automatic desperation to extinguish the flames. The poisoned constable never had the opportunity.

The apocalypse at Launch Terrace continued. Manhole covers detonated from their mountings on geysers of steam. The orange tentacles of *demon calamari* were emerging from the drains. DC Johnson squinted through the drifting smoke and couldn't believe his eyes. An old guy was standing on his porch holding a knife up in one hand and a tiny Yorkshire terrier up in the other, as if he was about to sacrifice the dog to a higher power. It was another curiosity in a grotesque and ludicrous night, with so many distractions that Demitrius wasn't even noticed. A boy in pyjamas was taking swipes at a flying *batgoil* with a tennis racket, and a woman with wild grey hair was prodding *sinistars* with a broom stick, saying: "Horrible smell! Horrible smell!" Over, and over, again. Policemen started ripping fence posts from people's front gardens, setting one end on fire to deploy as weapons.

Stephen Ashcroft observed all this horror with guilt churning in his guts. It looked like a battle from an age lost, long ago. It was his discovery causing this havoc, yet Satan had written the book, not him. He had discovered the gun, yes, but his finger had not pulled the trigger. He was wondering if this had made Oppenheimer feel any better when suddenly there was a gigantic jolt under his car. He couldn't have known what it was. A man-hole cover had sprung up and bounced against the undercarriage of the rental with such a force it felt like he had driven over a land-mine. The Ford started to rock on its mountings, from side to side, and a tentacle as thick as Ashcroft's forearm rose up and waved about in front of the car like an angry cobra. The adrenaline-inducing fear of the unknown, like seeing the wrong face in a mirror, was a terror shared by many that night.

The octopus-like tentacle swept forward and adhered to the windscreen. Underneath it there were pink suckers with needle-like protuberances convulsing against the glass, secreting a dribble of poison, or acid. He couldn't get out. He was too frightened to unlock the vehicle.

A second arm plastered itself onto the driver's side door. Hyperventilating with impotent terror flooding through his cramped body, another limb appeared writhing and squishing on the back of the Ford, which melted most of the rear screen-wiper before snapping it off. The Professor closed his eyes and clenched his fists, psyching himself up to make a break for it through the passenger door, but he was too late. He opened his eyes and saw an additional limb stuck to that glass also.

The car was now surrounded and the steel body-work groaned and whined as the tentacles began to squeeze. An Airbag inflated with a pop. Plastic door furniture cracked undone as the sides bulged inwards, and the rear window shattered. Ashcroft stared, at the young people in the next car, stared between that short distance and the obscene dripping limbs, at Tony and Sam. Their faces were shocked and bleak and helpless.

He lost sight of them as the transparency of the glass fractured into spidery cracks with a noise that sounded like a knife scraping across a piece of toast. He ducked instinctively to one side. The safety glass blew over him in a thousand glittering shards. He found the roof had become so low he could not straighten up. The tentacles flailed around in front of him, and he could smell that pungent chemistry lab odour of acid stinging his sinuses.

ZAXXON

Three more unclasped from the bonnet and converged through the absent glass onto his face. When at last he died, his soul was trapped inside the inner vicinity of the *Necronomicon*. That fate had befallen his enemy, Raul Caine, just six nights ago. Had he lived, the Professor would have testified that the time which had passed since seemed longer. The Ford was completely crushed, pulled underground like an unrecognizable lump of scrap disappearing under the hostile waves of a black sea.

DI Higgins was stricken. What was happening was impossible. When you got right down to the lead slugs, it was that simple. Blood was running down the kerb. Johnson had been seriously injured, his bones broken by something that had looked like a Damien Hurst exhibit. Most people thought the gates of Hell had been opened. A second tactical unit arrived, with additional ammunition for the three able-bodied members of the original team, but their training had never involved neutralising demons. Another *snarler* had materialized and now only seven men remained from both teams. A stinking starfish-shaped thing wiggled passed his shoe. Smoke clouds, alive with flashing blue and red lights, drifted down the road. Guns flashed and crackled. Empty MP5s were dumped in favour of pistols. It was all beyond the Detective Inspector's experience, and beyond his comprehension.

DS Augur handed his superior the radio, and Higgins was just yelling for further reinforcements when a red executive car broke through the cordon at the intersection with Gloucestor Road. It was a new-model Saab. There were two people sitting in it, a young man and a woman who was an ace behind the wheel. She drove fast and confidently, weaving between the bodies and the wreckage and the rents in the road surface. She pulled a handbrake turn, almost dropping the vehicle into a fissure, and stopped outside #21 near a blue MG BGT. Her companion cranked open his door, reached down and picked a 9mm semi-automatic pistol from a dead man's hand. He slammed the door.

Seeing them seemed to lower the volume of the war to DS Augur's ears. He took three steps nearer the car. The appearance of the couple exactly matched the descriptions of the Private School Savages! It took DI Higgins, himself, just two seconds to concur that it was them. A short moustachioed man with a book clenched under his left arm (who they knew was Demitrius Kiriacou) climbed into the MG, and started the engine. He roared off towards the main road, chased by the red Saab, in turn followed by the couple in their Volkswagon, at a pace the policemen would never have believed possible of the old car.

They knew there was a pattern here, somewhere. An explanation of connections, nevertheless they could not see it. Logic itself had been destroyed, alongside drill, and protocol. There was nothing left to cling to. DI Higgins learned that his helicopter was grounded, again, with technical difficulties. He swore. His last order was to send pursuit vehicles after the three fleeing cars. These words were barely out of his mouth when his throat turned into a fatal bloody wound, as a *batgoil* alighted on his shoulder and ripped out his neck.

ZAXXON

CHAPTER – 27

"Re.solve"

Police drivers aren't allowed to deploy any manoeuvre in public places that involves losing control of their vehicle. They have to adhere to their own set of rules and that gives the villain the edge because he will drive in any and everyway he can to get away. The broken cordon at the entrance to Gloucestor Road was a kind of start-line in Demitrius's mind. He went through it first. There were no police cars behind him in the beginning, he was being tailed by a powerful red Saab, and the driver was good. The Cypriot quickly found himself having to press the MG to the limits of its capability, and drive to the limits of his ability. The Succubus didn't care about public safety either. She commanded the car like a rally driver, a skill she had 're-collected' from a drunk named Arthur, long ago.

She switched the Saab into manual gear 'Sports Mode'. It was a very different vehicle to the MG in every respect, specifically much heavier. So at the top end of speed and acceleration, the cars had similar handling characteristics. Tony and Sam chugged along in the little old VW, lagging further and further behind, allowing cop cars to roar passed them into an unseen distance, but they knew where they were going. The Cypriot took the initial first round-about near Broadmead at about 65 mph. Lillith took it slightly faster. The back-end of her heavy vehicle spun out with a squeal of rubber and narrowly missed the front bumper of a taxi cab. Thorn was terrified by the 'G' forces he was experiencing at this speed, clutching hard the 9mm handgun as though it was a lucky charm. Lillith's foot pressed even harder on the accelerator.

Demitrius brushed a woman on a bicycle with his wing mirror, and knocked over a KEEP LEFT sign on a traffic island. He drove right or left, through red traffic lights or green, pulled every trick he had ever learnt yet still his rear-view mirror was filled with the persistent headlights of the Saab.

He crossed the swing-bridge near the Watershed at 80mph. For a moment the MG physically left the ground and landed momentarily out of control with a long skid. So did the Saab. A police car going slightly slower over the same obstacle skidded all the way across the road and smashed into a shop window. Demitrius wrestled with the steering wheel until he regained command of the MG, when two police Vauxhall Cavaliers with all their red and blue lights twirling pulled onto his tail. He cut every corner as he tore out of the city centre at speeds up to 90mph. Lillith moved ahead and nudged the rear bumper of one of the Cavaliers. Its driver would have called this a 'pit manoeuvre'. It abruptly slid sideways and crashed into a safety barrier.

For a brief moment the alternately flashing headlights of the doomed police car illuminated Lillith's face. Demitrius saw she was laughing. His eyes met hers in the mirror, for a split second, and she smiled at him. He grinned back, yet some vital thing was wrong inside him. Despite the fact that this was the race he had waited for, all his life, he felt cold and empty. His guessed that his soul had been spent summoning the demon hoards he had left behind in Launch Terrace. He couldn't think about it. In fact his soul was locked in the *Necronomicon* while his body still lived. The ancient book lay on the seat beside him.

Both drivers changed down a gear in order to take the steep hill of Park Street. The one remaining Cavalier hung back until the Saab passed it then re-accelerated. Thorn was terrified by the speed they were going. He could take a shot-gun blast to the chest, and be healed half a minute later. It shouldn't have been relevant, but as his loved one drove like a woman gone mad he felt his fear of crashing as though his blood had turned into sand. He was beginning to interrupt Lillith's ability to steer the Saab.

"Please, slow down!" he begged her. *"Please!"*

"Shut up!" bellowed the Succubus. She breasted the hill and went after the MG doing twice the speed limit in a 30mph zone. "I will *not* let him go!"

Holding the forgotten pistol in one hand, Thorn reached across and grabbed Lillith's elbow and pulled on her arm to somehow make her slow down. It caused her to lose control of the car. The Saab swerved against the side of a parked RAC rescue van with a screech of metal and a shower of bright sparks. Nevertheless, she managed to pull away. With an unmistakable noise the second Cavalier crashed, somewhere behind the Saab, on the hill. Now there were no police vehicles in pursuit. The road straightened out into a less populated area. Lillith stopped, for the first time, at a red traffic light.

"Oh, thank goodness!" exclaimed the Incubus, heaving a huge shuddering sigh of relief.

The Succubus put the engine into neutral and took the gun out of Thorn's hands. A woman with a blue-rinse hair style was leading a poodle over the crossing. She peered curiously through the windscreen. Lillith pointed the gun at the side of Thorn's head. She slid her thumb down the pivoted button to disengage the safety catch.

"I'm sorry, Rupert," she said. "I don't need you anymore."

There were two loud reports, and a blood spray. The side window shattered. The woman, with the dog, screamed. The Succubus reached passed him, opened the passenger door, and pushed his dead body onto the road. Slammed the door, and put the Saab into first gear. The poodle's fur was blue-rinsed the same colour as its owner's, and it was running around in distressed circles on the end of its lead. The woman was still yelling when Lillith moved off with a squeal of rubber, and almost ran over the desperate animal. The engine roared. The car reached over 50mph within a few seconds.

Once he had lost sight of pursuit Demitrius slowed down to a more leisurely pace. There was no police presence, neither ahead nor behind. He took the turning onto the country road which would bring him to Ashton Court in a few minutes. And then those familiar pear-shaped headlamps were coming right up behind him, again! The crazy fly bitch behind the wheel switched the lights to full-beam and completely blinded his rear view. He pressed his foot to the mat, using both sides of the road to lessen the cornering, and she fell behind a little. A motorcycle came round the bend and suddenly Demitrius was in the wrong lane! He over-compensated to avoid it and rode up the grass verge and almost lost the car into a ditch. He wrestled with the steering, bumped back onto the Tarmac and roared ahead.

He had made two modifications to the MG in preparation for fleeing to the ruined manor house tonight. He had taken the bulb out of the frame of the registration plate, and created a separate circuit for the brake lights linked to a button on the dashboard. He knew this particular road so well he could have driven it blindfolded. Now was the moment to find out if the woman behind him knew it as well as he did, and to learn if she knew where he was going. He switched the lights off.

Lillith knew the where and when of the Dimensional Window. Somehow she had always known it. The man with the *Necronomicon* wasn't the Artist. To have raised such a legion he must have evolved into a Necromancer because of the grimoire, and this would make him a formidable opponent. Lillith guessed he was travelling to the Window, also, taking the book to where she was destined to be herself, to the same event horizon in geography and time. The route he was taking confirmed it. Lillith had driven this road earlier in the day to survey the terrain, put it to memory. Yet at night, even to her eyes, it seemed like a different world. When the brake-lights of MG disappeared she had the equivalent of 70% less guidance to proceed. She had to slow down, rapidly. A rally driver has a navigator sitting beside them. Lillith was starting to miss that reassurance.

ZAXXON

At 11:40 pm the country park at Ashton Court was cordoned off behind a locked gate. The Cypriot reached it half a minute before the Succubus. He accelerated towards the perimeter, a flimsy iron fence hung between two squat redundant gate-houses, and rammed through it with the essence of an umbrella being blown inside-out. He broke a headlamp, mangled the front grill, yet the MG was intact enough to sustain the pace. He roared down the dusty winding road to the manor house, night shrouding the grassy hills and woods on either side. After Lillith went through the gateway, herself, she decided to take a short-cut. She turned the steering wheel and forsook the tired road surface for the grass. This way was almost 'as the crow flies'. Faster, and slippery, but it was true rallying. She was in her element.

The changing chaos in the headlamps would have confused other motorists. The Succubus was approaching a peeling whitewash fence of worm-ridden wood around the courtyard of the ruined building, from one side. She drove along the edge of the forest, changing gear continuously. She made the heavy car do things it had never been designed to. A wooden log, concealed in a hollow in the terrain, ripped something underneath. The car persisted to pull its weight, leaping over hillocks and slithering along dips in the grassy downs. Glancing between the dashboard instruments and the way ahead, Lillith noticed that the fuel gauge was dipping, almost imperceptibly. Something must have torn. A line connected to the petrol tank, maybe; or the tank itself. It didn't matter. As the white fence came into view, the race was over.

The Succubus arrived at high speed and drove through the barrier like it was made of balsa wood. Although the stones in the driveway rattled beneath the undercarriage, she lost no traction. Pulling one final stunt, Lillith stamped on the clutch, turned the wheel to the right, and pulled the handbrake. With a huge scrunch of gravel, the Saab skidded around the bonnet of the old roadster in a 240 degree broad-slide, leaving it almost in the middle of the courtyard and parked at an angle, bumper to bumper, with the smaller car. The Succubus turned the engine off. She got out, leaving the lights on full-beam, like the one unbroken lamp remaining in the MG.

She stretched her legs, breathing hard, feeling as agitated as a child that has just stepped off a fair-ground ride. She was experiencing an unusually high level of post-adrenal euphoria that could easily have been mistaken for happiness. All was comparatively quiet, except for liquid dripping to the ground, the hissing of engine coolant, and the tick-tick-tick of cooling metal. The cars looked like they had been driven a thousand miles. The air was cold for a July night, and tainted with the pungent odour of petrol. It was forming a puddle near her sensible shoes. The Necromancer was standing in a pool of light looking at her with an almost sexual interest. Tucked under his arm was the Devil's book: the thing she had been hunting all her life, since being disgorged like vomit from the bole of a tree sixteen days ago.

"That was fantastic driving," he said to her. "I rate you highly."
"It took me ten seconds to learn the skill."
"Yes, I know how it's done. I did it to a dog, once. You are Blight, aren't you?"
"Yes. Does that frighten you?"
"No."
"It should do. What is your name?" she asked him.
"Demitrius."
"Well, Demitrius…" *give me the book or I'll kill you*, she thought like a razor.
Take it, if you can, he offered telepathically.

She locked her viridescent gaze with his bottomless brown eyes. He felt as though someone was massaging his head. Gently at first, then as if their hands were beginning to press. He recognized his memory-cards were safe. This was an attack using the 'Touch'. The Cypriot fumbled through his brain searching for his own telekinetic ability. It was like reaching out for a balloon rising in front of him. He grabbed it out of the air and transferred the power onto the bitch's own head, focussed it, and then started to press.

She chuckled. "So that's how you want it, then. A contest of strength."

"Duelling this way was a tradition of honour, long ago."

"You speak true. Place the *Necronomicon* on the ground between us."

Demitrius dropped the book onto the gravel. The Succubus stepped up to him until they were close enough to spit in each other's eye. She laid her hands on his shoulders, and he did likewise. It gave the fight a curious kind of intimacy. They started to squeeze. Their eyes began to glow with a small, dull, light.

I'm going to send you back to Hell! The Cypriot thought.

I sense your emptiness, Lillith responded. *You've already lost, little man.*

Now, that wouldn't be fair, would it? he questioned rhetorically. *You can't see the future. Not even on a 'Reach'. No one can.*

I don't need to prognosticate. It doesn't matter if you win or lose, Demitrius, because you have no soul.

So what?

So when you meet your end, it will truly be *an end.*

Each squeezed more forcefully, the light in their different coloured eyes becoming a mutual, brightening, cream hue. Demitrius winced at the pain.

The Necronomicon *will return my soul,* he considered, optimistically.

You are too late to use that conjuration before the dimension gate opens.

So there IS such a conjuration!

You do not have sufficient time to cast it.

I'm taking the book with me, demon bitch! You are the one that cannot win because until I am restored inside that coldness makes me invincible!

They crushed each other even harder. The bright glow was illuminating drops of blood leaking from the corner of the Succubus's mouth. She had a cynical thought.

I think that the ink in the grimoire has driven you mad.
It was the best thing to ever happen to me.

The luminosity was a blazing whiteness. Demitrius snorted snot from his nose, and then realised it was blood.

No. I suspect it was the worst for us both.

Their skulls started to crackle at the same time and then, suddenly, both imploded inwards. The bodies fell, and the *Necronomicon* lay forgotten beside them on the harsh gravel.

*   *   *

Sam dawdled along in the Beetle doing 45mph in a 60mph zone. They were alone on the road, no police cars had passed them in the last five minutes. Tony was trying to re-channel his pessimism into a more constructive attitude. Going into battle made such meditation difficult. They had been talking about how to deal with Demitrius, a conversation tainted with a shared fear. Tony had extended his arm through the open passenger side window and swung the baseball bat around experimentally in the breeze. The capacity for violence was within him. Maybe it is somewhere in all of us, but Tony couldn't visualise the fight. His imagination was inhibited by something like a shroud. He didn't want to think about it, it made the top of his head spin. Drawing up to Ashton Court park, with theory now about to become reality, he felt as if they were driving towards a cliff.

ZAXXON

If the Dimensional Window opened before they got there, it would all be academic. Whether or not he actually desired to hit anyone with a bat would be an irrelevance. He had agreed to fight the Cypriot, again, but it seemed an insurmountable and unimaginable obstacle. Maybe he really *wanted* them to arrive too late. He would not ask Sam for the time. He wished it to be an enigma because another part of him, which he did not understand, was actually very brave. Here was risk, and mystery, and glory for the taking. The adventure would end soon, for good or ill, nevertheless *it was an adventure*. Tony and his lover were immersed in an archetypal battle of good against evil. Most people only experience that when they play a game's console, or hire a DVD to watch from the safety of their own armchairs.

The couple approached the perimeter. Sam looked down at her slim gold-plated watch. It was nine minutes to midnight. Someone had broken through the gate before them leaving twisted ironwork on either side of the entrance. She accelerated into the park. No lane markings were to be seen on this old road. Just ruts, and cracks, and dust twisting in the headlamps. Driving around the final bend they saw the lights in the courtyard, revealed almost theatrically. Tony's skin prickled with the most powerful deja-vu he had ever experienced. Aspects of the gutted house were lit up like a sound-stage seen from a distance, and he felt a primordial familiarity about the scene. He didn't want to recognize it, he couldn't, but he had definitely seen this before. The weight of past history, going back many lives, was calling him to arms. A force far more terrible than Demitrius was coming.

The couple pulled into the driveway with a long crunch of gravel. Sam parked parallel to the fence, at a near 90 degree angle and 40 feet away from the other cars. She left her headlights on also, to shine into the bright pool. They looked around the area. Sam found the *Necronomicon* on the blood-soaked stones. She picked it up with the expression of distaste that was common to most people who touched it. She looked happy, but held it away from her, in both hands, like a tray of worms. They also discovered something shocking: two headless bodies, one lying upon another. A strange woman - and Demitrius. Tony couldn't grasp the mechanics of how they had died. Of course he was relieved, his biggest problem had been solved for him, but he had questions.

"How could this have happened?"
"It doesn't matter how," replied Sam. "It's a gift."
"There could be a maniac with a rifle hiding somewhere around here!"
"These people didn't die from bullets. Look at them."
He stepped forward and glanced at the corpses. He grimaced. "So what did happen?"
"Maybe they attacked each other with magic and they both died."
"That makes a lot of sense. Bullets alone wouldn't have done this much damage."
"We should cover their faces."
"They don't *have* faces."
"Then let's destroy the book."

She walked up to the Saab. She could sense Tony's eyes on her, watching her face in the headlights, perhaps seeing her nostrils flaring at the odour of petrol. Or maybe he was just looking at her shape in tight blue jeans and a clingy red blouse. Victory was at hand and her excitement was like eroticism.

"This car is venting fuel," Sam exclaimed. "Let's burn it!"
Tony crouched by the Saab and investigated underneath it. Then he stood up. "You're not going to believe this. There's at least two and a half gallons of petrol under here and it's still leaking."
"Take the book," she said.

He took it out of her hands and her excitement evaporated because of her own deja-vu. Was there an account of her acts in past lives somehow recorded in her unmapped DNA? Through her own sub-conscious memory she recognized the stink of petrol like it was an auger of doom. She had never liked the smell of it. Was the reason something to do with what was happening here, and now?

"Stand well back, Sam," said Tony, observing her retreat. "Further!" When she was standing over 35 feet away, he opened his Zippo and flicked a spark. He held out the flame at arms length. "Here we go!" he exclaimed, and then paused.

"What's the matter?" she asked.

He muttered quietly: "Where's the third man?"

"Which man?"

"I could have sworn there were *two people* in this car, so someone may still be in it. Unconscious, slumped out of sight, needing assistance."

For some reason she didn't believe that. "Check it, then."

He placed the book on the bonnet of the Saab, snapped closed his warm Zippo and pushed it into his pocket. He took hold of the chrome door-handle in his fingers. "Tell you what, Sam, he nearly got fried. If there *is* someone in here they're a lucky bastard!"

He peered inside. He had to conclude there was no one present, but he did not emerge empty handed. He slammed the door, and held up a Browning 9mm pistol in his right hand. He waved it at Sam, smiling deliberately. She laughed. Tony fiddled with the catches until the magazine dropped out. He counted the rounds that remained, then pushed them back into it. He slid the magazine into the butt and pulled the slide like he had seen done on television. He felt powerful.

"There's still four bullets in it," he stated, proudly.

"It could be very useful. Now's the time to burn that horrible thing."

He pushed the gun into the waistband of his jeans at the small of his back, and tucked the *Necronomicon* beneath his left arm. With his other hand he fished the Zippo out of his front pocket. "Let's finish this!"

He sparked a flame at the first roll of his thumb and tossed the lighter under the Saab. He retreated to his girlfriend. She was standing a safe distance away, to his left, near the centre of the courtyard. Yellow flames caught and flourished suddenly with a sound similar to striking a muffled kettledrum. They were like two kids lighting a hijacked firework with unanticipated and astonishing consequences.

Tongues of fire snaked up into the back of the car. The fuel tank exploded with a staggering noise and a blaze of fire climbed into the black sky, towering above them. The couple were nearly knocked off their feet by the rush of hot air and a scrap of burning shrapnel nicked Sam's cheek. The bonnet popped open on its hinges as if punched from underneath by a fire-resistant troll. All the side windows burst. Thick red flames bulged from every breach.

Tony stepped forward. He stared raptly at the fire he had created with a sense of Neanderthal achievement, its purpose temporarily forgotten. As the car was consumed, he held the *Necronomicon* limply under one slightly singed arm and didn't notice the Dimensional Window whisper open behind his girlfriend.

"Well do it, then," Sam shouted. "Throw the book into the fire!"

The area was illuminated by a glistering variation of oranges, reds, and yellows. Then the status quo changed. Sam looked down wonderingly at her own feet and saw a blue light that should not exist. She felt her chest constrict with dread. Her shadow was impressed on the ground by a radiant blue rectangle from an unknown source that originated over her left shoulder. Slowly, very slowly, she turned in that direction.

There was a doorway into a fluorescent void floating a few inches above the ground. It looked as incongruous as a gun battle in a library. The thing was seven feet high and a fluid-substance like black smoke was bubbling out of the base of it. This mantle reeked of evil. As it was rolling ponderously over the gravel, towards the headless bodies, its leading edge changed continuously like the exploring fingers of a virus.

Sam called her lover's name, with a quiet force. Tony swivelled round and she pointed downwards. He took in the situation. The blue thing was obviously the Dimensional Window, but what was the black stuff? Sam used one hand to beckon him without actually looking at him. The rippling black mass had captured her complete attention. Tony walked over and stood slightly behind, and to one side, of her. The oily black smoke was progressing towards the corpses like a gunpowder fuse attached to a potent bomb. Then the couple observed it being absorbed into the gaping necks of Demitrius and the strange woman. They began to grow back what they had lost, like a graphic animation in a horror film. Tony's flesh crawled. Fear immobilised him, such as a fox exploring the night and then being frozen in lamp-assisted gun-sights.

The detritus of their heads withdrew from dust and stone. Pipes grew into brain stems. Yellowish material clotted into cerebral components. Bone shards, large and small, jumped in to re-form their skulls. Arteries were reconnected. Skin covered skull, hair covered skin, and they started breathing. Then they rose to their feet, like the twins of Lazarus.

Tony stared. Their features had been reconfigured wrong. Demitrius had one green eye and one dark brown. The woman had his debonair moustache. Some of his hair had become silver. Her ear had an absurd twig of wood stuck in it like the stem of a dead plant. Both had pieces of grit and gravel integrated into their faces. A lumpy cheek bone, a distended nose. Masks worn in a robbery that are designed to intimidate as much as the possibility of violence. They were a mishmash of each other, and their former selves.

That's Demi's best jacket, Tony thought.

The woman raised her right hand. Sam's long blonde hair rose of its own accord, crackling with static. She cried out. She was being tugged towards the stranger like her hair was wrapped around the fist of a schoolyard bully. The stranger entwined her fingers into Sam's locks, and jerked her around to face Tony. He saw a tiny piece of quartz embedded in the corner of the woman's eyelashes. It looked like a teardrop. The mismatched eyes themselves were dancing with an illusion of emotional life in the reflection of fire, but actually they were bland with hatred.

Tony held the *Necronomicon* even tighter under his arm. He reached behind his back for the 9mm automatic. The thing that used to be Demitrius stepped forward, and Tony stayed his hand. Not because of him, but because of the other one. The index finger and thumbnail of her free hand had become pink translucent blades threatening Sam's neck. The points looked sharp, living glass knives that were pink inside because of the blood vessels infused through them.

"Who are you?" Tony asked them.

"Always the same opening question," exclaimed the pair, speaking simultaneously with a single booming voice. "And Hell is always the same answer."

Tony stared at the impossibility they could be alive. "Did you kill these two people?"

"*Zaxxon* kill each other all the time."

"Why?"

"It's in their nature. It makes for a more velvety night."

"What do you want?"

"I want the *Envisage of the Four Flowers*."

The young Artist played for time. "I read some of the *Necronomicon Galaxion*, myself. Do you expect the experiment will work?"

"Of course it will. The introduction of global telepathy was my finest idea."

"He's lying out of his arse!" shouted Sam. Then somehow she giggled.

ZAXXON

The Dark Lord looked directly into Tony's left eye. Like pushing a soft, cold, spike into Tony's soul. "I'll say this only once: *I lie all the time.* Do you understand?"

"You mean you lie *sometimes.*"

"Hand over the book. I am the Entity in Command of the same Hell that your woman will languish in, if you don't."

"You are..." He could barely bring himself to say the word: *"Satan?"*

The two bodies in his control chuckled, simultaneously. "That tickles me every time! There exists none other above me, in the ranks of all horror vicinities."

Tony couldn't grasp their predicament. Sam had stopped laughing, and seeing her face made him feel helpless. "If I give it to you, will you let her go?"

"You will give it to me. You always do."

"Don't listen to him!" Sam shouted.

"Welcome to the *Tri-cycle of Being.* You and I have fought many times in passed eons, over this book."

"So it *has* happened before..."

"You know it has. But there are always variations."

A flaming fragment had been licking the undercarriage of the MG. Finally it burnt through to something that mattered, and the car exploded with a noise like an artillery shell being fired next to their ears. There was a shocking yellow flash. Burning pieces blew everywhere and a wall of heat singed them as it passed. Bits of the car fell out of the sky and crashed around them, as if seen in slow-motion. Tony was lucky not to have been killed when a buckled door landed in front of him. But in a way this was a good result. Now there were flames between himself and the pair possessed.

"How whimsical fire can be," the Prince of Darkness observed. "I didn't expect that thus my last point has been proved."

"But did I expect it?" Tony asked, cannily. Although his ears were whining, the explosion seemed to have focussed his mind. "What am I thinking, now?"

"You've been a telepath four times in our last six battles. I could see right into your head, then, read your deepest thoughts, your every fear. Those were the easiest of victories."

"But I'm not telepathic now," Tony said, considering the Browning 9mm hidden behind his back. He could feel the near-by fire warming the front of his body.

"It didn't matter," Satan continued. "I always cheated. I threatened to destroy your lover's body and soul and you returned the book to me without exception. The strange thing is, on paper, you are always supposed to win. Because you are a *Seraphin*. Your last name isn't really Newman. Do you know of what I speak, Anthony?"

"Don't talk about it..."

"Your divine name is *Nemamiah*. Remember your compassion for the defenceless? The quintessential holiness you basked in when you were a child? The way the sun always makes you sneeze? The déjà vu?"

Tony felt as if his limbs were chained. "Stop it..."

"You are *Nemamiah*, the Angel of Just Causes, the protector and defender of the helpless. And you always have been."

Tony screamed: "It's impossible! I won't accept it!" But he was flying in the face of every verifier he had ever suppressed.

Sam said: "I thought it would be something like this..."

The book was still clamped clumsily under his left arm. With his other hand, Tony reached for the small of his back, and pulled the weapon from his belt. He swung the heavy gun up to the front and pointed it at Satan's female host. He thumbed back the hammer, staring down the sights at the confusing visage of the thing that held Sam, their faces rippling in the heat. Then he lowered the muzzle. He did not have a clear shot.

The thing that used to be Demitrius started walking around the flames towards him. Tony swung his Browning to the right, like a scene transition in a DVD, and pulled the trigger three times. The gun jumped against the meat of his hand as he fired into Demitrius at point blank range. The bullets made thumping sounds and threw him onto his back. He lay still, and bled. Tony swivelled the weapon back onto the Dark Lord. "Let her go, or I'll blast you away as well!"

Satan laughed with a chilling *basso profundo*. "You can't do me harm with that trinket. These two are already dead, by your own limited understanding." Tony had no reply. Demitrius was getting back onto its feet, and said with a booming voice: *"See me rise!"*

This was what Tony had been afraid of. He prayed, silently, and raised the 9mm one last time. He aimed it at Demitrius's fringe and blew the top of his skull off. His last bullet did extensive damage. The thing had a head like a psychopath's fantasy of a Christmas decoration, but still it would not go down. It shambled directly up to Tony and took the smoking gun out of his hand, bent the barrel round until the muzzle was touching the stock, and then passed it back. Tony threw it into the fire and felt tears pouring down his cheeks. How could they survive against these odds?

"Angels don't cry," Satan observed.

This angered Tony. "Have it, then," he said, taking the *Necronomicon* out from beneath his arm. The thing that used to be Demitrius held out his hands to receive it, but Tony dropped it on the gravel. "Take it."

The thing bent down at the waist, to pick it up, slowly. The undersides of his hands touched the grimoire with a crackle of sparks that smelt like urine. Tony's attack was sudden. He reached into the hole in Demitrius's skull, swallowing his revulsion, thrust his fingers into the cavity and extracted the cold brain. The Cypriot's absurdly disparate eyes rolled up in his sockets and he dropped to one side, inanimate. The brain was heavy, and dripping. Tony tossed it into the fire and was just wiping his hands on his jeans when Sam screamed. He turned on the spot, experiencing a terrifying personal dread. There was blood all over her neck. The monster had cut her throat. He wailed, without hope.

"She's still alive, *Nemamiah*. It's a scratch. But next time I will pull her heart out," Satan stated.

"Take the thing," Tony sobbed. "You can have it." He picked it off the ground.

"Give it to me, voluntarily. You have to place it in my hands."

"Don't!" Sam cried out. "I understand everything now!"

Tony swallowed the salt in his tears. "What are you talking of, my love?"

Satan spoke: "She is trying to say that if you give me the book it will save the Earth."

"No! He's lying again! It is the other way round!" she shouted.

Tony couldn't think clearly.

The thing holding Sam clamped a hand over her mouth. "Return the *Necronomicon* to me and I may let her live. And I will do with the book *whatever I want to do.*" He was starting to shout: "Because it is my own book! *My property! I WROTE IT!!*"

Tony was feeling even more terrified, and intimidated. "What will you do?" the Artist asked him.

"I'll tell you, *Nemamiah*, because I tend to tell the truth more when I'm in a rage. I'll tell you just for the extra pain it will cause you. I will re-introduce the book back into the Material Plane. Place it in the hands of the most evil man in the world, and it will cause an Armageddon. That is all. This has happened six times before!"

"And, if I don't give it to you…"

"Then I'll kill your lover. Yes."

Tony looked at Sam; at the hazel eyes of his secret wife under the fragranced bed sheets of the night, and he moaned: "I can't avoid the darkness!"

"The only thing dark about you, is your shoes," Satan opined. He looked down at Sam. "Well, woman, tell him of your love. Tell this *Seraphin* that he must give me the book within the next ten seconds or you will most certainly die. I'll rip your heart out and squeeze it over the fire. Tell him, now. And if you want to say anything else, if you decide to turn your heart into a spade, you can do that also. But they will

be your last words, of that I can promise. I'll count slowly."
He unclasped the hand from Sam's mouth.

"10…"

"Throw it in the fire," she said to Tony.

"9…"

"I can't do it, Sam! Everyone I knew in Bristol is dead!" He was blubbering.

"7…"

"I'm prepared," she gasped. "Be rid of it now, or it will never end. We'll be going around and around in circles like this forever!"

"5…"

"I can't let you die!"

"4…"

"If you truly love me, you *will* burn it."

"2…"

"Then, I must."

"1…"

She smiled at him, ruefully: "I'll be seeing you on the Other Side."

Satan killed her, then. Plunged the transparent knives through the back of Sam's ribcage with a sound like breaking twigs, tore out her still beating heart and placed it on her body. The knives changed into fingers. He looked at the Angel, then down at the corpse, and an expression of confusion crossed the unnatural features of the woman he possessed. The Seraphin felt only hatred.

"You couple of idiots!" Satan exclaimed. "The Tri-cycle of Being is altered for the first time since records began! Do you know what you've done?"

"What?"

"When you give me the book to save your own skin, you will become me, Sam will become you, and I will become her."

"That won't happen. You obviously haven't been keeping up with current events." He took the *Necronomicon* out from under his arm.

"But if you don't give it to me, I will kill you also. You must know that."

"Just try it. Come over here and threaten me again. I'll smash your face in!"

The Prince of Darkness appeared stupefied. "But... you can't *actually destroy it*."

"- Didn't think I would, did you?"

He changed tack. "Think of all the power you could enjoy, being me."

"Worth nothing compared to love," said Nemamiah. "And you took mine. Look," he added, "I'm holding your book so far over the fire I'm singeing my hands!"

"You'll nullify all the Dimensional Gates!"

"I'm burning your precious thing..."

"But what will happen to me?"

"You will disappear and no one will care. Most people never even believed you existed."

So the angel dropped the *Necronomicon*, but saw his revenge dashed. It defied gravity, hovered towards Satan as if it was suspended by invisible wires. Nemamiah remembered it could not be damaged with 'The Flare', and watched as it moved away from him above the flames. His anger almost became helplessness. Sam may have died for nothing.

It was like seeing the final train home leaving the station, last thing at night, when the world widens with the mystery of where to sleep. Worse than that, like there were indescribable creatures hunting for him on the platforms. Then he noticed the book was shimmering through more than just the heat and joined the one-sided battle. It was being taken out of his hands with telekinesis, a psychic power he could command himself. He pursed his lips, wrapped his mind around the grimoire, and started pulling.

"I'm impressed," boomed the Dark Lord. It was moving out of his grasp. "I may let you live long enough to bury your lover."

ZAXXON

The Angel's focus slipped. It hovered back towards Satan. He re-doubled his efforts. "Do you have enough time for this dance before the Dimensional Window closes?"

"The gate shuts after I exit." It was floating back towards Nemamiah. He continued: "When I have re-possessed my property, I'm taking you with me." He knitted Lillith's brow with supreme concentration. "Don't imagine I will allow your soul to escape pain!"

The Seraphin was losing grip on it again. The monster growled triumphantly. He could not be allowed to have it, so, with a yell of defiance, his enemy jumped into the fire. He took hold of the *Necronomicon*, and smote it down into the flames. Began jumping on it, in a rage, to stop it bouncing back. The crusty cover ignited. The hems of the Seraphin's jeans caught fire and the soles of his trainers were melting, but the book was burning. Satan boomed impotent threats. It was over.

Nemamiah retreated, patting the flames from his denims. Then he heard a bellow of perplexity from the other side of the fire. He looked up and saw the consequences of his victory. It was the most beautiful thing he had ever seen.

The spine of the burning book had contracted, and opened. From the corners inwards, fire engulfed page after page of the ancient vellum. Delicate blue things were rising from the charcoal, little spirits making sighs of joy. They were pretty, and shining, and flying around in circles. Some gave him kisses, and others rubbed against Sam's body. Even from where the Seraphin was standing he could see that they were healing her. It was as if every soul that had ever died because of interaction with the *Necronomicon* had somehow become trapped in it. They had lent the book its power, but that power was borrowed, and now those prisoners were escaping to wreak havoc on the engineer of their prison. There were so many of them their combined light outshone the fire. They crashed against Satan, repeatedly, like an ocean against sand.

Some of the spirits were addressing recognizable forms; wild-haired women, intellectuals with swords, crusaders from the Middle Ages. The little ones cuddled Sam's heart, which began to beat again, the heart of the world. The Dark Lord was battered backwards. His strength was so depleted he had to let go of the body of the woman he had possessed. Lillith fell lifeless, to one side. After that his essence became black smoke. Though it was difficult to see, the spirits rammed that also. They wreaked their vengeance losing none of their joyous potency. Sam suddenly gasped, and sat upright, holding a slim hand to the middle of her chest.

The smoke around the Devil's core was diminishing as though it was a germ smothered in white corpuscles. What was hidden beneath that mantle was revealed, like the brightening lights of a ship emerging from a fog bank. The green colour of his life force was exposed. More spirits were freed and attacked this new vulnerability. Sam stood up, a little unsteadily, and walked around the fireworks into her lover's arms. They hugged one another's solid, living, warmth. Whispered words that tickled and hushed in their ears.

"I know you're an Angel," Sam said, "but may I call you Tony? Please!" she cried, "*Can I still call you Tony?*"
"Of course you can, my darling. I am Tony. I'm the same man."
She sighed. "I deeply love you."
"And I, you."

Still holding each other, they turned and watched the climax of the battle. A ghost of an older man with a beard swept around them.

"Look!" Sam exclaimed. "That's the Professor!" A woman's spirit with curly hair was following him about, trying to cuddle him at every opportunity. "And that other must be his daughter, Stephanie."

ZAXXON

The souls were dancing because the greatest of evil in any Plane of existence was being disarmed. A teenaged boy with a spotty face was leaping and jumping, like a dolphin, with pure happiness. Jason and Patrick Dreyer's souls were chasing each other in and out of blue sparkles like children. Demitrius's ethereal shape floated by holding his favourite Playboy mug. The war against Satan was almost over. The power being released from the burning book was relative to the shrinkage of his vital energy. Soon he was reduced into a pathetic pea-nut sized blip. It made mewling noises as it was finally kicked out of the Material Plane. The glittering blue assembly of souls rose far, far, up into the night sky. The cycle was broken. The Dimensional Window disappeared. And Tony knew that there would never be another.

Printed in the United Kingdom by
Lightning Source UK Ltd., Milton Keynes
137424UK00001B/101/P